W9-BYH-765

A
Difficult
Boy

A Difficult Boy

M. P. BARKER

Holiday House / New York

Copyright © 2008 by M. P. Barker
All Rights Reserved
Printed in the United States of America
www.holidayhouse.com
3   5   7   9   10   8   6   4   2

Library of Congress Cataloging-in-Publication Data

Barker, M. P. (Michele P.), 1960–
A difficult boy / by M. P. Barker. — 1st ed.
p. cm.
Summary: In Farmington, Massachusetts, in 1839, nine-year-old Ethan experiences
hardships as an indentured servant of the wealthy Lyman family alongside Daniel, a boy
scorned simply for being Irish, and the boys bond as they try to right a terrible wrong.
ISBN-13: 978-0-8234-2086-5 (hardcover)
[1. Indentured servants—Fiction.   2. Social classes—Fiction.   3. Prejudices—Fiction.
4. Irish Americans—Fiction.   5. Swindlers and swindling—Fiction.   6. Massachusetts—
History—1775–1865—Fiction.]   I. Title.
PZ7.B250525Dif 2008
[Fic]—dc22
2007037059

ISBN 978-0-8234-2244-9 (pbk.)

HOLIDAY HOUSE is registered in the U.S. Patent and Trademark Office.

For my parents,
who continue to think
everything I do is wonderful,
even when it isn't

And for Joe,
for love, patience, and
really, really good dessert

Chapter One

Farmington, Massachusetts, April 1839

"I don't want to go." Ethan curled his arms around his knees, drawing them to his chest.

The hay whispered beneath Pa's shoes as he crossed the haymow. He sat next to Ethan, his long legs stretched out in front of him. The early afternoon sun slanted through the cracks between the barn's boards, casting bars of light and shadow across Ethan and his father.

Ethan wished he could stay here forever in the sweet musty haymow; stay here watching the barn swallows swoop and dive and return to their young nestled snug against the roof's peak; stay here listening to the comfortable rustle of Tess in the stall below, tending to her new calf; stay here sitting with his father, not moving, not saying anything, because all there was to say now was good-bye.

Pa put an arm around Ethan's shoulders and drew him in. "The truth of it is, son, I need you to go." The striped light cast harsh shadows across Pa's lean features. Ethan couldn't remember when his father didn't have gray circles under his eyes or creases around his mouth and across his forehead. But this was a kind of tired that Ethan hadn't seen before. Pa blinked hard, as if his eyes hurt. "I thought we settled this," he said. "It's a good opportunity for you. If you mind your work well, maybe in a couple of years Mr. Lyman will teach you to clerk in his store. It's a good skill to learn." He tousled Ethan's thick brown hair. "You don't want to grow up a dunderhead about business like your father, do you? Remember how much time it took Mr. Lyman to help me straighten out my account book?" He laughed, but Ethan didn't join him.

It was all about business, wasn't it? At night, when Pa and Ma thought Ethan was asleep, he'd heard them talking of how much they owed Mr. Lyman for the mortgage on the farm and their account at the store. When Mr. Lyman had come over with the indenture papers, all the talk had been of Ethan learning a skill, but that hadn't been the half of it. Money—that had been the other half. Who would have thought one boy's work could make the difference between keeping and losing a farm?

So he'd pretended to believe that it would be an adventure to go across town and live in the big white house with the great columns. He'd tried to feel proud that he'd be working like a man, even though he was only nine. He'd almost convinced himself, until a few minutes ago, when Pa had told him that the Lymans' Irish boy, Paddy, had arrived to fetch him. Then his chest had grown tight with panic, and he'd bolted out of the house and into the barn.

Ethan's stomach knotted. He wasn't sure whether he was more afraid of what would happen if he left or of what would happen if he stayed.

Pa handed Ethan his hat. "It's only a few years. George and Mercy Lyman are good people. They never made me feel a fool for being backward with my accounts. You'll like it there if you set your mind to it. Now come on down. Paddy's waiting."

Ethan wiped his sleeve across his face and followed his father down the ladder. Ma waited outside with a basket of food and a cloth-wrapped bundle containing his clothes. Chloe and Maria hung back behind her, suddenly shy of their big brother. He wondered if they'd miss him. Benjamin still slept in his cradle; he wouldn't even notice Ethan was gone.

"Well, Ethan." Ma set down bundle and basket. She wiped

her eyes on her apron before she cupped Ethan's face in her callused hands. Her look made something ache deep inside his chest. "I put some caraway cakes and bread pudding in your basket. I'm sure you'll have better at the Lymans', but I just wanted—" She knelt in the dirt and hugged him hard.

He breathed in the familiar smell of her: harsh odors of sweat, sour milk, and soiled nappies, sweetened by cinnamon, nutmeg, and molasses from the morning's baking. The ache in his chest threatened to split him in half. He squeezed his eyes closed so he wouldn't shame himself with tears. If only he could carry the feel and smell of her with him.

Someone cleared his throat and spat into the dirt. Ethan opened his eyes and looked over Ma's shoulder. A strange boy stared back at him, his gray-green eyes cool and hard. The boy was perhaps fifteen or sixteen years old and not much taller than Ma.

So this was Mr. Lyman's Irish boy, Paddy. Red hair, a faded shade halfway between rust and straw, stuck out any old how from under his battered brown cap. Freckles peppered his pale face, and his ears stood out like teacup handles. His body was all sharp angles and knobby joints, as though someone had glued his skin right to his bones and had forgotten to put the muscles in between.

Paddy's feet scuffed in the dirt. The cuffs of his broadfalls exposed bony ankles and gnarly feet that looked tough enough to go bare in January, never mind a mild April afternoon. He reminded Ethan of an old stocking stretched long and thin, worn and frayed at heel and toe and cuff.

Ethan's mother sniffled as she released him.

"Now, Hannah, he's only going to the other side of town, not the other side of the world," Pa said.

"It might as well be, for all that we'll see of him," Ma replied sharply.

"Don't be silly. We'll likely see him in a few weeks or so," Pa said. "And no doubt Mr. Lyman will let him visit now and then."

Ethan winced at the reminder of how long it might be before he'd see his family again. The three hours' walk to the Lymans' might have been three days, or three weeks even. He knelt to hug Pa's arthritic old dog, Scratch, burying his face in the dog's coarse, dusty fur, delaying his last farewell to Pa. Finally, he stood up straight and solemnly held out his hand to his father, the way men were supposed to say good-bye. Pa swooped him up in a hug that pressed his ribs hard around his lungs and heart. Ethan's glance strayed over Pa's shoulder and caught Paddy staring at them with a peculiar light in his gray-green eyes. Paddy lowered his gaze quickly, but Ethan still felt the boy watching from beneath his pale lashes.

"Who'll look out for him at Mr. Lyman's?" Ma asked as Ethan hefted his bundle of clothes and Pa handed Paddy the basket of treats.

His eyes still downcast, Paddy shrugged. "S'pose it'll have to be me, won't it?"

Ethan's insides squirmed. Paddy didn't sound interested in anything that needed looking after.

"Right, then," Paddy said. "Let's be off or we'll be late for chores." He walked with a brisk long-legged stride, not looking back to see if Ethan followed.

Ethan glanced back at his family, the dusty brown house, the weathered barn and swaybacked shed. He tried to hold them fast in his mind, like a picture in a book. When he looked ahead, Paddy was already well down the road. Ethan trotted after him, clutching his bundle to his chest. They'd gone all the way past the schoolhouse and beyond Potter's farm before Paddy slackened his pace.

Ethan swallowed hard. Make the best of things, Pa always said. "So—so your name's Paddy?" he asked.

One of Paddy's shoulders lifted and lowered. "That's what they call me," he said, as though somebody's name and what people called him weren't necessarily the same thing.

"Why do they call you that?"

"Because I'm Irish."

"But you don't like it."

Paddy's mouth twisted. He shifted Ethan's basket to his other hand. "Clever of you to notice."

"Why?" Ethan asked. "Why don't you like it, I mean?"

Paddy's eyes narrowed. "Tell you what, lad. I'll call you 'fool' for a week or so and see how you like it." His voice had an odd slant to it, his sentences all ending on an upward lilt. When Paddy said *you,* it sounded more like *ye,* sliding into the next word so that it almost seemed a part of it. His *a*'s had round, soft shapes instead of the flat, straight ones Ethan was used to hearing. But there was hardness enough in the *t* and *k* sounds, which clicked like a bolt being shot home.

Ethan wondered if the Irish boy always spoke in riddles. "What *is* your name, then?"

Paddy stared hard at Ethan. He seemed to regard the question as a challenge or a threat. Then his face softened. "Daniel. Daniel Linnehan," he said carefully, as if he wanted to make sure he said it exactly right.

"Then I'll call you Daniel, or Dan, or whatever you like."

Daniel's eyebrows bunched together. He took a deep breath and nodded. "Daniel, then. But not in front of himself."

"Himself?"

"Mr. Lyman. Or herself, neither."

"Do you like working for the Lymans?"

Daniel shrugged. "I'll be liking it better when I leave."

"Why? Is your family very far away?"

Daniel's spine stiffened. He spun around to face Ethan. "Don't be asking me any questions unless you're sure you want to know the answers." His face closed up like a door slamming shut.

The rest of the journey was long, dusty, and silent.

"So you're Gideon Root's boy." Mr. Lyman's eldest son, Silas, swept a hand through his sweaty blond hair as he studied Ethan. Two other men stood with him in the Lymans' barnyard, staring Ethan up and down the way they'd inspect an ox standing for auction.

Ethan snatched off his hat with a hasty "Yessir."

The barrel-chested man standing next to Silas grinned at Ethan. His flat hat squashed his dark hair onto his forehead and made his chubby cheeks seem even rounder. "Not very big, is he?" Laughter lurked behind his brown eyes. "Maybe we should send him back until he grows some, eh, Phinney?" He winked at the third man, who let out a wheezy chuckle. Their laughter scalded Ethan's ears.

Silas's long face remained solemn. "How old are you?" he asked. His frown warned that he might take the other man's advice.

"Nine. Ten in August. And I can work hard." Ethan squared his shoulders and drew himself up straight, trying to look as big and strong and old as he could. For the whole long, silent walk, he'd wanted nothing more than to turn and run back home, but now that Silas seemed inclined to send him away, all he could think about was what Pa had said in the barn. *I need you to go.*

The first man elbowed Phinney's ribs. "Introductions, Phinney. Where's our manners?"

Phinney swept his hat off and grinned. "Phinneas J. Wheeler. Pleased to meet you." He was slightly built, with hands and feet that seemed too big for his body. His eyes, hair, and clothes were all the same murky brown, as though someone had rinsed him in the tobacco juice that dribbled out of the corner of his mouth when he laughed.

The first man bowed low and presented his right hand for Ethan to shake. "Rufus Pease. You stick with Phinney and me, and you'll learn a thing or two, boy."

"Silas!" The call came from a one-story ell at the back of the house. A girl stood on the step, tossing scraps to the poultry. Her brown dress and baggy green apron made her look as plump as one of the hens. But her round face and smiling eyes seemed friendly. "Are Mr. Pease and Mr. Wheeler staying to tea?" she asked.

"We will if there's any of your currant cake left, Lizzie," Mr. Pease shouted back.

"I take it that means yes," Lizzie said with a laugh.

When the girl had disappeared into the house, Mr. Pease winked at Mr. Wheeler. "If only that Lizzie Stearns looked as fine as she cooks, I'd marry her tomorrow." He bowed toward Silas. "Unless, that is, you want her for yourself."

Silas's mouth twisted in exasperation. "Lizzie's our dairymaid," he told Ethan. "You'll be helping her and Paddy with the milking. You can milk a cow, can't you?"

"Of course I can." Ethan thrust out his chest and put his shoulders back, trying to look even bigger and stronger than before.

Silas turned to Daniel. "Show him where to put his things, then bring him down. We'll see how he does."

"Look, Mrs. Lyman, the new boy is here," Lizzie said, smiling at Daniel and Ethan as they entered the kitchen.

Ethan tried hard not to gape. The huge whitewashed room dwarfed the dark little kitchen at home. Pewter and tinware gleamed from shelves and mantel. Barely a spattering of flyspecks marred the white ceiling. At home, whole constellations of them covered the plaster, along with patches of gray and tan where the roof had leaked or where a pumpkin in the attic had rotted and oozed pulpy orange slime onto the ceiling below.

The bustle and noise, at least, were familiar. Just like at home, the Lyman kitchen seemed full of women and girls hard at work baby-tending, tea-making, and preparing for milking. And just like at home, the kitchen was rich with smells. Ethan picked out woodsmoke, vinegar and horseradish, nutmeg and cinnamon, sour milk and soiled nappies, and the smoky-salty-sugary-greasy aroma of ham.

A tall, broad-shouldered woman, Mrs. Lyman worked at a big table in front of the fireplace. Two girls who shared Mrs. Lyman's dark hair and eyes and long nose worked alongside her, slicing meat and bread and cakes and rinsing pickles for the evening's tea. One of the girls looked about Ethan's age; the other looked a few years older and a decade more serious. At a side table, a third, smaller girl changed a nappy for a toddler who squealed enough for three babies.

Ethan gave Mrs. Lyman an awkward bow and tried to say "Good day." The words caught in the back of his throat and came out as "Guh-uh-uh."

The younger of the girls at the big work table snickered.

"Zeloda!" the older girl said. "Mind your manners."

"Don't be silly, Florella. It's not like he was company." Zeloda wrinkled her nose at Ethan.

"It's not charitable to laugh at the afflicted." Florella lifted her chin high as she spoke. "Is it, Mama?"

Mrs. Lyman raised an eyebrow. "The boy's only bound out. That doesn't make him afflicted."

"Isn't he dumb?" Florella sounded disappointed that Ethan wouldn't give her any scope for charity. "Why can't he talk, then?"

"I'm not dumb!" Ethan's words had no trouble bursting out this time.

"He's not dumb, only stupid." Zeloda stretched out the last word so that it dug under Ethan's skin like a splinter.

Mrs. Lyman clapped her hands. "Girls, that's enough! We'll find out soon enough whether the boy is quick or not. Get to your chores and let him get to his."

"Don't mind Zeloda," Lizzie whispered. "It's only words." She wiped her hands on her apron and introduced herself. Her sparkling cinnamon-brown eyes made Ethan want to smile in spite of the sting of Zeloda's teasing. Lizzie nodded toward the children at the side table. "That's Ruth and Aaron, Mrs. Lyman's youngest." Ruth couldn't have been much more than five years old. She was dark-haired like her sisters, but with blue-gray eyes and a babyish round face. Aaron let out a shriek that set Ethan's ears ringing.

"I hope you like it here," Lizzie added, as if she were telling Ethan a secret.

Ethan followed Daniel up a steep, narrow staircase to a stout door with a heavy bolt set above the latch. A second flight of stairs led to an attic full of squash and pumpkins, drying herbs and seedpods, discarded furniture and broken tools. Great fan-shaped windows arched like a tom turkey's tail across each end wall. On one side, a string of small rectangular windows along the eaves overlooked the barnyard and the road heading south; on the other side of the house, another row of little windows yielded a view of the road leading north, back toward the common, back toward home.

He peered out the big fan window at the back of the house, which overlooked Mr. Lyman's fields and orchards. The land swept down toward the glistening ribbon of the Farmington River, then back up again to the blue-green Berkshire foothills in the distance. It wasn't the view, however, that enchanted him, but a tiny figure perched on the windowsill.

A little wooden horse stood guard over the attic, rearing back on its haunches, mane and tail flying. The wood glowed softly in the mellowing afternoon sun. If he touched it, he was sure the bunched-up muscles would feel warm and ready to spring into life. "He's beautiful," he murmured, reaching out a finger to caress the figure.

A hand snatched the horse away. Daniel stood over him, his eyes dark and narrowed, his mouth twisted. The horse disappeared into his pocket. "Don't be touching what ain't yours." He tossed Ethan's basket onto the floor, grabbed the bundle from his hand, and sent it tumbling. "Time for chores," he said, and headed downstairs.

The cow next to Ethan cocked her tail. He sidestepped to dodge the hot yellow stream that splattered the floor. He followed Daniel to a big brindle cow who munched her supper uneasily, pawing the floor and tossing her head between bites.

"This is Nell," Daniel said, dropping a well-worn stool near the cow's back feet.

Ethan looked at the cow, then at the stool, then at the bucket, then back at the cow. He didn't look at Daniel.

"Well?" Daniel folded his arms across his chest. "You do know how to milk, don't you?"

Nell's hind feet stepped about as if she were trying to dance a reel.

"Of course. I do it all the time at home." But Tess never danced around the way Nell did.

Daniel tapped his foot and rolled his eyes. "You can't. Oh, this is grand. They send us a lad who can't even milk."

"I can too!"

"Show me." Daniel hooked a foot around one leg of the

stool and shoved it next to the cow. He dropped the bucket under her belly. Nell rattled her horns against the stanchion boards.

"I—I'm just waiting for her to stand still."

"She'll stand still when you pail her out. Or would you be wanting her to burst, now?"

Gritting his teeth, Ethan sat at arm's length from Nell's haunches and reached out a hand. It couldn't be that hard. He'd managed all right with Tess, and one cow was just like another.

Only they weren't. Tess's udder had hung down loose and low, the teats as big as Pa's thumb, wrinkly and rubbery and a perfect handful for Ethan to pinch off at the top and squeeze the thick stream of milk down. Nell's bag was high and tight, with teats barely as big as the tip of Ethan's pinkie. He could fit only his thumb and forefinger around one. When he squeezed, a thin warm trickle ran down his hand, along his arm, and up his sleeve. He bit his lip and tried again, his fingers now wet and slippery with milk. The teat slid between them and popped out of his grasp.

In the next instant, Ethan was on the floor. One moment he'd seen a hoof flashing in front of his face. The next, the stool was gone and he was sitting in a pile of fresh manure.

Chapter Two

Ethan took a shuddering breath, half expecting to find his chest crushed or his head broken, but the only thing that hurt was his rear end. When he tried to get up, he found that Daniel's hand gripped his braces. He realized that the other boy had pulled him away from Nell's sharp hoof.

Daniel yanked Ethan to his feet. "You want to be getting your bloody head bashed in? Who the devil ever taught you to milk like that?" His voice dripped with contempt.

"Our cow doesn't kick." Ethan plucked at the seat of his trousers. A glob of manure splatted to the floor. He backed up and tried to rub the rest off against the wall.

"She wouldn't kick if you'd milk her proper." Daniel righted the stool and set the bucket back under the cow. "Like this." He sat close up against Nell's flank. Bracing the bucket between his knees, he turned his face toward Ethan and laid his cheek against Nell's side. "If you're afraid, she'll be afraid, too. You get right in here and she sees there's nothing to be scared of." He put his hands out, tucking his left arm into the crook of Nell's hock.

Fear, Ethan thought, was probably the last thing on Nell's mind. Murder was more likely.

"Then you get yourself a good handful of her. She's not got much of a teat to grab onto, so you got to be taking a bit of the bag, too." Daniel's long fingers grasped an inch of Nell's bright pink udder along with the tiny button of her teat.

Ethan noticed strange ragged patches of white flesh on the older boy's hands and forearms, unfreckled and paler than the rest of his skin. The discolored spots distracted him until a steady stream of milk spurted from between Daniel's fingers and hissed into the bucket below, drawing Ethan's attention back to the lesson.

Nell's hind leg cocked back. Ethan opened his mouth to shout a warning. Daniel jabbed his left elbow sideways into the cow's hock, stopping the kick before it had time to start. Nell tried again. Daniel jabbed again. The kick turned into a harmless pawing in the hay, as though all Nell had meant to do was readjust her footing. After Nell settled, Daniel's left hand moved back to the cow's udder and joined his right in a steady one-two rhythm. "See? You get right in there and she hasn't space to swing. And if she tries, you can stop her."

"But how did you know?"

"Felt it here." Daniel pressed his face tighter against the cow's flank. A corner of his mouth curled. "And saw it in your face."

Ethan's cheeks warmed.

"S'pose this one's too much for you. Go do Patience." Daniel jerked his right elbow toward a placid brown cow who stood with her joints so slack she seemed to be eating in her sleep.

Ethan moved toward Patience, then stopped. "No."

Daniel's hands missed a beat, but he didn't look up. "No?"

"You wanted me to do Nell. I'll do Nell."

Daniel cocked his head to blink at Ethan. His pale eyebrows gathered, then smoothed. He shrugged. "Suit yourself. Just remember you're milking a cow, not playing the bloody pianoforte."

Ethan clenched his teeth and planted himself against Nell's side, his left arm poised against her hind leg. From the corner of his eye, he could see Nell's cloven hoof and, next to it, Daniel's feet, bare and bony and filthy. He felt Daniel's eyes on him, waiting for the next opportunity to scold and sneer. Ethan reached for the cow's udder and grasped teat and bag just as Daniel had demonstrated. When he felt Nell's muscles bunch against his forehead, he stiffened his arm, jabbing his elbow into Nell's hock when her heel came off the floor. Her foot came back down, hard and fast, and stayed there.

His first squeeze brought the milk out in a feeble trickle. The next squeeze was better. The milk came in only a thin string compared to the ropy stream Daniel had produced, but it came. He had the bucket a quarter full before Daniel's feet disappeared and the weight of being watched vanished.

Ethan was used to working hard: chopping wood, picking stones in fields and garden, hoeing, digging, hauling wood and water. None of it seemed to use the muscles that milking Nell did. His fingers cramped, and he lost the rhythm of pinch and squeeze. The stream of milk faltered into short spurts.

He gradually became aware of motion around him. Stanchion boards rasped open, and the cattle clomped out of the barn. He heard the scrape-scrape-scrape of someone mucking out the barn. His wrists and the backs of his hands tingled, but he forced his fingers to keep moving.

The cows murmured in the barnyard like children waiting for a friend kept after school. He heard the men chatting and laughing outside. Laughing at him, no doubt. His fingers kept moving, though his shoulders felt rigid. The milk went from small spurts to drops to nothing. He pressed his lips together and tried again, forcing his fingers to continue working the udder that was now soft and loose in his hands.

Something nudged his leg. Daniel's feet reappeared next to Nell's. "Let's have a look, then."

"I can do it." Ethan felt sure Daniel wanted him to give up, to be sent home in disgrace.

Daniel crouched and shouldered him away. He put a thumb and forefinger at the top of one teat, then gently slid his fingers down. Nothing came out. After repeating the test with the other three teats, he nodded. "I s'pose that'll do." He gave Nell a parting slap on the rump and walked away.

Ethan stared after him. Daniel paused at the door to the cattle yard. "Well, are you going to be leaving her in all night?"

"You call that washing up?" Daniel grabbed Ethan's arm and shoved him back in front of the pump. He tossed a little scrub brush into the tin basin that sat under the spout, sending a splash of water into Ethan's face and down the front of his shirt and vest. "There," he said, flicking a glob of soft brown soap onto Ethan's cheek. "Hands *and* face. Ears, neck, nails. The lot."

"How can I finish washing my buckets with you boys blockading the pump?" Lizzie dropped the last two milk pails on the floor with a hollow thunk.

"It's this new lad," Daniel said. "You'd think he'd never laid eyes on a pot of soap before."

The cold water that Ethan splashed on his face did little to cool his burning cheeks. If not for Lizzie standing there, he'd have doused Daniel with the contents of the washbasin. Instead, he scrubbed at his face and hands with all the fury he wanted to set loose at Daniel.

"He'll learn," Lizzie said. Ethan looked up from his rinsing to see her offering him a towel. Her smile faded as her nose twitched and her gaze drifted down to Ethan's trousers. "Oh, dear," she sighed. "Couldn't get it all off?" Without waiting for a reply, she rummaged under the sink and came up with a battered brush and whisk broom. She led Ethan to the doorway of the little ell and stood him on the threshold so she could brush and scrape the manure off into the yard.

Two furry bodies twined around Ethan's ankles, then bolted into the house.

"Now the bloody fool's let the cats in," Daniel growled. He took off in pursuit. Ethan heard the thud of Daniel's feet, a shriek, a thwack, and a couple of feline yowls. He hoped Daniel hadn't struck the cats.

"I'm sorry," Ethan said, twisting around to see if Lizzie's work was doing any good.

"*I'm* the one who let the cats in," Lizzie said. "Don't mind him." She shrugged in the direction Daniel had gone. "That's just Paddy being Paddy." She gave Ethan a final brush, then quickly stepped aside as the two cats hurtled out, Daniel stomping behind them.

"They didn't get into the cream, did they?" Lizzie asked.

Daniel shook his head. He yanked Ethan back into the ell and slammed the door.

"There," Lizzie said. "Best I could do, I'm afraid. Good thing your trousers are brown."

"S'pose it'll have to do," Daniel said. With a loud sigh, he grabbed Ethan by the shoulder and tugged him toward the kitchen. "Right, then. Let's see what else he don't know how to do."

"Not like that. You want to be wearing down the carpet? And by the seat, not the back." Daniel picked up a bright yellow chair to demonstrate.

Ethan smothered a groan. There seemed to be a right way and a wrong way to do everything around here, and whichever way he chose was always the wrong one. Now there even seemed to be a right way to set the chairs around the table for the evening's tea.

Mrs. Lyman and the girls had already laid the table with starched white napkins and blue-edged dishes as delicate as eggshells. A platter of cold ham formed the centerpiece, flanked by bowls of gleaming burgundy-red pickled beets and cabbage. Bread, pies, cakes, and pastries paler and more delicate than any Ethan had ever seen covered nearly every inch of the white tablecloth. His stomach fluttered with apprehension at all the things on the table that a misplaced elbow or hand could spill or break.

The chairs bumped against his shins as he carried them, but better bruised shins than more scoldings. In a few moments, he'd lined up a neat row on his side of the table. He stood back to await his next order.

Daniel came around and inspected the chairs. He moved the first one an inch to the left. He moved another chair a few inches to the right, and a third a fraction of an inch back. Ethan's jaw tightened. Finally, Daniel nodded. "That'll do." He retreated to the kitchen and returned with an old ladder-back chair with a grease-stained rush seat. From the way Daniel thunked it down, Ethan guessed that nobody cared much how this chair was handled.

"Whose is that?" Ethan asked.

"Mine," Daniel said.

With a rustle of skirts, Mrs. Lyman swept into the room. Florella and Zeloda followed close behind. Florella carried two puddings, while Zeloda brought in the steaming teakettle. Somehow Mrs. Lyman conjured up spots on the crowded table for all the new dishes.

Daniel seemed to shrink when Mrs. Lyman entered. He cleared his throat. "Excuse me, ma'am. What chair would you like me to be setting for him?" He jerked his chin toward Ethan. Although he spoke to Mrs. Lyman, he directed his eyes at the table, his head bent, his shoulders rounded. His voice changed as well as his posture, losing some of its sharp edge, though not all. Something hard lurked under his deferential tone, like a tiny bone lodged in his throat.

Mrs. Lyman gave Ethan a weary glance, as if he were yet another platter that needed a space on the table. "The table's crowded enough with all the help we have to feed," she said. "He can stand."

Ethan gulped. *Stand?* He hadn't stood for meals since he was five. From the corner of his eye, he thought he noticed Daniel watching him, but when he turned to look, Daniel had dropped his glance.

Daniel dragged a foot along a thin red stripe in the parlor's carpet. Without looking up, he asked, "Only for today? Or for always?"

"Until I say he can sit," Mrs. Lyman said. She wrinkled her nose. Ethan realized that in spite of his double scrubbing and Lizzie's brushing, there was no erasing the ground-in smear on the seat of his trousers or the smell of souring milk on his shirt—a fine impression for his first day in her house.

The parlor seemed to explode with noise and people as Silas and the two farmhands came in, talking and laughing, at one door. Lizzie entered from another, carrying Aaron and leading Ruth by the hand.

Ruth squealed and dashed toward Silas. The work-weariness faded from the young man's eyes as he picked her up and balanced her on his hip.

"Silas." Mrs. Lyman frowned at him as if he were a great stupid dog who might bite his little sister.

The muscles under Silas's eyes tightened. Like Daniel, he seemed unable to look directly at Mrs. Lyman. "Sorry, ma'am." He let his sister slither out of his arms and onto the floor.

Mrs. Lyman tugged Ruth's dress straight where it had ridden up her legs. "You must be ladylike, Ruth. You are not a monkey." Her voice softened when she addressed her daughter. She touched the tip of Ruth's nose with her finger, making the girl giggle. A hint of a smile crossed Mrs. Lyman's mouth. She kissed Ruth's forehead as she fixed the girl's hair ribbon.

"Yes, Mama." Ruth's voice was dutiful, but her eyes strayed to Silas's, and they shared a smothered smile.

The household milled around the table for a few moments, then stilled as footsteps in the hallway announced Mr. Lyman's entrance. It reminded Ethan of how the children in school would fall silent when the teacher came in. Daniel and Silas stood at attention with their eyes averted, as though waiting for the master's examination.

Mr. Lyman stood in the doorway for a moment, surveying the assembled household. Ethan noticed that Mr. Lyman and Silas had the same serious, deep-set blue eyes: Silas's the soaring blue of a crisp autumn sky; Mr. Lyman's, the grayish blue of winter. Father and son shared the same strong nose, dimpled chin, and high forehead. While Silas's profile was lean and sharp, the flesh under Mr. Lyman's chin and at his neck had thickened with age. Stern lines ran from Mr. Lyman's nose to the corners of his mouth, and a severe crease separated his eyebrows.

When Mr. Lyman's glance settled on Ethan, all the sternness washed out of his face. He gave Ethan the smile he always gave Ma and Pa when they came into his store, as though he were greeting an old and cherished friend. "Ah, young Mr. Root." He strode over and patted Ethan's head. "And how are your parents?"

"Well, sir," Ethan said softly.

"And your sisters? And the baby?"

"All well, sir." Ethan spoke carefully, feeling his tongue threatening to thicken and tangle up inside his mouth.

"It's a fine thing having a baby brother, isn't it?" Mr. Lyman glanced fondly from Silas to the baby in Lizzie's arms, then back to Ethan.

As far as Ethan could tell, all a baby brother meant was more noise, confusion, and smells in the house, and Ma always being too busy, too tired, too something or other else for anything but Benjamin. But it would be rude to say that to Mr. Lyman, wouldn't it? "I—well, I don't know. I mean, he doesn't do anything yet."

Mr. Lyman, Mr. Pease, and Mr. Wheeler burst into laughter. "Oh, that's good, boy, very good," Mr. Lyman said. "'He doesn't do anything yet.' I must remember that. Well, you'll see. You'll see." He surveyed Ethan up and down. "You've started your chores, then, hmmm?"

"Yessir." Ethan ducked his head, hoping Mr. Lyman wouldn't comment on his state of cleanliness.

"Well, then," Mr. Lyman continued. "You're to help Silas with the farm chores most of the time. A few days a week, I'll need you at the store, sweeping, tidying up, delivering parcels, helping unload the wagons when they bring in the goods. And now and then Mrs. Lyman and the girls will need you in the kitchen garden." He nodded toward his wife, his face relaxing into a fond smile. "Think you can manage that, boy?"

"Yes, sir."

Mr. Lyman ruffled Ethan's hair again. "Good boy. How did he do with the milking?" he asked Silas.

Silas looked to Daniel. Daniel's head tilted almost imperceptibly down, then up, just once. "Paddy says he'll do," Silas said.

Mr. Lyman frowned. "Paddy?"

"I've put Paddy in charge of him. He can show Ethan his chores as well as anybody. No sense taking my time on what Paddy can do."

"Just see you don't learn too much from Paddy." Mr. Lyman wagged a finger under Ethan's nose. "You know what they say about the Irish." He let out a hearty laugh and clapped Daniel on the shoulder.

A muscle quivered in Daniel's cheek. He didn't laugh. Neither did Silas, Ethan noticed, and Lizzie only pressed her lips together. But everyone else laughed.

"Indeed," Mr. Pease said. "Like the thieving Irishman who went to heaven."

"To heaven?" Mr. Wheeler said, taking his seat. "Don't you mean the other place?"

"Well, you'd think so, for he'd stolen his neighbor's pig and eaten it." Mr. Pease shook out his napkin and tucked it into his collar. So did Mr. Wheeler and Daniel. The Lymans, Ethan noticed, laid their napkins tidily in their laps.

He watched the others carefully, as his mother had told him to, so that he wouldn't embarrass himself with poor table manners, and so he could learn how he was supposed to fit into the household. At the head of the table sat Mr. Lyman with his wife and older daughters on either side of him. Lizzie had returned from putting Aaron to bed and taken her place beside Florella, while Silas sat next to Zeloda, with Ruth in his lap. Mr. Pease and Mr. Wheeler sat at the end of the table near Ethan and Daniel. Since he didn't have a lap anyway, Ethan finally tucked his napkin into his shirt the way the hired men and Daniel did.

Mr. Pease continued his story. "Anyway, eventually Mrs. O'Malley died. And so, after a bit, did Paddy. So there's Paddy, standing before the seat of judgment, with Mrs. O'Malley and her pig there, too, ready to charge him with the crime and call out judgment upon his head. Paddy, of course, says he only borrowed the pig and he'd meant to give it back.

"'You never,' Mrs. O'Malley says. 'For didn't you eat it all up?' And the pig confirms the tale. In pig, of course." Mr. Pease made a little squealing noise that set the children giggling. Ethan couldn't help smiling along with them.

"Then Paddy says, 'How can you say I didn't return him, when there's that very pig standing beside you? It only took a bit longer to get him back to you than I was expecting.'

"Well," Mr. Pease continued when the laughter had died down. "Nobody could deny that he was right, however they tried to look at it. So there was nothing for it but to let the sly rascal into heaven after all."

Mrs. Lyman leaned back in her chair and wiped her eyes. "Oh, Mr. Pease, where do you find such tales?"

"All true, ma'am." Mr. Pease laid a hand over his heart. "I swear on my honor, which is more than an Irishman can do, eh, Paddy?" He elbowed Daniel. "No offense, of course." His eyebrows rose as Lizzie held a plate under his nose. "Ah, currant cake. Lizzie, you are a jewel," he said with a blissful sigh. He put a thick piece of cake on his own plate, then reached across Daniel to lay a slice onto Ethan's plate. He followed it up with heaps of baked goods, cold ham, pickles, and preserves, until Ethan's dish was buried beneath a mountain of food. Daniel, meanwhile, had to sit back and wait to eat while Mr. Pease's arm passed back and forth under his chin.

If Ma had served such a tea at home, instead of the usual bread and milk, Ethan could have eaten all that Mr. Pease had given him and still not had enough. But today the currant cake tasted like ashes, and the white bread stuck in his throat like a clump of wool.

Mr. Pease winked at Ethan. "Eat up, boy. Don't be shy. No lumps of soap here, I promise."

"Soap?" Mr. Wheeler prompted.

"Haven't you heard the story about the Irishman who went to the city and mistook a barber shop for an eating house? The barber sets a basin of suds and a ball of soap before him and goes to fetch his razor. When he returns, the basin is empty, the soap is gone, and Paddy's wiping his mouth on a towel. 'Oh, no, sir, you didn't need to bring me a knife, now. I'm finished,' says Paddy. 'The soup was lovely, but I must say that turnip was just a wee bit undercooked.' "

While everyone laughed, Daniel hunched lower over his plate, drinking and eating as though he were the only one at the table and the meal required his full attention. He raised his eyes only when Silas addressed him with instructions about tomorrow's work.

At first, Ethan welcomed Mr. Pease's jokes. Daniel deserved it, after all, for being such an ill-tempered lout. Eventually, though, the jokes grew stale and Mr. Pease's laugh grated. Ethan almost felt relieved when, after several thwarted attempts, Silas managed to change the subject.

Ethan considered his future in the Lyman household. He prayed he'd spend more of his time working in the store than Mr. Lyman had predicted. Other than Lizzie, Mr. Lyman was the only one who'd seemed pleased to see him. The rest were indifferent at best, and at worst—

He glanced over at Daniel. The weeks and months and years ahead seemed impossibly long.

In the rapidly fading light, Ethan surveyed his new home. The northwest corner of the attic served as the boys' bedchamber. The bed was piled with bolster and pillows, sheets and blankets, all tidily arranged as if they sat on a real bedstead instead of on a straw-filled tick laid on the floor. Next to the bed stood a battered chest and table. A chipped redware pitcher and bowl sat on the table, along with a couple of towels, a redware mug, a hairbrush, a toothbrush, and a small scrub brush with bristles softened and splayed from long use. Daniel set a bucket of water down under the table.

In the graying light, Ethan retrieved the lump of cloth that held his clothes. "Where do I put my things?"

Daniel opened the chest and shoved his small pile of clothes to one side. Ethan leaned over to drop his bundle in. Daniel grabbed his wrist and let the trunk slam closed. "Wait," he said. He took Ethan's bundle in one hand. With the other, he grabbed Ethan's elbow and led him toward the table. Daniel dropped the bundle, opened a drawer, and pulled out a candle stub. He struck a lucifer against the ragged lip of the pitcher.

"What're you doing?" Ethan asked.

Daniel lit the candle. He put a hand on Ethan's neck, tipping his head downward. "Making sure you got no lice."

Ethan squirmed away. "Of course I haven't."

"Nor fleas, neither. You'll not be putting your things in with mine if you got fleas." Daniel grabbed Ethan's shoulder and held him still.

"I don't have fleas," Ethan protested. Not this time of year, anyway. April was too early for fleas.

"I'd like to be seeing for meself."

"What difference does it make?" Ethan didn't know anybody who didn't have fleas by midsummer.

"You'll be giving 'em to me, and the next thing herself'll see me itching, and she'll be thrashing me for a filthy Irishman, and I'll not be having that, understand?"

Daniel's talk of thrashing made Ethan decide that he'd better let Daniel have his way. Biting his lip, he stood still while Daniel poked through his hair for nits and checked his arms for fleabites. A lump clogged his throat and moisture pricked his eyes. He clenched his fists, digging his nails into his palms to quell the urge to slap Daniel's hands away.

Apparently satisfied with his examination, Daniel released Ethan. "S'pose you'll do." He opened Ethan's bundle of clothes and shook out each item before placing it in the chest, making sure there were no moths or worms or beetles that might contaminate his own clothes. Finished with Ethan's clothes, he planted the candle stub in a cracked saucer caked with tallow. Then he lifted the water bucket he'd brought upstairs and filled the pitcher. He set the bucket down and pointed to another that sat a few feet away. "Two buckets—see? That one for waste, this one for clean water. Don't you be getting 'em mixed up and don't be throwing nothing out the windows. Understand?"

Ethan nodded.

Daniel stripped off his shirt and began to wash. While Daniel's back was turned, Ethan hunted for the little basket Ma had packed for him. He didn't feel hungry so much for the food itself as for something that tasted and smelled of home. Earlier, he'd thought of trying to soften Daniel's temper with an offering from the basket. Now he didn't consider sharing so much as a crumb. He wouldn't give Daniel anything. Ever. Not even if he were starving.

As Ethan picked up the basket, something small and furry squirmed out and scurried away among the squash. His stomach lurched. Two more furry somethings crawled around inside the basket, feasting on Ethan's treasures. In his imagination, he screamed and flung the basket—mice, food, and all—across the attic. Or better yet, at Daniel, and the mice would bite his homely face and tear at his hair. Ethan wished he could turn into a mouse so he could bite Daniel to his heart's content. Then he'd slip away through a crack and run home.

Home.

And Ma and Pa would greet him like the prodigal son in the Bible and he'd never have to leave again and . . . and . . .

The truth of it is, son, I need you to go.

Ethan let the basket fall. He pressed his face against the cold window glass until he realized that Daniel was speaking to him. The Irish boy's face was red from scrubbing. With his wet hair slicked back, his features looked pinched and angular. Like a fox, Ethan thought, and a half-starved, mangy one at that.

"Will you be washing, or will you be standing there all night?"

Numbly, Ethan gave his face and hands a cursory rinse before undressing for bed.

"Me own side's by the window." Daniel stripped off his broadfalls and threw on an old shirt. "You keep to your side and don't be hogging the covers, understand?"

Clenching his teeth, Ethan crawled into bed while Daniel blew out the candle. He settled himself as close to the edge of the mattress as he could, stiffening when he felt Daniel slip into bed next to him, grab a handful of covers, and turn his back. Ethan stared up at the ceiling, silently releasing the tears he'd held back all evening.

He hated it: hated the big white house with everything so clean and fine that he was afraid to breathe; hated every cow in the big barn, especially Nell; hated all the farmers who'd stood outside laughing while he'd been milking; hated Mrs. Lyman, who wouldn't let him sit at dinner. But most of all he hated the gawky, ugly boy lying in bed next to him.

Daniel pitched about in the bed. He yanked all the covers over to his side, then kicked them off again, shoved his pillow away, then pulled it back and thumped it down. He made a grumpy, huffing noise and flung himself out of bed, dumping sheet and blanket onto Ethan's head.

Cautiously, Ethan tugged the covers away from his face. A fan-shaped piece of star-spattered sky framed Daniel's silhouette. He stood at the window for a long time, his hands splayed like spiders against the glass.

Just as Ethan began to wonder if Daniel was going to sleep standing up like that, the boy swung away from the window. Ethan couldn't see exactly what Daniel was doing, only the lighter gray shape of Daniel's body drifting among the attic's shadows. When the lower half of Daniel's form disappeared, Ethan guessed that Daniel had put his trousers on, the dark cloth hiding his pale legs. When Daniel's shirt seemed to sink into the floor and the padding sounds of Daniel's feet faded away, Ethan knew that Daniel had gone down the stairs and outside.

Ethan crept out of bed to see what Daniel had been staring at. A cap of stars hung over the black outlines of the western mountains. He picked out the road and some vague dark shapes that might have been trees. He stared until little flecks of rust and amber fuzzed his vision. For a moment, he thought he saw something moving along the road. He rubbed his eyes, and the blacks and grays settled back into their proper shapes. No, there was nothing. Daniel was mad, that was all. Mad, as everybody said the Irish were.

Ethan settled back in bed. His slumber was shallow, his dreams uneasy and full of Daniel's cold gray eyes, the men's mocking laughter, Nell's hooves flashing in front of his face, and of trying and trying to run away home, but being unable to find his way back.

He woke in a panic, not knowing where he was. The only things that he recognized were the waking cries of songbirds announcing the last hours before sunrise. As his mind cleared and he remembered where he was, he heard a shuffling noise next to the bed. A gray shape loomed over him.

Daniel flopped onto the mattress and quickly fell into a snoring slumber. Sunrise, Ethan realized, would come too soon for both of them.

Chapter Three

Daniel scraped a shovel through the mess of sodden straw and manure that covered the barn floor behind the stanchions. He drew together a steaming heap and pitched it out a small side window. "Like this, see?" His shovel rasped against the slick floorboards. "Get it all off or the floor won't dry proper, and then the boards'll rot, and there'll be hell to pay."

When he'd risen that morning, Ethan had sworn not to talk to Daniel unless it was absolutely necessary. He'd managed all the way through the morning's feeding and milking. But he wouldn't stand for being treated like a simpleton. "I know how to muck out a barn," he said.

Daniel squinted and looked Ethan up and down. "Aye. And you said you knew how to milk a cow, too, didn't you?"

Ethan lowered his eyes, his cheeks growing hot.

"And watch your step, 'cause I'm not picking you up if you slip and fall on your arse."

Ethan scraped the mess together into a pile below the window. His shoulders jarred when the shovel caught on a protruding nail head or an uneven board. The reek of urine and manure filled his throat. He clamped his mouth shut against the smell. He'd thought cleaning up after Tess had been a chore. But the Lymans owned fifteen Tesses, and all of them seemed to have waited until milking time to relieve themselves. He sighed and dug in again.

Daniel laid his own shovel aside, took up a pitchfork, and began to walk out.

"Where're you going?" The question came out of Ethan's mouth before he remembered his vow of silence. He wrinkled his nose. Sometimes questions seemed to spring out of him as if they had a life of their own.

Daniel glanced back over his shoulder. "You have your chores to do. I have mine."

Ethan grunted and scraped and dug and pitched, finding a rhythm that kept the work going without requiring any thought. He heard Silas and Mr. Pease and Mr. Wheeler working above and around him: the rustling noises in the loft overhead as one of them pitched down hay or straw, the steady thock-thock of another one splitting wood in the yard, the rattle of chains and tools as a third sorted the things he'd need for his day's work. Meanwhile, the sheep and cattle and pigs and chickens bleated and lowed and grunted and cackled to each other in the yard.

There were so many sounds that he didn't notice the new noise until he'd nearly finished mucking out. The sound was not quite humming, not quite singing, and not quite talking, but somehow all three at once. It continued as a steady presence underneath the talking and the animal noises, like the sounds of crickets and frogs on a summer evening, the kind of sound that would lie unnoticed underneath all the other sounds until everything else was silent. Except this sound wasn't comfortable and familiar like crickets and frogs. He felt cold as he heard unfamiliar words with ghostly intonations. But ghosts didn't walk in the day, did they?

He set his shovel aside and followed the voice until he reached the stall where Mr. Lyman kept Ivy, his dainty chestnut mare. Ethan peeked inside.

Daniel stood nose-to-nose with the mare, Ivy's chestnut forelock mingling with the Irish boy's disheveled mop of pale rusty hair. The strange humming-singing-talking voice came from Daniel, sounding as though it came from somewhere deeper than his throat. His strange, soft words were full of shushing and whooshing sounds, muted *c*'s and *t*'s that clicked gently together instead of clattering, and rumbling *w*'s and *v*'s that vibrated like humming bees.

Ethan couldn't make any sense of the words, but the mare seemed to understand them. She murmured back to Daniel as she huffed at his hair and his cheek. Daniel's hands moved over the mare's neck as if he were performing a magical incantation. Little clouds of dust and loose hair danced around him before they settled to the floor.

Ethan held his breath. He let it out when he saw that Daniel merely burnished the mare's coat with thick handfuls of twisted straw. He seemed changed, although Ethan couldn't explain how. He was still trying to figure it out when Silas came through the barn, a rake and shovel in his hand.

"What's he doing?" Ethan whispered. He feared that talking any louder would break the spell.

"What—Paddy?" Silas shrugged. "Tending to the horse. That's part of his chores." He didn't seem to see anything extraordinary about the way Daniel tended to a horse.

For a second Ethan saw what Silas did: just an ordinary boy grooming an ordinary horse. Then Daniel smiled up into the mare's face and said one of his magic words to her, and the spell took shape again.

"But what's he saying?"

Silas laughed and patted Ethan's shoulder. "Oh, that's just some Irish talk. Paddy says she's the only one who can understand that Gaelic of his."

At Silas's laugh, Daniel turned. His face went blank, as if he'd been far away and it took an effort to recall himself.

"Mrs. Lyman wants the privy cleaned out this morning," Silas said. "Why don't you take Ethan once you're finished up in here?"

Daniel nodded as Silas turned away. When he looked down at Ethan, his features sharpened. "You finished mucking out?"

Ethan glanced from Daniel to the horse, unsure whether he'd only imagined the transformation. Somehow the mare had smoothed the roughness and angles and sharp edges off Daniel. But they were all back now.

The Lymans' necessary was set at the edge of the hill just behind the house, so that the waste fell into a dark, airless, stench-filled, fly-ridden, closet-sized cavern cut into the slope. Daniel and Ethan took off their cravats and tied them over their faces to filter out some of the smell, but their eyes still watered, and they had to take turns retreating for air as they worked. Ethan was more than eager to be the one to trundle the wheelbarrow to the manure pile at the top of the kitchen garden, even though it listed to the right and the wheel kept getting bogged down in the newly thawed soil.

When he returned, he wondered if he looked as ill as Daniel did. The older boy's freckled face had a greenish sheen to it. Or maybe he was only tired from having wandered about all night. Ethan wondered again where Daniel had gone. He set down the wheelbarrow and picked up his shovel to go back to work. Then he noticed the peculiar look in Daniel's eyes, as though he were suddenly oblivious to everything around him—to Ethan, the privy, even the stench and the flies. He seemed to be staring at something far away and yet inside himself at the same time.

31

"Daniel?" Ethan said cautiously.

Without acknowledging Ethan, Daniel picked up his own shovel and went back to work. He moved as if his body were present but his mind and soul were somewhere else entirely. Even though he forgot to pull his cravat back up over his nose, he didn't seem to be affected by the smell anymore. Ethan wondered how he did that and where his mind had retreated to.

By the time they were finished, Ethan was drenched with sweat and sure that the odor would live in his nose and the back of his throat for days. Still, he'd done a good, hard morning's work. Surely Daniel would be pleased with him now.

Daniel blinked against the sun for a moment, as if he'd just woken up. Clearing his throat noisily, he spat several times into the dirt. He glanced back and forth from the bottom of the privy to the pile of manure Ethan had mounded up at the top of the garden.

Good job. Time for a rest, Ethan hoped he'd say.

Daniel nodded. "That'll do." He gathered his shovel and pitchfork. "Though it'd'a been better if you'd'a put it closer to the garden."

"Not like that." Daniel snatched the wrinkled little seed potato from Ethan's hand. "You're cutting 'em up to plant 'em, not to be making a bloody stew." He took several pieces from the basket and thrust them under Ethan's nose. "Look. You been cutting 'em so half of 'em got no eyes, and the other half got two or more." Grabbing Ethan's worn little pocketknife, he began to demonstrate. "Like this, see?" With a few deft motions, he sliced a potato into eight pieces, each with one little nubbin of an eye just starting to sprout. He jutted his chin toward the hill Ethan had just planted. "And you got to be planting 'em deeper so the vermin won't be getting to 'em before they sprout. Whoever taught you to plant potatoes, anyway?"

"My father."

Daniel went quiet for a long moment, his eyes growing distant. Then he shivered like a cow shaking off flies. "Your da, eh? Well, you mustn't'a been listening very well, then."

Ethan bit his lip, irritated that Daniel was right. Pa had taught him the right way to cut and plant the seed potatoes. He'd just been paying more attention to getting the work done quickly than getting it done right. But he wasn't going to admit that to Daniel. He'd been foolish enough to think that if he kept up with Daniel step for step, shovelful for shovelful, through all their chores, the Irish boy wouldn't possibly have any reason for complaint. After three days of trying his best to please Daniel by working just as hard as he could, he should have known it was hopeless. "All right," he growled, snatching his knife back. "I can do it."

"Fine. Then make a proper job of it, eh?" Daniel stood over Ethan, arms folded, to supervise the planting of the next two hills. When he seemed satisfied, he grunted, "That'll do," and turned back to his own work, shuffling his feet to keep his shoes from falling off. He wore a pair of battered brogans that didn't look much different from the potatoes they were planting. Ethan didn't think they gave him much more protection from the shovel than the soles of his leathery feet. But at least they slowed him down so that Ethan had half a chance of keeping up with him.

By the end of the morning, Ethan was only two hills behind Daniel in his planting. Arms and legs aching, he groaned with relief when Lizzie called them in for dinner.

Daniel squinted against the sun, surveying Ethan's work, each hill of potatoes marked with a little stick. "S'pose that'll do," he finally said. He turned to head toward the house, then looked back over his shoulder at Ethan. "Even if your rows are crooked," he added.

Ethan panted as he dragged the last box inside. It was his first afternoon working at Mr. Lyman's store, and already he'd worked up as much of a sweat as he did mucking out the barn. He'd despaired when he'd first seen the load of crates and sacks and barrels crammed into Mr. Palmer's wagon. Ethan and the teamster had hauled down box after barrel after sack after package, and each time they had returned to find the wagon apparently just as full as it had been before. But bit by bit the load had shrunk and the mound of goods in Mr. Lyman's back room had grown, until finally Mr. Palmer had wiped his forehead and said, "That's the last of 'em."

Ethan leaned against a barrel and waited while Mr. Lyman and Mr. Palmer made notes in their account books. Then the burly teamster shook Mr. Lyman's hand, clapped his dented straw hat back onto his head, and was gone. Ethan straightened, presenting himself for Mr. Lyman's next orders.

The storekeeper peered down his nose at Ethan and gave him a curt nod. "Well, that's a decent hour's work for you, boy." He smiled. "You may be small, but you can certainly work hard. Your father would be proud of you."

"Th-thank you, sir." Ethan felt a warmth grow inside his chest at the idea of making Pa proud.

Mr. Lyman tucked his chin in tighter and made a little humming noise in his throat. Ethan wasn't sure, but the noise sounded vaguely pleased. "Do you think this work will suit you, then, boy?"

"I—I hope so, sir."

Mr. Lyman sat at his desk. He laid his ledger down and set his pen in the inkwell. With a deft motion, he flicked his coat-tails out from under his backside. "And how are you and Paddy getting along?"

Ethan's mouth snapped shut. It took a moment for his mind

to shift to the new subject. "Oh, um, f-fine, sir." He wondered if Daniel had been telling tales about him to Mr. Lyman or Silas. He thought Silas was satisfied with his work, but Daniel—well, Daniel was never satisfied with anything, was he?

Mr. Lyman nodded. "He's not giving you any trouble, then?"

"N-no, sir," Ethan said hesitantly, remembering how Pa had cautioned him against complaining.

"Now, now, boy. You must be honest with me. What's he done?"

"I—well, not anything, really. I mean, he's showing me what to do, like Silas says he should." What exactly could he say about Daniel? When Ethan thought hard about it, the Irish boy really hadn't *done* anything, had he? Maybe he'd been rude and ill-tempered, but he hadn't struck Ethan or cursed him, though he sometimes looked on the verge of doing so. All he'd done was make Ethan work harder than he'd ever worked before. Mr. Lyman surely wouldn't fault him for that. No, it wasn't anything Daniel *did,* exactly, just the way he *was*—as Lizzie said, *Just Paddy being Paddy.* "He's just not very friendly, that's all. He seems cross all the time. Cross and unhappy." Ethan surprised himself with the last word. Until just now, he'd never given much thought to how Daniel might feel—if he had any feelings at all.

Mr. Lyman's eyebrows lifted. "Unhappy?" He laughed. "What reason could he have to be unhappy?"

"I—I d-d-don't know, sir." Ethan pondered the question a bit and made a guess. "His—well, he's got no family, has he?"

Mr. Lyman shook his head. "A tragedy, that. Quite the tragedy." But he didn't elaborate, and somehow Ethan felt it would be rude to ask.

Ethan suddenly saw Daniel's moodiness in a different light. "I didn't really think about it that way before. I s'pose that, maybe, well, sir, I s'pose maybe if my mama and papa and everyone who liked me was gone, maybe I'd be unhappy, too. Wouldn't you?"

"Gone," Mr. Lyman repeated. He reached into a cubbyhole in the desk and pulled out a little silver oval, a bit bigger than a watchcase. When the storekeeper opened the case, Ethan caught a glimpse of a tiny portrait. "Gone," Mr. Lyman said again, his eyes growing sad and distant. He closed the case and put it away gently, as if it were a flower he didn't want to crush.

"D'you s'pose that's why he's so cross all the time?"

Mr. Lyman shivered away the peculiar expression and put a thin smile on his face. "Don't be silly, boy. That was a long time ago. Now he has everything a boy could want. More than his parents ever could have given him."

"Oh." Ethan scratched his head, trying to fathom the mystery that was Daniel. "I guess he just doesn't like me, then."

"Well, don't fret over it, boy. He's merely envious. Already you're showing more promise than he ever did."

"I am?" Ethan's puzzlement over Daniel faded with the comforting thought of his own superiority.

"Indeed, yes. If he wouldn't persist in his—his—Irishness . . . If he would only resolve to be more like an American, well, then, he could be as successful as I'm sure you'll be."

"I will?" Ethan stood up a little straighter. Wouldn't Pa be pleased that Mr. Lyman expected him to be a success!

"If—" Mr. Lyman raised a finger to emphasize the *if.* "If you apply yourself and study and work hard. It's what your father wants for you, isn't it?"

"I—I think so."

"He did a wise thing sending you here. It's a smart man who knows his own limitations."

Ethan felt confused. He liked what Mr. Lyman said about Pa being smart and wise, but he wasn't sure about that part about limitations.

"He wants the best for you. And he knows you'll have it here, that I can do things for you he can't, teach you things he can't."

Ethan nodded slowly. "Yessir. That's what he said the day I left. Though I don't quite understand all of it."

"If you don't understand, boy, you only need to ask." Mr. Lyman leaned forward in his chair, his blue eyes warm with sympathy.

"Those papers he signed, 'bout the indenture, and all. It's complicated, isn't it?" Pa had shown him the papers, but there had been so many big words in such curvy handwriting that it had made his head spin trying to read them all.

Mr. Lyman shrugged. "A lot of words, but it's really a simple business transaction. You work for me, and in exchange, you learn a trade. Two trades, in your case, so you can count yourself lucky. There's few better than Silas to teach you husbandry, and few better than myself to teach you business, if you'll forgive my vanity." Mr. Lyman chuckled. "There are other responsibilities, as well. You're to conduct yourself properly, and I'm to make sure you have a proper moral upbringing. Nothing so difficult there, eh?"

Ethan shook his head, although he had a feeling that *proper* in the Lyman household might be more complicated than *proper* in his own home.

"And you get your room and board and one set of clothes a year. So don't be too eager to grow out of them." His eyes twinkled at his joke. "But you're liable for any damages you'd cause to me. Not that you would, of course." He dismissed the idea with a wave of his hand. "Oh, and you can't marry without my permission." Mr. Lyman cast him a slantwise glance. "You don't have any secret lady friends that I need to worry about, do you?" His mouth pursed in a suppressed grin.

Ethan made a face and shook his head.

"Well, then, there you have it. Now you just work hard and learn as much as you can, and you'll be surprised how quickly the time will pass. Before you know it, your nine years will be up and you'll be leaving us a better man than you came."

Nine years, Ethan thought. For him, that was a lifetime.

Ethan fitted a smooth oval stone to his sling and squinted one eye shut. He studied the three cackling crows perched on the fence. The first was Mrs. Lyman, who'd pulled his ear and made him go without breakfast because he'd come to the table uncombed and unwashed after morning chores. The second was Nell, who'd kicked the bucket from the evening's milking all over his trousers and shoes. And the third one—the largest and the one who cackled the loudest—that one was Daniel.

That'll do. That'll do, the Daniel-crow seemed to say.

"'That'll do. That'll do,'" Ethan mocked back. The sling whistled over his head. The stone bit the fence rail with a satisfying crack, right next to the Daniel-crow. With a shriek, the three birds flew up, black silhouettes against the setting sun.

Ethan's stomach rumbled, making him think of the plate of tea cakes left over from the evening meal. Lizzie had said she would set them aside for him and Daniel. He trotted up the road and back toward the house, pointedly ignoring Daniel, who sat on the chopping block sharpening his pocketknife.

The kitchen was empty. Ethan walked over to the little side table where the plate of cakes sat neatly wrapped in a blue checkered cloth. He'd barely lifted a corner of the cloth and taken one of the round white cakes when somebody grabbed his wrist and spun him around.

"What d'you think you're doing?" Daniel whispered. "You fancying a thrashing already?"

"B-but Lizzie said . . .," Ethan stammered, surprise turning to anger. Daniel might be able to boss him around in fields and barn and attic, but he had no right to lord it over him in the kitchen, too. "You heard her. She told Silas she set them by for us."

"What Lizzie says don't mean much once she's gone home. You want something in this house, you'd best be asking for it, if you know what's good for you, understand?"

Reluctantly, Ethan let the cake fall back onto the plate.

Daniel nodded toward the door. "Silas is in the parlor. Ask him quiet. You don't want to be disturbing Lyman and herself."

Ethan's chest tightened. He couldn't even breathe without Daniel dogging him. Well, he didn't want the stupid cakes anymore. He yanked his hand away and spun on his heel. As he turned, the button on his shirt cuff caught a ragged thread in the cloth covering the cakes. The cloth came with him, dragging plate, cakes, and all behind it. The plate smashed to the floor and cakes bounced across the kitchen.

"Now you've bloody done it!" Daniel shoved Ethan away from the mess. "Fetch the broom."

Ethan had just picked up the broom when he heard another crash, not of breaking crockery, but of something large and solid slamming hard against a wall.

Chapter Four

Ethan spun around to see Mr. Lyman clutching Daniel's frock, pinning him up against the wall. Daniel squirmed, his feet barely meeting the floor. Ethan expected Daniel's face to be frozen with the same fear that knotted his own stomach. Instead, his eyes were blank with resignation.

"The boy's not here a week and you're already teaching him to steal, Paddy?" Mr. Lyman twisted Daniel's cravat to force the boy to look at him.

"I wasn't stealing." Daniel's voice rasped against Mr. Lyman's choking grip. "Lizzie said—"

"None of your lies." Mr. Lyman slapped Daniel across the mouth to silence him.

Ethan closed his eyes, fighting the sick feeling in his stomach. He wanted to run, but his legs seemed to be melting beneath him. When he opened his eyes again, he saw Mr. Lyman drawing his fist back to punch Daniel. Without willing it, he opened his mouth. "Please, sir. It wasn't his fault." His voice came out in a tremulous squeak.

Mr. Lyman whirled. "What did you say, boy?" Anger distorted his distinguished features into a frightening mask.

Ethan watched Daniel fall to his knees. The front of his frock reddened as blood dribbled from his mouth. "He didn't do it." Ethan's voice was almost a whisper. He backed up until the big worktable stopped him. "I did." He closed his eyes and ducked his head, waiting for the blow to fall.

When it didn't, Ethan opened his eyes to find Mr. Lyman peering narrowly from one boy to the other. Mr. Lyman spun toward Daniel. Ethan gasped as the storekeeper kicked the Irish boy. Daniel curled up around himself and moaned. "That's for stealing," Mr. Lyman growled. Whirling, he backhanded Ethan across the face. Ethan staggered, his cheek burning. "And that's for lying." Ethan cringed against the table, wishing he could crawl underneath it. "Now clean up this mess," Mr. Lyman said. "Then upstairs with the two of you. Don't show your faces back down here until it's time for chores tomorrow."

Ethan held a hand to his stinging cheek and stared.

"Well, boy? What are you gawking at?" Mr. Lyman raised his hand again. "Get moving before I lose my temper."

"Yessir." His vision blurring, Ethan ducked his head and lunged for the broom.

Mr. Lyman spun out of the room as abruptly as he'd entered it.

Ethan's body turned limp and heavy. He grabbed the table for support as his knees crumpled.

Daniel moaned and slowly uncurled. "Is he gone now?"

Ethan managed a feeble "Uh-huh." He dropped his broom and knelt beside the older boy.

Daniel drew himself to his hands and knees. Ethan decided he must still be dizzy from the blow, for he could have sworn Daniel almost smiled. "Didn't take you long, eh?" Daniel said. "Not here a week and you're on his bad side already."

"Are—are you hurt?" Ethan asked.

Daniel shook his head. He pulled out his handkerchief and mopped his bloody lip.

"Why didn't you tell on me? You don't even like me," Ethan whispered.

Daniel shrugged. "Never said I didn't." The handkerchief muffled his voice.

"You never said you did."

Daniel leaned on Ethan's shoulder and pulled himself to his feet, leaving bloody finger marks on Ethan's sleeve. "Well," he said in a low voice, "I don't like to be making up me mind about a person too quick. Anyway, it'd hardly be fair now, would it? Letting him thrash you and you not even knowing the proper way to get hit."

Ethan rubbed his cheek and gaped. Maybe it was true what they said about the Irish being mad.

The boys cleaned up the mess in silence. It wasn't until they had retreated to the attic that Ethan mustered the courage to speak again. "What did you mean by—"

Daniel hissed Ethan to silence. He crouched at the head of the stairs and cocked his head.

Ethan heard footsteps in the hall below. He tensed as the sound stopped at the door at the bottom of the attic stairs. Metal slid against wood, then a bolt clicked home. Daniel wouldn't be wandering anywhere tonight.

Daniel's mouth twisted in an ironic grimace. "Could be worse. He could'a come up." He padded up the last two stairs and shuffled across the attic. "What did I mean by what?"

"Uh—" Ethan tried to remember what he'd been asking. "About there being a right way to get hit."

Daniel snorted an odd, humorless laugh. "You just have to be knowing a few tricks, is all." He pulled his frock off over his head. "You see, Lyman, it's just knocking you down that he's after," Daniel said, unbuttoning his vest and dropping it on the bed. "So the sooner you fall, the sooner he'll stop hitting you. But you have to do it so he thinks he's got a proper lick in at you, but without really letting him." He shrugged his braces off his shoulders and untied his cravat.

"You mean, he didn't—didn't hurt you?"

Daniel gingerly touched his mouth, then his ribs. His cheek

twitched when his fingers probed his side. "Well, not as much as he thinks he did." He took Ethan's arm and led him toward the window. "How 'bout you?" Turning Ethan's face toward the fading light, his long fingers probed the red mark on Ethan's cheek. "Not bad," Daniel said. "Prob'ly won't even bruise." He gave Ethan a push toward the little table. "Put some cold water on it and it'll be fine. Least we didn't get a switching."

"S-switching?"

Daniel raised an eyebrow. "You never been switched?"

Ethan shook his head. "Pa mostly gives me extra chores. He says he might as well get some good out'a me being bad, and hitting never got any kindling chopped." Ethan took one of the rags from the table and sloshed some water onto it. "Why'n't you just tell him I did it?" He held the rag to his face. The cool moisture eased his throbbing cheekbone.

Daniel soaked a cloth and held it to his mouth. "Wouldn'a mattered. I'd'a just got thrashed for lying, too." Daniel's eyes narrowed over the rag. "How come you told him you done it?"

"I—I don't know." An hour ago, Ethan would have sworn that nothing would have given him greater joy than to see Daniel on his knees, his face blooming bright with blood. Instead, he'd only felt sick to his stomach. "It was the truth," he said, although he hadn't told the truth for its own sake. All he'd wanted was to make Mr. Lyman stop. He sat down on a fat warty squash that was nearly as big as he was. "Does he—is he like that all the time?"

"Not if you do your work proper and keep your mouth shut and mind your manners and stay out of his way. And don't be dropping anything. And don't be making him angry. And—"

"It's not right."

"I never said it was. That's just the way it is." Daniel's voice was as matter-of-fact as his words.

"Aren't you afraid of him?"

"Nah. He'll only knock me about a bit, then let me be. Why waste your time fearing something that can't kill you?" Daniel put his rag aside and dug through his pockets. "Besides, every now and then when he's not looking, I settle up with him." He drew out a handful of broken tea cakes and offered them to Ethan. "Here. I'll eat the bloody ones if you're squeamish." He picked out a few pink-smudged cakes and kept them for himself.

Ethan gasped. "Wha—"

"'S'all right. There's no broken crockery in 'em." Daniel's mouth twisted into something that was almost, but not quite, a smile. He blew a little dirt and pocket lint from a bit of tea cake and popped it in his mouth. "No sense throwing all Lizzie's good baking to the chickens, eh?"

Ethan twisted the button on his shirt cuff until it couldn't turn any more. He released it and watched it twirl back into place. Strange how something so small could cause so much trouble.

Mr. Lyman cleared his throat. "Well, boy, there's no need to look so timid. I'm not going to bite you. I only want to talk to you about last night."

Getting bitten was the least of Ethan's worries. He shifted his weight from one foot to the other, hanging back out of Mr. Lyman's reach. "I'm sorry, sir. I won't do it again, I promise," he blurted, although he wasn't sure what he was promising not to do.

Mr. Lyman smiled and nodded. Seated at his tall secretary, he looked like a benevolent judge, with no trace of the fierce disciplinarian of last evening. "I'm sure you mean that now, but a bad influence is hard to fight off."

"Sir?"

Mr. Lyman's face grew serious and thoughtful. "You may think I was rather . . . severe . . . with you boys last night. But you must understand that while you're in my care, I'm responsible for keeping you on the right track. For making sure you're . . . well disciplined. Do you understand?" His words were steady and even, with no sign of temper.

"Sir?"

"Discipline." Mr. Lyman seemed to savor the word like a sweet on his tongue. "Discipline is the key to raising a boy. It's why your father sent you here. Did you know that?" His chair squeaked as he shifted his weight toward Ethan.

"No, sir." Pa hadn't said anything about discipline.

"Your father is a kind man. Indulgent. It does no harm to indulge a girl. But a boy . . ." Mr. Lyman shook his head. "Discipline," he repeated. "A well-disciplined boy makes a successful young man. Look at Silas. How many men do you think would have the management of three hundred acres at twenty-two years old? But he didn't get that way by himself. Discipline was the key." Mr. Lyman pointed a finger, as if the word hovered in the air before him. "And a well-disciplined boy has to be careful of whom he looks to for an example." The finger turned on Ethan. "Do you understand?"

"An example?"

"Do you think your father would be pleased if he learned you were picking up bad habits from a liar and a thief?"

"No, sir."

"No, indeed." Mr. Lyman's sigh sounded heavy with weariness.

Ethan dropped his head and began worrying at the button again. Would Mr. Lyman tell Pa that Ethan had turned into a thief and a liar not a week after leaving home? Would Mr. Lyman send him back in disgrace?

Mr. Lyman continued. "Paddy has always been . . . difficult. Of course, he can't help it; it's his nature. You don't know how I've struggled to curb his temper, his willfulness, his stubbornness. But he's still a difficult boy: unruly, clumsy, full of mischief. He could lead an unwary boy down the wrong path, and we don't want that, do we?"

"I—I don't suppose so, sir." Ethan twirled the button, drawing up a little twist of cloth at his wrist. The cuff dug into his skin.

"If Paddy tries to lead you astray, you come and tell me, and I'll set him right."

"Right?" Ethan gave the button another twist. His pulse thudded against the twisted cuff, an uncertain rhythm under his fingers.

"You can help me make sure he's headed down the right path. You want to help Paddy, don't you, boy?"

Ethan nodded as if he understood. It seemed important to Mr. Lyman that he understand, almost as if it would make the storekeeper sad rather than angry if he didn't.

Mr. Lyman settled back into his chair, resting his hands on his knees. "I don't know what's to become of that boy when he leaves here. A man needs intelligence and discipline, but Paddy . . ." He sighed as if he'd suddenly grown weary. "His birth deprived him of the first, but I thought I could give him the second. If the boy's fit to do no more than serve, at least he could serve well."

"Serve, sir?"

Mr. Lyman raised his head. "Yes, of course. It's the way the world works. Some are fit to rule and some are fit only to serve. Do you understand?"

"I—I think so, sir." Ethan wondered which Mr. Lyman thought he was. He twisted his button one more time.

"That's a good boy." Mr. Lyman hooked a thumb into his vest pocket. "So you just remember to come to me when you see him going wrong. Can you do that?"

Ethan chewed his lip. He wasn't sure he wanted Daniel set

right if it meant more bloody lips and bruised ribs. But he had to give Mr. Lyman an answer. "I understand, sir," he said.

"Good. That's settled, then." Mr. Lyman opened a small black ledger and dipped his pen in the inkwell. "Now, on to business. You'll have to pay the cost of the breakage. You know that, don't you?"

"Me?" Ethan's voice squeaked.

"Well, your father, of course. I'll add it to what he already owes. You'll pay it off in time." Mr. Lyman blotted the notation and closed the book. He leaned forward. "I'm glad we had this little talk. I trust you'll give me no further trouble."

"No, sir. I'll try, sir."

"Good, good. After all, we don't want your father hearing you've been a difficult boy, do we?"

"No, sir." Ethan twisted his button again. He felt a snap, and it came away in his fingers.

Chapter Five

"Why is Ethan sad?" Ruth asked from her perch on Silas's shoulders.

Ethan wondered how Silas put up with his littlest sister. They'd barely left the meetinghouse when Ruth had demanded to ride home on Silas's back. Now she sat drumming on her brother's tall hat and surveying the lumps of newly plowed and planted earth like a queen viewing her realm from her coach.

Silas cupped Ruth's shoes in his hands to keep her from swinging her muddy feet against his chest and dirtying his black tailcoat. His Sabbath clothes made him look very elegant, accentuating his broad shoulders and trim waist. Only his callused, square-fingered hands marked him as a farmer rather than a lawyer or a minister or a storekeeper. He shushed Ruth's question, but Zeloda had already latched on to it.

"Ethan's sad because his mama and papa don't want him no more."

"Zeloda!" Silas snapped.

Ethan dug his fists deeper into his pockets, bending his head so that his hat brim would hide his reddening face. He focused on walking a narrow line along the straggling border of tufted weeds at the edge of the road. If he concentrated very hard on keeping to the line, he couldn't possibly hear anything Zeloda said.

"That's a horrible thing to say," Florella said. "They're

probably just sick. That's why they didn't come to meeting today." Her tone of studied kindness stung Ethan harder than Zeloda's tease.

Ethan stared back toward the center of town. It was half an hour's walk back to the common, then another three home. If Pa or Ma were sick . . .

"Don't be ridiculous," Silas said. "It's a long walk from Stackpole's Mountain, especially after a week of planting. And with the way the roads are today—" He shook a glob of sticky mud from his shoe.

Silas was right, Ethan thought. With so much work to be done in the spring, Pa and Ma rarely went to church in April or May. As often as not, Pa spent the Sabbath breaking it: doing those little bits of jobs that took fifteen minutes or half an hour here and there; little jobs that Pa said the Lord surely wouldn't credit as work. He shook his head. He'd known from the start that it might be weeks before he'd see Pa and Ma again. It would have been foolish to expect to see them at church this morning. Still, it would have been nice if they'd come. If they'd come, he could have asked Pa if Mr. Lyman was right about discipline and all that.

Silas shook his finger at his younger sister. "As for you, Zeloda, you need to mind your manners."

"I don't need manners around *him*." Zeloda jutted her chin in Ethan's direction. "He's only here 'cause his papa doesn't pay his bills and can't afford to keep him."

Ethan clenched his fists inside his pockets. He wished Zeloda were a boy so he could knock her down.

"You shouldn't talk about Mr. Root like that," Florella said. "It isn't Christian to mock the poor." She gave Ethan a prissy little smile.

"We're not poor!" Ethan cast a despairing glance at Silas.

Silas stepped between Ethan and the girls. "It isn't Christian to mock anybody," he said. He swung Ruth down from his shoulders. "Girls, take Ruth and get along home."

Ethan looked away from the girls. It was all a lie. Pa and Ma *weren't* poor. They were just *having a little trouble,* as Pa said. They *did* want Ethan. They hadn't sent him to Mr. Lyman's just to get rid of him. But if they weren't poor, if they did want him, why had they sent him away? Something tugged at his sleeve.

Ruth's cold-reddened lips puffed out in a sympathetic knot. "Don't worry, Ethan," she said. "If your mama and papa don't want you, you can stay with us. Just like Paddy."

Just like Paddy. Ethan closed his eyes and wished he could sink into the mud and never rise up again. He barely felt Ruth's hand squeeze his, then let go. He didn't notice the larger hand resting on his shoulder until Silas gave him a little shake.

"Don't mind them. Ruth and Florella mean well. They just don't know how to say it. And Zeloda . . ." Silas took a deep breath. "She's her mother's daughter." He patted Ethan's shoulder and nudged him forward. "Don't worry. Maybe your parents will come next week. Or the week after."

Ethan's face brightened. "Or maybe even this afternoon. Maybe they'll go to the afternoon service. D'you think so, Silas?"

Silas hesitated a moment before answering. "Maybe." He nudged Ethan again, and they started back to the Lymans'.

By the time Ethan and Silas arrived, Mrs. Lyman and her daughters were laying out dinner: a chicken pie and bread and cakes and puddings baked yesterday, and the usual complement of pickles and preserves.

Silas rubbed his hands together and stooped in front of the fire. It crackled brightly after the chilly service and the cold walk. Ethan hovered near Silas, basking in the heat radiating from the black iron fire frame.

Heavy footsteps announced Mr. Lyman's arrival. Ethan slipped behind Silas and hunkered down in his jacket, his head bowed, his shoulders rounded. Already he'd learned Daniel's trick of making himself small and inconspicuous when his master was around.

Mr. Lyman stalked into the room and surveyed the table. The line between his eyes deepened, and his mouth curved downward into a scowl.

The room grew quiet when Mrs. Lyman and her daughters noticed Mr. Lyman's expression.

The storekeeper turned to his wife. "Mrs. Lyman, is Lizzie here to dinner today?"

"No. She went home after milking." Mrs. Lyman's dark eyes narrowed as she, too, spotted the flaw.

Ethan shivered in spite of the fire. He couldn't see the point of Mr. Lyman's questions, but he knew they meant trouble for somebody.

"Are we expecting a guest?"

"No, dear."

Mr. Lyman tugged the front of his tailcoat straight and rubbed his hands together. "That's what I thought. Where's Paddy?"

"He went to wash up," Florella said.

Mr. Lyman raised his chin and shouted toward the kitchen. "Paddy! Come in here!"

Daniel's face, pink and shiny, peeked through the doorway. "Sir?" His wet hair was combed flat against his head, but already little tufts had strayed from their place and stuck out however they pleased. He tied his cravat around a damp, drooping collar.

"I said, come here."

Ethan's stomach writhed at Mr. Lyman's tone. Whatever was coming, he didn't want to see it.

Daniel entered the parlor slowly, keeping the table between himself and Mr. Lyman.

"Come *here!*" Mr. Lyman pointed to the carpet directly in front of him.

Daniel edged around the table and stopped at the spot indicated.

"Have you forgotten how to count, you Irish idiot?"

"No, sir."

"Then why are there too many chairs around this table?"

Ethan did a quick mental inventory. There was Mr. Lyman's big chair with the arms, then the four yellow painted chairs, Daniel's swaybacked rush-seated chair, and one of the ladder-backs that the hired men usually sat on. One chair too many.

Daniel frowned at the errant seat as if it had walked into the parlor on its own. Mr. Lyman's hand across Daniel's mouth directed the boy's attention back to his master.

Mr. Lyman's toe tapped out a muffled rhythm on the carpet. "Well? I'm waiting for an answer."

"I—well, sir, I remembered you let me sit to dine on the Sabbath when I first come, so I thought you'd be wanting Ethan to do the same. I thought he could have me chair, and I could—"

Mr. Lyman's other hand came up this time. Daniel staggered at the blow. He would have fallen into the table if Mr. Lyman hadn't grabbed him by the front of his shirt and pivoted him away. He shook the boy hard and shoved him against the wall. Ethan winced when Daniel's head met the edge of the mantel.

"You *thought?* You're not here to think, boy. You're here to do what you're told. No less and no more. If there are to be any more chairs set out, Mrs. Lyman or I will tell you, understand?"

"Yessir," Daniel said mechanically, his eyes blank. A tendril of blood trickled down his chin.

"B-b-b—" Ethan felt words trying to come out of his mouth. He wasn't sure what he could say that would do any good, but it didn't feel right not to say anything. Silas's fingertips dug into his shoulder. Ethan glanced up. Silas moved his head slightly from side to side.

Mr. Lyman whirled toward Ethan. "Do you have something to say, boy?"

Ethan looked past Mr. Lyman at Daniel, still suspended in Mr. Lyman's grip. Daniel moved his head from one side to the other, just once, as Silas had done.

"N-n-no, sir," Ethan said.

"I hope not." Mr. Lyman relaxed his grip on Daniel. "Now take those chairs away, both of you, and get out of here." He shoved Daniel against the wall and stepped aside.

Daniel wiped his mouth on his sleeve, took a broad step around Mr. Lyman, and picked up the offending chair.

Silas released Ethan's shoulder and gave him a little push forward. Ethan picked up Daniel's chair and followed him into the kitchen. As he passed Zeloda, she crossed her eyes and stuck out her tongue. Florella hissed at Zeloda and pinched her elbow.

Daniel stood by the kitchen fireplace, dabbing his lip with his shirt cuff. He spat a mouthful of blood into the fire, then explored his mouth with his fingers, as though counting his teeth. "And they tell me I'm no Christian," he mumbled, his mouth still full of fingers. "You'd think he'd be giving his arm a rest of a Sunday, wouldn't you? More fool me for believing he might." He spat again.

"Are you—are you hurt very bad?"

"Nah. No teeth loosened and nothing broken but me head, and that's no loss when you're an Irish idiot, is it?" He rubbed the back of his skull, then looked at his red-stained fingertips.

"You're bleeding," Ethan said.

"S'pose so." Daniel wiped his hand on his trousers.

Ethan looked from Daniel to the parlor door. "But—but what about our dinner?"

"No dinner for you and me today, Sunday or no. When he says get out, you don't come back 'til he sends for you. Unless you're wanting a thumping, too. 'S'only beans anyway." Daniel nodded at the squat brown bean pot sitting on the kitchen table. Ethan wouldn't have missed the beans much, but he couldn't help thinking about the chicken pie and the cakes.

Daniel took his brown woolen frock from its peg by the door. He shrugged himself into it, then leaned against the wall and closed his eyes, his lips pressed together. His face turned so pale that Ethan wondered if he was going to be sick. After a moment, he took a breath, opened his eyes, and grabbed his cap. Before putting it on, he lifted his hand to his head again. Ethan saw the pale orange hair turning a shade darker around Daniel's fingertips.

"That looks bad." Ethan pulled out his handkerchief. "Here."

Daniel folded the cloth into a pad and held it to the back of his head. He went to the outside door and began to open it, then paused with his hand on the latch. Slowly, he closed the door, letting the latch fall quietly back into place. He returned to the kitchen table and stared down at the bean pot. Using Ethan's handkerchief for a pot holder, he lifted the lid. His tongue flicked at his bleeding lower lip, and his mouth worked for a few moments as he watched the steam curl slowly up from inside the pot. A little bit of color returned to his cheeks. With a resolute tilt to his chin, he pursed his lips. He spat a bloody mouthful into the pot, stirred the contents, and replaced the lid.

Daniel set his cap firmly on his head, pulling the brim down low over his forehead. Without a word or a glance to Ethan, he walked out, his steps long and certain.

* * *

"Daniel! Daniel, wait!" Ethan shouted, running down the road. The cold stung his ears and cheeks, but the running warmed him soon enough. He was gasping for breath and damp with sweat when Daniel finally stopped and turned around.

"What?"

"Where're you going?" Ethan asked.

Daniel rubbed his head. "None of your business. I don't need you telling himself me doings."

"Me? What did I do?" Didn't Daniel want to be friends? Why else had he set a chair for Ethan?

"Only got me head bashed and me dinner missed." Daniel rubbed hard at the back of his head, as if to remind himself of the trouble Ethan had caused. His eyelids puckered and he bit his lower lip.

Ethan's mouth worked for a few moments before he could get the words out. "But I—I didn't do anything. I never asked you to set a chair for me." His damp shirt felt like a layer of ice forming around him.

Daniel stopped and stared at Ethan. His gray eyes matched the threatening sky. "I shouldn't do it now if you begged."

Ethan folded his arms across his chest to hide his shivering. "Fine. Keep your stupid secret. Who wants to go anywhere with you, anyway?"

"Then why are you still following me? Why don't you find yourself some *children* to play with?" Daniel said the word *children* the way he might have said *maggots.* He waved his hand at Ethan in dismissal—the hand that still held Ethan's handkerchief. The boys stared at the handkerchief, then at each other, their jaws set and their eyes unyielding. Daniel crumpled the cloth and threw it on the ground.

"Mr. Lyman was right." Ethan tried to make his voice as cold and harsh as the wind.

Daniel began walking again, his strides growing longer and faster.

"You're stubborn and bad-tempered and . . . and . . ." In his fury, Ethan couldn't remember the rest of Mr. Lyman's words, so he reached for some of his own. "And mean . . . and nasty . . . and . . . and I hate you! Do you hear that? I hate you!" Ethan shouted.

Daniel stopped with his back to Ethan, his shoulders slack, his hands limp at his sides. Ethan felt an instant's satisfaction that he'd said something that had stung. Then Daniel whirled. "Good!" he shouted. "Maybe you'll leave me be, then!" He turned and continued stalking down the road.

"I hate you!" Ethan shouted again. He searched for the worst insult he could fling. "I hate you—*Paddy*!" he shrieked. "Paddy—Paddy—Paddy—Paddy—Paddy!"

The name seemed to hit Daniel between the shoulder blades. His stride faltered, his head drooped, and his hands clenched and opened at his sides. Within a few steps, however, he squared his shoulders and cocked his head, as if the name now slid over him without touching him anymore. He didn't look back again.

Although he couldn't see Daniel's face, somehow Ethan knew that he'd disappeared into that mysterious place inside himself. Ethan tried to walk off in the opposite direction, but the mud seemed to hold his feet fast. He stared after Daniel until he disappeared from sight. Even though it was Daniel's form shrinking into the distance, it was Ethan who felt small.

Chapter Six

"Just a minute, Ethan," Mr. Lyman called out as Ethan followed Silas down the meetinghouse steps.

Ethan cringed. He glanced toward Silas for a clue about how he should act, but Silas was already heading over to join the other young men clustered around Clarissa Smead as thickly as flies around a jelly jar.

"Ethan," Mr. Lyman repeated.

With a sigh, Ethan resigned himself to facing Mr. Lyman alone. He wondered what he'd done now. For the whole afternoon service, he'd sat up in the gallery with Silas and the rest of the choir, as far away as possible from Mr. and Mrs. Lyman. Unless Mr. Lyman was a sorcerer, he surely couldn't have noticed the two or three times Ethan had nodded off during Mr. Merriwether's sermon. "Yessir?" Ethan said cautiously as he turned, wondering if taking his hat off or bowing would take the edge off Mr. Lyman's temper.

He was surprised to see both Mr. and Mrs. Lyman smiling as if they'd completely forgotten the noontime upset over the wayward chair. "There's someone I want you to meet," Mr. Lyman said. He stepped a little to the side to present the couple with whom he'd been chatting.

Ethan decided that both hat-tipping and bowing were in order when he recognized the owner of the sawmill and his wife. "G-good day, Mrs. Ward. . . . Sir," he said, bowing first to the sawyer's wife, then to the sawyer.

"You've met already, then," Mr. Lyman said.

"Yessir. Pa always takes me when he has to go to the sawmill," Ethan said, feeling a little less nervous. He loved Mr. Ward's mill, with its great saw ker-chunking up and down, spewing sawdust everywhere while it chewed the logs into boards. It was a pity Pa had to go there only once or twice a year.

"So you're working down to Mr. Lyman's now, eh, young Mr. Root?" Mr. Ward asked, his blue eyes crinkling at the corners when he smiled.

"Yessir," Ethan said, flattered that Mr. Ward called him *Mr. Root* instead of just *Ethan*.

"He has a great deal yet to learn, but I think we'll get along, won't we?" Mr. Lyman raised an eyebrow.

Swallowing the chalky lump that rose in the back of his throat, Ethan said, "I—I hope so, sir."

Mr. Ward's eyes searched the common. "Peter! Sol! Come here, boys!" he shouted in the booming voice he usually used to make himself heard over the racket of his mill.

Two chubby-cheeked boys about Ethan's age stopped chasing each other and joined their parents. The boys had the same brown eyes and curly dark hair that strayed from underneath their blue woolen caps. Except for a slight difference in height, they could have been twins. Ethan had seen Peter—or maybe it was Sol—down at the mill once or twice, but he'd never had much chance to get to know either of them.

"The Wards live just down the road from us. I—" Mr. Lyman paused and put his arm through his wife's. The couple exchanged a sociable smile. "—*we* thought you ought to get to know some boys a bit more . . . suitable. Boys your own age," Mr. Lyman added, nodding toward Peter and Sol.

"They're suitable when they've a mind to be, just like all boys," Mrs. Ward said with a laugh that made her cold-flushed cheeks even pinker. She tucked a straying curl of dark brown hair back under her bonnet. "Ethan's staying at the Lymans'," she explained to her sons. "Why don't the three of you walk home together and get acquainted? Your father has some business to talk over with Mr. Lyman." With a smile, she took Mrs. Lyman's other arm and gave it an affectionate squeeze. "And we ladies would like to have a chat."

Mrs. Lyman smiled back, looking not nearly as stern as she had at dinner.

"Where do you live?" Peter, the older boy, asked as they walked. He squinted at Ethan and curled his lip. "I've seen you at the meetinghouse and maybe now and then at the mill. But you don't go to our school."

"I s'pose I will too, this winter," Ethan said. Not the summer term, though; Silas had told him he'd be needed on the farm all summer. "But I used to go to the district five school, up on Stackpole's Mountain," Ethan added.

"It's not really a mountain," Peter said scornfully. "Just a big hill."

"But everybody calls it that," Ethan said. "Pa says it was a mountain when the Stackpoles started living on it years and years ago, but there's been so many of them that they wore it all down."

Peter and Sol both laughed, and Ethan felt a little more at ease.

"C'mon up to the house," Peter said, breaking into a run. "There's plenty of good sticks in the brush pile we can use for playing soldier."

Ethan followed the boys up the road to the Wards' large red house. They rooted around in a pile of branches behind the barn until they found a proper stick for Ethan. Then they declared war, chasing each other across pastures and fields, shooting each other out of trees, and dying in noisy and dramatic agony. First, they were rebels and redcoats, then Indians and settlers. Their rifles became swords and lances, and they played knights jousting on the tourney field. The swords and lances became cutlasses, and they were pirates boarding a treasure ship. The cutlasses had just turned to spears, and they were in the midst of becoming cannibals in the Sandwich Islands when a tall dark-haired boy leaned over the fence and shushed them.

Ethan recognized Mr. Ward's oldest son, Joshua, who usually assisted his father at the mill. He was a little older than Daniel, maybe eighteen or so. He walked with a spring to his step and a jaunty air, as if life rested lightly on his shoulders. "Ho now, lads. Aren't you supposed to play *quietly* on the Sabbath?" But he was grinning and his blue eyes sparkled.

"Oh, Joshua. We were only being cannibals," Sol said.

"And were you going to pass the Sabbath by eating a few missionaries?" Joshua laughed. "Now what would Mr. Merriwether say about that?"

"We weren't really going to eat anybody," Peter said.

"You can eat anyone you like for all I care, so long as you're quiet about it." Joshua winked. "And you keep your mouth closed when you chew."

"I thought you were keeping company with Clarissa Smead this afternoon," Peter said. "I guess you couldn't charm her into asking you to tea after all."

Sol snickered.

Joshua's eyes lost a little of their sparkle. "She—um—she was otherwise engaged."

"Prob'ly with Silas Lyman or Francis Tolliver," Peter said to Ethan in a whisper deliberately loud enough for Joshua to hear. Then he sang out, "Joshua likes Clarissa! Joshua likes Clarissa!" Sol quickly joined the chant. Joshua looked as though he couldn't decide whether to be angry with his brothers or just ignore them.

"It looked to me like everybody likes Clarissa," Ethan said, a little baffled by the spell she seemed to cast over all the young men. Dainty as Ruth's china doll, she'd been dressed up in a striped silk gown and pink bonnet and shawl that looked too thin for such a blustery day. Ethan supposed she'd meant to look pretty, but in his opinion she'd only looked too stupid to know enough to wear a cloak. Then again, she probably had no fear of taking a chill with so many young men around her to ward off the breeze.

Joshua seemed to notice Ethan for the first time. "Aren't you the boy working over to Mr. Lyman's?"

Ethan nodded.

"How d'you like living with that Irish devil they have over there?"

"He's always cross," Ethan said with a shrug, pretending it didn't bother him.

"I'd watch my back if I were you," Joshua said. "Those Irish are unpredictable. I heard of a family out in Southwick who hired themselves an Irish girl for their dairying. She was neat as you please and worked as hard as the day is long. Or so it seemed. . . ." He let the unfinished story hover over them for a moment.

"What happened?" asked Sol.

Joshua stooped to the boys' level and fixed each one with wide eyes. "She hadn't been there a week when she cut their throats while they slept"—Joshua slashed a finger across his neck—"and made off with silver, jewelry, money, and all." He stretched himself back up to his full height and patted Ethan's shoulder. "So you'd best watch yourself if you don't want to wake up with your throat slit. Especially a boy like you."

Ethan ran a finger under his collar. "Like me? What do you mean a boy like me?"

Joshua shrugged. "Oh, you know." He tapped an index

61

finger against his temple and winked. "Simple," Joshua said. "Like your father."

Peter chanted, "Sim-ple, sim-ple! E-than's pa is sim-ple!" In a moment, Sol had joined in.

Ethan's cheeks burned. He knew what simple was. Simple was Martha Cooney, whose face was shaped like someone had folded it up and then unfolded it wrong, who couldn't do more than recite her ABCs, even though she was all of sixteen. That wasn't Pa at all. Pa knew lots of things. Pa could take a tool that you'd swear had no life left in it and somehow make it do for another season. Pa could reach inside a cow that was having a hard calving and turn the calf around and make it come out right. Pa could tell you the names and ways of the animals and birds that hid in the hay fields and woodlots. Pa could tell a story so you'd think you could see it all happening in front of you.

"My pa is not simple, and neither am I!" Ethan clenched his hands into fists, ready to fling himself at Joshua.

Joshua wrinkled his forehead and spread his hands in apparent surprise. "I heard that your pa had to bind you out because he was too simple to keep his books straight."

"Liar!" Ethan launched himself at Joshua. Peter and Sol grabbed Ethan's arms and held him back while he kicked and struggled to be free.

Joshua laughed. "Now, now, little man, who are you to be calling folks liars?" He gave Ethan a patronizing pat on the head. "You want proof?"

"You can't prove it and you know it!"

"Stop your noise and I will." Joshua gestured toward the house. "Come inside and listen for a bit."

Peter and Sol relaxed their hold and Ethan shook himself loose.

"Coming?" Joshua smirked. "Or are you afraid to find out the truth?"

"I'm not afraid." Ethan followed the Ward boys into the kitchen.

Joshua marched into the parlor, leaving the door between the two rooms ajar so the boys could hear. The three of them hunkered down by the doorway.

"Your brothers still out playing with that Root boy?" Ethan heard Mr. Ward ask.

"Oh, they're having a jolly time together. Didn't you go to school with Mr. Root?" Joshua asked, his voice all innocent curiosity.

"Well, he was just a bit of a lad when I was finishing school. Your aunt Kezia, she's closer to his age." Mr. Ward chuckled. "Said she never could tell what Hannah Bartlett saw in him, slow as he was."

Peter and Sol held their fists up to their mouths to stifle their giggles.

"Slow?" Joshua asked.

"Oh, yes. The master used to say Gideon Root's writing might as well be Greek, the way he made his letters and numbers upside down and sideways and backwards and inside out. At first the master thought Gideon was playing some sly schoolboy trick to mock him. But when he couldn't beat it out of him, the master had to give it up and admit that Root wasn't being sly, only stupid."

Peter and Sol snorted into their fists.

"They used to call him 'Simple Gideon.'" Mr. Ward sighed. "Children can be cruel sometimes. But he grew up well, Gideon did. He's a hardworking man, and you couldn't find a better-hearted, more honest fellow. It's not just book learning makes a man, you know, Joshua."

Ethan's empty stomach turned cold and leaden. Mr. Ward's praise was no balm for the stab of *Simple Gideon*.

"And now Root's boy is over to the Lymans'. At least Gideon won't have to worry about him there. George will do right by him, you can be sure of that. Ah, well, it's a pity Root hasn't gotten any better at doing his figures."

It wasn't true. It couldn't be. And yet . . .

Ethan thought of how Pa struggled over his accounts, complaining that the fives and the twos and the sixes and the nines got all jumbled up. At the time, Ethan had thought Pa was only joking. But just a month ago, Pa and Mr. Lyman had spent hours together at the store, untangling the scribblings in Pa's dog-eared brown copybook, comparing them to Mr. Lyman's ledgers, patiently straightening out the debits and credits.

Ethan slumped against the wall. Peter and Sol stared at him with shining, laughing eyes. They didn't need to say the word; he could see it in their faces: *Simple*.

As Ethan ran from the house, the Ward boys' singsong refrain rang inside his head: *Sim-ple, sim-ple! E-than's pa is sim-ple!* No matter how hard he ran or how far he got from the Wards, he couldn't outrun their voices shouting in his brain. He'd gone well past the Lymans' before he realized that Sol and Peter's chant had yielded to another voice echoing in his head. This voice had a barbed lilt to it as it said, *Tell you what, lad. I'll call you "fool" for a week or so and see how you like it.*

Ethan was surprised to see the cattle yard empty by the time he arrived back at the Lymans'. He'd lost track of time, wandering aimlessly after his flight from the Wards'.

Daniel was milking Nell when Ethan came into the barn. Although Ethan walked lightly, he saw Daniel's shoulders stiffen when he entered. But the older boy didn't turn around.

Ethan twisted his hands together. The fingernails of one

hand worried at a healing blister in the web of skin between the thumb and forefinger of the other. "Daniel," he said. His voice came out in a croak.

Daniel's only response was a change in the tilt of his head. Ethan tried again. "I—I—"

Daniel's hands continued to squeeze the milk out in an unfaltering rhythm.

Ethan's fingers worked some more. The thin new skin forming over the blister split. The spot burned as the salt from his hands worked into the opening. He rubbed his thumb hard across the sore and cleared his throat. "I'm sorry." There. He'd said it.

Daniel's hands stopped, then started again.

"I shouldn'a called you Paddy."

One of Daniel's shoulders lifted, but he kept his forehead pressed to the cow's flank. "Everyone else does."

"But it's wrong."

"How can it be wrong if everyone does it?"

"Because you hate it. I shouldn'a said it. It was—it was mean, and I'm sorry."

"You'll be saying it again."

"No, I won't." Ethan edged closer, standing just behind Daniel's shoulder. "I promise."

Daniel turned his head away. All Ethan could see was unruly red hair and ears and Daniel's neck growing pink near his collar. "I thought you hated me," Daniel said. His fingers grabbed harder at Nell's teats, his rhythm growing quicker. One hand slipped. A stream of milk splattered on the edge of the bucket, spotting Daniel's trousers with white.

Nell's head bobbed, and her right hoof came up. Ethan stuck out his left foot and blocked the kick before the older boy had time to react. Daniel finally turned his head. Instead of the sullen scowl Ethan had expected, Daniel's mouth was set

65

askew, his teeth gnawing at his lower lip. He didn't seem to understand anything Ethan had just said or done.

"I don't hate you, Daniel."

"Why?" Daniel asked blankly.

Ethan blinked at the challenge. "I—I—I don't know."

The two boys stared at each other for a long moment. Then Daniel tilted his head over his shoulder. "Go do your chores."

Ethan turned to fetch a stool and a bucket.

"But not like that," Daniel called after him. He rose from the milking stool and stared Ethan up and down.

Ethan realized that he still wore his Sabbath clothes. With the luck he'd been having today, he'd never make it through chores without getting milk and manure all over himself. He didn't know whether his stomach churned more over a possible thrashing or the prospect of a second missed meal. He put his blistered hand to his mouth and sucked on the tender spot.

He cast a despairing glance at Daniel, but Daniel's face had disappeared beneath the frock he was slipping off. Ethan's vision went brown and fuzzy as Daniel dropped the big woolen shirt over him. The frock draped like a blanket almost to Ethan's ankles. He had to roll the cuffs back four times before his hands showed. Even then, the sleeves hung past his knuckles.

"S'pose that'll do," Daniel said. "Mind you don't trip on the hem. I'm not picking you up if you fall on your arse." He picked up his milk bucket. "And don't you be expecting no beans with your tea. I hear Zeloda and Mr. Lyman et 'em all up at dinnertime." His lips parted, exposing a row of surprisingly even teeth that looked out of place in the rest of Daniel's pinched, homely face. Until that moment, the nearest thing to a smile Ethan had ever seen on Daniel's face was an ironic twist that looked more like pain than pleasure. Until that moment, Ethan would have said Daniel didn't know how to smile.

Chapter Seven

"Why so glum, Ethan?" Lizzie asked.

Ethan shrugged off her question and picked up the digging bar. The iron chilled his fingers. He'd been out of sorts all morning, even though he usually enjoyed helping Lizzie in the kitchen garden. There was a friendly ease to her that was missing from the rest of the Lyman household.

A pile of long, twiggy branches waited at the end of the row where they would plant the peas. The branches would go into the holes Ethan made with the digging bar and would provide a framework for the peas to cling to as they grew. Ethan and Lizzie had planted two rows so far. The pea brush looked like a miniature forest springing up in their wake. A gloomy, dead forest, Ethan thought. The day was overcast and windy, threatening snow more than rain. He had a hard time imagining the bare branches covered with white blossoms and fat green pea pods come July. Today it felt as though spring were in full retreat, and it would never stop being gray and dismal and cold.

"Lizzie, does your pa owe Mr. Lyman a lot of money?" he finally asked.

Lizzie poised her hands on her hips. "Now, that's a rude sort of a question. Why ever would you want to ask . . ." She frowned. "Oh. That's not why I work here, Ethan. It's different from you and Paddy. I'm not bound out. The Lymans pay me by the day, like Mr. Pease and Mr. Wheeler."

Ethan rubbed his hands to warm them up. "So—so why *do* you work here, then?"

"When I was about thirteen, Mrs. Lyman hired me to help out after Ruth was born. Then she wanted help with the gardening and sewing and such. Pretty soon she wanted help with the dairying, too, so I started coming nearly every day, and, well . . ." Her shrug sent her shawl slipping down one shoulder. "Here I am."

"Do you like it?" Ethan thudded the bar into the narrow trench they'd dug for the peas.

"Mrs. Lyman pays well enough, and I like nice things." She pulled her ragged shawl tighter around her, crossed the ends over her waist, and secured it behind her back with a snug double knot.

Ethan pursed his lips doubtfully. Lizzie's stained and faded brown flannel dress was the color of an overdone Indian pudding. The combination of her ancient dress, her frayed shawl, and her murky yellow apron made her short, plump body look like an old chair whose stuffing had settled in all the wrong places.

"I don't wear my nice things here, silly! Not to get milk and manure and soil all over." Lizzie laughed. She seemed to be the only one in the Lyman household who could laugh without looking to anyone else first to see if laughter would come amiss. Her laugh always made Ethan feel warm inside. He liked her gingerbread-colored eyes that turned up at the corners when she smiled. But she wasn't pretty, at least not the way people thought pretty should be. The young men in town admired girls like Clarissa Smead, who was slim and delicate with translucent white skin and long, elegant hands. "Besides," Lizzie continued, "I have to think about my wedding, don't I?"

Ethan nearly drove the digging bar through his foot. He

leaned heavily on the bar to regain his balance. "Who—when—you're getting married? To who?"

Lizzie glanced over the high garden fence, toward the field where Silas struggled to pry loose a boulder. "I don't know. But someday I will, and I should have some money and things set by, shouldn't I?"

"Uh—I s'pose so. But do you like working here?"

Lizzie untangled a branch from the pile. "It's as good as anywhere else, I suppose."

"Mrs. Lyman—she—does she—did she ever hit you?"

Lizzie looked up sharply. "If she did, I'd be off like a shot, and who'd make her prize-winning butter and cheese for her then? Just because she pays my wages doesn't make her better than me."

"I can't leave, though, can I? That's what being bound means, doesn't it?" Ethan said.

"I'm afraid so. There's lots of legal papers and things, aren't there?" She shook out the pea brush. "It won't be so bad, Ethan. Just do your work as best you can and keep out of trouble."

He nodded and moved on down the trench. That was what Daniel said, too. Ethan glanced toward the bottom of the garden, where Daniel was digging a bed for onions. "Daniel can't leave either," Ethan said. He thrust the iron bar into the soil.

"Daniel who?"

"Daniel—you know—" Ethan made a small gesture toward the bottom of the garden. A little parade of chickens trailed after Daniel, gobbling up worms and grubs in his wake.

"Oh." Lizzie followed Ethan's glance. "I'd forgotten he had any name other than Paddy."

One of Daniel's brogans flapped open at the toe. "He needs new shoes," Ethan said.

"He needs trousers, too, unless he intends to stop growing

this year. I'm sure Mr. Lyman'll get him some, once he notices. Or once Paddy asks." She centered the end of a branch in the hole Ethan had drilled with the digging bar.

"He won't ask." Ethan and Daniel had quarreled about it that morning, after one of the calves had stomped on Daniel's bare foot. Daniel's idiotic refusal to ask for what he needed had soured Ethan's mood.

"But Mr. Lyman is supposed to buy him clothes. It's part of the indenture. It always is. At least that's what I've been told." Lizzie grasped the branch close to the ground and shoved it into the soft earth. "Well, he usually gets Silas's castoffs, but it's the same thing, really."

"He won't ask Silas, either." Ethan sighed. "He doesn't make sense."

"I think Paddy only makes sense to Paddy," Lizzie said.

"Doesn't he have any friends?"

Lizzie peered brightly at Ethan from under the flopping brim of her calico garden hat. "Aren't you his friend?" she asked in a teasing voice.

Ethan rammed the bar into the loosened earth three times, making a neat little round hole. "I mean boys his own age, like from when he was in school."

Lizzie frowned and shook her head. She tamped the earth down around the branch with her toe. "He's so odd—the way he talks, the way he looks, the way he just *is*. The other boys tormented him something awful."

Ethan helped Lizzie set the last few pieces of brush. She fetched the peas she'd left soaking in a bowl. Kneeling next to the row, she sprinkled some of them at the base of the brush, then sat back on her heels and stared down the garden toward Daniel. "One winter, three or four years ago, Joshua Ward took a notion that he couldn't abide Paddy's red hair, so he and his friends set on him and cut it off."

"Joshua Ward?" Ethan said. He watched Daniel place his spade, step on it, and turn the earth in a steady mechanical rhythm. He couldn't picture Daniel three or four years younger any more than he could picture him without his willful shock of marmalade-colored hair. It wasn't hard, though, to picture Joshua Ward bedeviling him.

"I don't think I've ever had such a fright," Lizzie continued. "When I came on them, there were four of them holding Paddy down on the ground, and Joshua kneeling on Paddy's chest with his pocketknife in his hand. I was sure they'd killed him. Paddy lay there so still, and there was hair and blood all over the snow. The blood was only because Paddy'd hit one of them in the nose trying to get away, but I didn't know that." Her lips turned up in a wan little smile. "I imagine they heard me screaming all the way to Boston. But it scared the boys away." She spread another handful of peas in a tidy line. "It was so odd." She rocked back on her heels, her forehead creasing. "After they left, Paddy lay there in the snow, ever so still, for such a long time, just staring up at the sky with such a—a—" She swallowed and looked down at her row of peas as though she could find the right word spelled out in them. "—such an empty look in his eyes, that I thought perhaps the fright had stopped his heart, like you read about sometimes in the newspaper." She shuddered again, then forced an uneasy laugh. "It nearly stopped *my* heart, I can tell you that."

Ethan realized he'd left off planting to hear the story. Hastily, he dropped clumps of peas down in the bare spots until he caught up with Lizzie. "Did Mr. Lyman thrash him?" he asked.

Lizzie scattered peas faster as she talked. "Why? It wasn't Paddy's fault. Anyway," she continued, scrubbing at her muddy fingers with her apron, "Papa and Mr. Lyman had a long talk with Mr. Ward. After that, the boys mostly left Paddy alone for the rest of the term. But he didn't go back to school the next winter." Reaching the end of the row, Lizzie picked up a hoe to push the soil onto the newly planted seeds.

Ethan did the same. The blades of their hoes pushed toward each other from opposite sides of the row, piling up a little hump of dirt at the base of the pea brush.

"Lizzie—"

"Mmm-hmm?"

"Are you Daniel's friend?"

Lizzie looked toward the bottom of the garden. Daniel had finished digging. He smoothed the soil with a rake, now and then stooping to collect a stone and toss it into a wheelbarrow.

"Paddy doesn't want any friends," she said. "He's always so cross."

"But do you like him?"

"What difference would it make?"

Ethan shrugged. "Maybe he'd be less cross if he thought somebody liked him."

Lizzie laughed. "Maybe he'd be less cross if he wasn't Irish."

Ethan struggled with a bit of brush snagged on his sleeve. "Do you really think so, or is that just what everybody else says?"

"You ask a lot of questions for such a little boy."

Ethan tugged impatiently at the branch. "I'm just trying to figure things out."

Lizzie reached through the brush and freed Ethan's sleeve. "Maybe some things aren't meant to be figured out. Maybe some things just are."

Chapter Eight

For the first two weeks of April, the season had pivoted between winter and spring. By Ethan's third week at the Lymans', it seemed to have finally decided which it wanted to be. The air turned sweet and moist, and songbirds returned to join the crows and sparrows that had stayed the winter.

The change affected everybody's mood. Mrs. Lyman hummed as she laid breakfast on the table, though she still didn't offer Ethan a chair. Mr. Lyman shared laughing endearments with his wife, gently teased his daughters, and made silly faces and babbled nonsense at Aaron. Even Daniel's perpetual scowl eased a little.

"What's that on your plate, boy?" Mr. Lyman said to Ethan.

"M-me? Uh—sir?" Ethan ducked his head in anticipation of a scolding or worse.

"Hardly enough to feed a sparrow, from the looks of it." Mr. Lyman pushed a platter of fried salt pork and potatoes down the table. "Silas, put some food on that boy's plate. Paddy's, too."

Daniel's head bobbed up, and he pressed his lips into a thin line.

"They've worked hard all week. They've earned a hearty meal," Mr. Lyman said.

"Thank you, sir." Ethan overcame his surprise enough to remember his manners. All Daniel said was "Sir," without the thanks.

"They'll be working even harder today, sir," Silas said. "I want to get that new wagon shed finished."

"Well, eat up, then, boy," Mr. Lyman said with a smile that seemed as warm and genuine as the spring morning. "We don't want your father hearing that we're starving you, do we?"

"No, sir." Ethan forced himself to smile back. Perhaps it was only the winter that made Mr. Lyman cross. Maybe his mood would change and his temper grow milder as the days did. Ethan scooped a thick layer of jam onto his fritters. Surely things would get better now that spring had well and truly arrived.

If Mr. Lyman was particularly jovial that morning, Daniel seemed especially moody. Not that Ethan was surprised. Silas needed some boards cut for the shed, which meant a trip to Mr. Ward's sawmill.

Ethan held his breath as the oxcart rumbled to a stop in front of the mill. Joshua and Mr. Ward were helping another man load boards into a wagon. Ethan glanced around cautiously but didn't see the other two Ward boys. He hung back by the oxcart's tailgate, trying to make himself invisible, and noticed Daniel doing the same.

"Good day, Mr. Ward, Mr. Smead," Silas said, shaking hands with the men all around. To Joshua, however, he only gave a curt nod.

The air felt thick with tension. At first Ethan thought he imagined it because of the story Lizzie had told him about Joshua and Daniel. Then he noticed that Silas and Joshua eyed each other like two mistrustful dogs.

Joshua wiped his forearm across his brow. He'd evidently been doing a hard morning's work; his shirt drooped with sweat. "Will you need someone to help you unload once you get home, Mr. Smead?" he asked courteously.

Mr. Smead thumbed back his tall straw hat. "I'd appreciate that, Joshua. If your father can spare you, that is."

Mr. Ward looked hesitant, glancing at the load of logs in Silas's oxcart.

"Don't worry about this job. I've got plenty of help here," Silas said quickly, gesturing toward Daniel and Ethan.

"All right, then. But come right back. There's plenty needs doing around here, and most of it too hard for Peter and Sol to handle . . . if I could find 'em in the first place. Funny how they seem to disappear when there's work to be done." Mr. Ward shrugged, seeming more amused than annoyed. He rubbed a handkerchief across the back of his neck and looked around. "Well, if it isn't young Mr. Root!" he said, noticing Ethan. "Why don't you see if you can find Peter and Sol? If they're going to waste their time, they might as well have company, eh?"

Ethan shook his head. "No, thank you, sir. I need to help Silas. Besides, I want to see how the saw works."

Mr. Ward laughed. "Always working, huh? Just like your father. I never saw such a fellow for hard work as him. Keep on that way and you'll do him proud, boy."

Joshua grinned behind his father's back. Ethan's face grew hot as the older boy tapped his forehead and mouthed the word *simple*. He seethed quietly while Mr. Ward and Mr. Smead settled their accounts. When Silas acted as if Joshua weren't there, he couldn't help feeling pleased.

"All right, then, I'll be off," Mr. Smead said. "Silas, don't you forget, now, about Saturday. Mrs. Smead won't be the only one disappointed if you don't come to tea." He winked and clapped Silas on the back.

Ethan was surprised to see both Silas and Joshua turn slightly pink. Silas glanced over at Joshua, pressing his mouth into something Ethan could only describe as a smirk. "Oh, I'll be there, sir," Silas said. "You can be sure of that."

After unloading the logs, Silas helped Mr. Ward secure one

onto the log carriage, ready to be sawn into boards. Meanwhile, Ethan and Daniel brought the oxcart around to the lumberyard below the mill, where they would pick up the boards after the cutting was done. It was a good spot to watch all the workings of the mill, from the flume that rushed the water down to the turbines, to the network of shafts and gears and belts that moved the giant blade up and down. It was also far enough away from the pounding and clatter that he could talk to Daniel without Silas and Mr. Ward hearing. He nudged Daniel. "Silas and Joshua don't like each other very much, do they?" he said.

"Not when they're both always making calf eyes at Clarissa Smead," Daniel said. He watched the first boards come skidding down the long poles that acted as a slide, sending the lumber from the mill to the yard below.

"She likes Silas better, though, doesn't she?" Ethan asked.

"Oh, she does, does she?" While Silas and Mr. Ward readied the next log up above, Daniel grabbed the first board and dragged it toward the cart. "And why is that?"

Ethan fumbled with his answer. He liked Silas better. Why shouldn't everybody else? "He's older and bigger. And he's not mean. And anyway, Mr. Smead asked Silas to tea, not Joshua."

Daniel coughed. "It ain't Mr. Smead that Silas is mad for, is it, now? As for Clarissa, she'll be liking whoever suits her mood today. And next week she'll be liking the other one, or someone else entirely. Silas'd be smart to look closer to home and leave Clarissa Smead to Joshua Ward. If ever anybody was deserving each other, it's them two."

"Oh," Ethan said, although he didn't understand what Daniel meant. He never understood anything to do with girls, or why the young men went all foolish over them. He was a little disappointed that Silas's hostility toward Joshua was over something so trivial. "I thought maybe Silas didn't like Joshua because he's your friend." He helped Daniel stack the boards together.

Daniel laughed harshly. "Why ever would you be thinking Joshua was me friend?"

"No, no," Ethan said hastily. "I meant Silas. I mean . . . I mean I thought maybe Silas doesn't like Joshua because Silas is your friend. He is, isn't he?" Ethan had noticed that Silas never laughed at Mr. Pease's Irish jokes. Daniel never drooped his head and hid his eyes in front of Silas, the way he did around Mr. and Mrs. Lyman. There was something about the way Daniel and Silas spoke—not exactly easy, but like they were equals, and that they knew things about each other that nobody else did.

Daniel spat out another laugh. "Silas is Mr. Lyman's son."

"But Silas likes you, doesn't he?"

"He's a fair man. Can't say he favors his da much. 'Cept for his face. Maybe it's his ma he takes after."

Ethan laughed at the thought of blond, blue-eyed Silas taking after Mrs. Lyman with her dark hair, black eyes, and sharp, narrow face. "Even I can tell he doesn't look anything like his mother."

Daniel thumbed his cap back and tilted his head. "And how would you know that? His ma died before you was ever born."

Ethan wondered how many more surprises Daniel and the Lymans had in store for him. "She died before—? But—Florella and Zeloda and Ruth and Aaron—" He felt as though he were babbling while he tried to figure out which child belonged to which Mrs. Lyman.

"Herself's ma to the girls and the baby, all right. But not to Silas."

The stack of boards had grown to half a dozen now. Daniel nodded for Ethan to grab one end and help him carry them to the oxcart.

"I wonder what she was like. Silas's mother, I mean."

"Don't know. I never asked. I fancy she had yellow hair. Where else would Silas'a got it?"

"D'you s'pose he ever misses her?"

"Who?" Daniel asked, shoving the boards into place. "Silas or himself?"

Ethan couldn't imagine Mr. Lyman missing anybody. That would have been a weakness, a lack of discipline. But Silas . . . Ethan was about to say how sad it must have been for Silas to lose his mother, but he bit his tongue. Silas, at least, still had his pa and his home, his stepmother, a baby brother, and three little sisters. What did Daniel have?

"There. That's the last of it," Silas said as Daniel shoved the final board into the oxcart. "Why don't you boys head back while I settle up with Mr. Ward? I want to stop by Mr. Harris's on the way home and see when he wants to hire the team for his plowing. The two of you can make a start unloading the wagon and getting to work. Paddy, you can show Ethan what to do."

Paddy. Silas always called Daniel *Paddy.* Ethan hadn't thought about that when he'd wondered if the two might be friends.

They'd barely gotten out of sight of the mill when the sound of laughter made Ethan's shoulders stiffen.

Peter and Solomon Ward played in the orchard next to the road, wrestling and tumbling among the apple trees. Peter glanced up and shouted, "Look, Sol, Mr. Lyman's let his idiots loose!"

Ethan's fists tightened until his nails dug into his palms.

Daniel nudged Ethan's elbow. "You don't hear nothing. You don't see nothing."

Peter and Sol scrambled to the tree nearest the road and

swung from its lower branches. "Sim-ple! Sim-ple!" the boys sang in chorus. "Ethan's pa is sim-ple!"

Ethan gathered himself to lunge after them.

Daniel gripped Ethan's elbow harder. "Mr. Ward oughtn't to'a let his pigs to run loose," he said without missing a step. "He oughtn't to fatten 'em on cabbages, neither. Shameful, the way they're squalling and breaking wind over there loud enough to scare away the customers, ain't it?"

"*You're* the pig, Paddy Linnehan!" Peter shouted. "Wait 'til I get Joshua. He'll thrash you for a coward and a liar and a thief and a—"

"Aye," Daniel called back. "He might, if he wasn't too busy swooning over Clarissa Smead."

Ethan struggled to follow Daniel's example and not turn his head to see whether the Ward boys followed. But the jeers faded until Ethan could hear nothing but the squeak of the cart's wheels and the oxen's plodding steps.

Daniel cleared his throat and spat into the dirt. "Them two. If I had a tongue as sharp as theirs, I could mow an acre an hour, just by standing there talking at it."

Ethan grinned at the idea of acres of hay collapsing to the ground as the Ward boys shouted and teased and talked. "Why doesn't Joshua like you?" he asked.

Daniel lifted one shoulder. "It couldn't be because the first time I met him, I punched him in the stomach, could it, now?" His mouth twisted.

"You did?" Ethan grinned in surprise and admiration. "Why?"

"He said if I was Irish, then me da must be a thief and me ma must be a—" Daniel shook his head, as if suddenly remembering Ethan's age. "Anyways, I hit him where he was softest. And didn't his face turn a lovely shade of green, too!" The twist in Daniel's mouth curved upward.

"What did he do then?"

"He couldn't do naught, when all the carrying on brung out the schoolmaster." The twist reversed itself. "The master must'a switched me half the afternoon, trying to make me apologize."

"Did you?"

Daniel shook his head. "No one made Joshua apologize to me, now, did they? Me da nearly strapped me, too, when I come home, 'til I told him why I done it. Then he said 'twas a sorry thing I didn't hit the bas—" Daniel caught the word halfway out—"—the devil twice whilst I had the chance."

Ethan nearly stumbled. It was the first time he'd heard Daniel mention that he'd ever had a home other than the Lymans', that he ever had a father. "What's he like? Your pa, I mean?"

Daniel's eyes started to fade into that blank look. "He was me da," he said.

Was, Daniel had said. Not *is.* Ethan's curiosity about the fate of Daniel's parents was so strong he could taste it. But Daniel's face closed up like a shuttered window, and Ethan knew that the time for questions was over.

"Well, that's done with," Daniel said, tossing his pitchfork into the cart. He squinted at the sun.

"Do we have time for another load?" Ethan stared out at the mounds of manure they'd scattered across the field. Tomorrow they'd plow it, then the next day they'd plant it to mangel-wurzels, the big beets that Silas used to feed the cattle over the winter.

Daniel shook his head. "Enough time to fetch it, but not enough time to spread it about before we got to get the cows in for the milking." He stretched until his joints popped. He jerked his chin toward the road that led to the far pasture where the cattle had been grazing all day. "And since they're already out here, I s'pose we got no choice but to stay with 'em until it's time to be bringing 'em in, eh, lad?"

Ethan studied Daniel carefully. Where normally he approached his chores with dour concentration, he'd seemed almost cheerful when Silas had sent them to the farthest corner of the farm to work, as if he liked nothing better than to spend the afternoon flinging manure about. At first Ethan had supposed that it was just being out of range of Mr. Pease's teasing that pleased Daniel. But there was something else, something vaguely expectant about his posture and face.

"So—um—what do we do until then?" Ethan asked, sure that there was some chore or other that needed doing. There always was.

But Daniel wiped his hands on the seat of his trousers as if he were finished for the day. "Can you keep a secret, lad?" he asked.

Ethan's heart jumped. "A secret?" he repeated. "Of course I can. Better'n anyone."

Daniel glanced over one shoulder, then the other, although there was nobody but the oxen to see or hear them. He stooped so that he and Ethan were nose to nose, then he grabbed Ethan's arm so hard that it hurt. "Come along, then. But if you tell anyone, I'll thump you worse than Lyman, understand?"

Ethan was disappointed to find that Daniel's secret place was only the pasture where they'd turned out the livestock after the morning's feeding and milking. Just a little bit south of the field where the boys had been working, the pasture was sheltered in a little hollow scooped out of the land so that it seemed like the world began and ended at its edges.

As they neared the stone wall that bordered the field, Daniel's legs stretched into long, eager strides. The lash twitched in his hand, as if he were impatient with the oxen's slow pace.

When they reached the wall, he flung off his frock and cap and tossed them to Ethan along with the lash. "Here. Mind these. And mind the team."

Ethan glanced at Mark and Luke. The oxen drooped their heads sleepily. "Where're you going?"

But Daniel had already vaulted over the wall and broken into a run. Ethan clambered up onto the wall to watch.

He heard a wild shriek, like a scream and a whistle and a laugh all mixed up together. Then the sod thudded with clustered hoofbeats that vibrated through his perch on the wall.

"Daniel, look out!" Ethan shouted in panic.

Chapter Nine

Ivy galloped wildly across the field, a fierce tilt to her head. She headed straight for Daniel. Ethan was sure she'd trample him. She'd gone mad, and she was going to kill Daniel sure as anything—Daniel, who brushed her and crooned secret love-words to her every morning.

Daniel stood as still as a headstone, as trusting as a calf going to slaughter. It was all Ethan could do not to close his eyes.

But the mare did stop, tearing up a shower of clods as she skidded to a halt. She threw herself up on her haunches and shrieked again. The placid mare Ethan knew was now a wild thing, pawing the air and snorting, shaking her mane and swishing her tail as if she were tossing off some outer skin. She dropped back to the ground, bouncing on her front hooves and kicking her back legs out behind her.

Then, incredibly, Daniel and Ivy began to dance. The mare circled and swayed and capered around the boy while he feinted left, then right. She whirled to meet him, arching her body around him, then wheeling on her haunches. The pale, frowning mask Daniel usually wore turned soft and bright as a grin parted his lips and his cheeks reddened with exertion. His unruly hair flopped on his forehead, the sun making the dull orange strands glow like pale copper.

It was a dangerous dance; one slip or stumble, and Daniel would be crushed beneath those sharp flashing hooves. But

Daniel reveled in it, taking wild chances that made Ethan hold his breath.

Ethan realized that the dance had a purpose. Ivy's circles and arches herded Daniel in a meandering line toward the wall. Every now and again, the mare drew close enough to nudge Daniel's chest with her nose or to prod at his pockets. Then Daniel would laugh and spring away, each time a little closer to the wall.

At last Daniel's back was against the wall. The mare swiveled before him, bobbing her head from side to side to keep the grinning boy cornered. He raised his hands in surrender and praised her in their secret language. Ivy arched her neck and pressed her forehead against Daniel's chest, pinning him against the stones. Her nostrils quivered, and a happy rumble sounded in her throat.

Daniel pulled a handful of carrots from his pocket. He laid a piece of one across his palm. With comical delicacy, the mare brushed her lips across his hand. The carrot disappeared. When three more pieces vanished in similar fashion, Ethan began to laugh.

Daniel and the mare turned toward Ethan. "She's grand, ain't she?" he said as he rubbed Ivy's cheek.

Ethan nodded. "Aren't you afraid she'll step on you?"

"Nah. She'd never do naught to me. Just a big baby, she is, ain't you, lass?"

The mare's ears twitched. She prodded Daniel for another carrot.

Ethan wondered how often Daniel stole carrots from the root cellar for Ivy, and whether Mrs. Lyman would notice her supply steadily dwindling. "What if Mr. Lyman catches you stealing?"

Daniel tilted his head and pursed his lips. "We-l-l-l-l, whose horse is she?"

"Mr. Lyman's," Ethan said, although he wasn't sure Ivy would agree.

"And whose carrots are these?" Another one disappeared between Ivy's lips.

"Mr. Lyman's."

"So how can it be stealing when I'm feeding Lyman's carrots to Lyman's horse?" Daniel scratched the mare's chin. She bobbed her head as if in agreement.

Before Ethan could respond, Daniel grabbed the mare's mane and leaped onto her back, the motion so swift and graceful that it looked as if the mare herself had swept him up. She spun on her hind legs and bolted across the field.

Ethan had never seen anyone ride the way Daniel rode Ivy. She galloped recklessly, every now and again dipping her head and flinging up her heels. Daniel clung fast, sometimes bent low over her neck, sometimes riding straight and tall, his hands buried in her mane, his legs wrapped tightly around her body. He laughed as they ran: a harsh, joyful noise like the crows made when they feasted in the corn. As they leaped imaginary obstacles and ran circles around the cows, it seemed to Ethan that they were no longer Daniel and Ivy, but some new fantastic creature that was neither horse nor boy but both at once. Ethan half expected this new creature to sprout wings and fly.

At first, it felt wonderful to watch, but after a while sitting on the wagon and watching weren't enough. He wanted Ivy to dance for him, too.

Daniel finally steered the mare back to the wall. Her flanks and withers shone with sweat. He slid from her back and thumped her shoulder fondly. Finger-combing his sweaty hair away from his eyes, he settled his cap in place. "We have to walk for a bit now," he said. "To cool her off. She won't mind if you come. The boys'll stay put, I fancy."

Indeed, except for occasionally rolling their cud around on

85

their tongues, Mark and Luke seemed to be napping. Ethan jumped down and joined Daniel. The mare plodded behind, the old Ivy again, with no trace of the wild mare who'd danced around the field a few moments ago. Ethan rubbed his eyes, wondering if he'd dozed in the sun and dreamed it all. But Daniel's shirt had wet patches under the arms and along the back where his braces crossed, and the mare's long winter hair curled with sweat. She huffed and shook the damp mane from her neck.

"Who taught you to ride like that?" Ethan asked.

"She did." Daniel cocked his head toward the mare.

"But how?"

Daniel shrugged, as if it had been so long ago that he could hardly remember. "I just kept getting on until I stopped falling off, that's all."

Ethan looked up. The mare's back seemed impossibly high. He imagined falling onto the hard ground from that height over and over. Then he imagined flying across the fields, the wind tearing at his hair and his face, and the falling didn't seem such a high price to pay. "Can you teach me?"

In a moment, the Irish boy became the old Daniel again, who looked at the world with a sullen frown. His hand went up to the mare's neck, and he placed himself solidly between Ivy and Ethan. "I can't. You'll fall and you'll run to Lyman, crying about what I done to you."

"I wouldn't. Didn't I say I wouldn't tell?"

Daniel's face struggled for a long time. For a moment, Ethan thought he would relent. Then his mouth hardened. "Aye," he said. "And you said you wouldn't call me Paddy, neither."

The late-afternoon chores passed in awkward silences as Ethan wondered how to recapture Daniel's trust. Now and again, Daniel would seem ready to say something, but instead he would tighten his mouth into a firm line and turn away.

After tea, when the boys had finally retreated to the attic, Daniel stood for a long time, staring out the rear window at the disappearing sun. He reached into his pocket and pulled out the little wooden horse. The reddening sun streamed in through the fanlight and rippled across the tiny figure so that it seemed to move.

"He's beautiful," Ethan said. "He looks just like Ivy did this afternoon."

Daniel turned away from the window, blinking hard.

"Does he have a name?"

"Horse, I s'pose. He's only wood. It's not as if he'd care." But Daniel's finger caressed the horse's back as gently as if it could really feel his touch. He sat on the floor next to Ethan and held his hand out flat, the way he had held it out to feed the mare. The wooden figure lay on its side, cushioned in his palm.

Ethan cast a wary glance at the other boy. Daniel nodded. "Only to look at, mind. Not to keep."

Ethan picked up the horse, running his finger over muscles so finely sanded that the figure felt more like glass than wood. He laid it reverently back in Daniel's palm. "Did you make it?" he asked.

Daniel shook his head. "Me da did. He gave it to me when we come over."

When we come over. Ethan held his breath. Until that moment, Daniel's Irishness had been vaguely connected with his pale orange hair, his odd way of speaking, the secret language he shared with Ivy, and his reputation for questionable morals. The fact that Daniel had come from an entirely different land and had traveled across an entire ocean and most of Massachusetts to reach Farmington had never settled on Ethan's

87

imagination before. Now it landed with its full weight, transforming Daniel into a boy who had been places, a boy who had seen things. Daniel was a boy who had had an adventure.

"What was it like in Ireland?" Ethan asked.

Daniel shrugged impatiently. "How should I know? I wasn't but four when we come."

"Don't you remember any of it?"

"A bit."

"And?"

Daniel chewed his lower lip. "Green. Green and wet." He nodded as if pleased with his summary.

"Was it pretty?"

"Oh, lovely. For them that had money." His mouth made that funny twist of his. "See? Not so different from here, eh?"

"You came over on a ship, didn't you?"

"I'm hardly the one you'd be seeing walking on water, now, am I?"

"Was it very exciting?" Ethan's head filled with images of sailors scrambling monkeylike in webs of rigging, hoisting billowing sheets of snowy canvas, of a gallant captain swaggering across the deck, leading his weather-toughened crew across the sea in the face of raging storms, ferocious sea monsters, and treacherous pirates.

"Aye, if you find it exciting to be spending a coupl'a months crammed into a dark rat hole smelling like a privy, with everyone crying and puking all the time, and barely room to walk about without stepping on someone—if you can stand at all without the floor sliding out from under you." He shivered a little, and Ethan remembered how green Daniel had looked the day they'd cleaned out the privy. He wondered how many bad memories that dark, foul space had evoked.

"Didn't you ever go on deck and look at the sea?"

"Folk'd come up now and again for a bit. But me ma was

too sick most of the time to take me about." His voice softened and he shook his head. "She hadn't no stomach for the sea."

"But—but when you did go up . . . what was it like?"

"Wet. Wet and gray."

"That's all?"

Daniel's hands flapped at his sides. "What'd you have me say? I wasn't but four."

"Were you afraid?"

"I was four."

Ethan sighed. He could never get a story out of Daniel all at once. He had to draw out one answer at a time, always wary that the next question would poke Daniel the wrong way. "What about your pa? Did he get seasick, too?"

"Me da was already here waiting for us."

"Already here?"

"Well, he had to get work first before he could send for us, didn't he, now?" Daniel's voice grew impatient, as if any idiot should have known that.

"Oh." Ethan mulled the idea over for a while. "You must have been happy to see him again."

"Again?" Daniel cocked his head toward Ethan.

"Well, yes. I mean, after all those months . . ."

"Months? Lad, I never seen him at all before the day we got here."

"You never—? You mean he was gone four *years* before you came?"

"We were lucky. Some folk never got sent for at all."

Ethan puzzled over what it might be like to wait and wait and never get sent for. He studied Daniel's face to see if it was safe to ask any more questions. "What did your pa do? I mean, for work?"

"Build things. Canals and dams and mills and houses and such."

"Was he sorry to go? Did he miss you and your mama? Did your mama miss him very much?"

Daniel crossed his arms over his chest and frowned. "Why ever are you asking so many questions for?"

"Just trying to be friendly, that's all," Ethan said hastily.

"Why?" Daniel's eyebrows rose, and he looked truly bewildered.

"Everybody needs friends," Ethan said.

"Not everybody." Daniel uncrossed his arms and studied the wooden horse again.

"But you have friends, don't you? From school, maybe?"

"I'm too old for school."

"I mean when you used to go."

Daniel shrugged. "Who wants to be friends with the likes of Joshua Ward?"

"Oh." Ethan winced to recall that, for a little while, he had wanted to be friends with the likes of Joshua Ward's brothers. "I wish I'd'a seen Joshua Ward's face when you hit him."

Daniel shook his head. "I don't fancy it'll happen again. I'm not fool enough to tackle him twice." But the corner of his mouth curled upward. Then he was on his feet again. He placed the horse on the windowsill overlooking the western landscape. "I could teach you, maybe, in a year or so, when you're bigger," he said, more to the horse than to Ethan. "To ride, I mean. If you promise not to tell."

"Of course I wouldn't."

Daniel nodded without turning away from the window. "Your da's not simple, and neither are you." Although the comment had nothing to do with horses, wooden or real, in a funny way Ethan understood that it was all connected somehow. Daniel headed for the stairs, leaving the horse to stand guard.

"Where're you going?" Ethan asked.

"Privy."

The sun disappeared behind the mountains, the sky deepened from turquoise to indigo, and Daniel didn't return. The sky was black and pinpricked with stars when a noise roused Ethan from an uneasy dream. It took him a moment to come fully awake and realize that it was Daniel throwing off his clothes and putting on the old shirt he usually slept in. Daniel tiptoed over to the window, ran a finger once along the wooden horse's back, then slipped into bed. He fell into a restless sleep, tossing and pulling at the blankets and muttering in that strange language he shared with the mare.

Chapter Ten

Mr. Bingham's nose almost touched the page as he followed the loops and crosses of his numbers and letters. Ethan was amazed that such handsome letters could flow from the pen of someone with Mr. Bingham's cramped posture and feeble eyesight.

A tall, reedy man in his late twenties, Lucius Bingham had grown stoop-shouldered from years of having to peer too closely at the world in order to bring it into focus. Spectacles as thick as the bottoms of tumblers perched on his nose, their lenses blue-tinted to protect his eyes from the light. The blue glass turned the clerk's amber-colored eyes an unearthly shade of milky green, so that his irises seemed to float inside the glass of his spectacles.

"Is it very hard minding Mr. Lyman's books?" Ethan asked.

"Hard?" Mr. Bingham's head bobbed up. His questing eyes sought but didn't quite meet Ethan's. "I shouldn't say it's harder than any other work. It's all a matter of—" He tilted his head as he sought the word.

"Discipline?" Ethan guessed.

Mr. Bingham chuckled. "Discipline? What has that to do with accounts? No—no, it's—umm—accuracy, precision, paying attention to details." The muscles around his eyes relaxed. A flash of milky green showed in his spectacles as he found the word. "Order." He spoke to himself more than to Ethan. "Yes. Order . . . hmmmm. Now how could I forget that? . . . So simple. Simple . . . And logic, logic, of course. It's all logical.

92

Logic and order, yes." His head tipped to one side, his squint settling firmly on Ethan this time. "Well, I suppose there's a bit of discipline to that, isn't there?"

"Did it take you a long time to learn what all the books are for?"

"Oh, well, a bit . . . a bit. Until I saw the logic of it."

"Can you teach me?" Ethan asked. If he learned how the books worked, maybe he could help Pa sort out his accounts. If he only understood how it all worked, maybe he could figure out some way to pay off the debts sooner, some way out of his indenture, some way to get back home again, where he belonged.

Mr. Bingham chuckled and peered more closely at Ethan. "You're a bit young for all that, aren't you? Bore you . . . bore you to tears . . . yes, to tears."

"I'm old enough to go out to work. I'm old enough to learn about money and accounts and—and everything."

Mr. Bingham's sandy eyebrows rose. "Everything? Surely not . . . not everything." He smiled kindly.

"Wouldn't it please Pa—and Mr. Lyman, too," Ethan added hastily, "if I could be learning while I work here? I'm sure you could teach me ever so much more than I could learn in school."

"Well . . ." Mr. Bingham drew himself up a little bit straighter. "Perhaps . . . perhaps."

"I have to work in the summers now, 'stead of going to school. If you taught me some about figuring and all that, I wouldn't get behind, would I? I bet if you taught me, I'd go back to school in the winter smarter'n anybody there."

Mr. Bingham patted Ethan's shoulder. "Ambitious, are you?" he said. "Like me when I was your age. All right, then." He slipped his fingers under the page, his palm showing through the onionskin-thin paper. "This is the waste book, see—cheap paper because it's only the quick notes we take as the day goes by. In here we write down everything just as it happens: sales, purchases, credit, cash . . . right away, you see, so we don't forget . . . don't forget." His nose dipped closer to the page, as if an entry there had suddenly caught his attention. "Yes. Don't forget. Hmmm." His voice drifted off, his head nodding over the book. For a moment, Ethan thought Mr. Bingham had fallen asleep, but then the clerk bobbed back up so quickly that Ethan nearly jumped.

"Then, at the end of the day—or maybe sometimes during the day, if it's quiet . . . quiet, yes . . . we copy everything in a neat, fair hand—very neat, mind—into Mr. Lyman's journal." His long fingers reached under the counter, where two red-and-brown marbled volumes rested. He lifted the top one, thudded it onto the counter, and flipped it open at random.

Ethan recognized Mr. Bingham's handsome swirls in some entries, but most were in a stronger, more vertical hand. "Who writes in this one?" he asked.

"Oh—ah, depends . . . depends. On a quiet day, or when Mr. Lyman's away, I do the entries. But if he's here, he takes care of them. To spare my eyes, you see . . . you see. Very wearing on the eyes, bookwork. Yes, indeed, very wearing." The muscles around Mr. Bingham's eyes squeezed tighter, in what Ethan supposed was a blink, but when the blink was over, Ethan could see no more of the clerk's eyes than when they'd been closed. "Or he takes them home to work on, so I needn't stay late after closing. Because of my mother, you see."

"Um . . . your mother?" Ethan asked. Mr. Bingham and his mother and sister rented a little house near the common. Ethan didn't know what had happened to Mr. Bingham's father, though Ethan supposed he must be dead. There was also a brother who had moved out west. The clerk always kept the most recent letter from his brother in his pocket and would read it when anyone asked.

"Not well. No, not well at all. Mr. Lyman's good . . . very good about it." Mr. Bingham smiled, exposing a chipped tooth and the gap where its neighbor had once been. "Lets me go before my time if she's poorly, you see." His head bobbed toward Ethan. He placed a hand on the boy's shoulder. "You've a good master, Ethan. Very good." He took off his spectacles and rubbed them with his handkerchief. "There aren't many would give work to a man with eyes like mine."

"How—how bad are they?" Ethan said. "I mean, if you don't mind me asking. . . ."

Mr. Bingham held his hand about a foot in front of his face. "I can see perfectly well to here with my spectacles." The hand moved to touch his nose. "Here without 'em. And beyond here . . ." He gestured around the store. "They let me see shapes, mostly . . . shapes. And these are the best I've had yet . . . best yet . . . mmmm. Got 'em from a peddler last year." When he bent down, his nose brushed Ethan's ear. "But don't tell Mr. Lyman, eh?" he whispered, his chuckle tickling the boy's cheek. Mr. Bingham straightened. He nodded toward Ethan, one eye squeezed tighter than the other, a finger to his lips. Then he glanced down at the journal and remembered the lesson he'd been giving Ethan. "The journals," he murmured. "What about the journals? Oh, yes. The day's debits and credits all get copied into the journals, you see? Just in the order they happened . . . happened."

Ethan nodded.

"And then Mr. Lyman has his ledgers in the storeroom."

"The big brown books?"

Mr. Bingham nodded. "Everybody has his own page, all in order. Your father would be under the Rs, and he'd have his own page with everything that he owes and everything he's paid all written up . . . written up together. Then when he wants to check his account, Mr. Lyman just looks it up in the ledger for him. You see?"

"What about the other book?" Ethan asked, remembering the small account book Mr. Lyman had pulled out of his secretary and written in after the incident of the broken plate.

"Other?"

"The black one. The one Mr. Lyman carries back and forth from the house. What does he do with that one?"

"I don't know . . . don't know. I don't take care of that one. . . ." Mr. Bingham squinted hard as he thought. "He's a very busy man, Mr. Lyman . . . very busy. It must be hard to remember all the things he has to do . . . things to order . . . bills to be paid . . . debts owed to him. Perhaps he uses it to remind himself . . . remind himself. . . ."

"Mmmmm-hmmm." Ethan propped himself on the counter, supporting his weight on his elbows and letting his feet dangle so his toes brushed the floor. He flipped pages in the journal. Mr. Bingham had been right; it was boring—just lines of words and numbers. How, he wondered, was he going to pay attention closely enough to learn what he needed?

Mr. Bingham cleared his throat. "It's not just numbers though . . . not just numbers. There's a story in every one of 'em . . . a story. You can see who's making a new dress . . . new dress. See? Mrs. Aldrich bought twelve yards of calico . . . calico. If you can see the story behind it, then it all makes sense . . . makes sense."

Ethan nodded. He stared at the page harder, looking for familiar names, trying to figure out their stories. For a few minutes, the entries remained a meaningless jumble, then, like untangling a thread, he found himself able to tease loose some sense from it. Mr. Bailey had a sweet tooth; he'd bought a pound each of horehound candy and lemon drops. Mrs. Holcomb was making extra money sewing shoe uppers and braiding straw for hats. "It's like a puzzle," he said. "Like a game." Seeing it that way, all of a sudden it wasn't quite so boring anymore.

"Not a game . . . no, no . . . this is serious," Mr. Bingham scolded.

"Well, it has rules, doesn't it?" Ethan said. "And you're not s'posed to cheat."

Mr. Bingham had to laugh at that. "No," he said. "You're not supposed to cheat . . . to cheat."

"Oh, dear," Mrs. Nye said, shaking her head. "That number never seems to get any smaller, does it?" She laid an arthritis-twisted finger along the entry in Mr. Lyman's journal.

"Don't you mind that, Mrs. Nye," Mr. Lyman said. "Your credit's always good here."

"You're a very patient man," she said with a smile.

"You'll pay me when you can," he said, taking her elbow. "Now sit down and I'll put your order together."

Ethan didn't think he'd ever seen Mr. Lyman so gentle, not even with Mrs. Lyman or the baby. He guided Mrs. Nye to a chair as though she were as fragile as a butterfly. Ethan wondered how such an insubstantial-looking old lady could ever have gone out at all times of day, in all sorts of weather, mid-wifing just about every woman in town.

Mr. Lyman took Mrs. Nye's list from her hand and sent Ethan and Mr. Bingham bustling about the store for her goods. Ethan had caught a glance at the list, and it had seemed nothing but a bunch of indecipherable scribbles. He wasn't sure how Mr. Lyman knew what to get.

Ethan carefully wrapped a piece of paper around the three nutmegs that Mr. Lyman had told him to fetch. When he came up next to Mr. Lyman to put the tiny parcel in Mrs. Nye's basket, the storekeeper was measuring out a bolt of blue calico against the yardstick affixed to the counter. As he measured, he and Mrs. Nye chatted about who'd visited her lately and what news she'd heard, how the weather affected her arthritis, what Mrs. Lyman should do for the baby's rash . . .

Ethan found himself staring at the cloth unrolled across the counter. At first, he didn't quite understand what had drawn his attention. Then he realized that Mr. Lyman was measuring each yard a good two to three inches short. He blinked. No doubt the storekeeper was distracted by Mrs. Nye's conversation and wasn't paying attention. "Sir—" Ethan said tentatively.

Mr. Lyman looked down at Ethan, following the boy's glance to the cloth on the counter. "Yes, boy?" There was a knife-edge in the storekeeper's voice, and the gray-blue eyes that had been all warmth and softness for Mrs. Nye turned to steel. He tugged the cloth to properly meet the end of the marker. But he didn't go back to remeasure the rest.

Mr. Lyman's stare felt like a spider crawling across Ethan's face, down his neck, around his shoulders, then back up to the top of his head again. His hands itched to brush it away and cover his face and head against it. "Ah—I—uh—nutmegs. Here," he choked out, placing the parcel in the basket and backing away quickly.

"Thank you, boy. That will be all."

Ethan nodded dumbly and retreated to find a paper of pins to add to Mrs. Nye's order. But he couldn't help surreptitiously watching Mr. Lyman as the storekeeper finished measuring the cloth out. Although he couldn't see quite as well, he was almost certain that the last two yards measured short again.

"Lemon!"

"Peppermint!"

"Lemon!"

Peter and Solomon Ward came into the store, Peter clutching something in his fist, and Sol struggling to take it away.

Ethan retreated into a corner of the shop, wishing himself invisible.

"It's *my* penny! I say what we can buy," Peter said, shoving Sol aside.

"It's *my* penny now." Joshua stepped in behind his brothers, separating them and snatching the penny from Peter. "And you won't get it back if you don't stop acting like a pair of heathens and—" He swept his hat off and bowed deeply to Mrs. Nye, giving her a delighted grin.

Mr. Ward followed Joshua in, muttering to himself and flipping through a small account book. Like Joshua, he tipped his hat and bowed to Mrs. Nye, but there seemed to be something a little sad in his face when he greeted her.

Peter and Sol wandered off to admire the pocketknives on display in one of the glass cases while Joshua chatted with Mrs. Nye and Mr. Ward placed his order with Mr. Bingham.

"Pins!" Mr. Lyman said. "Boy, where are those pins?"

"H-here," Ethan said, coming out of his corner cautiously. He was relieved that the Wards all seemed too busy to notice him. He added the paper of pins to the parcels on the counter next to Mrs. Nye's overflowing basket. The tiny woman would never be able to carry it all home unless she had a wheelbarrow sitting outside.

"That's all of it," Mr. Lyman said. "No, wait," he added as Mrs. Nye rose from her chair, leaning on her cane. He took a spool of cheap blue ribbon from the shelf behind him, measured out a length and snipped it off. Smiling at Mrs. Nye, he tucked it into one of the parcels. "No charge." Her face glowed as if he'd given her a length of solid-gold chain.

"Here's a chance for Peter and Sol to earn their penny back," Joshua said. He snapped his fingers and waved his brothers over, then divided up basket and packages between them. "Ma'am?" He held out his arm for Mrs. Nye. Beaming like a girl, she allowed Joshua to escort her from the store, the boys trailing behind.

Mr. Ward shook his head and made a little tut-tutting noise. "A shame, a true shame . . ."

Mr. Lyman nodded sagely. "It *is* sad to see her health failing so. And her all alone in that great big house."

"That great big house. Yes, there's my problem."

"Your problem? Surely it's hers, Robert."

"Well, it would be if I hadn't sold her the lumber for her new roof and clapboards last year. She hasn't paid more than fifty cents on her account. I can't carry her on my books forever, George." He thumbed through his account book. "But God help me if I have the heart to see her turned out over it. Joshua adores her; she's always been like an old auntie to him. And how could I face my Abby, knowing that I evicted the woman who delivered all our babies?"

Mr. Lyman smiled. "Indeed. How could you face any mother in this town? And yet—" He ran his finger along the edge of the counter. "It would be a mercy, wouldn't it? If she were to be taken out of that house."

"That doesn't sound very charitable, George. You know she has no family left since her daughter died. She'd have to go on the vendue."

Ethan stifled a gasp of horror. He didn't entirely understand how the vendue worked, except that it was like an auction in reverse, with the town paying the lowest bidder to take care of an orphan or a widow or a pauper who had no family to take them in. Whenever Pa and Ma fretted about money, the specter of the vendue lurked about the household like an evil spirit.

"What charity is it that would leave her rattling around that dark, drafty house, growing older and sicker there, perhaps to freeze for want of fuel or to stumble into the fire with no one to rescue her? Wouldn't she be safer, healthier, if she were to move in with, say, the Ingersolls and have a great happy family around her, pleased to feed and shelter her in return for the pittance the town pays for her keep?"

"Yes. Well. When you put it that way . . . that way . . ." Mr. Bingham said, joining the discussion.

"Surely some people are better off with someone else to take care of them," Mr. Lyman said.

"I suppose you're right," Mr. Ward said. "I see, though, that *you're* still carrying her on your books. That was quite a stock of goods you sold her today. I don't suppose she paid for any of it, did she?"

Mr. Lyman shrugged.

Mr. Ward continued, "It's easy enough to talk about letting someone go on the vendue, but hard enough to do it. I wonder what if it was me? What then? Do you ever wonder about that, George?"

Mr. Lyman shook his head. "It would never be the likes of us, Robert. Men like us, we'll always be our own masters."

"Well, shouldn't every man be?"

Mr. Lyman leaned across the counter, warming to his argument. "It's all well and good to *say* every man should be his own master, but you'll agree, surely, that some men are better off with a master over them—men who can't master themselves."

"Yes," Mr. Bingham said. "Yes . . . the drunk, the feeble . . . feebleminded, the cripple—"

"The poor," Mr. Lyman concluded.

Mr. Ward propped his elbows on the counter. "Surely some

are poor through no fault of their own. Would you make slaves of the poor, then?"

Mr. Lyman shook his head. "I'd have them taken care of. Relieve them of their burdens. Some men are weakened by vice, some are weak by nature. The former don't deserve the benefits of property. The latter are only burdened by it."

"Burdened?" Mr. Ward asked.

"Yes, burdened, as a simpleminded mother is burdened with the care of a child. Now, which is the true charity—" He put his palms together before him. "—to leave child and mother together out of sentiment, or to turn the child over to someone who can tend it properly?" He separated his hands and held the right one out, palm up.

Ethan couldn't help but shiver, thinking about his own father. Did Mr. Lyman believe Pa was simple, like the Ward boys did? Worse, did Pa believe it, too? Was that why he'd sent Ethan away? Ethan shook his head. It wasn't—it couldn't be true.

"Of course both would be better served if they were separated," Mr. Ward agreed.

"Exactly. The child is well reared,"—Mr. Lyman lifted the palm representing the child—"and the mother is freed of a burden too great for her." He turned the other hand palm-up and moved his hands up and down as if they were the balances of a scale. "But leave them together,"—he brought his hands together again, this time closed into opposing fists—"and both are destroyed. So, too, it is with men and property."

"And *women* and property?" Mr. Ward asked with a half-smile.

"I was speaking hypothetically." Mr. Lyman smiled and spread his hands wide again.

"Yes, but Mrs. Nye's debts are real. As real as this counter." Mr. Ward knocked on the wooden surface.

"As is our responsibility to her. The weak—women, children, paupers—they are all our concern, are they not?" Mr. Lyman reached under the counter and drew out a piece of paper. "I'll buy out your note," he said.

"What?" Mr. Ward backed away from the counter, startled.

"The promissory note you have from Mrs. Nye."

"Charity, George?" Mr. Ward shook his head doubtfully. "To me or to her?"

"Business. I can afford to carry the debt longer than you can. She'll pay me. Eventually."

Mr. Ward shook his head as Mr. Lyman wrote out the paper. "You're a better man than I am, George."

After Mr. Ward had left, Mr. Lyman pulled out his black notebook and began to write in it, humming to himself a little as he did. Mr. Bingham bustled about, putting back tins and covering the barrels and boxes that he'd opened to fill Mrs. Nye's order. As he swept up a spill of flour, Ethan mulled over everything he'd heard, making a mental list of questions to ask Mr. Bingham later about promissory notes and debts and the vendue.

"Well, boy?"

Ethan's head snapped up at Mr. Lyman's voice. Mr. Bingham had disappeared into the back storeroom; Ethan could hear the clerk muttering to himself as he looked for something. Ethan and Mr. Lyman were now alone in the shop. "Sir?"

Mr. Lyman opened a tin of lemon drops and held it out. Ethan's mouth puckered yearningly toward the sweets. Mr. Lyman chose one for himself, then gestured for Ethan to do the same. Ethan took one but didn't put it in his mouth.

"I hope you learned something useful today," Mr. Lyman said. "It's an intelligent boy who knows when to speak and when to keep silent, hmmm?" He raised one eyebrow.

Ethan nodded dumbly, not feeling particularly intelligent at all.

Mr. Lyman pressed his lips together, the way Pa sometimes did when he was trying to figure out how to explain something so that Ethan could understand it. "You see, boy, everything's a lesson—to those who are intelligent enough to learn it."

"A l-lesson, sir?" What, he wondered, was he supposed to have learned? That Mr. Lyman could cheat Mrs. Nye and be kind to her all at the same time? That maybe the vendue wasn't so very bad?

Mr. Lyman warmed to his lecture. "If we learn, we become strong. Successful. I know. I've learned." He gestured at the evidence of his success that surrounded him. "If we don't, if we let events overcome us, we become undisciplined, weak." His nose wrinkled over the last word.

"Weak, sir?" Ethan repeated, feeling a bit that way himself. Mrs. Nye was weak, he could see that. But she couldn't help it, could she? She was just old. His head started to go all fuzzy, the way it did when the schoolmaster would explain something far beyond his grasp.

"Weak. It all comes down to discipline and intelligence." His voice broke off, and he cupped his chin in his hand. "A lapse of discipline can be fatal. Fatal," he said softly, as if he were talking to himself. His eyes drifted back to Ethan, and he resumed his lecturing tone. "You think I'm exaggerating, but I know what I'm speaking of, boy. I know." Mr. Lyman's index finger tapped his breast.

Ethan nodded as if he understood. But what did discipline and intelligence have to do with Mrs. Nye and her debts? "And . . . and intelligence?" he asked.

"Why else did God give us intelligence if not to rule the weak and the foolish?"

"I d-don't know, sir. Maybe He wants us to help them."

Mr. Lyman's hand caressed the black leather that covered his account book. "And what better way is there to help them, boy, than by relieving them of those burdens that are too great for them to bear?"

Chapter Eleven

"Will you be needing Ethan today?" Silas asked his father at breakfast.

"Why?" Mr. Lyman responded.

"Ivy needs shoeing, and I thought he could go to the farrier's with Paddy."

Mr. Lyman set his coffee down and raked a glance across the two boys at the end of the table.

Ethan and Daniel kept their heads bent over their meal. Ethan's eyes darted to the side, and Daniel's did the same. Their glances met with a flicker of raised eyebrows.

"Why send two boys on an errand that takes only one?" Mr. Lyman asked.

"I thought Paddy could show Ethan a little about managing the horse."

A hopeful flutter quivered around Ethan's heart at the thought of tending Ivy, of wooing her into murmuring her mysterious love-noises to him, the way she did for Daniel. He bit the inside of his mouth to keep from smiling. Best to keep still. Mr. Lyman hadn't said yes yet.

The storekeeper nodded. "Good idea. Then the next time you can send the younger one alone. No point in losing half a day's work from the bigger lad on a chore the little one can do."

Ethan could barely swallow his eggs. To be allowed to take the mare out by himself was more than he'd wished for. He turned to nudge Daniel.

But Daniel only stared straight down at his plate, while crumbs from his bread dribbled between his clenched fingers and onto the tablecloth.

"Be back by dinner," Silas said. "Make sure Mr. Hemenway charges you fair." He handed Daniel the little brown book that he used to keep track of the farm accounts. "Sometimes he forgets she has only four feet."

Daniel's mouth twisted as he took the little book and stuck it in his pocket. "Aye, I'll mind what he does." He turned to lead the mare away, but Silas laid a hand on his arm to stop him.

"And don't let me hear about you riding that horse, understand?" Silas said in a voice so low Ethan barely heard it.

The bemused quirk left Daniel's mouth, and he nodded dully.

Daniel led the horse with long strides, the mare's head nodding sociably at his shoulder. Ethan sighed and wished his legs were longer. He was tired of always trotting to keep up with Daniel. "Are you angry with me?" he asked. Daniel had been sullen and silent all the time he'd been haltering the mare and taking her out of the barn. Ethan had tried to help, but Daniel and Ivy both had shrugged him off like a bothersome insect.

"It's naught to do with you, lad." But Daniel's fingers tightened possessively around the lead rope, and the mare's head tilted toward him, closing Ethan off.

"Silas said I was s'posed to help, that's all."

"Help me out of a job, you mean," Daniel snapped.

"I don't want to take her away from you." Even as he said it, Ethan realized it wasn't entirely true. There was nothing he'd like better than to have Ivy adore him the way she adored Daniel. But why couldn't they both take care of her?

Daniel's stride lengthened. "It's naught to do with what you or I or even Silas will be wanting. It's about himself getting the best use of us."

Ethan bristled at the idea that he and Daniel were no more than rakes or hoes or shovels to Mr. Lyman. He stopped and folded his arms across his chest. "What if I say I don't want to do it?"

Daniel's lower lip curled as if it couldn't decide whether to turn up or down. "Lad, I wouldn't have you saying 'won't' to Lyman." He stroked Ivy's cheek. "Still, I'd not be minding if you could manage to be a bit slow about the learning, eh?" Daniel and Ivy started walking again, this time at a pace more suited to Ethan's legs.

"How did *you* learn?" Ethan asked.

Daniel's hand circled the mare's nose. "She and I—we come here the same day," he said simply, his voice matter-of-fact and unbarbed. Daniel tugged at a bit of Ivy's forelock that had become trapped under the halter strap. He finger-combed the coarse hair and swept it to one side so it wouldn't hang in the mare's eyes.

For most people, that would have been the beginning of a story. For Daniel, it *was* the story. "So what happened?" Ethan asked when he realized the tale wouldn't come without his prompting.

"Well, we weren't neither of us glad to be there. We had that much in common, didn't we, lass?" Ivy's attention strayed to a vivid green patch of new grass. Daniel started to tug her head away, then relented and let her snag a mouthful of the sweet young growth.

"So that was your job, then, when you started? To take care of Ivy?"

"After a bit. Himself wanted Silas to tend to her, but Silas didn't want to be bothered. So he taught me how."

"He didn't want her?" Ethan's voice rose in astonishment. How could anyone not thrill at the chance to tend Ivy?

"Silas thinks horses are foolish," Daniel said.

"What?" Ethan realized that as they walked, he'd wandered across the invisible boundary that Daniel and Ivy had drawn around themselves. Daniel's hand eased on the lead rope, and Ivy stretched her neck across Daniel's body to give Ethan a quizzical inspection.

"Foolish," Daniel repeated, "ain't they, lass?" He rubbed the mare's neck. "Just like Irishmen."

The mare tossed her head and planted her feet, eyeing the shiny thing with suspicion and distaste.

"There, lass. It's only a peddler's cart," Daniel said. "You seen 'em before."

The cart was pulled off to one side, empty shafts angled to the ground. Tinware bright as silver was arrayed in the cart as temptingly as the wares in Mr. Lyman's store. Milk pans and tin kitchens and lanterns and teapots and coffee pots and mugs sparkled as if freshly polished.

Daniel led the mare up to the cart. "See?" he said. "T'ain't nothing to be fearing, is it, lass?" He walked the mare around the cart until her tail stopped swishing and her ears tipped forward. Once he'd calmed Ivy, Daniel glanced around the farrier's yard. He nodded at a bony gray gelding tethered alongside the shop. "Now there's a sorry excuse for a horse, eh, lad?" he asked.

The gelding looked as though someone had taken parts from several different horses, tossed them randomly together, and sewn them into a skin about a size and a half too big. The horse's enormous head hung from a short snaky neck that looked ready to collapse from the weight it had to bear. Knobby, stick-thin legs ended in dinner-plate-sized hooves fringed with a luxuriant growth of long silvery hair. The horse's mulish ears flopped, his nostrils quivering with a soft humming that sounded very much like a snore.

"Yessir, I would have to say that is the absolutely most ugliest horse you boys will ever see, should you live to be a hundred and twenty-seven," said a throaty voice behind the boys.

A man approached from the back of the farrier's shop. At least it mostly looked like a man, though Ethan thought there was something a bit trollish about him. He was barely Daniel's height, but wide enough in the girth that Ethan would have had trouble reaching around him. His once-black spencer had faded to bluish gray, and the short jacket was spotted with unidentifiable stains. His striped vest had trouble meeting around his middle. Ethan expected buttons to burst in all directions with the man's next breath. The man blinked slowly through his spectacles at the boys, his moss-green eyes reminding Ethan of a turtle's.

"Your humble and obedient servant, Jonathan Stocking." He fastened a wayward button on the flap of his broadfalls and tugged his vest down to cover the gap between vest bottom and trouser top. "That's my cart and that's my horse." At his gesture, the vest rode up, exposing a white band of shirt across his middle. He tugged the vest down again and buttoned his jacket closed over it.

The gelding rumbled an affectionate greeting to Mr. Stocking. The peddler thumped the horse's hide from neck to shoulder, raising a trail of dust clouds. Eyes half closed, the gelding leaned into the thumps, his ears twitching to attention. "And a damn ugly beast you are, ain't you, Phizzy?"

The peddler's voice had an odd slant to it, words gliding lazily into one another, not at all like the clipped nasal tones of Ethan's neighbors. It reminded Ethan of a southern revival preacher who'd visited Farmington a few years ago. Mr. Stocking was older than the usual run of peddlers who passed through town. Gray tinged the stray wisps of hair poking out from his tasseled knitted hat, and his cheeks prickled with a smattering of silvery stubble mixed in with the brown.

Mr. Stocking squinted one eye at Ivy. "Now *that*, my boys—" He waved a hand at the mare. She flung her head up and snorted. "That," Mr. Stocking continued, "is a horse."

Stepping away from the gelding, Mr. Stocking scraped the ground with one foot and began to recite: "'He paweth in the valley, and rejoiceth in his strength: he goeth on to meet the armed men.'" The little man pulled himself up to his full height and threw back his head contemptuously. "'He mocketh at fear, and is not affrighted. . . . He swalloweth the ground with fierceness and rage: neither believeth he'"—Mr. Stocking cupped a hand to his ear, alert to an imaginary noise—"'that it is the sound of the trumpet. He saith among the trumpets, Ha, ha!'" Mr. Stocking's hand flew up in a wild gesture, his jubilant "Ha, ha!" sending Ethan jumping back two full steps. Ivy's head bobbed, and her throat gurgled in something that sounded like a chuckle. Mr. Stocking's nostrils flared wide. He turned his head this way and that like a questing hound. "'And he smelleth the battle afar off, the thunder of the captains, and the shouting.'"

It was a fine speech, although Ethan couldn't help wondering how anybody, whether horse or human, could smell thunder and shouting.

Daniel's eyes narrowed under the shade of his cap. "*He's* a mare."

Mr. Stocking took an affronted step away from Ivy and peered down at her nether regions. "Ah, so she is, so she is. Well, I fancy she could do her share of pawing in the valleys if she had a mind to, eh, son?"

Ivy cast a placid eye on Mr. Stocking. To Ethan, she looked

like the last horse in the world—except perhaps for Mr. Stocking's gelding—to be pawing in valleys and laughing at trumpets.

"What is that—Shakespeare?" Daniel asked.

"Scripture, son, Scripture. Job. A man I'm well acquainted with, in spirit, if not in fact. 'I will not change my horse with any that treads but on four pasterns. When I bestride him'—er, her, in this case—" He raised an eyebrow toward Ivy. "'When I bestride *her*, I soar, I am a hawk; she trots the air; the earth sings when she touches it; the basest horn of her hoof is more musical than the pipe of Hermes. She's of the color of the nutmeg. And of the heat of the ginger. She is pure air and fire. She is indeed a horse, and all other jades you may call beasts.'" He bowed toward Ivy with a flourish of his hat. "'Indeed, my lord, it is a most absolute and excellent horse.'"

The skin on Ethan's arms and neck prickled. It was just exactly as Daniel and Ivy had looked racing across the field last week. Daniel's eyes widened and his mouth dropped open. Then he caught Ethan staring at him and clapped his jaw shut and fussed with Ivy's halter. Ivy arched her dainty neck as if preening at the words.

Mr. Stocking cleared his throat, tugged vest and spencer down, and tweaked his cuffs. "*That,* my boys, is Shakespeare, and the next best thing to Scripture for divine inspiration. A man who has those two books has a library in his keeping." Mr. Stocking's reptilian glance swept Ivy from nose to tail. "So, is this fine beast yours?"

Daniel's mouth hardened into a sneer. "Oh, aye. And I got a dozen more back to home just like her or better. I feed 'em on naught but Seville oranges and Scotch cake and raspberry cordial."

A gold tooth winked from the corner of Mr. Stocking's mouth when he smiled. "Ah, I suspected as much when I heard you speak. You're an exiled Irish prince, then."

Daniel tugged at his frock. "Oh, aye, and these must be me royal robes, then, eh?" Ethan wondered that the acid in his voice didn't burn the peddler.

But Mr. Stocking's grin only widened, exposing yellowing teeth, square like a horse's. "Well, I imagine you only dress like this so's not to make folks uncomfortable in your exalted presence."

Daniel pressed his lips together, an angry blush scalding his cheeks.

Mr. Stocking's nose jutted forward. "Now, son, I'm not mocking you. I'm only listening to your horse."

Daniel stepped back, sheltering under Ivy's chin. He nudged his head against her neck. "Even a horse could tell you I ain't nothing and ain't never going to be."

Mr. Stocking's gaze traveled slowly from Daniel's cap to his toes and back, then wandered to the mare's face before finally settling back on Daniel. "Indeed, son, you *ain't* nothing," he said. It was curious, Ethan thought, how his emphasis on the one word changed the whole sentence. "What you *are*, I couldn't rightwise say, but that horse knows, don't she?"

"It ain't no prince, anyways."

One of Mr. Stocking's eyebrows settled on the rim of his spectacles. "Well, there's princes and there's princes, ain't there?"

Daniel scowled, his eyes challenging the peddler's stare. Daniel blinked first. Then he snorted. "What you're saying is every man's home is his castle, and every man's a king to his dog, eh? Well, sir, I got no home nor dog nor horse to call me own, and ain't likely to, so you needn't be wasting any of your peddler's flatteries on me. I got no money to be buying your wooden nutmegs with."

The folds of Mr. Stocking's eyelids gathered as he turned his turtle-gaze onto Ethan. "There's courtesy for you. I take your brother for a prince and he takes me for a thief."

Daniel drew in a sharp breath, as if the peddler's words had stung, though Mr. Stocking's voice had been jovial.

"You want to find your thieves, son," Mr. Stocking continued, "you look to your storekeepers. Now you might—*might*, mind you—find a peddler dealing in the odd wooden nutmeg, though I've never seen such things myself. But a storekeeper'll steal the teeth out of your mouth and sell 'em back to you for ivory shirt studs quicker'n you can blink. And if you did, he might steal the blink, too."

Daniel's chin lowered, but not much. "I can't debate you there."

"Mr. Lyman—our master, that is—he's a storekeeper," Ethan explained.

"Aye, and he got no love for peddlers, neither," Daniel added, his voice prickly. "I'd not be crossing his path, if I was you."

Mr. Stocking pulled a brown ropy twist of tobacco from his pocket. He cut a plug off and slipped it into his mouth. "Sounds like you got no love for him, neither, son." A brown dribble trickled out of the corner of his mouth. He wiped it away with the back of his hand. "A hard man, your Mr. Lyman?"

Daniel shrugged. "You might say that."

"Why not hire yourself to another, then?"

"I can't." Daniel smoothed Ivy's mane. "I'm bound."

Mr. Hemenway emerged from his shop, wiping a sooty forearm across his sooty bald head.

The peddler tilted his head toward the farrier. "Now just to show a peddler can play you fair, I'll step aside for a real horse."

Daniel squinted and tilted his head. "You were here first. We ain't in no hurry."

Mr. Stocking bowed as elegantly as a man of his stature and girth could. "Go ahead, son. Phizzy and I will have a visit with your brother while yon smith works."

"He ain't me brother no more'n I'm an Irish prince." Daniel's voice had a peculiar rasp to it, and he turned sharply away.

Mr. Stocking made a thoughtful "humphing" noise as Daniel led the mare over to the farrier. The peddler turned his head and spat a long brown stream that arced over the trough and splatted into the dirt beyond. "Now, I've seen some peculiar boys in my day, son, but that is one of the peculiarest," he said.

"He was awful rude," Ethan admitted. "But you shouldn't' a teased him 'bout being a prince."

Mr. Stocking watched Daniel discuss terms with Mr. Hemenway. The boy's grubby brown cap and the big farrier's shiny soot-streaked scalp bent together over Silas's little brown account book. Ivy's nose kept light but constant contact with Daniel, whose hand strayed now and then to her neck or cheek. "I'd say your brother looks to be as hard a servant as your Mr. Lyman is a master."

"He's not my brother," Ethan said.

"Mmmm. So he said, didn't he?" Mr. Stocking's spectacled squint bobbed from Ethan to Daniel and back. "Nor quite your friend, either, eh?"

Ethan twisted a bit of his frock between his fingers. "I—I don't know. We're only bound to the same master."

Mr. Stocking made a thoughtful noise in his throat as he studied the way Daniel held the mare still for Mr. Hemenway. Ivy pressed her forehead to Daniel's chest, her ears cupped beneath the boy's chin to catch the magic words that trickled from his lips.

Mr. Stocking's fingertips rasped against the stubble on his chin. "Your friend's bound all right. Only not the way he thinks."

The boys had passed well over an hour at the farrier's. While Daniel had held Ivy to be shod, Ethan held Mr. Stocking's mirror so the little man could shave over a milk pan that had long ago lost its shine. Then the peddler held Ethan's eyes and ears with the contents of his wagon. Besides the tinware, Mr. Stocking's goods included the common peddler's sundries: spices and ribbons, combs and patent medicines, handkerchiefs and essences. But Mr. Stocking somehow transformed the wares into exotic treasures, presenting each one with a magician's flourish and tales of mist-shrouded lands, pirates and explorers, kings and queens, quests and battles, betrayal and treachery, so that a common brown nutmeg seemed more precious than an emerald.

Although Ethan was sure Mr. Stocking's tales were exaggerations, if not outright lies, he couldn't help listening, openmouthed, spellbound as much by the way Mr. Stocking's oratory swung from *ain't*s to eloquence as by the wonder of his stories.

When the farrier finished with Ivy, he set to work refitting a loose shoe for Phizzy, and Mr. Stocking's talk turned to horses. He began by praising Ivy's finer points, followed by an assortment of tales about horses historic, horses legendary, and horses entirely imaginary. Somehow he even managed to coax Daniel out of his cynical squint and cajole him from curt retorts to actual conversation.

At last, the peddler broke up the party. "Come along, Phizzy," he said. His horse nodded lazily and backed into place between the wagon's shafts with the bored ease of familiar routine.

"Why do you call him Phizzy?" Ethan asked.

"T'ain't really Phizzy. It's just an abridgment of Mephistopheles." Mr. Stocking bent to tighten buckles and fasten traces. Little puffs of dust followed his hands as they brushed against Phizzy's body.

"Mephizzz—" Ethan couldn't quite get his mouth around the name.

"Mephistopheles?" Daniel raised a pale eyebrow. "Is that Scripture or Shakespeare?" He stepped forward to adjust the harness on his side of the horse.

"Neither." Mr. Stocking came around to the horse's head. "I was maybe a few years older than you when I acquired him, and I wanted to give him the grandest name I'd ever heard." One eyelid lowered slowly. "Only you see, I didn't know then that Mephistopheles was just a fancified name for the devil. Not altogether unappropriate, though, I must say."

"He acts like the devil?" Daniel untied the reins from where they'd been bunched at Phizzy's withers and smoothed them across the horse's back and onto the wagon seat.

"No, but he runs like it. Wouldn't know to look at him, though, would you?"

Ethan could barely imagine the gelding mustering up a slow walk, never mind a run. "Where'd you get him?"

"I was working on this farm down Pennsylvania way. One of the mares busted out just as her season was coming on her. Found her four days later and fifty miles away. When Phizzy came out, we knew she'd been up to some fine tricks while she'd been gone. From the looks of him, I'd say his dam must've—" Mr. Stocking peered over his spectacles at Ethan and coughed delicately. "—hem—dallied—with anything remotely equine she met. And maybe a few things as wasn't."

Ethan's jaw dropped. "But—but—a horse can't have more'n one pa—can he?"

One of Mr. Stocking's scraggly eyebrows twitched. "So they say. All I know is when she came back, she was mighty tired. And I swear she was smiling. Anyway, when she foaled Phizzy, my master took one look at him and turned purple. It wasn't just the ugly he minded, see, but with them legs, he was sure Phizzy was bound to be a cripple. He had half a mind to shoot him, half a mind to drown him, and half a mind to give him to the first blind man who came down the road." Mr. Stocking tilted his head at Mephistopheles, who watched him through sleepy eyes. "Well, I was young and softhearted, and I figured I'd do just as well as a blind man, so I said to him, I said, 'Mr. Griswold, if you'll give me that colt, I swear in three years, he'll beat any critter you've got on this here farm.'"

"And—and did he?" Ethan asked.

Mr. Stocking tugged Phizzy's forelock and patted the gelding's forehead. "Well, they never caught us, did they?" The gelding's head bobbed lazily.

"So you stole him," Daniel said.

"Mr. Griswold gave him to me, remember? Only being kind'a simple and trusting, I neglected to have him put it in writing." Mr. Stocking waggled a stubby finger at the boys. "Let that be a lesson in business to you fellas. Anyways, when he saw how that colt was shaping up, he began to see the money bags. Imagine bringing a beast like that to a race, huh? Who'd ever think he could win? But he could, see, and that's how we made our living the first few years." Mr. Stocking patted his stomach. The vest had ridden up a full three inches by now, the lower button straining hard. "But I got a little roundish, see, and had to come up with another line of work." Mephistopheles nuzzled Mr. Stocking's belly and fluttered his lips over the peddler's buttons as if he'd pick them off for a snack. The peddler scratched the gelding's ears with one hand while his other searched his pocket. He pulled out a stale-looking biscuit and blew the lint from it.

"And that's why you're a peddler?" Ethan asked.

Phizzy took Mr. Stocking's offering with a slobbery wiggle of his rubbery lips. Mr. Stocking dried his palm first on the seat of his trousers, then on Phizzy's neck. "I've been about every sort of traveling something you can think of, except a toe dancer. I've been a circus rider, a juggler, a writing master, a singing master, a dancing master, and an actor." Mr. Stocking drew himself up to his full height and placed a hand upon his chest. "I've been heroes and scoundrels and wizards and kings. And even a queen or two, when the company was short of the fairer gender."

Ethan smothered a giggle at the idea of Mr. Stocking bewigged and begowned, reciting in a falsetto voice.

"Seems to me," the peddler continued, "with all there is to see and do, it's a crime, a pure and unholy waste, to plant your-self down somewheres and never get up again."

"Where'll you go next?" Ethan asked.

"I've been all the ways down to Florida, and all the ways up to Canada." Mr. Stocking's index finger swooped down toward the ground, then up toward the sky as he spoke. "So I estimate there's only one way left for me, ain't there?"

"West," Daniel said almost reverently, as if he were talking about the Promised Land.

"That's the place." Mr. Stocking's hand disappeared into his pocket and extracted a crumpled piece of paper. Ethan caught a brief glimpse of bold letters and exclamation points as Mr. Stocking gave the handbill to Daniel. "Yes, indeed. You want adventure, son, you go there."

A tremor of excitement and trepidation quivered inside Ethan. "Won't you be scared?"

Mr. Stocking wreathed one arm around Phizzy's nose and held the other in the air, finger pointing to the heavens. "'We mocketh at fear, and are not affrighted.'" A chuckling whicker from Phizzy echoed Mr. Stocking's *Ha, ha!*

"Mmm-hmm," Daniel said, his head bowed over the paper. "Ain't old Phizzy a bit on for such a trip?"

"Appearances are deceiving, son, deceiving. Mephistopheles would no more be still than I would. You couldn't part us any more'n you could part Castor and Pollux, David and Jonathan,

Lewis and Clark, Napoleon and Bonaparte. It's not every day you find a horse like this one." Mr. Stocking gave Phizzy's shoulder a proud thump.

The dust from Phizzy's hide must have caught in Daniel's throat. He turned away, coughing into the handbill. Ethan thumped Daniel's back three times hard before he finally straightened, eyes glistening, cheeks red. "I daresay." He wheezed between the words.

Mr. Stocking cocked an eyebrow. "It's more'n looks makes a horse, son." His spectacles winked at Daniel. "With some horses, there's no training 'em for love nor money. Some— they'll mind you fine, but it's only their dinner they're looking out for. But every now and then, you'll come across a horse who'll give you his soul. Maybe he'll mind someone else if he has to, but for you he'll run or pull or jump until his heart bursts." He ran a tender hand down Phizzy's neck. "When you get a horse like that, it don't matter whose name is on a piece of paper. That horse knows who he belongs to, and there ain't no telling him no different."

Mr. Stocking's turtle-gaze loitered over Ivy, then pinned Daniel hard. "And there ain't no telling you, neither, is there, son?"

Chapter Twelve

"D'you think it's true?" Ethan asked. "What he said about Mephis—Mephis—about Phizzy, and all—all the other things he told us?"

One of Daniel's shoulders rose and fell under his frock. "Maybe half. He's a peddler, after all." The lead rope dangled loose between Daniel's fingers. Ivy trailed behind him like a dog walking to heel.

They turned south down the back road that led over Slocum's Brook. The quiet, narrow lane meandered between swampland and woodlots and parcels too rocky to till. It was the long way back to Mr. Lyman's, shadier and less traveled than the broad main road that ran between pastures and fields. They still had hours yet until dinnertime, and Daniel seemed intent on using every second.

"He was right about Ivy," Ethan said after a long silence.

"Aye, she's grand, ain't she? 'A most absolute and excellent horse,'" Daniel quoted.

"Not that. I mean, it don't matter what anybody else thinks. Ivy thinks she belongs to you."

Daniel frowned and rubbed his chin. "I don't s'pose nobody'll be wanting her opinion on it."

If Mr. Stocking was right about Ivy, Ethan mused, then maybe he was right about Daniel being a prince. Ethan's head floated with visions of coaches and castles. He became so caught up in his fancy that he was startled when he realized that Daniel had led the mare off the road into the woods.

"Where're you going? That's not—" Ethan stopped short when Daniel grabbed a handful of Ivy's mane and swung himself up onto her back. "But—but Silas said—" Ethan sputtered.

Daniel thumbed his cap back. "Silas said not to let him *hear* about me riding, didn't he? I'll not be telling him. Will you?" He reached down a hand. "Come on."

"I—I—I can't," Ethan said, though his heart danced at the idea. The specter of Mr. Lyman's discipline loomed too large.

Daniel straightened and shrugged. "Suit yourself, then." His legs tightened on Ivy's sides, and the mare stepped forward. "I'll meet you by Stearns's orchard," he said over his shoulder.

A tiny empty space opened up inside Ethan and grew as Daniel and the mare receded into the woods. He lurched into a run, his shoes hissing through the leaf mold underfoot. "Daniel, wait! Wait for me!"

Ivy stopped and gave Ethan an inquisitive glance. She nodded, seeming to second Daniel's invitation.

"All right, lad. No need to shout." Daniel slid closer to the mare's rump. "Here—you sit in front. That way I can keep you from sliding off."

Ethan held out his arm for Daniel to grab and jumped when he felt Daniel pull. He ended up sprawled on his belly across the mare's back. He blinked at Daniel's grimy naked toes dangling below his face.

"Ah, well. It's a start, I s'pose." After a bit of twisting and tugging on Ethan's braces and trousers, Daniel righted Ethan and turned him so he faced forward.

Ethan grabbed a double handful of Ivy's mane. "All right. I'm ready."

"No, you ain't. You got to hold on with your legs."

Ethan clamped his knees tight around Ivy's sides. He felt

her warmth through his trousers, felt the rhythm of her breathing. If he stayed very still, he was sure he'd feel her heart.

Daniel clucked to Ivy and shifted his body in some mysterious way.

"Oh!" Ethan said, tipping from side to side. He clung harder with his knees, but it was like trying to ride a barrel. Out of the corner of his eye, he saw Ivy's tail slap at Daniel's calves with barely contained fury. When he looked forward, he saw Ivy's ears bent flat against her head.

"She doesn't like me," he said.

"It's 'cause you sit like a sack of grain. No, like a kettle. A sack of grain'd at least have some give to it, wouldn't it, now?"

"I'm going to fall off." Ethan shifted his rump as he slid first one way, then the other. The bony ridge of Ivy's spine jarred against his backside.

"Aye, if you keep sitting like that. You got to . . . you got to . . ."

Ethan twisted to watch Daniel's face. Daniel frowned, tipped his cap off, and scratched his head hard. "Hmmm. I never had to talk it before." His body shifted. He seemed to be analyzing what each muscle and joint was doing when. "Let's start with your legs, eh? And then we'll move up."

Daniel's legs seemed to dangle loose from his hips. Ethan's own clamped viselike at the knees, so tight that his thigh muscles trembled.

"You got to make your legs long, see? You got to feel like they was a couple big long ribbons that you'd like to wind 'round her sides and tie under her belly."

"But your legs *are* long," Ethan protested.

"Well, they weren't when I was your age, now, were they?"

Ethan chewed his lip. "You said you fell off."

"Oh. I s'pose I did." Ivy's hooves thudded softly in the damp leaves as Daniel thought. "But I didn't have no one to hold me on, now, did I?" he finally said. "Now let go your hands and just use your legs like I told you. It's having your knees clapped on so hard that's got her jumpy."

Ethan imagined stretching his legs all the way around Ivy's round rib cage and tying his ankles in a neat bow underneath her. As his muscles stopped squeezing in and started stretching down, Ivy's belly swung gently from side to side like a fat, lazy pendulum. One coppery ear stood erect, twitching front to back.

"There, see? She can feel it, too," Daniel said. "Now, just keep your legs on her like that, like—like—like Lizzie maybe sewed your trousers to Ivy's ribs, see?" One of Daniel's hands let go of the rope and moved toward Ethan's waist. Ethan's middle tensed.

"I ain't going to tickle you. I just want to see what you're doing with your back." Daniel pressed a palm against Ethan's spine. "You're—you're like a board here." He nudged the small of Ethan's back. "That's no good. But you can't be loose like a string, neither. It's like—like—ah, I don't know." He untangled Ethan's hands from Ivy's mane and placed them on his waist. "Here, *you* feel what it's like."

Ethan groped at Daniel's hips, then his spine, then his waist. "I can't tell anything," he said. It felt so silly he had to laugh.

"Maybe you could if you'd stop giggling like some fool girl. Here—like this." Daniel slid forward so that Ethan's shoulders rested against Daniel's chest, his spine along Daniel's belly, their legs touching. "Can you tell what I'm doing now?"

Ethan concentrated, then nearly squealed with sudden understanding. "I see! It's like your top's all still, but your bottom moves with her, and your middle's sort of like a—like a—a hinge."

"Well, not quite a hinge, but nearly so."

"Let me try," Ethan said.

Daniel slid back again. Ethan felt the mare's steps move

through him, legs to backside to hips to belly. The mare's ears pricked forward.

"Look, Daniel, I *am* riding! And Ivy likes it!"

"Well, she's maybe not minding you so much. But you ain't riding. You're only not falling off. It ain't riding 'til you can tell her what to do and have her do it."

"Oh." Ethan chewed his lower lip. "How do you do that?"

"Well-l-l-l-l . . ." Daniel scratched his head. "I don't exactly know. I mean, I just sort'a think what I want to do, and she does it, see?"

"She reads your mind?"

"Of course not. It's more like—like I get to thinking about having her walk faster, say, like this." Ivy pushed forward with longer strides. "And while I'm thinking in me head, me body's thinking about it, too, and that's how she feels what I'm thinking. Or sometimes it's the other way 'round, and I can feel her wanting to run or jump, and I just say, all right, then, lass, and go along with her."

"It sounds so easy."

"It is—now. But I et a lot of grass and dirt and such before I knew the way of it."

"Well, then show me the right way."

"I don't know if I can. I can maybe tell you a bit how it feels, but to say you got to move your legs this way or that, or shift your arse just so . . . It'd be like trying to teach somebody to walk. You can do it fine without thinking, but let you start saying, 'I've got to put me foot down so, and bend me knee just this much,' and you'd be getting so muddled up with how much there is to it, you'd fall over."

"Then how am I s'posed to learn?"

Daniel sighed. "You can begin by not jabbering so many questions at me. Just be quiet and feel what she's doing, all right, lad?"

Ethan reached out with all his senses, trying to find the mare's rhythm. He felt the soft one-two-one-two of the mare's hooves, felt the same rhythm in her belly as it swayed between his legs, the same rhythm in Daniel's chest as Ethan leaned against him, and the same rhythm in his own body as hips and legs and spine responded to Ivy's motion.

Silencing his mind and body to concentrate on Ivy heightened all his senses. Warmth surrounded him: the mare between his legs and under his hands, Daniel at his back, the dappled April sun lightly toasting him through his woolen frock. A soft haze of red-tasseled maple blossoms and barely breaking yellow-green leaves softened the trees with memories of autumn and promises of summer. When he closed his eyes, he could feel the heartbeat of the earth waking up to the new season. The sun made warm patterns of gray and red and orange on the insides of his closed eyelids as the mare walked from shadow to sun to shadow again. There were no Lymans, no chores to get back for, no debts to work off, nothing but him and Daniel and Ivy and the woods forever and ever.

Then the earth bounced underneath him, and he had to open his eyes. His seat rose from Ivy's back and plopped down again with a jarring thunk that clanked his teeth together. He'd no sooner landed than he was back up again, then down once more.

"Wh-wh-at-at're you-ou-ou do-o-o-ing?" His words vibrated in his throat with each jounce.

Daniel slowed the mare, but not enough to break her bouncing gait. "Trotting," he said. Ethan felt Daniel's body rise and fall with the mare's, as if he'd somehow glued the seat of his trousers to her spine.

"How-ow-ow-ow d'you-ou do-o that-at-at?"

"Same's walking. Just follow what she does. Go up when she does, and down when she does."

It was impossible. As soon as Ethan could figure out that the mare was down, she was already up again. "I ca-an't."

Daniel's legs shifted behind him. "Well, then, we'll have to run."

Ethan's panicked "No!" was smothered by a rush of terror and delight as the mare sprang forward and they burst out of the woods. For an eternal second, he thought they'd plunged off the edge of the world and hung suspended in a great green-and-blue bubble. They'd cantered halfway across the field before he realized that they were running across a bowl-shaped meadow that rolled gently down to a pond. Ivy's body gathered and stretched and landed, the flex and release of each muscle precise and distinct. The grass flashed beneath her hooves, but Ivy and Ethan and Daniel seemed not to travel at all, but to float while the bubble of grass and sky whirled by them. Ethan wanted to cry out with the joyous terror of hanging poised between flying and falling.

Daniel laughed for both of them, a harsh exultation, like a raven's cry. But all too soon his laugh turned into an unfamiliar word with the slant of a curse to it. Ethan's nose was suddenly buried in coarse chestnut hair as Ivy's canter broke into a jarring trot, bursting the bubble that had held them.

Ethan's head still swirled with the motion of the canter. The grass and sky rocked around him, like a pan of water sloshing after being jostled. "What?" he asked.

"It's that bloody peddler fella again," Daniel said.

Ethan looked toward the pond. A flash of brightness struck his eyes as the sun glinted off Mr. Stocking's spectacles. Mephistopheles, stripped of his harness, peered lazily over the peddler's shoulder.

Daniel sighed and nudged Ivy toward the peddler.

"For such a homely boy, you surely do some of the prettiest riding I ever seen," Mr. Stocking said.

"Ain't you got some tinware to be selling or some such?" Daniel asked.

Mr. Stocking crossed his arms. "Ain't you got some fences to fix or some fields to plow?"

"We ain't wanted back 'til dinner. Not much point in going where we ain't wanted, is there?"

Mr. Stocking guffawed and spat a fat, juicy stream. "Son, you got some way of turning words around. If you could tame that brogue, I could make a peddler of you for sure." His eyes narrowed behind the glasses while one finger traced the roll of flesh under his chin. "Then again, it might be handy to have someone who knows a little Irish talk, what with all your tribe moving into Springfield and Westfield and Pittsfield and all them other fields. You could help me sell a pile of teapots to your town cousins."

"I got no kin in any of them places."

"No?" The peddler tugged his ear. "No, I don't s'pose you do. Ah, well, it'd be a shame to waste you on peddling anyways. Now, the circus—that'd be the place for a man of your talents. Such riding!" Mr. Stocking nodded to himself. "It's on account of your race, I imagine. Equines are in the Irish blood, so they say—passed down from father to son."

"Me da never sat a horse in his life. Me grand-da neither, from what I been told," Daniel said coolly.

Grasping his lapels, the peddler struck an exasperated pose. "You're bound to take offense, no matter what I say, ain't you, son?"

"I ain't taking nothing. I'm just wondering how you come to be here."

"Just following your advice. You said your Mr. Lyman is death on peddlers, so here I am, giving him a wide"—the peddler's arms spread to indicate just how wide—"berth. Anyway, it'd be a waste of a perfectly good horse-riding day to spend it peddling . . . or farming, hmmm?" One eye closed solemnly behind the peddler's spectacles. "And Phizzy's feeling a bit sprightly now he's got his shoes fixed, ain't you?" The only show of energy the gelding made was a slight pricking of his ears. "What we want to know is, what took you boys so long to join us?"

Ethan twisted to share a wide-eyed glance with Daniel. "You followed us!"

Mr. Stocking chuckled at Phizzy, who responded with a throaty gurgle. "Now how could we'a followed you if we got here first? You'd'a got here quicker going by the road, though."

"We weren't in no hurry," Daniel said woodenly.

"Daniel was teaching me to ride," Ethan said.

"And a pretty sight it was, too." Mr. Stocking lowered an eyebrow at the boys. "But how's that mare when it comes to serious riding, huh?"

"Serious?" Daniel repeated.

"I mean a challenge. A race."

Daniel smothered a laugh. "You wouldn't be meaning against Phizzy, now, would you?"

"Well, I don't see no other contenders."

"Won't be much of a race."

Mr. Stocking cocked his head, the sun blinking off his glasses into Ethan's eyes. "Are you that sure you'll win? Or that afraid you'll lose?"

"I ain't afraid." Daniel nudged Ethan in the small of the back. "Off with you, lad."

Ethan grabbed Ivy's mane stubbornly. "But I want to ride, too."

Mr. Stocking waved a hand at the boys. "Oh, let your friend ride. It'll even the odds a bit. You must admit, sir, that you have the advantage of us in age and"—Mr. Stocking patted his bulging vest—"ahem, and girth." He scratched his chin. "Now, what'll be the stakes?"

"Stakes?"

"What'd be the point in racing, son, if there wasn't no prize at the end?" The peddler's scratching fingers wandered from chin to ear to scalp. "Hmmmm. If you win, you can pick anything out of my goods." He gestured toward his wagon. The winking tinware lay hidden beneath a worn canvas.

"I got nothing to give you," Daniel protested.

"No matter. No matter." Mr. Stocking glanced around the field, then snapped his fingers. "Wait. There is something. . . . If we win, let's say you give me the loan of your mare for, oh, a quick gallop around this field . . . if she'll have me."

"Oh, she'll have you all right. It's you having her I'd be minding."

Mr. Stocking shook his head. "Do you think I'd abandon three hundred dollars' worth of goods for fifty dollars' worth of horse? Anyway, you're going to win, ain't you, son?"

"All right, then," Daniel finally said. "One turn 'round the meadow. Will you be wanting a few seconds' lead?"

Mr. Stocking grinned as he shed his spencer and hat and undid his vest buttons. "Now that's very big of you, son. Damned if you ain't a gentleman, even if you ain't no prince." His round form bobbed in a bow.

Any other time, Ethan might have giggled as he watched the little man climb onto the horse as gracelessly as a piglet clambering into a trough, but the prospect of the race made something stir inside him, like a bird gathering itself for flight.

Daniel selected a starting point. Ethan sensed a sudden keenness in the older boy, like a hound put onto a scent. He twisted to look at Daniel's face. The Irish boy's jaw set tight with concentration.

The peddler and his splay-footed gelding looked like something from a fairy story about a troll and an ill-made horse. Yet for all their absurdity, Ethan saw something impressive about them. Perhaps it was the way Phizzy's massive head sat poised on his scrawny neck, ears standing at attention, nostrils quivering eagerly. Or perhaps it was the way Mr. Stocking and Phizzy seemed fused together, the same way Daniel melded with Ivy to become a new creature both human and equine. Ethan's heart fluttered. Perhaps the peddler had been telling the truth about Phizzy after all.

The riders lined up their horses. Mr. Stocking's eyes glimmered as he swept the boys and the mare with an appraising glance. Daniel returned the peddler's gaze measure for measure. Then the peddler nodded and settled deeper into his seat.

"I calculate I still have a few pounds on you, son," Mr. Stocking said.

"I'll give you three seconds, if you like," Daniel offered.

"Fair enough." Mr. Stocking's spectacles flashed at Ethan. "Do you want to say go?"

Ethan wanted to shout, "Oh, yes!" but he could only nod. He took a deep breath to steady his voice. "Ready?" he asked.

Mr. Stocking somehow managed to fold his roundness into Phizzy's withers and neck.

As Ethan counted to three, Daniel pushed him down until he was bent double over Ivy's withers.

"Go!" Ethan shouted.

Phizzy lurched forward, showering Ethan and Daniel with clods of earth. Ivy skipped and strained impatiently as Daniel held her in place. The agreed-upon three seconds seemed more like thirty as Phizzy's dappled rump bobbed farther and farther away.

Then Daniel's weight shifted, he let out a sharp cry, and Ivy leaped into the race.

Chapter Thirteen

Ethan felt like a dry leaf spun into a cyclone. Any second he and Daniel and Ivy might whirl apart and be flung to pieces. At first, he could sense nothing but Ivy's coarse mane slapping at his face and his own urgent clinging with hands, arms, legs, soul. His only thought was, *Don't fall off. Don't fall off.*

Sounds broke through the blur: drumming beneath them as Ivy's hooves met and left the earth so fast that Ethan couldn't separate one footfall from the next, Ivy's greedy inhaling and moist exhaling, Daniel's steady stream of Gaelic-laden magic words.

Then Ethan was aware of another set of drumbeats and breaths, another set of words.

Phizzy galloped ahead of them, his legs flying any old how in such a bizarre galumphing run that Ethan wondered if the gelding's knees and hocks were in their proper places or if, perhaps, he had a few more than his proper share. The shaggy tufts of hair at Phizzy's fetlocks fluttered like birds flapping around his heels. It was a ridiculous gait, and yet Daniel's body crushed Ethan lower against the mare, and he uttered a word that Ethan was sure was a curse. "Sweet Jesus! I can't catch the bloody beast!"

They crested the hill and turned along the high side of the meadow. Chestnut hair whipped Ethan's eyes. He blinked, and the horse in front loomed larger. The chanting over Ethan's head turned roughly musical.

Phizzy's hoofbeats pounded out a deeper, louder rumble. His rider's voice changed from a vague hint of words into something Ethan recognized as song.

The peddler hadn't lied about being a singing master. His sturdy baritone barely shuddered, even with the jostling of Phizzy's hooves. Ethan almost laughed when he identified the song as "Happy Land," Ma's favorite hymn. Mr. Stocking was just reaching the part where *Sickness and sorrow, pain and death are felt and feared no more.* Only he'd changed the words to *Lameness and founder and moldy hay are felt and feared no more.* Canaan's fair and happy land apparently had room in it for horses, at least in the peddler's world.

As Ivy gained on Phizzy, Mr. Stocking's singing increased in volume and tempo. He'd changed to a fuguing tune, and Ethan was certain the peddler sang all four parts: "Fly swifter round, old horse of mine, and earn the welcome hay."

They crossed the upper meadow that way, Ivy's nose close enough for Phizzy's tail to tickle her, but never getting any closer. Daniel's spell intensified. His words danced around each other and blended into one great continuous word. He squeezed himself together like a tightening spring, pressing Ethan nearly flat into Ivy's mane. Ethan turned his head, and suddenly he was looking Mr. Stocking in the eye.

The peddler sang tenor now: "Oh, may my horse in tune be found, even though he's big and round."

Peddler and horse both shone with sweat. Mr. Stocking's spectacles flashed, and then there was nothing but swirls of green and brown in front of Ethan's face. His ears vibrated with Daniel's whoop ringing over his head. Ethan would have laughed, too, if he'd been able to breathe.

They pounded for the downhill slope that would lead them back to the start. The crush against Ethan's back eased, and he sucked in a long, laughing breath. Mr. Stocking's singing fell far away from them. Ivy's gallop felt like a stone skipping across the surface of a pond, skimming over the meadow, then touching with a splash of torn dirt and grass, then skimming again. Ethan's excitement was tempered by the breathless fear that the whole adventure would end in a disastrous plunge. His hands throbbed from his grip on Ivy's mane, fingernails digging hard into palms. His back and shoulders groaned with the tension of his crouch. He had long ago lost the feeling in his legs. He'd never been so afraid or so sore in his life. The ride would surely kill him. He wished it would never end.

Then, in the heartbeat between one stride and another, Ethan sensed something different about the mare's pace, the tone of Daniel's voice, Daniel's posture.

There was a drumming just behind Ethan's left shoulder, a wheezing breath along Ivy's flank. The gray muzzle, nostrils flared and red-lined, crept up by Daniel's calf, then Ethan's, then by Ivy's withers.

The layer of sweat on Phizzy's hide had turned his pale gray coat to white-flecked iron. His head bobbed raggedly, as if his neck had tired of holding it. Mr. Stocking's fun and frivolity had disappeared behind a mask of sweat. His mouth hung open, but there were no more songs coming from his lips. Then the moment passed, and Ethan found himself looking at the back of Mr. Stocking's head.

"No!" His hands jerked at Ivy's mane. "Come on, Ivy! You can beat him! You can do it!" He felt a brief surge of gratification as Ivy's ears flicked and she drew closer again, then he grunted with the thud of an elbow in his side.

"Quiet, you!" Daniel hissed over his head. "I'm the one riding this horse."

But Ivy dropped farther behind on the downhill slope, her muzzle back against Phizzy's rump. Frustration clawed at

Ethan's belly. Couldn't Daniel see that Phizzy was tiring? Surely Ivy had enough left in her to surge ahead.

But the starting point flew past with Ivy still at the gelding's flank. She passed Phizzy only after the peddler had reined the huffing gelding to a stop. Ivy trickled to a canter, then a trot, then a walk, before Daniel stopped her well past her rival.

Fists balled, Ethan twisted to look up at Daniel. "How could you lose? Ivy should'a beat him! She should'a!" He wanted to pound Daniel's chest with his fists and curse him for his incompetent riding.

His face passive, Daniel slid to the ground. "Hush. You don't know nothing about horses, lad." He reached up to help Ethan down.

Ethan snubbed the offer, even though his legs felt limp. He clutched Ivy's shoulder to keep from collapsing. Eyes stinging, he opened his mouth to fire a stream of accusations at Daniel.

Daniel cut him off with a cool look. "Fix your hat. We'll be walking her out a bit now."

Ethan snatched the straw hat from his head and wrestled with the dents. "We could'a won," he muttered. He tried to stalk away, but his legs wobbled, nearly dropping him onto his knees. Daniel took his arm and forced him to walk alongside the mare, away from Mr. Stocking and Phizzy.

Ivy's withers gleamed damply, but she held her head neatly poised, flared nostrils questing for a treat from Daniel's pockets, as if she had forgotten her recent humiliation. Could it have been her fault? Ethan wondered. Was she one of those horses who were all show and no go? No. Ethan was sure Ivy would have run herself to death for Daniel, but he had just stopped trying.

They walked the mare for a long time before Daniel turned back toward the peddler and his gelding. Ethan's stomach clenched at the sight of Phizzy standing wilted and straddle-legged. His nose nearly touched the ground, ears flopping like dead leaves, sides heaving in and out. Mr. Stocking's hands moved over the horse, massaging legs, inspecting feet. He pulled a rag from his pocket and wiped Phizzy's sweaty hide in soothing swirls and sweeps, working his way toward the horse's drooping head. His arms circled Phizzy's muzzle and propped the horse's nose against his belly so that Mr. Stocking could look into Phizzy's eyes. Murmuring soothing endearments, the little man stroked Phizzy's cheek. It was only when the boys drew right alongside that Ethan realized Mr. Stocking's hands were trembling.

"Sir?" Daniel held Ivy's lead rope out to Mr. Stocking.

Mr. Stocking stared blankly at the redheaded boy. The little man's face now had a grayish tinge to it. His shirt clung damply to his thick body, and his hair lay flat and wet against his scalp. A dullness had replaced the playful glow in his eyes. Even his spectacles no longer winked in the sun. Studying horse and rider, Ethan wasn't quite sure which supported the other.

Mr. Stocking drew himself up straight and cleared his throat. The hand holding the rag drifted shakily about his vest as if to tidy it. The two horsemen traded a long, level glance that seemed to hold a world of unspoken dialogue. "That was a long three seconds you gave us, son," Mr. Stocking finally said.

"Have your ride. Ethan and I'll walk Phizzy out for you." Daniel gently took the reins from Mr. Stocking's hand and turned them over to Ethan. "Shall I give you a leg up?" Daniel's voice was calm, without a hint of the sarcasm that Ethan would normally have expected.

The little man blinked. He looked first at his own horse, then at Ivy, before his eyes locked again on Daniel's. He started to shake his head, but Daniel pressed Ivy's lead rope into the peddler's hand.

"We'll mind him fine for you." Daniel touched the gelding's sodden hide as if it were silk. "You were right, sir," he said. "That horse can run."

Ethan gaped, mystified. Anyone could see that Phizzy was dead tired. Ivy was breathing hard, too, but she pricked her ears forward and pawed the ground as if she were ready to go another round and then some.

Mr. Stocking finally accepted Ivy's rope. The dullness behind his spectacles began to glow again. "Yes, I was right. And not just about the horse." Something solemn and unspoken passed between the riders, over Ethan's head.

After Mr. Stocking had trotted Ivy away, Daniel's hands began to work over Phizzy. He murmured the magic words that Ethan thought belonged only to Ivy. Ethan's insides squirmed. Daniel hadn't even winced over relinquishing the mare, and now he was using Ivy's words on another horse. The betrayal was complete.

"You—you *let* him win!" Ethan spluttered.

Daniel didn't answer, but Ethan read confirmation in the other boy's eyes. Daniel shrugged apathetically, as if the race hadn't mattered to him after all.

"Why?" Ethan demanded.

Daniel led the gelding forward into a shuffling walk. Phizzy rested his nose heavily on the boy's shoulder, as if he needed help carrying his own head. Daniel's gray-green eyes narrowed at Ethan, the way the schoolmaster's did when Ethan lost the way of figuring a simple sum. "He said this horse'd die for him. I'm not needing to see it proved."

Ethan barely tasted his dinner, even though Lizzie had made her best veal pie. It seemed as though four days' worth of astounding events had happened in the four hours that they'd been gone: meeting Mr. Stocking and Phizzy at the farrier's; the riding lesson and the race; the way Daniel had shown no concern over his loss, and Mr. Stocking no joy in his victory; the way the peddler had pressed gifts on Daniel, even though the boy had lost the race; the way Mr. Stocking and Daniel had solemnly shaken hands at parting, like men of equal stature.

Perhaps this afternoon, Ethan mused, he could prod Daniel into explaining everything. Perhaps they could mull over the old handbills Mr. Stocking had dug out from under the wagon seat and given to the boys: yellowing and brittle advertisements emblazoned with horses or proclaiming the glories of western lands. Perhaps Daniel would show Ethan the fat little book that the peddler had given him, and they could puzzle out whether there really were any horses in Shakespeare.

Mr. Pease roused Ethan from his meditations. "Did you see that tin peddler poking around today?" he asked casually. "A soggy kind'a fella with a bony nag pulling his cart."

Ethan's bread stuck in his throat. He took a sip of cider, but it only seeped into the doughy lump and made it swell. He saw Daniel's knife pause briefly on its way to his mouth, his scarred knuckles whitening on the handle. But he took in the mouthful calmly and chewed with deliberate care.

"He didn't dare show his face near the common," Mr. Lyman said.

"Did he have any news?" Lizzie asked, leaning forward.

Mr. Pease rocked back in his chair. "News? Hmmmm, well, he'd just been through Springfield a few days since." His eyes drifted toward Daniel, his mouth slanting mockingly. "He says the Irish are thick as fleas in Cabotville now."

Everyone stared at Daniel for a moment. His head

remained bent over his plate, as if he couldn't feel the weight of their eyes upon him. A trace of pink crept up his neck.

"They're talking of building their own church," Mr. Pease continued.

Mrs. Lyman wadded her napkin into a ball and threw it down next to her plate. "A Papist church? Well, I never!"

Mr. Pease paused to chew a bulging mouthful of pie. "Oh, and he admired your horse, sir." He waved his knife in Mr. Lyman's direction.

Ethan shifted his weight to stand closer to Daniel. He met Daniel's warning glare and tilted his head in a tacit vow of silence.

"My horse?"

"Your horse and the boys riding her."

For a moment everyone seemed frozen, glasses or knives poised halfway to their mouths. The air felt charged and heavy, the way it did when a thunderstorm was about to break. Then there was a clatter of crockery and a startled shriek near the head of the table.

"Ruth!" Silas said. "See what happens when you play at the table? Now look what you've done."

A rusty brown puddle oozed from Silas's overturned mug, across the tablecloth, around Silas's plate, and into his lap. He lifted his arm to reveal a dark, dripping spot on his sleeve from his wrist to his elbow.

Ruth stood at Silas's knee. Her lower lip quivered as she stared down at the soggy brown rosette on the bosom of her yellow dress. She snuffled miserably. "But I—"

"Hush now." Lizzie leaned across the table to mop at the puddle with her napkin. "Oh, look, and all over Mr. Pease, too!" In her haste to clean up the mess, she nearly sent the pickled beets into Mr. Pease's lap to join the cider, but Mr. Wheeler steadied the bowl in time. She hurried around the table, snatching up napkins and attacking the pool of cider to keep it from dripping onto Mrs. Lyman's carpet.

Silas stood, patting futilely at his trousers with his own dripping napkin. Ruth had one pudgy fist clenched around a handful of Silas's broadfalls. Her crimsoning face puckered into an imminent wail.

"Oh, Silas, you're soaked," Mrs. Lyman said.

Silas gave his stepmother a sheepish look. "At least nothing's broken." He pulled his chair away from the table. Scooping the now-bawling Ruth into his arms, Silas nodded toward Mr. Pease. "Come on, Rufus. I'll lend you a shirt."

Mr. Pease waved a careless hand toward Silas. "Awful decent of you, but I'm fine."

"Suit yourself." Silas frowned. He retreated with Ruth to the kitchen, followed by Lizzie, her hands full of sopping napkins. She paused in the doorway, scowling at the mess. Then Ruth wailed and Lizzie disappeared into the kitchen.

The remaining members of the household stared at their dinners a moment, as if they'd forgotten what they were for. Finally Mr. Lyman began to eat again. Ethan sensed a communal sigh, then the rest of the household lifted their knives.

Daniel ate with deliberate speed, as if he wanted to hasten the end of the meal. But Ethan's appetite had vanished, and he merely pushed the remnants of his dinner around his plate. Mr. Lyman helped himself to another slice of pie and a second piece of gingerbread. Mrs. Lyman cast restless glances at the dark spot under Silas's plate, as if she wanted to snatch the tablecloth away and put it in to soak without delay. She finally breathed an impatient little sigh and poked at her own dinner.

As the meal continued in silence, Ethan began to breathe a little easier. But Mr. Lyman hadn't forgotten after all. He waited until he'd cleared his plate before asking, "What was that you were saying about my horse, Rufus?"

Mr. Pease's mouth curled up at the corners. "Only that this peddler thought she was a fine animal. And the boy riding her a fine horseman."

Ethan reached under the table for Daniel's elbow. Daniel's arm was rigid in his grip.

"The boy riding her?" Mr. Lyman repeated slowly. "What boy was that, Paddy? Ethan?" Ethan felt the cold blue eyes boring into him, but he couldn't look up from his plate.

"Oh, him," Daniel said carelessly. "We seen that peddler down to the farrier's. We talked a bit about horses and such while we were waiting for Mr. Hemenway. He must'a thought we rode down 'stead of walking."

Mr. Pease persisted. "But I'm sure he said he saw someone riding. A chestnut mare, he said, and a boy with hair nearly as red as the horse, riding like he'd been born on horseback, that's what this peddler said. He said it was a fine thing to see." Mr. Pease grinned at Daniel as if he expected to be thanked for the compliment.

"Only one boy?" Mr. Lyman probed. Ethan's forehead grew damp before his master's searing eyes.

"No. No, I'm sure he said two. Yes, that was it: a second boy sitting in front, hanging on for dear life."

Zeloda snickered.

"I see." Mr. Lyman's chair hissed across the carpet as he rose. "Paddy. Ethan. I want to talk to you out in the barn."

Daniel stood slowly, his hand clenching Ethan's shoulder. When Ethan looked up into his eyes, they were as cold and hard as granite.

"Well, now you can't say you never been switched," Daniel said. "At least he didn't make you drop your trousers."

"I—it wasn't so bad for me." Ethan had endured nine swift stinging blows to his rear end: one for each of his years. "But you—" Ethan hefted his shovel to hide his shudder. "But he—he *beat* you." Daniel's switching hadn't even started until Mr. Lyman had battered Daniel to the barn floor with punches and kicks. And it had been Daniel's back, not his backside, that had met the switch, with no frock or vest or shirt in between to soften the blows. Mr. Lyman hadn't stopped at sixteen.

"What did you expect? I done all he said. Disobedience, lying, leading lads astray." Daniel's shrug turned into a wince. "Not that I ain't done worse. Or been beat worse." He moved carefully, as if to keep vest and shirt from rubbing against his back while he wielded the digging bar.

"I thought he was going to kill you." Ethan shivered.

Daniel snorted and spat in the dirt. He rammed the iron bar hard into the fence-post hole. "What'd be the point in that? He'd not be getting much work out of me if I was dead, now, would he?" He wiggled the bar back and forth, loosening the earth for Ethan to scoop out with his spade.

They worked together for a few minutes in a silent rhythm. Daniel heaved the bar up and down with strokes as regular as the saw at the mill. Ethan slipped the shovel in during the pauses. He tried to study Daniel's face, but all he could see under the brim of the other boy's cap was the tip of a sharp sunburned nose, an angular chin, and a mouth clenched in a firm line, distorted where Daniel's lip was starting to swell.

"We should tell somebody," Ethan said at last.

"Eh?" Daniel's head came up. He blinked and lost his rhythm.

"What he does—I mean, Mr. Lyman—he can't hit us like that. It isn't right."

Daniel blinked again, his eyes tightening at the corners. Then his lips curled and he began to laugh and shake his head.

"What?" Ethan said.

Daniel shoved the bar down with a dull thud. "We done what he said, lad. Your da would'a punished you, wouldn't he?"

A tangle of worms squirmed blindly, as if in dread of Ethan's shovel. "Pa would never'a done that. It's not the same at all."

Daniel thumped the bar again. The earth turned paler as he broke through the topsoil to the sand below. "And who would you be telling, then? The selectmen, maybe? I'm sure they'd be believing the likes of us, with himself the chairman of them all. Or maybe you'd rather be calling on the justice of the peace, who's only Lyman's brother? Or maybe the overseers of the poor? I'm sure they'd not be half distressed over Lyman thrashing his lads for lying and disobedience."

"I—uh—" Ethan's shovel scraped up the side of the hole at an angle so steep that nearly all the dirt fell back down. "I could tell Pa. If I told Pa, he'd—"

"He'd what? Take you home? And who'd be paying his debts then, eh? What'll he do if Lyman calls in his note?"

Ethan felt a cold lump in his stomach. He stared down into the hole at the golden sand that the digging iron had stirred up. He remembered being four, maybe, or five, and watching Pa dig. He'd seen the yellow sand under the black loam and clapped his hands, thinking it was gold. Pa had laughed so hard that he'd had to sit down. Ethan knew better now. It was just sand, so worthless not even the worms would live in it. If he dug forever and ever, all he'd ever find was sand.

He flopped down on his belly and picked up a tin scoop to scrape the dirt from the bottom of the hole. He bit his lip, thinking about what Daniel said, how it changed everything. All these weeks he'd been holding on to the thought that soon he would go home. Next Sunday maybe, or the one after that, Pa and Ma would be there at the meetinghouse, and he'd tell them all about the Lymans and Daniel and himself. Then Pa would make it right so Ethan could come back home. Maybe Daniel could even come with him. Three Sundays had come and gone without Ethan's plans coming to light. But one week or even two hadn't seemed so long to wait for Pa to make everything all right. Now it didn't matter anymore—one week or two or twenty—or even if he saw Pa tomorrow.

Ethan's knuckles scraped hard against the side of the hole. He dug blindly, like the worms, until he felt Daniel's hand on his shoulder.

"Here—that'll do, lad. Help me set the post." Daniel pulled Ethan to his feet. He nodded toward the mound of earth they'd raised up. "Nice lot of worms, that," Daniel said. "Tell you what—when you come back from meeting tomorrow afternoon, I'll show you how to fish."

"Nah, nah. Not like that. He'll just come off." Daniel took the hook and worm out of Ethan's hands. "You got to thread it right through him." He put one end of the worm to the sharp end of the hook and deftly slid the worm on, so that when he was done, hook and worm seemed all of a piece. He cast the line out into the river. He handed Ethan a second hook and line. "Here. Now you do it."

Ethan's worm slid out of his grasp and tumbled into the grass, where it squirmed blindly, seeking a hiding place.

"Do it again. And don't stick yourself."

Ethan picked up the struggling worm. He held worm and hook up close to his face, like Ma eyeing a needle for threading. This time the hook stuck, although the worm ended up gathered sloppily along it like a stocking that had fallen down around somebody's ankle. He held it out for Daniel's inspection.

Daniel squinted one eye at the mess on the end of the line. "It'll do. Now toss it in."

Ethan cast the bait out as hard as he could. It landed with a satisfying plunk a few yards from Daniel's, the cork floaters bobbing in tandem on the surface.

"Now what?"

Daniel eased himself back in the grass and pulled his cap down over his eyes. "We wait."

"Oh." Ethan drew his knees up to his chest and wrapped his arms around them. He watched the lines for a few minutes. Nothing happened.

"Daniel—"

"Mmm-hmm?"

"Why don't you go to meeting with the Lymans?"

Daniel shoved his cap back with his thumb and squinted at Ethan with one pale gray-green eye. "You know it's not me own church."

"But—but aren't you afraid?"

"Afraid of what?"

"Hell. Mr. Merriwether says—"

"How do you know he's right? Maybe it's you lot as are all going to hell." Daniel tugged his hat back down over his eyes.

Ethan's stomach felt cold and heavy. That couldn't be. They couldn't all be wrong, Ma and Pa and Mr. Merriwether, and—and everybody.

The corner of Daniel's mouth twitched. "Don't worry, lad. I'll be right down there with you. I ain't heard a Mass nor seen a priest for five years or longer."

The line at the end of Daniel's pole jerked tight. He sat upright and shoved his cap back. He teased the line, tugging it and letting it go slack, testing what was on the end. Whatever it was pulled back. He jumped to his feet and struggled with the line for a few minutes, then drew in a shimmering silver-sided fish about ten inches long. He gave Ethan one of his rare grins. "Ain't very big, but it's something."

More serious questions dulled Ethan's pleasure in the catch. "Aren't you afraid?" he asked again.

Daniel eased the fish free of the hook, then pulled a ball of twine from his pocket. "Cut me a piece," he told Ethan. "'Fraid of what?"

Ethan measured out an arm's length of twine and cut it off with his pocketknife. "Hell."

"I got enough to be afraid of in this life without fretting over the next, don't I, now?" Daniel ran the twine through the gasping fish's gills. He tied a loop to secure the fish, then fastened the free end of the line to a bush that straggled over the river's edge.

That couldn't be right, Ethan thought. He'd never seen Daniel afraid of anything. Not the mare, not the Lymans' prize bull, nor the sow when she was nursing. Not even Mr. Lyman. Yesterday, during their punishment, Ethan was certain it wasn't fear he'd seen in Daniel's bowed head and lowered eyes, but only resignation.

Daniel set the tethered fish in the water and handed Ethan the hook to bait.

Ethan chewed his lower lip as he pondered the fate of Daniel's soul. Maybe he really was a heathen, after all. "Don't you believe it? Heaven and hell and all that?"

"Dunno. But if I could make me own heaven, I'd put no Lymans in it."

"What would be in it?"

Daniel leaned back in the grass. "Lots of Sunday afternoons to fish. And horses. Lots of horses."

Ethan laughed. The worm slid onto the hook more easily

this time, with only a few puckers in the middle. "And hell? Do you think there's a hell? Do you think there's fire and sulfur and people burning forever, like Mr. Merriwether says?"

Daniel sat up slowly and stared out across the river. He hugged his knees to his chest as if he'd suddenly grown cold. When he finally spoke, Ethan could barely hear him.

"Oh, aye. There's fire all right," Daniel said. "Fire and mothers and babies crying and naught you can do about it."

Chapter Fourteen

"Satisfaction."

"Satisfaction?" Ethan repeated. Mr. Bingham nodded. "Satisfaction," Ethan said yet again. "Well, it's when you're happy about something. Like when you've had enough to eat, or are finished working and feel pleased about it?" He ended the statement on an upward slant, like a question. It was too simple. Surely it couldn't be the right definition.

"Yes . . . yes. Very good . . . good. Now, how would that apply . . . apply to a mortgage?" Mr. Bingham's milky green stare fixed Ethan.

"Um . . . um . . . I don't see . . ." Sometimes Ethan felt as though his brain would burst from all the new things Mr. Bingham was teaching him. The figuring was bad enough without having to learn a new language, too: words that Ethan had never heard of before or, worse, words that meant something entirely different in business than they meant in the rest of Ethan's life. And why did Mr. Bingham have to make him figure so many things out for himself instead of just telling him? He pressed his lips together and thought hard. What could be satisfying about a mortgage? All it meant was that you didn't really own what you thought you owned and that you owed somebody piles of money and you'd never pay it off and . . . "Oh, I know!" he exclaimed, the answer flaring in his brain like a newly lit fire. "If you paid off your mortgage, then you'd be satisfied, wouldn't you? Because then you'd really and truly own your house. And the person you owed the money to, he'd be satisfied, too, wouldn't he? Because he'd have all his money back."

Mr. Bingham clapped Ethan so hard on his back that he nearly knocked the boy from his perch on the flour barrel. "There! That's thinking . . . thinking for you!" he said. "That's exactly it. Now . . ." He reached under the counter for the dog-eared book of legal forms.

Ethan groaned. "You mean there's a piece of paper to go with that, too?"

"There's always a piece . . . piece of paper," Mr. Bingham said. "To keep everybody honest, hmmm?" One eye closed slowly. Then he stooped over the book, his nose almost touching the pages as he looked for the proper form to show Ethan.

A long shadow crossed the threshold and fell across the page. "I hope you're keeping him busy, Mr. Bingham," said a deep voice.

"Pa!" Ethan whirled to stare at the gaunt figure in the doorway. He took two leaping steps toward the blue-coated man, then froze, halted by the sudden thought of what Mr. Lyman might tell Pa about him.

Pa's long, thin jaw softened with his laugh. "What is it, son? Now that you're a working man, you're too old to hug your pa?"

"I—no, Pa." Pa's smile warmed Ethan's insides. But the momentum of his rush had been broken. The feel of Pa's arms around him was different somehow. Even though they touched, it seemed that there was a space between them. Pa didn't seem to notice. He squeezed Ethan's arms, pretending to check how his muscles had grown.

The door to the back room clicked open. "Gideon." Mr. Lyman came forward, both hands out to grip Pa's in a firm handshake. "So good to see you. Your family's well, I hope?"

Pa nodded with something that looked like relief. "Yes,

thank you. Hannah had a bit of a fever this week past, but she's much better now."

Better? Ethan felt a chill. He wanted to ask, but Pa and Mr. Lyman had the look of men with more important things on their minds than a boy's questions.

"Nothing serious, I hope?" The storekeeper laid a sympathetic hand on Pa's shoulder.

Pa shook his head. "I'd like to take Ethan home for a little. Only tonight and tomorrow. He'll be back Sunday afternoon. It'd do Hannah a world of good to see him again."

Mr. Lyman raised one thick eyebrow at Ethan. "Hmmmm . . . We'll see. We'll see," he said. "Gideon?" He extended a hand to invite Pa into the back room.

Ethan wished he could make out the words in the low murmur of voices on the other side of the door. If Mr. Bingham hadn't been there, he'd have pressed his ear against the wood to listen. But the clerk set him to sweeping up the shop and fetching kindling for the little box stove. When Pa emerged, his long face looked more solemn than usual. Ethan held his breath as Pa and Mr. Lyman shook hands.

"Well, boy, it seems you're to have a holiday," Mr. Lyman said.

But Pa wasn't wearing his holiday face.

Ethan and his father had gotten well beyond the common before Ethan mustered up the courage to ask, "Is Ma really all right?"

"She's fine now. Still a bit weakish, but she'll mend." Pa smiled crookedly. "To tell you the truth, son, I've had my hands full tending to us all. I tend to forget how much work your mama does 'til she's laid up."

"You should'a sent for me. If I'd'a known, I'd'a come home. I could'a helped. . . . I could'a done your chores and—"

Pa gave Ethan a gentle shake. "What good would you have

done if you'd come home and taken sick, too? Then I'd have had one more to take care of, and you losing days or weeks of credit for working at Mr. Lyman's."

"You should'a sent word to Mr. Lyman that you needed me," Ethan insisted. "I could'a helped."

"Don't fret about it, son. It's over and done with." Pa took Ethan's hat and rumpled his hair. "Besides, I need you more over there, don't you see?"

Ethan nodded even though he didn't understand.

Pa twirled Ethan's hat between his hands, first spinning it on his finger like a top, then flipping it brim over crown over brim. "Working at Mr. Lyman's must be doing you good. Look how tall you've gotten. I bet you can even knock my hat off now."

Ethan stared at his father. They hadn't played the hat game in ages. Ethan would try to capture Pa's hat while Pa would try to fend him off. When Ethan was very little, Pa would end the game by swooping Ethan into the air and letting him take the hat. Ethan had long been too big to be swooped up. The last time they'd played, the game had ended in a wrestling match that dissolved into laughter. It seemed silly and childish now. Maybe he was too old for it.

Pa's brown eyes creased deeply at the corners, teasing him, telling him Pa wasn't too old for the game. His hat did look much closer than it ever had before, even though Ethan couldn't have grown all that much in barely a month. The sun winked on the watery blue sheen of the jay's feather in Pa's hatband, daring Ethan to try. Ethan gathered himself, jumped, grabbed. Pa dodged, but not quickly enough. In one bound, Ethan captured the hat. Pa's eyes widened and his mouth made a surprised *O*. Ethan's face mirrored his father's. Both of them stared at the faded black top hat in Ethan's hands, as if it had jumped there all on its own.

Pa laughed. "Guess I misjudged how much you've grown." He gave Ethan's ragged straw hat a comical frown and slapped it onto his own head. Holding his head stiff, as if afraid the hat might fall off, Pa winked at Ethan.

Ethan nestled Pa's hat on his own head. As hard and hollow as a bandbox, the stiff black felt sat heavy on his temples and brow, casting a band of shadow across his vision. It was warm from Pa's head and smelled of tobacco and sweat and hay and barn. Ethan tipped his head back, so he could see from under the hat's brim. His eyes met Pa's and they laughed together.

After nearly a month of living in the Lymans' big white house, Ethan couldn't help noticing how stark and shabby his home looked, its dirt front yard barely a yard at all, but only an extension of the road. He'd never thought twice about the bones and broken crockery that lay outside the kitchen door, the chickens pecking in the slop bucket. But now all he could see were the cracked, weathered clapboards, the moss furring the roof with green, the refuse scattered in the yard. He thought of Mrs. Lyman and her flowers and her broom applied daily to her stone walks, of Silas and Daniel raking the yards clear of chicken droppings and rubble.

Scratch lay in a sunny corner of the yard, his tail sweeping a happy arc in the dust. Whining a greeting, he rose stiffly and limped over to lick Ethan's fingers.

Chloe darted into the yard, a faded rag baby clutched to her chest. She danced around Ethan and Pa as they made their way into the kitchen, where Maria was preparing bread and milk to go with their tea.

"Efan's home!" she started to sing out, but Pa scooped her up and silenced her with a kiss.

"It's a surprise," he said softly. "A surprise for Mama."

"What's a surprise?" a voice called out.

Ethan ducked under a strand of drying nappies and ran through the kitchen into the best room.

Ma was lacing up her dress with one hand and settling Benjamin with the other. Her brown eyes seemed to have faded to the shade of weathered wood, shadowed with ashy circles underneath. Frizzes of chestnut hair straggled from beneath her cap. Surely there hadn't been gray in Ma's hair when Ethan had left.

"Mama?" Ethan said tentatively. He hadn't called her "Mama" in years—ever since Massey Dunn had told him that only babies and girls said "Mama" and "Papa." Big boys said "Ma" and "Pa." But now it was "Mama" again, and he envied the baby, who only had to squeak to draw her around him like a cloak against hunger, pain, and fear.

Ma smiled, reaching out with her free hand. "Oh, Ethan, don't you look fine!" She held him at arm's length, looking him up and down so long, he felt his face grow red.

Maybe it was wearing Pa's hat that made him look so, Ethan thought. Ma looked fine, too, now that she was smiling, though when she hugged him, her arms felt thin and trembly. Pa's hat tumbled off, landing on the floor with a hollow clunk.

Then her gaze shifted toward the doorway. "Well, Gideon!" she said softly, her eyes blurry with tears.

Pa leaned against the doorjamb with Chloe in his arms, a grin spreading across his face. "Now, Hannah, didn't I promise I'd bring you something special from the store?"

"I had a talk with Mr. Lyman, and I didn't like everything I heard," Pa said. He leaned against the fence, knotting a twist of hay between his long fingers while he watched Ethan milk Tess. "He said he's been forced to—to discipline you."

Ethan's hands pumped at Tess's teats. The milk made a

brittle splash in the bottom of the pail. He pressed his forehead harder against Tess's flank. Funny how her hide suddenly felt so much cooler than his own skin. "I'm sorry about the plate and everything, Pa. I'll work extra hard to pay for it, and—"

Pa's long, thin fingers sat heavily on Ethan's shoulder. "It's not only a plate, son. Lying, stealing, disobedience. We taught you better than that."

Fingers, udder, and pail melded into a blur of pinks and browns. Only the hollow sound of liquid against wood told Ethan that the milk still squirted into the bucket. "I'm sorry. I won't do it again."

Pa crouched next to Ethan. "Son, you have to realize how important it is that you do well at Mr. Lyman's."

Ethan couldn't meet Pa's eyes. "I don't like it there. Can't I just stay home?"

"You know we have a contract. There are penalties if I break it."

Penalties. That was what Daniel had said, too.

"Mr. Lyman's giving you a better home than we can, better food than you've had in your life. He's teaching you things I can't, things you need to learn. . . ." The weariness in Pa's voice stung Ethan harder than anger would have.

Ethan bit the inside of his mouth, tasted blood on his tongue. It hadn't been a lie, then, what Mr. Lyman had said about Pa sending him away to be disciplined.

"Your mama and your sisters and the baby," Pa continued, "they're all depending on you, just like they depend on me. You can't come running home just because things don't suit you. Remember what I said the day you left?"

I need you to go. The weight of that need sat harder on Ethan's shoulders than Mr. Lyman's switch. He nodded, chewing at his lower lip to stop it from trembling.

But Pa was remembering a different thing. "Remember

what I said about setting your mind to be happy? It seems to me you've set your mind to be unhappy, and so you are. Like that Paddy."

Ethan winced. "His name is Daniel. He's my friend."

"Mr. Lyman says he's full of mischief and he sets you a poor example."

Ethan looked up. Pa's face had never seemed so long and stern before. The space between them suddenly looked like miles instead of only a few feet. "He's not so bad as everybody thinks, Pa. He's only lonesome."

"Ethan, son. You've got a good heart. If you had your way, you'd take in every stray dog and orphaned bird you come across. But the world's a hard place, with plenty of folk ready to take advantage of good-hearted people."

Tess's udder sagged loose in Ethan's hands, the milk coming in trickles now. Pa's long fingers ruffled Ethan's hair. He fought the longing to close his eyes and lean into the familiar caress. "No. He's not like that," Ethan insisted.

"He's a good six or seven years older than you. Why doesn't he have any friends his own age?"

"They all laugh at him on account of he's Irish and he talks different and he has red hair." Surely Pa would understand that. If Pa remembered what it felt like to be taunted, he'd feel kindlier toward Daniel.

"If the boy has no friends his own age, there's more reason to it than something as foolish as red hair. Maybe it's because he's a troublemaker."

"He's not, Pa! He's not!" The vehemence of his own denial surprised Ethan. He'd never dared to contradict his father before. But Pa had never been wrong before, had he? Pa wasn't supposed to be wrong. "Daniel works hard. Really he does. And he's good with the animals, and he teaches me things, and—"

Pa's voice hardened. "That's enough. Paddy's been given

more than anyone in his position has a right to expect, but all he does is scowl and sulk and make trouble where there is none."

Ethan opened his mouth to deny Pa's accusations. But he couldn't tell Pa how Daniel came to his defense against Mr. Lyman's switchings, Mrs. Lyman's pinches and slaps, without telling all the ways he'd gone wrong, all the ways he'd been a disappointment and a failure. Worst of all, he couldn't bear to have Pa confirm that Mr. Lyman was right—that Pa had sent Ethan away because he was too soft to give Ethan the discipline he needed.

Ethan turned his face against Tess's side as he stripped the final drops of milk into the pail.

"I know you've no choice about working with him or living with him," Pa said. "But when your time's your own, I don't think it's a good idea for you to spend it with this Paddy fellow, do you understand?"

Ethan picked up the pail and swiveled off the stool, away from his father.

Pa took the pail. It bumped Ethan's thigh and Pa's knee as it hung between them. "Mr. Ward has a couple boys your age. I think you'd be better off spending your time with them, don't you?"

"The Wards?" Their chant of "Sim-ple, sim-ple! Ethan's pa is sim-ple" echoed in his head. But telling Pa about it would be like saying it himself. It would be like making it true. "I—I dunno," Ethan muttered. A month ago, there was nothing he couldn't tell his father. Now, suddenly, he couldn't tell him anything. Anything but "Yessir."

The pail shifted to Pa's other hand. He picked up Ethan's hat, perched atop a fence post. "That's the way." He settled the hat onto Ethan's head. It slipped sideways over one eye. "Your mother and I have enough worries without wondering what sort of company you're keeping while you're away from home."

"Y-yessir."

Pa's hat brim cast a band of shadow across his face. "And I don't want to hear any more about Mr. Lyman having to discipline you, understand?" The band of shadow divided Pa's features like a mask, the light touching only his angular jaw, lined hard and deep around nose and mouth.

"Discipline?" Ethan repeated, adjusting his hat. "N-no, sir."

Ethan's bare feet padded a silent and solitary path across the darkened kitchen toward the cellar. He eased the door open and peered down the stairs. The tiny circle of light from the candle seemed a feeble defense against the yawning blackness below. The cellar's silent darkness seemed alive, waiting to swallow him up, just as it had swallowed Daniel.

Ethan quelled his fear and padded down the stairs, concentrating on the small charmed circle within the candle's light. He held the candle high, sending the dark retreating behind barrels and crocks and boxes and bins. The smells of vinegar, rotting cabbage and apples, and damp earth stung his nostrils.

Daniel sat on one of the boxes of sand that held last fall's root vegetables. His knees were drawn up to his chest, his arms wrapped around his legs. His head was bowed against his knees, and he rocked back and forth, murmuring in his secret language.

"D-Daniel?" Ethan said softly, then again, louder, when Daniel didn't reply. "Daniel!"

Daniel's head jerked up. He blinked twice, hard, at the light and took in a gulping breath. He turned away, rubbing his face with the heels of his hands. "Ah, lad, I must'a been dreaming," he said. His voice sounded as though it stuck in his throat. The dark shadows and red rims around his eyes looked like something different from rubbed-out sleep.

"Are you all right?" Ethan asked.

Daniel coughed. "Aye . . . Aye," he said hoarsely. "A bit damp and dusty is all." His cough turned into a rough laugh with a hiccup at the end. "Least I'm too big for him to shut up in the potato bin." His eyes fixed on the light the way a dog's eyes might fix on a scrap of food. "You still fancy knowing what it's like on a ship, lad, just pinch out your candle."

Ethan suppressed a shiver. He wove his way between a pair of barrels and hoisted himself onto the box next to Daniel. He set the candle between them. "Why are you being punished?"

Daniel shifted to sit cross-legged, facing Ethan. "Can't you guess, now?" His fingers plucked at the puddle of tallow at the candle's base.

"We had to sit in the parlor 'til bedtime, listening to Mrs. Lyman read from Scripture," Ethan said. "It was all about stealing."

"Aye. Zeloda saw me going down to the root cellar after some carrots. Himself was standing at the top of the stairs when I come back up."

"Did you tell him they were for Ivy?"

Daniel's shoulders rustled his shirt. The shirt was untucked and ballooned around him like a skin that he'd never grow into. "Don't you think he knew that? He said—" His eyes drifted toward the candle. "He said if I was that mad for carrots, I could stay down here and have me fill of 'em."

"Oh. Did he thrash you very bad?"

A shudder worked its way down Daniel's back. "It wasn't the thrashing I was minding so much as missing me ride." There was something else, Ethan guessed, that Daniel had minded more than either, but he couldn't figure out what it was.

Ethan dug into his pocket for something wrapped in his handkerchief. "Ma gave me some cake to take back with me. You can have it if you like. I had plenty to eat at tea." He unwrapped it and laid it on the box. "Oh," he sighed. The cake had dissolved into a pile of crumbs. "It's broken."

Daniel moistened his fingertips, pinched some crumbs together into a lump, and stuck it in his mouth. "It's fine, lad." He licked his fingers noisily and took another lump of crumbs. "How was your visit?"

Ethan stuck his thumb in the warm tallow. "It was all right, I s'pose." It wasn't entirely a lie, nor entirely the truth. Some of it had been fine: working like a man alongside Pa to put in the potatoes, start Ma's kitchen garden, fix fences, mend the shed roof. Doing three days' work in a day and a half. Feeling a happy sort of exhaustion that his work made up somehow for not being there while Ma had been sick, for not knowing they'd needed him. Curling up on his old bed in the attic with the marmalade cat warm and purring at his back. Teasing Maria and Chloe and not even getting scolded for it. Catching Ma watching him across the table, wearing a smile that looked as if she'd been saving it up ever since he'd left.

But then he'd noticed the lines around Ma's eyes, how she seemed to get tired so quickly. He'd noticed, too, that there'd been no singing in the evenings, less noise in the house alto-gether. Even the secret glances that Ma and Pa exchanged—the ones that used to warm Ethan inside like a swallow of good sweet tea—even those had changed. Something new about the tilt of an eyebrow or the curve of a lip that Ethan had caught passing between them had made his insides go still and dull.

Daniel's hand stopped halfway to the cake. "As good as all that, eh? Something wrong to home?"

"No. Not really. I mean, Ma was sick, but she's all better now. Mostly." Ethan watched the wick curl, blacken, crumble inside the flame, the tallow oozing down in thick, slow drops.

Something that was not candlelight flickered across Daniel's face and was gone. "Is she, now? Are you sure?"

"I—well, that's what Pa says." Ethan pinched a bit of soft tallow from the top of the candle. It seared his fingertips.

"And what else did your da say that has you looking as if you just felt the end of herself's spoon on your knuckles?"

"Pa says—he says I'm not to keep company with you anymore." Ethan peeked at Daniel's face.

Daniel seemed to be concentrating on a pair of shriveled cabbage heads hanging from the ceiling in knobby brown fists. "Oh, aye? And how're you s'posed to be getting your chores done, then?"

"I mean, after chores—in the evenings and on the Sabbath. He says you make trouble for me."

Daniel folded the ends of Ethan's handkerchief over the remains of the cake. "Your da's right. You oughtn't to be spending time with liars and thieves." He set the little bundle in Ethan's lap.

"But—but you're not!"

Daniel hopped off the box and paced the cellar, tethered within the circle of yellow light. "Ain't you heard me with your own ears and seen me with your own eyes? Ain't that what I been locked up for all afternoon and evening?" The flame bent and twisted with the breeze from Daniel's passage, turning his shadow into a dark, dancing ghoul against walls and ceiling, around barrels and boxes and bottles.

"But that's different! That don't count!"

Daniel stopped in front of Ethan. The flame straightened and stilled. "You ain't but nine, lad. Who're you to be saying what counts and what don't? You'd best listen to your da."

"But if I do, then you won't have anybody." Worse, though, Ethan thought, was imagining life at the Lymans' without Daniel's company to ease the time between work and sleep.

Daniel's body moved carelessly inside his shirt. His face

twisted before he turned away. "I got Ivy. She's been enough for me this long."

"He wants me to make friends with the Wards."

"Oh . . . well, he don't know them, now, does he?"

"He don't know you, either."

Daniel slowly turned back, shaking his head. "Neither do you, lad."

Ethan frowned at the cake in his lap. He fumbled in his pocket. "I brought you something else."

Daniel's little horse stood in Ethan's palm. The flame made its sides seem to heave in and out, its nostrils quiver with breath, its mane bob along its proudly arched neck.

Daniel stood frozen for a moment, a muscle trembling below one eye. He pressed his lips together and drew in a slow, steady breath. In one long stride, he was in front of Ethan, his hand closing gently around the horse. "Ta, lad," he murmured.

"Ta?" Ethan asked.

"It means thanks."

"Is that Irish?"

Daniel shook his head. "But it's how—it's how me da would'a said it."

Chapter Fifteen

"She'll go bald if you keep brushing her like that," Ethan said. Ankle-deep tufts of copper hair carpeted Ivy's stall. But the hair kept coming, and there was still no sign of her bare skin.

"You can help if you like," Daniel suggested. He'd already brushed out most of Ivy's loose winter hair and burnished the mare's coat so that even in the shadowy stall she glowed softly. Now he gently brushed out the tangles in her mane. The mare arched her neck and crooned at his shoulder.

"Why should I spend my Sunday working?" Ethan's lower lip jutted out.

Rain thudded on the barn roof. The relentless downpour had made the Lymans decide to stay home instead of going to the meetinghouse for afternoon services.

"You can do her tail," Daniel said.

Ethan gave the thick chestnut hair a halfhearted swipe with his brush.

Daniel rubbed his thumb up and down the inside of Ivy's ear. The mare closed her eyes and leaned toward him, her upper lip quivering. A delighted grunt rumbled deep within her throat. He responded with a secret word that sounded like the happy whicker Ivy made when she greeted him.

"That means horse, doesn't it?" Ethan asked. He tried to repeat the word, but it sounded more like he was clearing his throat. "It means horse, or mare, or something like that. It must, because it's what you always call her."

Ethan thought he saw a splash of pink color Daniel's cheek. "Umm—no—that ain't it. You say it like this: '*a mhuirnín.*' And it don't mean horse."

Ethan tried again, but he still couldn't get his mouth to shape the word. "Well, what does it mean?"

Daniel retreated to the mare's forelock and mumbled something.

"What?"

Daniel took an audible breath. "Sweetheart, or darling, or some such."

Ethan lowered his head and grinned at the mare's tail, giving it three hard sweeps with his brush. "Can you teach me? Teach me to talk Irish, I mean?"

Daniel's "no" was brisk and definite. "I don't fancy having a great spoonful of cayenne jammed down me throat. Nor do you, I'll wager."

Ethan swallowed, his imagination already stinging his mouth and nose. "B-but you talk it—"

Daniel stepped out from the mare's shadow and waved his brush at Ethan. "Only out here, see? Never in the house, and never when himself is around. Nor herself neither."

"Mr. Lyman did that? With the cayenne, I mean?"

Daniel nodded. "That was me first day here. The day she come. And she and me—" He rubbed the mare's forehead. "We both slept our first night in the barn." He twisted her forelock into a rough rope, then untwisted it and smoothed it out again. "It's a pity," he said softly.

"What's a pity?"

"A pity I can't be taking her when I leave."

"Why not?"

Daniel rolled his eyes. "I ain't daft as all that, lad. I'd go to prison for sure now, wouldn't I?" His hands cupped the mare's chin, his forehead pressed against hers. "To be shut up forever, away from the light . . . It'd be worse than death." A tiny shudder quivered along Daniel's shoulders. Ivy nuzzled his fingers. He stroked the mare's cheek. "Sorry, lass. I couldn't do that for nobody. Not even you."

"You could buy her."

Daniel let out a horselike snort. "Oh, aye."

"You told me you'll get your wages when you're twenty-one. Why couldn't you buy her? Even if it's not enough all at once, maybe you could pay for her a little at a time. Maybe . . ."

"Oh, and Lyman'll sure want to be selling her to me." Daniel gave Ethan a skeptical grimace. "He'd not let me have her just for spite."

"You won't know unless you ask."

Daniel harumphed and returned to his brushing. "Some things you can know without asking."

Ethan perched on the edge of the upper haymow and spread his arms. If he closed his eyes, the drop to the lower mow seemed to last longer, and in that final second before he landed in a cloud of hay dust, it would feel like flying. He pretended that the rain thudding on the roof was the flapping of a thousand eagles' wings all around him, and he was the biggest one, the king of the eagles. He stayed an eagle until the dust from his landing made him sneeze. He wiped his nose on his sleeve and picked himself up to fly again.

"Hey! What the bloody hell you playing at?"

"Just—just playing, that's all." Ethan flopped down on the hay as Daniel came up the ladder.

"Playing at breaking your bloody neck is what you're at." Daniel's head appeared at the edge of the lower mow.

"I'm bored." After grooming Ivy had lost its appeal, Ethan had remembered how he and his friends Massey and Ira used to play at flying on rainy afternoons.

"Well, play at something else."

"What?" Ethan rolled over onto his stomach and thumped at the hay, stirring up swirls of dust.

Daniel hauled himself the rest of the way into the mow and flopped down next to Ethan. He pulled out the fat little book Mr. Stocking had given him. The corners were already frayed and the pages dog-eared. "We could read some of this Shakespeare that peddler gave me. There's one I thought might be about Ireland, 'cause there's a lot of Macs in it."

Ethan yawned. "Is it?" One toe squirmed in the hay, working a round hole through the dried grass.

"Nah. They're all Scottish. But there's witches and kings and murders and ghosts and such. In between all the speeches." Daniel shook his head. "I can't see why they take so long to say a thing. Nobody can say 'good day' without making a bloody speech out of it."

"Sounds boring."

"I thought so, too, first time I tried it. But then I saw it's like doing a puzzle, trying to figure out what they're saying. And some of it's lovely when you read it out loud." Daniel held the book a couple of inches away from his nose, like Mr. Bingham bending over Mr. Lyman's account books.

"I don't want to read. I want to *do* something." The need for movement twitched through Ethan's legs and arms, like an unsatisfied itch deep inside him. He stuck his head down into the hay and tumbled end over end. "Don't you want to play anything? You must know some games."

"And who'd be teaching me to be playing games, now?"

"Didn't you see anybody playing games when you went to school?"

Daniel slapped his book shut. "Oh, aye. I learned lots of games there from Joshua Ward and his lot. Like 'See Paddy Run,' and 'Knock Paddy on His Arse.'"

"Oh." Ethan watched a bug crawl through the hay.

"Lizzie was s'posed to come up this afternoon and help Ruth with making some rag babies," Daniel said.

Ethan snorted in disgust.

"I ain't saying you should be making dolls, lad. But Lizzie's a good one for storytelling, and maybe she knows some games, too. If herself don't forbid stories and games on the Sabbath."

Ethan rolled away from Daniel. "I don't want—" he started to say, then sat up. "Wait here."

Daniel's mouth curled. He made a noise that sounded like a cough. "And where else would I be going?"

Ethan scrambled to the edge of the mow and flipped himself down onto the barn floor. He landed with a satisfying thump that shook him from his heels to his shoulders. He peeked out the barn door at the gray screen of water slanting down relentlessly between the barn and the house. He took a deep breath and ran, stomping hard in all the puddles.

Ethan returned to the barn with his arms full, a rag wrapped around the odds and ends Lizzie had given him: bits of paper and scraps of wood, pencil stubs, string, pieces of cork, and feathers. Daniel sat on a barrel next to Ivy's stall, his sharp nose buried in his book. He raised an eyebrow as Ethan entered, then returned to his reading.

"Are there any horses yet?" Ethan asked.

Daniel kept his face in his book. "None to speak of. But there's a ghost sat down to dinner."

"Least he gets a chair." Ethan set his bundle down and picked up a ragged broom.

Daniel grunted something that might have been half of a laugh. "What you got in there?" he asked over the edge of his book.

Ethan shrugged. "Things." He swept the barn's center aisle.

Although Daniel seemed to be reading again, Ethan felt the older boy's eyes follow him around the barn. When Ethan peeked at him, Daniel returned to his book, a finger tracing the words, his lips pursed as he tried to decipher them.

Ethan sat next to his bundle and opened it so that he could take something out without Daniel seeing what else was inside.

"You don't want to be hearing 'bout this ghost, then?" Daniel asked. "He's all over blood and such."

"I'm busy." Ethan pulled his knife out and began carving the thing in his hand.

"If you were wanting a bit of lunch, I'd think you could'a asked Lizzie for something nicer than an old beet, couldn't you?" Daniel finally said.

Ethan bit his lower lip to keep a smile from dribbling out. He finished cutting the top off the beet, sliced off the taproot, and shaved the cut places round. "I'm not going to eat it." He set the beet aside and returned to his bundle. He pulled out nine pieces of kindling, carried them to the far end of the barn, and set them on end, like soldiers standing at attention in a neat triangle. He dusted his hands on the seat of his trousers and retrieved the beet.

Both of Daniel's eyebrows rose as Ethan took the book out of his hands and replaced it with the beet. "What're you after, lad?"

Ethan tilted his head toward the pieces of kindling. "Haven't you ever seen ninepins before?"

Daniel rolled the beet between his hands, smearing his palms red with the juice. "I never played. I told you I don't know any games."

"Well, then, I guess I'll have to teach you."

"I can—almost—reach it." Ethan stretched for the shuttlecock trapped in the crotch where the beams met. He dug his stockinged toes into Daniel's shoulders, but it was like trying to stand on a board laid edgewise. "Can't you get me any higher?"

"Not unless you stand on me head. You could'a just climbed up for it, you know." Daniel's hands tightened on Ethan's ankles as the boy wobbled.

"This is better. It's like being in the circus."

"How would you know? You never seen one."

"Mr. Stocking told us all about it." Ethan stretched again, his fingertips brushing the end of a feather. "Al-most—got—it. Can you stand on your toes?"

"You think he really done all he said? Dancing and singing and acting and such?"

"I don't know. I can't see him acting a girl's part." Grabbing one beam for balance, Ethan wriggled the shuttlecock into his hand. "Wearing a gown and talking like this: 'Oh, my dearest darling sweetheart! Kiss me! Kiss me! Kiss me!'" Ethan's voice went high and squeaky when he chirped the silly love-words. He finished with loud, smacking kiss-noises. Daniel's shoulders shook violently, and he made funny wheezing sounds. "Stop it, Daniel! I'll fall!"

The boys went down together in a noisy tangle of arms and legs, Ethan making a lumpy but safe landing on top of Daniel's bony limbs.

"Ow! Get off!" Daniel growled, but Ethan could barely make out the words between the cackling sounds coming out of Daniel's throat.

Ethan untangled himself and rolled away. Somehow he'd managed to hang on to the shuttlecock. "It was your fault. You wouldn't stand still."

"It was your fault for making me laugh," Daniel said.

"My fault? You're the one who—" Ethan stared at Daniel,

who lay slumped on the floor, red-faced and breathless, that odd sound still gurgling in his throat. "I made you laugh?"

Daniel rubbed his sleeve across his eyes and nose. "Is that so strange, now? I'd'a thought—"

He was interrupted by the creaking of the barn door. Both boys flung themselves upright and forced their faces stern and sober.

"What do you think you're doing?" The rain dribbled off the rim of Silas's hat, puddling at his feet. He crossed his arms and frowned at the boys.

Ethan hid the battered shuttlecock behind his back. "Nothing."

"We were only having a bit of fun," Daniel said. The grin began to fade from his mouth, but stopped halfway, leaving an odd twisted smile there.

"Fun." Silas studied Daniel's face hard, as if he'd never seen it before.

"Ethan was showing me some games. Ninepins and shuttlecock and such." Daniel picked up the broken shingle he'd used for a paddle.

"On the Sabbath."

"They say God rested on the Sabbath."

Silas's mouth pursed. "I don't think God spent the seventh day playing shuttlecock."

"Pity. Maybe if He'd'a spent more time playing shuttlecock with Adam and Eve and less time making rules, maybe we'd still be in Paradise."

Silas turned his head, coughing so hard it bent him over. When he turned back, his frown was firmly in place. "Mr. Merriwether would call that blasphemy."

Daniel shrugged. "I'm a Papist. Me whole life is blasphemy to Mr. Merriwether."

"I don't imagine your Pope spends his Sabbath playing games, either."

"You won't tell, will you?" Ethan pleaded. "We didn't break anything."

Silas reached out toward Ethan. Reluctantly, Ethan yielded the shuttlecock. Silas pointed to a shingle-paddle lying on the barn floor. Ethan picked it up and handed it over. "It's time for chores. Go fetch the buckets and bring the cows in. Lizzie'll be along in a little bit." He studied the bit of cork, fledged with ragged and bent feathers. "I suppose she gave you this?"

"Just scraps and things she said nobody'd miss. She won't get in trouble, will she?"

"Go do your work." Silas waved the shingle at the boys.

Daniel shrugged into his frock and pulled his cap down low over his eyes. "C'mon, lad." He tossed Ethan his frock and headed out into the rain.

Ethan retrieved his shoes. He hopped as he pulled the trampled-down backs up over his heels. "Don't be cross, Silas. We didn't mean no harm. I only wanted to make him laugh."

"Laugh?" Silas's eyebrows gathered. "Is that what all that noise was?"

"Haven't you ever heard him laugh before?"

Silas smoothed the shuttlecock's bent feathers. "I can't say I ever have," he said. He seemed to be talking to himself, as though he'd forgotten Ethan was there.

"Are you coming, lad?" Daniel shouted from the yard. "I ain't moving them cows by meself."

"Coming!" Ethan called back, snatching up his stick. As he turned to shut the door, he saw Silas step out to the middle of the barn, bouncing the shuttlecock on the shingle. Silas caught the shuttlecock, threw it high into the air, and slammed it hard with the paddle. It thudded against the far side of the barn and bounced back to his feet, where he crushed it beneath his boot.

Chapter Sixteen

Daniel was restless.

Most nights, the boys dropped off to sleep within minutes of crawling under the sheet. But now and then, Daniel would roll back and forth, pull the blanket over his shoulders, push it away, flatten the bolster, fluff it up again, then finally lie still, trying to fool Ethan into thinking he slept. Ethan could tell from his breathing that he didn't. On those nights, Ethan would drift to sleep, only to wake a few hours later to find a cold spot in the bed where Daniel had been.

Several times, Ethan had vowed to find out where Daniel disappeared to. But no matter how hard he'd tried to keep his eyes open, they would droop shut long before Daniel rose and slipped down the stairs and away to his secret destination.

When Daniel fidgeted with the blankets and thumped the bolster before settling down for the night, Ethan resolved once more to discover the older boy's secret. He forced himself to keep breathing deeply, steadily, as he listened to Daniel pad across the floor and slip into his clothes. Ethan opened one eye and peeked over the crook in his elbow. The western fan window framed Daniel's head and shoulders in silver-blue moon glow. Ethan wondered what made him stare out that window first thing in the morning and last before bed, his fingernails digging into the sill, one hand clutched around his little wooden horse. Daniel made a strange sign with his right hand, then grabbed the tiny horse, stuffed it into his pocket, and headed down the stairs.

Ethan clenched his fists and counted to ten to make sure Daniel was out of earshot before he dressed and followed him.

Daniel was out of sight by the time Ethan pulled the back door closed behind him, but it wasn't hard to guess where he'd gone. Ethan followed the road beneath the western fan window. It curved down the hill between the rye fields and to the lower pastures, orchards, and hay fields. Blue-green by day, the rye glimmered silver in the moonlight, whispering to itself in the breeze. Ethan kept to one side of the road, hidden in the shadow of the apple trees that lined the way. He would have passed Daniel by if he hadn't heard him talking in his strange and secret language.

The moon hung low in the sky, like a big golden peach nibbled at one edge. Daniel waded through the grass a dozen yards from the edge of the road. Ethan carefully followed, keeping close to the ground in case Daniel turned. About fifty feet from the road, Daniel's head bobbed lower and lower, as if he were sinking slowly into the ground.

Ethan shivered. Maybe the stories everybody told about Papists and pagans and their secret midnight rituals were true. He bit his lip. No, that was stupid. Witches and magicians and ghosts and goblins only existed in stories that old people told to scare babies into behaving. He didn't believe any of that— anymore. Still, his heart thudded against the ground as he crept snakelike through the grass.

He drew in a nearly audible breath when he realized that Daniel wasn't being sucked into the earth but had merely gone down a little embankment. He patrolled a rough square in the center of a large flat area at the bottom of the bank as though pacing off a measured distance. He would pause now and then to pick up a rock or a fragment of something Ethan couldn't see. Then he walked on again, made a sharp turn to the left, and paced off the next side of his square.

He repeated the walk several times, then went to the center of the square and sat down. The angled shadows showed a slight depression with raised edges marking the line that Daniel had paced. In its center, where Daniel sat, there was a mound about five feet square. Daniel dug his fingers into the mound, hunting for something. He pulled out an object and threw it. He threw a second and a third, aiming in a different direction each time. The fourth landed a couple feet from Ethan.

Ethan reached out and picked it up. It was a triangular lump, smooth on two sides, rough on the third, and it shed powdery dust on his fingers when he rubbed it. He moved his hand so that the moonlight fell on it. He was disappointed to find only a piece of broken brick. Still, he put it in his pocket.

He felt as though he watched for hours, but Daniel did almost nothing. He talked to himself for a bit, but it was all in Gaelic, so Ethan couldn't tell what he was saying. Perhaps he was trying to conjure up some Papist magic, but his words had the rhythm of ordinary conversation, not the cadence of prayers or charms. And the conjuring, if there was any, produced nothing. Now and then he stood and poked around the mound or paced the square. Although his angular body and ill-fitting clothes made an eerie figure in the silvery moonlight, there didn't seem to be any purpose to his actions. Mostly, though, he just sat.

Ethan's eyes grew heavy with waiting. He closed them for a moment. When he opened them again, the moon was a tiny gold coin high in the sky. He glanced up with a start, afraid that Daniel had gone back to the Lymans' ahead of him and would discover him missing. He was relieved to see Daniel still there, sitting on the mound with his knees hugged to his chest. His cheek was pillowed on his knees, his face turned toward Ethan, his eyes closed as he rocked and hummed tunelessly to himself. The moonlight softened his features, making him look almost as young as Ethan. Ethan felt suddenly uneasy, though he wasn't sure whether it was from seeing Daniel so alone and unguarded or from fear that Daniel would open his eyes and discover him spying. Softly, he crept toward the road and headed back to the Lymans'.

Daniel didn't return until just before daybreak.

Chapter Seventeen

Ethan opened and closed the jackknife half a dozen times. He savored the way the blade eased out of the handle with the tiniest pressure of his thumbnail, then folded back into its groove, soft and neat as a whisper. The knife had caught his eye long before he'd started working for Mr. Lyman. Although there'd been no hope of getting it, he'd visited it every time he came to the store with Ma or Pa. Now, from the other side of the case, he called on it each time he was in the store, managing to find a second or two to reach in and stroke the cool cream-colored bone handle when Mr. Bingham's back was turned.

Today was the first time he'd dared to take it out. While Mr. Bingham waited on Mrs. Smead and Clarissa, Ethan had slipped his hand into the case to caress the knife. When he'd drawn his hand back, the knife was nestled in his palm, a perfect fit. He balanced it, noticing how it was heavy enough to have substance but not so heavy that it would tire his wrist. The sun smiled at him along the blade.

He glanced up. Mr. Bingham's head bent low over the waste book as he lined out Mrs. Smead's purchases. Clarissa fondled the silks and ribbons, chattering about what colors the *Lady's Book* said were in vogue this season in Paris and London.

Ethan crouched behind the counter to test the blade. When he drew it across his forearm, it cut through the fine hairs as easy as skimming cream.

"Ethan?"

His thumb flipped the knife shut, and he shoved it back into the case. It sat crooked in its row. He made a mental note to fix it as soon as he could. "Um—yes, sir?"

"Could you put this silk back while I wrap up Mrs. Smead's things?"

"Yes, Mr. Bingham." Ethan scurried across the store, nearly colliding with Mr. Lyman as he came out from the back room.

The storekeeper scowled. "Look where you're going, boy."

"Yessir. Sorry, sir. I just—um—I didn't see—"

Mr. Lyman clasped his hands behind his back and rocked forward on the balls of his feet. "You'd better learn to pay attention if you want to make anything of yourself, hadn't you?" Although his tone seemed jovial, he pinned Ethan with a sharp glare.

Ethan ducked his head. "Yessir. Sorry, sir."

Mrs. Smead turned toward them with a smile. "Good day, Mr. Lyman. I was afraid we might have missed you."

The storekeeper's face softened. "I would be sorry if you had." He returned Mrs. Smead's smile and gently pressed the hand she offered. "And how is Clarissa today?" His head bobbed toward the slender, dark-haired girl, who gave him a graceful curtsy. He fingered the soft shell-colored silk that Mr. Bingham had cut from the bolt. "An excellent choice, just what they're wearing in Boston. That pink will suit you perfectly. And I think it will suit the young men even more, don't you?" His smile widened as Clarissa blushed and fluttered her eyelashes.

Mrs. Smead laughed. "Oh, Mr. Lyman, you do flatter so."

A little tsk-tsking noise chortled merrily in Mr. Lyman's throat. "It's not flattery when it's the truth, is it, Mrs. Smead? Now, when are you ladies going to take tea with us? Mrs. Lyman would be delighted. And so would Silas." He raised his eyebrows with the last sentence.

"Silas? Oh, I'm sure he doesn't care a whit who comes to tea." Clarissa's curls bobbed as she tipped her head to a flirtatious angle.

Half a dozen bolts of silk lay in a shining spill of color on the counter. Ethan wound the tail of cloth back onto one fat bolt. He kept his eyes on his master, trying to will him back into his office and storeroom. But Mr. Lyman and Mrs. Smead settled in for a long chat about her relatives and his, the weather, the news from Springfield, and the new wares that Mr. Lyman wanted Mrs. Smead and her daughter to notice. Ethan tried to mentally steer them away from the case containing the knives. He held his breath as Mr. Lyman started toward the case, then spun toward the back of the store to show the Smead ladies some new lace that had arrived last week.

Ethan balanced the bolt of cloth on his fingertips, stretching up to replace it on its shelf. Just as he had it angled to slide into its place, the top fold of cloth slithered loose, and the bolt tumbled down. It rolled as it fell, sending a drape of pale pink over his head and shoulders. He grabbed blindly, relieved when the weight of the bolt settled safely in his arms. He clutched the cloth tight against his chest and held his breath, certain that his face was pinker than the silk that hid it.

He heard Mr. Lyman's voice. "What—" Then "Oh, my! Oh, my!" from Mrs. Smead.

The cloth shifted, and Ethan stared up into Mr. Bingham's blue spectacles.

"Dear, dear," the clerk muttered. "Dear, dear. Must be more careful. Yes. More careful. Here." He lifted the bolt out of Ethan's arms and laid it on the counter.

"Oh, my!" Mrs. Smead said again. "The boy is hurt."

"No, I—" Ethan protested. Then he saw the red smudges dotting the soft pink fabric. He followed Mrs. Smead's gaze toward his hands. His left palm was stained with a bloody smear from a cut so fine he hadn't even felt it. A sudden chill began at the top of his head and washed over his body, as if someone had dropped a handful of melting snow on him. He put his hand behind his back.

But Mr. Lyman had already seen.

"I—I'm sorry," Ethan said. "I'll clean it up." With his right hand, he pulled out his handkerchief and rubbed at the silk. A gray smudge appeared among the red ones. He dropped the handkerchief and backed away, both hands behind him now. The chill was replaced by a wave of heat that scalded his face and made his collar and cuffs feel suddenly tight.

"Let me see," Mr. Lyman said, his voice gentle.

Ethan shook his head, backing away until he bumped into the shelves behind him.

Clarissa's eyes narrowed behind her long lashes. "I hope that boy didn't spoil my silk."

"Oh, no. Oh, no," Mr. Bingham assured her. "It's already wrapped. I wrapped it myself . . . wrapped it myself."

"Come here, boy," Mr. Lyman said. "Show me your hand."

Ethan threw a pleading glance toward Mr. Bingham. The clerk nodded. Ethan bit his lip, stepped forward, and held out his hand, palm down. He was surprised that it didn't shake. His trembling was all inside, the tendons and ligaments vibrating like the strings inside Zeloda's pianoforte. At least the counter still separated him from his master.

Mr. Lyman grasped Ethan's wrist, his fingers tightening like a snare. Ethan's pulse hammered against Mr. Lyman's thumb. The storekeeper uncurled Ethan's fingers. A smear of blood ran along his thumb and across his palm. Mr. Lyman pulled out his handkerchief and dabbed at the blood, bending Ethan's thumb backward as he did. Ethan bit his lip and lowered his eyes.

"My, my. What have you done to yourself, boy?" Mr.

Lyman squeezed Ethan's thumb. A thin line of red welled up from the tip down to the fleshy pad of his hand. Even as his heart plummeted, Ethan couldn't help admiring how the knife had been so keen that he hadn't felt the smart of it until the salt from Mr. Lyman's hand pressed into the cut.

"I—it's nothing, sir." He glanced toward Mr. Bingham and Mrs. Smead, who bent over him with serious, sympathetic faces.

"Now, how did you do that?" Mr. Lyman's grip tightened, pulling Ethan forward, pressing him up against the counter. The drawer knobs dug into his belly and the front of his legs. Mr. Lyman's glare scorched him, trying to burn the answer out of him.

"I didn't mean to—" Ethan tore his glance away, searching for something safe to focus on. His eyes flickered over the case where the knife sat askew in the row, a fresh red thumbprint marring its glossy ivory handle.

Mr. Lyman made a satisfied humming noise in his throat.

Mrs. Smead put her hand under Ethan's chin and tipped his head up. She smiled reassuringly down at him. "There, now, Ethan, no need to look as if you're going to be eaten, is there?"

He tried to say "No, ma'am," but his throat thickened around the words. He swallowed and blinked hard.

"Boys must be brave as well as handsome, mustn't they?" Ethan's cheeks burned. "Oh, yes, you are a handsome boy." Mrs. Smead prattled on as though she could distract him with silly compliments. She patted his cheek. "Such long eyelashes, just like your mother. Any girl would love to have them. But isn't that just the way? Remember when your Silas was little, Mr. Lyman? All those lovely golden curls, just like your poor Delia had. Such a waste on a boy, when they'd only be cut off. . . ."

The color seeped from the storekeeper's face. His eyes

drifted away to a place that seemed even darker and more distant than the secret place inside Daniel. His hand knotted around Ethan's and squeezed, as if he were wringing out a damp rag. A tendril of blood crept along Mr. Lyman's wrist and darkened his cuff.

The door slammed, and in walked Mr. Cowles, a heavyset, middle-aged farmer who always spoke a little too loud and carried with him a vague odor of pigs, even when he was cleaned up for the Sabbath. Mrs. Smead and Clarissa stepped back as the farmer headed toward them, his boots clomping heavily against the floorboards. "Are you paying a good price for butter today, George?" Plates and glassware whispered and shivered as Mr. Cowles's voice boomed through the store.

The storekeeper's hand opened, and Ethan's flopped onto the counter like a dead thing, Mr. Lyman's handkerchief stained and crumpled in Ethan's palm.

Mr. Lyman turned toward the new customer, his lips working to recapture his best storekeeper smile. "As good a price as you'll get."

Ethan crept away from the counter, rubbing his hand back to life.

Mr. Lyman froze him with a glare. "Lucius, see to the boy, will you, please? We don't want any more silk ruined today." Although his tone was casual, his stern eyebrows gathered. "And Ethan and I will have a little talk later about carelessness, won't we?" His voice oozed patience and fatherly concern, but his eyes promised something entirely different.

Ethan curled himself into a ball, the sheet pulled over his head. He was almost asleep when he heard the rattle of the bolt in the door at the bottom of the stairs. He huddled motionless under the sheet as Daniel's bare feet padded like cats' paws up the stairs and across the attic floor.

"He wouldn't let me come up," Daniel said softly. "Not 'til all of 'em were ready for bed."

Ethan opened his eyes, gritty and sticky with the afternoon's tears. He winced away from Daniel's hand on his shoulder.

"Come on, lad. Let's have a look," Daniel said.

Ethan squeezed himself tighter, like one of those prickly winter caterpillars that would roll into a ball when he poked it. "It wasn't my fault," he said.

"You don't have to be telling me that." Daniel tugged at the sheet. "So are you going to let me have a look, or are you going to be a lump?"

Ethan uncoiled himself and turned over. He could just make out Daniel's silhouette, lighter gray against the black roof boards. "It's too dark."

"There's a bit of a moon. Come over to the window."

Ethan joined Daniel by the eastern fan window, where the rising moon drew a half-circle of pale blue on the floor. Daniel put his hands on Ethan's shoulders and tried to settle him on a big pumpkin, the last one left in the attic. Ethan shook his head.

"Oh. Switched you, did he?" Daniel tilted Ethan's head into the light. He touched Ethan's cheekbone with his fingertips, letting out a low whistle when Ethan winced and pulled away. "Didn't I tell you to watch yourself?"

"It wasn't my fault. I didn't spoil his stupid silk on purpose."

"No such thing as an accident, far as Lyman sees." Daniel stepped into the shadows and returned with a bag, a handful of rags, and a pitcher. "Off with your shirt, lad." He dampened a rag in the pitcher, then pulled some feathery greens out of the bag and wrapped them in the rag. "Put that on your face."

The leaves smelled peppery, but they cooled Ethan's throbbing face. "What is it?"

"Wormwood. Me ma used it for bruises and such." Daniel

pressed something smooth into Ethan's free hand. "Here. Saved you a rusk from tea."

Ethan stared at the biscuit, shiny like a stone in the moonlight.

Daniel tugged at Ethan's shirt. "C'mon, lad. I can't be fixing you up if I can't see what he done."

The shirt came off, and Ethan stood naked and shivering in the moonlight. He held the pungent rag to his face and gnawed at the rusk.

Daniel said something in Gaelic that sounded rude. "He must'a been in a fine temper to'a done all that. Go lie on your belly and I'll do you up proper."

Ethan settled on the bed, propping his chin on one hand and pressing the rag to the sorest part of his face. He shifted a bite of rusk from one side of his mouth to the other, trying to find a spot where it wouldn't hurt to chew. He heard Daniel open and close the trunk and make sloshing noises with pitcher and basin. Daniel's footsteps drew near, and a delicious coolness covered Ethan's back.

"What's that?"

"Just an old shirt. I put some of the wormwood inside it, so it's like a poultice."

The damp, fragrant cloth soothed the welts that ran from Ethan's shoulders to his backside. The wormwood drew the sting out, leaving behind a cool, fuzzy numbness. "It feels nice," he said around the last bite of rusk. "Ta."

Daniel made a funny startled noise and shifted out of Ethan's sight.

"He says I can't work in the store or go to meeting for two weeks," Ethan said.

"I don't fancy he'd want too many folks seeing how he marked you up."

"Maybe I shouldn'a called him a liar."

Daniel made a strangled noise that seemed to have a curse mixed up in it. "'Twasn't hardly very clever of you, was it, now?" he said. Ethan heard sounds that he recognized as Daniel's getting-ready-for-bed noises.

"He said Pa was stupid. He said Pa sent me away because they don't want me no more."

"Oh." The getting-ready-for-bed sounds stopped. "Your da's not stupid," Daniel said. "And he hadn't no choice about sending you here."

"And Mr. Lyman *is* a liar."

"Aye. But you'll have to say you're sorry for calling him so." Ethan heard the double swish of Daniel shrugging his braces off first one shoulder, then the other. Fabric rustled as Daniel stepped out of his trousers. The contents of his pockets made a muffled thud against the floorboards.

"I won't say I'm sorry. Not ever." Ethan sat up in bed, the damp shirt sticking to his back.

Daniel knelt and grasped Ethan's shoulders. "Aye, you will. Unless you're wanting another thrashing for breakfast tomorrow. And another for dinner and tea, as well."

"But I'm *not* sorry. He *is* a liar."

Daniel's fingers dug into Ethan's arms. "You'll say you're sorry, understand?" His voice was soft but insistent.

"If I do, I'll be a liar just like him."

Daniel sighed and loosened his grip. "Well . . . you can say you're sorry without having it be a lie, now, can't you?"

Ethan gathered the shirt around himself like a shawl. "How?"

"You must be sorry for some of what happened today."

"No, I'm not. Not one bit." But his voice faltered as he thought about another thrashing in the morning, and another and another until he said the right words.

"You're not sorry that cloth got spoilt?"

"Well-l-l-l—"

"You're not sorry you got thrashed? Or maybe you like being strapped."

Ethan shuddered. "Of course I don't."

"You're not sorry you missed your tea?"

"I—I guess I am." The rusk only reminded him how empty his stomach was. He wished Daniel had managed to steal three or four instead of only the one.

"You're not sorry I had the work of milking your cows while you was up here nursing your arse?"

"He locked me up. . . ."

"And you're not sorry he did?"

"I . . . I s'pose. . . ."

Daniel settled back on his heels and crossed his arms. "Well, then. You can say you're sorry for what happened, then, can't you?"

"I . . . I guess so."

"So you can tell Lyman you're sorry and not take back calling him a liar, see?"

"I—I—"

Daniel shrugged as if he didn't care anymore. "It's your own business, of course, if you'd rather be thrashed and starved for a week or two. It never done me any good. If you do it your way, he'll only win in the end. If you do it my way, you'll be keeping your pride *and* your skin." Daniel crawled over to his side of the bed and slid between the sheets.

"I hate him." Ethan settled under the covers and adjusted the shirt over his back. He pillowed his cheek against the rag, releasing more of the wormwood's scent as he crushed it.

Daniel wriggled to the far edge of the bed, avoiding the wet shirt and the growing damp spot spreading across the sheet and blanket. "Can't say I'm overfond of him meself."

"I wish he was dead."

The silence stretched out so long that Ethan thought Daniel had fallen asleep. But finally the Irish boy spoke. "I did, too, once. I said so to me ma. She told me if you wish someone ill, it only comes back at you in the end. So you're better to wish somebody good."

Ethan closed his eyes and conjured up the best wish he could. "Then I wish I was your brother."

Daniel stiffened. He held his breath for a very long time, then he spoke so softly that Ethan could barely hear him. "No. No, you don't."

Chapter Eighteen

"Silas, what's over there?" Ethan asked. He and Silas had been hoeing a field of pumpkin seedlings across the road from the secret place where Daniel sometimes went at night. If anybody knew what the spot signified, Silas might, and it might be a long time before there would be another opportunity to ask him.

"Grass," Silas said matter-of-factly, not looking up from his hoeing. "Not very good grass, mind you, but if I manure it well this season, it might do for a little hay next year . . . or maybe—" He didn't break his rhythm as he spoke; his hoe cut big even swaths through the weeds, leaving them behind to wilt in the blistering sun.

"No, no," Ethan said impatiently. "I mean there's something peculiar about it. There's a sort of funny bit." He pointed with his hoe. "Over there. You can't see it from the road, but—"

Silas straightened, wiping his forehead on his sleeve. He eyed Ethan sharply from under the shade of his tall straw hat. "And when were you wandering over there?"

"Just—just exploring. Sometimes. When I have an afternoon free, I like to walk around and see what's where. It's allowed, isn't it?"

"Yes, it's allowed." Silas ran his handkerchief along the back of his neck. "You don't know the story, then," he said.

Ethan shook his head.

"I thought everybody knew," Silas said. "Come on, then.

Let's take a walk." Still carrying his hoe, Silas strolled to the fence and hoisted himself over the rails with a smooth, easy vault that reminded Ethan of Daniel leaping onto Ivy's back.

Clumsily, Ethan climbed the fence and followed Silas across the road to the little rise where Daniel had nearly disappeared from view on the night Ethan had followed him. The site didn't seem nearly as foreboding in the daylight. The apple trees lining the road had leafed out and now cast soft pools of welcome shade instead of ominous skeletal shadows.

Silas and Ethan walked to the top of the bank and looked down. The ground fell gently away to a broad flat spot where the grass grew thinly.

A scrubby bush stood to one side of the flat space. The scrawny plant was about four feet high and nearly choked by brambles. Ethan noticed something familiar about the weaker plant's heart-shaped leaves. The wind stirred them, and he caught sight of a few stunted clusters of lilacs, long faded and starting to go to seed.

"It's here, isn't it? That funny bit you were asking about," Silas said.

"I think so." At first, Ethan couldn't find the square that Daniel had paced the other night. The raking shadows of the rising moon had revealed contours in the earth that the brightness of midmorning and the long, scraggly grass now hid. His bare feet felt what his eyes couldn't see. His toes found a depression a couple of inches deep. He felt a subtle difference in the earth and the grasses and weeds inside the depression from those outside it. He paced it off as Daniel had, finding the boundary by walking with one foot on the high side and one on the low. It was a rectangle, not a square, measuring about eight by ten paces.

The odd little mound in the center of the rectangle was easy to see even in the daylight, though it looked much smaller, no more than a foot at its highest point. The grass was thinner there than in the rest of Daniel's secret spot.

"It used to be Paddy's house," Silas said.

"His house?" Ethan's eyes widened as the puzzle fell into place in his mind.

"Most of the bricks and foundation stones are gone, whatever somebody could use again, and the cellar hole's filled in. But you can still find the shape of it." Silas pointed east, toward his own home, which stood like a white sentinel on the hill that overlooked the field. "You can see our place from here. And Paddy could see his house from our attic."

"What happened?" Ethan asked.

"It burned." Silas continued to pace the outline of the foundation.

Ethan shuddered.

"Paddy was a little older than you when it happened. He saw the light from the window upstairs and ran down here. We all came down after him, but there was nothing we could do. It was December, and it was hard to get water to put the fire out. We threw snow on it, but we didn't save much. It was already burning pretty badly when we got there. Nobody could get inside to help Paddy's family, although he tried."

"He—he went inside?"

Silas nodded. "He said he could hear his brother crying."

"Brother?" Ethan repeated, reeling with the new information.

"His brother, Michael. The child must have been three or four. But it was too hot. The house was falling down around Paddy, and he couldn't reach any of them. Nobody could. We had to drag him out. They made me hold him because he kept trying to go back in." Silas shivered all over, as if it had suddenly turned winter again. "You've seen the scars on him." He rubbed his forearms.

Ethan nodded.

"His arms and hands were all burned, and some of his hair burned off, too. Even so, he fought me. I held him down and put snow on his burns. I didn't know what else to do. I never heard anybody scream like that before. I thought he was dying. When we took him home, he was so sick. I don't know if it was from the cold or the burns or from—" Silas shook his head and closed his eyes. "Maybe all of it. He took a fever, and then he really *was* dying. The doctor even gave up on him."

"But he didn't die," Ethan said.

Silas shook his head. "Mrs. Nye," he said. "She wouldn't give up, even when the doctor said it was no use." With his hoe, he began to hack at the brambles that surrounded the feeble lilac bush. "So now you know."

Ethan picked up a lump of broken brick and studied it while he framed his next question. "Silas . . ."

"What?"

"Why does your father hate Daniel?"

Silas raised an eyebrow. "Daniel? Did he tell you to call him that?" Just like everybody else, Silas called Daniel *Paddy*. Well, not quite like everybody else. When Mr. and Mrs. Lyman or Mr. Pease or Mr. Wheeler said *Paddy*, it was more than just a name. Or rather, less. There was something sly about it that seemed meaner to Ethan than if they said *fool*. But when Silas said *Paddy*, it was just a name. No more than a name, but no less, either.

"No. I just—well, it's his name, isn't it?" Ethan watched Silas's face carefully from under the shade of his hat brim.

Silas nodded, his mouth drawn in a thoughtful line. "I'd almost forgotten—I haven't heard it in so long. I thought he'd forgotten, too."

"Your father won't even let Daniel keep his own name. Why does he hate him so?"

Silas blinked dully at Ethan, as if he didn't understand.

Ethan blinked back. "You see how he hits him," he continued. "When Paddy's folks died, he was left with nothing but debts."

Ethan couldn't understand what Daniel's father's debts had to do with the way Mr. Lyman acted. "What about this?" He spread his arms to indicate the field around him. "He had this, didn't he?"

"It was mortgaged." Silas didn't seem anxious to return to work. He kept chopping the weeds away from the pathetic little shrub.

"And now it belongs to you," Ethan said.

"To Him." Although Silas hadn't named *Him*, Ethan knew from the odd way he said it that Silas meant Mr. Lyman. Ethan cast a sidelong glance at Silas, whose profile was a younger, sharper tracing of his father's. Silas never addressed Mr. Lyman as anything but *sir*. Never *Papa* or *Pa* or *Father*. When speaking in Mr. Lyman's absence, Silas never said *my father*, but only *he* or *him*. Yet somehow it was always clear which *he* Silas meant, because he said the word in a different way from all the other *he*s and *him*s in his life. For Mr. Lyman, all Silas's *he*s and *him*s sounded as though they had capital *H*s, the way some people talked about God.

Or the devil.

Ethan shook off the thought. He threw a worried glance up at Silas, as if he feared the young man could hear what was inside his head. "So your father had to keep Daniel because of his indenture?"

Silas shook his head. "Paddy first came here to work off part of his father's debt. When Matthew Linnehan died, his creditors laid claim to his property—what was left of it—" He made a sweeping gesture that took in the remnants of the house and the scrubby land around it—"to pay his debts."

"Creditors?" Ethan asked.

"Well, as it turned out, He was the only one."

Somehow Ethan wasn't surprised. "So your father took the land and Mr. Linnehan's debt was paid off?"

Silas nodded. "Legally, that was the end of Paddy's obligation to Him, and His to Paddy. So then it was up to the overseers of the poor to take charge of Paddy, since he had no property and no family."

"Did they put Daniel on the vendue then?" Ethan asked, remembering his lessons with Mr. Bingham.

"The vendue is only for people who have a settlement here, people who were born in this town."

Ethan's eyes widened. "What happens if they're not?"

"Then they have to go back to where they're from. The overseers of the poor didn't want to pay anybody to take care of Paddy. They said he would have to go to the poorhouse in Springfield, because he was there first, when his father worked on the canals in Cabotville. But the overseers in Springfield said he was from Ireland, and that's where he'd have to go." Silas began to attack what remained of the brambles with his bare hands.

"All the way back to Ireland?" Ethan shuddered, recalling Daniel's description of the months he'd spent in the reeking, lurching, dark belly of a ship.

"But he didn't know or couldn't remember where he came from or if he had any family there. Still, they were going to send him anyway. I suppose they thought his passage was cheaper than having him on the town until he could earn his keep. You see, He could have let the overseers of the poor send Paddy away and have done with him. But He said Paddy could stay with us, and He worked out an indenture for him with the overseers, even though it would cost *Him* money in the end, since He'll have to give Paddy his wages when he's finished his service."

At least Daniel would get to keep his wages, Ethan thought. From what he understood of his own bond, he wouldn't even see his wages, since Pa would have to hand the money back to Mr. Lyman to pay his debt to the storekeeper. Ethan doubted there would be anything left over.

Silas continued, "He said it was the least He could do for the boy, even though He got nothing from the town or anyone for it."

The way Silas put it, it made Mr. Lyman sound compassionate and generous. But if he were all that generous, couldn't he have just made Daniel part of his family without any indenture at all? Ethan wondered. It seemed as though Mr. Lyman couldn't even be charitable—if indeed, Daniel's bond could be called charity—without imposing a legal obligation on the other person, with papers to be signed and prices to be agreed upon.

Ethan squeezed the brick hard, the rough parts biting into his skin. "But—but—"

"If He hated Paddy, He wouldn't have done that, would He?"

"But he beats him!" Ethan blurted. "He says Daniel's a thief and a liar, and all sorts of other things."

Silas shook his head. "He's only doing His best to raise Paddy not to be any of those things, just the way He did with me. Just the way He's doing with you."

"Do you think Daniel's a thief and a liar?"

Silas frowned, pondering the question so long that Ethan thought he wouldn't answer it. "He's never cheated me out of a fair day's work. But things go on that I don't know about, I imagine." Silas nodded, as if settling something inside his head. "Paddy's a difficult boy."

"So Mr. Lyman's right to hit him, then?" *To hit us*, Ethan added in his head, but he pretended he asked only for Daniel's sake.

"He knows His business." Silas's face began to close up. He wiped his hands on his trousers, his fingers now peppered with scratches from the briars.

Ethan guessed the conversation would be over soon. But he had to ask one more question. "But *you* don't hit Daniel." He knew it was true, even though he'd never asked. Daniel never drooped his head and hid his eyes in front of Silas. There was something about the way Daniel and Silas spoke—not quite as friends, but not as antagonists, either. "If it's right, why don't you hit Daniel, too?"

"He knows His business," he repeated. "And I know mine." Silas shouldered his hoe and turned away from the scrubby little lilac bush and the remains of Daniel's house. When they reached the road, he hesitated, turning to look back toward the house site, though it was now hidden behind the little hill.

"He must miss them awfully," Ethan said softly, thinking of Daniel and his family.

"Awfully," Silas repeated, his voice distant and strained. "Yes, I'm sure he does."

"They were all Papists, weren't they?"

Silas blinked hard, as if Ethan had just woken him from a dream. "They were Catholics, yes."

"Is it true what Mr. Merriwether says about Papists, that they're heathens and idolatrous and all that? That they're not even Christians? Do you think it's true that people like them go to hell?"

Silas held up a hand against Ethan's cascade of questions. "What I think isn't going to make a difference whether somebody's saved or not."

Ethan chewed his lip. "It doesn't seem fair, that somebody would go to hell just for belonging to the wrong church."

"They seemed like decent people," Silas said.

It didn't matter, though, did it? Ethan thought. That's what the minister said. Being decent didn't count for anything if you believed the wrong things. He felt heartsick for Daniel's family. But Daniel, he could still be saved. Was that what Mr. Lyman meant? "What about Daniel? Will he go to hell?"

Silas's face hardened, as if he'd drawn a set of shutters closed against something. For a moment he looked almost as old as his father. "There's worse things a boy can have on his soul than belonging to the wrong church."

Chapter Nineteen

"Why do I have to take my tea in the kitchen?" Ruth said, plucking at Lizzie's apron.

Lizzie swirled the last bit of icing onto an enormous cake. "Because Mrs. Lyman's having company." She turned to the fireplace to dip some water from the massive hot-water pot into the teakettle.

Ruth trailed after, one hand tugging Lizzie's skirt. "But Florella and Zeloda get to have their tea in the big parlor."

"Florella and Zeloda are almost grown." Lizzie gently maneuvered Ruth away from the steaming water. She scooped some coals onto the hearth and set a trivet on top of them.

"Paddy's bigger'n both of 'em. But he has to have his tea out here."

"That's different." Lizzie set the teakettle on the trivet to steep.

"Why?" Ruth trotted after Lizzie as she headed to the buttery to fetch some cream.

Lizzie rolled her eyes at Ethan and Daniel. Freshly scrubbed and combed, the boys stood in the doorway, waiting for her orders. Ethan pressed his lips together to smother a grin over Ruth's endless string of *why*s. He didn't think Lizzie would welcome his smile. Her face was damp and flushed from the frenzy of cleaning and dusting and sweeping and polishing and cooking that Mrs. Lyman had imposed on all the girls. She brushed impatiently at the tendrils of hair that crept out from her cap, its wilting ruffle flopping over her forehead.

Daniel stooped so that his eyes were level with Ruth's. "Lizzie's needing your help with the baby. And you're better at that than your sisters, ain't you, now?"

Ruth's eyes grew wide. "Really?"

Lizzie raised her eyebrows at Daniel, then turned an inquisitive glance toward Ethan. He shrugged. He didn't think he'd ever heard Daniel talk to Ruth before. Most of the time, the Lyman children and Daniel ignored each other.

Lizzie collected herself as Ruth looked to her for confirmation. "Of course. You're such a big help to me all the time, Ruth."

Ruth beamed, stretching herself to stand a full half inch taller. She strutted over to Aaron, who babbled and kicked in his high chair. The two stared at each other solemnly for a moment. Then Aaron emitted a smell that filled the kitchen. Ruth backed away, her lower lip working into a pout.

"Anyway," Lizzie added hastily, "you can have your own chair in here. And so can Ethan."

Ruth stuck a finger in her mouth. "But I like sitting on Silas's lap. Can he have tea with us?"

"Maybe you ought to'a stopped talking while you were ahead, eh, Lizzie?" Daniel teased.

Lizzie frowned, although her eyes recaptured some of their usual twinkle as she stepped past the boys into the cool dimness of the buttery. "And maybe *you* ought to fetch some chairs."

Daniel bowed low, like a character from his fat little book of Shakespeare plays, then spun away.

"What's got into him?" Lizzie whispered to Ethan. A cloud of flies rose as she lifted the cloth covering one of the milk pans and skimmed some cream into a little pitcher. "He never—I mean . . . well, I could swear he smiled."

Ethan shook his head, trying to puzzle it out. Part of it, he supposed, was that Daniel had managed to sneak in a brief, secret ride just before milking. The joy of it had stayed on his face all the way through milking, turning the cattle out to pasture, and returning to the house to wash up for tea. But Ethan couldn't tell Lizzie that. Instead, he said, "I think he's glad to have his tea in the kitchen."

Ethan was glad, too. Being exiled from Mrs. Lyman's company meant he'd have a chair to sit in to enjoy the treats that Lizzie and the girls had slaved over all day: orange fool and lemon pudding and syllabub and jumbles and white gingerbread and other things that smelled tantalizingly of cinnamon and nutmeg and mace and cream and raisins and brandy.

"No." Lizzie waved away the hopeful flies that hovered by the milk pan. "There's more to it than that." She draped the cloth over the pan and tugged it down around the edges. "Something different about him. It's like he's . . . not changed, but chang*ing.* Just this spring, it seems he's been, well, not as sour as he used to be. Haven't you noticed—" She laughed and stopped herself. "Of course you wouldn't. You don't know what he was like before you came." Her eyes narrowed at Ethan, then she shook her head. "Perhaps it's just Paddy growing up."

Lizzie'd seen it, too, then: something different about Daniel, the way he held himself, the way he set his face. Something that showed more and more as spring worked its way into summer. Ethan pursed his mouth, trying to figure it out as he followed Lizzie back into the kitchen. But the answer wouldn't come. "Maybe he's just glad he won't have to listen to Mr. Pease's jokes," Ethan said.

"Hmmm." Lizzie set the pitcher of cream on a tray already laden with puddings and cakes. "Well, Mr. Pease hasn't been invited for tea. Nor Mr. Wheeler, either. Mr. Lyman wants only one young gentleman at the table."

"Why?" Ruth asked.

Lizzie's lips pressed into a thin line.

Footsteps thudded down the back stairway, and Silas burst into the kitchen. "Lizzie! My collar won't stand. And look!" He flapped the ends of his cravat. "I can't get them even." He was decked out in his finest burgundy vest and black tailcoat, freshly brushed. His cheeks were pink from his recent shave, and a little dab of soapsuds lingered by his left ear. One corner of his starched collar stood properly at attention along his jaw-line. The other sagged like a wilted flower.

Lizzie's shoulders drooped momentarily, then squared as she stepped toward Silas. She wiped away the soap with a corner of her apron and tugged at the wayward collar. "Of course it won't stand. You've got it all wet." Her mouth couldn't seem to decide whether to smile or to frown.

"I'll have to change, then." Silas turned toward the stairs, then spun back, shaking his head. "No, there's no time. They'll be here any minute."

Something nudged Ethan's elbow. He turned to see Daniel standing nearby, a chair in each hand. He set the chairs down quietly and retreated to a corner of the kitchen, nodding at Ethan to join him.

"Here, let me see." Lizzie snapped the cravat off Silas's neck and fiddled with the edges of his collar. She creased and straightened it, then made several wraps with the cravat high around Silas's throat so that it forced the collar into its proper place. Silas had to hold his chin high, but the collar behaved. The result looked very elegant and very uncomfortable.

"Make sure you tie it good and tight," Daniel said.

Ethan stifled a giggle. Though Silas looked as though he wasn't listening, his ears reddened.

Lizzie's lips gathered in an unruly pucker. For a moment,

Ethan thought she might stick her tongue out at Daniel. Instead, she sighed and gave Silas's cravat a final tug. "There. It'll stay up fine once it dries. Just don't move your head too much until then."

Silas looked in the tiny mirror in the corner of the kitchen. "It's perfect. Lizzie, you're a wonder."

Mrs. Lyman appeared like a thundercloud in the doorway. "Silas, no dawdling, if you please. The Smeads will be here any moment." She swooped toward the table, captured the tray Lizzie had prepared, and swirled back toward the door.

"Yes, ma'am," Silas said meekly, like an oversized naughty boy.

Mrs. Lyman rustled into the formal parlor, which she and the girls had spent the afternoon preparing with a starched white tablecloth and napkins, flowers from the garden, and the best dishware and silver.

Silas rolled his eyes at Lizzie. Their mouths and noses wrinkled in a shared snicker. "Lizzie, no dawdling, if you please," he mimicked. He crooked his elbow toward Lizzie to escort her into the parlor.

Lizzie shook her head and backed away, wiping her hands on her apron. "I can't—"

Silas's forehead creased. "But you always take tea with us, Lizzie."

Lizzie shook her head again. "Mrs. Lyman wants me to mind the children."

Silas glanced around the room. He seemed to expect help to spring magically from the teakettle or the pudding dish. "Well, um, Paddy could mind them." He looked at Daniel, who seemed to be trying very hard not to make a sour face.

Lizzie's laugh sounded oddly brittle. "Oh, and I'm sure Paddy knows all about changing nappies and feeding babies."

She gathered a handful of her faded brown skirt. "Anyway, I can't sit to tea with the Smeads with my clothes smelling of cows and cheese and dirty nappies, can I?"

Silas wrinkled his nose. "I don't smell anything."

"It doesn't matter, Silas. I'll have my tea in the parlor tomorrow." But it did matter. Ethan could tell from the jagged sound of Lizzie's laugh and the way she had to work at making her mouth smile.

Silas tilted his head toward Lizzie, but the cravat made him wince and hold it straight again. "I only thought . . . I thought it would be better if you joined us."

Lizzie's eyelids fluttered. "Better?"

Silas cleared his throat. "I mean," he continued, "you and Clarissa are friends, schoolmates, aren't you?"

Lizzie's eyes tightened. "Friends?" She turned away and busied herself with straightening the tea things on the big kitchen table. "We did go to the same school before she went off to academy, if that's what you mean."

Silas's mouth relaxed. "There, you see? I thought it might put her at ease if she had a friend at the table."

Daniel winced. Ethan didn't understand the word that Daniel muttered, but he guessed that it was not a nice one.

Lizzie picked at a clump of dough stuck to her apron. "I hardly think Clarissa needs me to feel at ease."

The front door opened and closed, and feminine voices trickled down the hall. Silas shifted from one foot to the other, his head cocked toward the hallway.

"Si-las!" Zeloda's voice shrilled toward the kitchen.

Silas fidgeted with his cravat and collar. The damp corner drooped again. "Do I—am I all right?"

Lizzie raised her head slowly and gave him a thin smile. "Splendid."

Silas grinned and spun out the door. The hall burst into

greetings and giggles, soon muffled as Mrs. Lyman led the guests into the formal parlor and closed the door.

Daniel nudged Ethan toward the table. Ethan wasn't quite sure what had happened, only that it had dampened the sparks in Lizzie's eyes. He wished he could think of something clever to say to bring back her old smile, but all he could come up with was, "I'm glad you're having tea here with us, Lizzie."

Lizzie smiled with her mouth, but not her eyes. "So am I."

"He's a proper fool, Lizzie," Daniel said, in the gentlest voice Ethan had ever heard him use.

Lizzie's eyes sparked. "I'll thank you to keep your own counsel before you go calling people names, Paddy Linnehan." She bustled away to fetch a plate of bread and cakes from one of the side tables.

"Pity," Daniel murmured in Ethan's ear as the boys settled into their chairs.

"What?"

"Pity you can't find a way t'be spoiling Clarissa's silk today, ain't it?"

Chapter Twenty

"You'll see. There's nothing puts himself in a fine humor like a good string of trout on his breakfast table." The boys' catch dangled from Daniel's hand in a shimmering iridescent bundle.

"Can I carry 'em?" Ethan's voice echoed as they stepped from the dusty road into the cool darkness of the covered bridge. It couldn't have been a more perfect afternoon—an afternoon with no less than two miracles in it. Silas had granted the boys an unexpected afternoon holiday, and Ethan had caught the biggest fish of the lot.

"You'll drag 'em in the dust and spoil 'em."

"I will not!"

"Your arms'll get tired. You can carry 'em when we get nearer home."

"I can do it."

Daniel whirled, and Ethan found the end of the Irish boy's fishing pole poised against his chest. "Have at you, now," Daniel said, curling his lip in a teasing sneer.

Ethan blinked. "Have what?"

The pole drooped as Daniel sighed and rolled his eyes. "It's what they say in that peddler's book of plays." He resumed his stance, poised on the balls of his feet, fishing pole extended in one hand, fish held high in the other. "When they have a duel. If you'd read any of 'em, you'd'a known."

"Oh." Ethan's face lit up. Three months ago, no amount of coaxing could have induced Daniel to playfulness. Ethan wondered how many other surprises this new Daniel had inside him. Grinning, Ethan mimicked Daniel's posture. "Have at you, too!" he shouted, and flailed at his friend with his own pole.

The switches that Daniel had cut for fishing poles seemed to have a life of their own, bending the wrong way when one of the boys tried to score a hit, or wobbling when the boys tried to parry each other's blows, and generally doing exactly the opposite of whatever the boys tried to make them do. But that made the duel all the more fun. Ethan's giggles blended with Daniel's harsh barking laugh, echoing back to them from the bridge's rafters. By the time they reached the opposite side, both boys were red-faced and panting.

"Take that—" Ethan jabbed to the right. The end of his pole wobbled to the left. "And that—" With a whoop of laughter, he lunged, then retreated, backing up nearly to the mouth of the bridge.

Daniel dashed after him, feet slapping hard against the boards. He gasped in a breath, then suddenly stopped, his face returning to its usual blank mask.

"What?" Ethan said.

"Shhh." Daniel's hand twitched in a sharp slashing motion. "Listen."

All Ethan could hear was the water rushing under the bridge and a jay scolding them for disturbing his rest. Then he caught a high musical tone that sounded like a woman singing. It floated in on the breeze for a moment, then disappeared.

Daniel muttered something in Gaelic and made a quick gesture, touching his forehead, breast, and shoulders. Then he shoved his fishing pole and the string of trout into Ethan's hands and ran.

"Daniel! Wait!" Ethan plodded after, holding the fish high to keep from trailing them in the dirt.

Daniel stood in the middle of the road, his head tilting to the right and left like a questing dog's.

The singing grew stronger: a high, clear treble purer than any voice Ethan had ever heard in the singing school.

Daniel let out a ragged cry that seemed torn from his heart rather than his throat. He ran toward the sound and disappeared around a bend in the road.

The trees and underbrush near the river gave way to pastures and fields of silvery blue-green rye. Away from the muffling trees, Ethan could hear the singing more clearly. The sounds were at once familiar and foreign, like the gibberish of a dream voice.

Daniel stopped at the crest of a little hill, looking down at the road winding toward them from the east. He scrubbed at his face with his palms until his cheeks and forehead turned red. Then he paced, sweeping his hands through his hair so that it stood up in unruly spikes.

"What is it?" Ethan asked.

Daniel shook his head raggedly. "Naught. Naught but me being a fool." He stumbled toward the edge of the road.

Ethan squinted down the hill at an approaching wagon. It crept along at a leisurely stroll, the sunlight winking and shimmering in silvery lights on its contents. Daniel turned his back on the view and wiped his sweating face with his sleeve.

The wagon drew close enough for Ethan to recognize the serenely plodding horse and its globular driver. "Daniel, look! It's Mr. Stocking!" He waved at the peddler.

Daniel shrugged and headed in the opposite direction. "S'pose it is," he replied dully.

Mr. Stocking urged Phizzy into a trot, neatly pulling the splay-footed gray gelding to a halt in front of Ethan. "Well, if it ain't young Mr. Root." The peddler swept off his hat and bowed deeply. "I thought I recognized your physiografication. Didn't I say so, Billy?"

Ethan's gaze shifted to Mr. Stocking's companion: a boy, maybe eleven or twelve years old, slouched in the seat. Blond curls strayed out from under a deep blue cap that almost exactly matched the boy's eyes. He wore a spencer of the same blue material, with brass buttons that winked as brightly as Mr. Stocking's wares. Billy's face looked as if it might tend toward round-cheeked fullness if he weren't so lean. The leanness made his face a shade less than pleasant—that, and something hard around his eyes.

"Aye," Billy said, the sound tilting upward at the end. The word had nothing musical about it.

Ethan stared, trying to connect the boy on the wagon with the song. "That—that was _you_ singing?"

"Aye," the boy said again. His jaw tensed, as if the question were a challenge.

"Not a finer treble in three counties, eh, son? Pity it won't last more'n a couple more years." Mr. Stocking's spectacles winked as he glanced from the boy to Ethan. He nodded toward the fish in Ethan's hand. "'Pears you and your comrade-in-arms have had a successful day." He looked beyond Ethan to where Daniel lingered at the roadside. The peddler's mouth widened in a broad grin that fully exposed his gold tooth. He bobbed and leaned forward. "Good day, Mr. Linnehan," he called out. When Daniel didn't come any closer, he flicked the reins and drove the wagon over to the boy. "Looks like you boys're afoot today."

"Aye," Daniel said, his face closed and hostile.

"Hop aboard, then. No sense preambulating when you can ride in style, eh?"

"You're going the wrong way." Daniel crossed his arms

and jutted his chin in the direction from which Mr. Stocking had come.

"Ah, but that's the beauty part of this peddling scheme. I got no fixed itinerary." He accentuated the *tin* part of the word, laughing at his own pun.

Daniel remained stone-faced. "I don't fancy being thrashed again."

Ethan moved closer to Daniel. He'd once thought he'd never forget that switching, but the moment he'd recognized Mr. Stocking, all he'd thought of was the peddler's stories and gifts, the joy of the race, and Daniel and the peddler's enigmatic parting. With Daniel's words, the betrayal was suddenly fresh again. No wonder Daniel was angry.

"Thrashed?" Mr. Stocking repeated. "Someone saw us racing, huh? Oh, boys, I am sorry. I thought we were discreet as Pharaoh's wife."

Ethan's lower lip jutted out. "Nobody saw us. You told," he said.

Mr. Stocking pulled himself up straight. He tugged his jacket into place as it rode up his belly. "I did no such thing. I may be a peddler, but I never betray a confidence."

"You told Mr. Pease, and he told Mr. Lyman, and he thrashed us." The memory burned Ethan's cheeks.

The peddler lifted his hat and rumpled his thinning hair. "Now I never said a word about racing to a soul, and I'll swear that on Phizzy's rump. . . ." He rasped a finger across his chin. "But there was a fella . . . yes, a big strapping farmer-fella, nearly slick enough to make a peddler . . . yes, I did talk to him about you boys. I mentioned I'd been at the farrier's, and he asked if I'd seen two boys riding a chestnut mare. I said indeed I had, and commented on what an excellent example of equine-imity she was. Then he said that Irish boy, he's a rare one for riding, and I'd'a been lying if I disagreed, wouldn't I?

But we never talked about racing." He glanced up, as if the memory were written in the air for him to read. He shook his head. "No, no, can't say the subject was brung up. I was only complimenting your talents, not telling your sins, son."

"The riding alone was enough to get us thrashed," Daniel said.

"He don't let you *ride?*" The peddler's eyebrows arched nearly to his hat brim. "Now there's a damn-fool waste of time, sending two boys on an errand with a horse and not even letting 'em *ride.* You'd think a man as skinflintish as your Mr. Lyman would'a heard that time is money, wouldn't you?"

"Not when it comes to lads riding *his* horse." Daniel's eyes hardened to gray stone.

"And my carelessness cost you boys a thrashing." Mr. Stocking's voice softened, losing its playactor's bravado. The peddler shook his head and doffed his hat, his eyes soft behind his glasses. He swirled his gray-speckled hair into an unruly nest that matched the discomfort in his face. "My deepest and sincerest apologies. I wouldn't have no harm come to you boys, not with me owing you so much."

Daniel's frown eased into a neutral line. "*You* owing *us?*"

"Well, you, sir, particularly." The peddler pointed at Daniel. Phizzy's nose bobbed in agreement.

Daniel's pale eyebrows twisted in confusion. "For what?"

"An idea." Mr. Stocking settled his hat back on his head. "A very profitable idea." The peddler jerked a thumb over his shoulder. "Hop aboard, boys. I'll tell you while you ride." He nudged his companion with his elbow. "Go on, Billy, make some room for these gentlemen. Pile up the goods around 'em so no tattlers'll spot 'em."

"They're no more gentlemen than I am," Billy muttered as Ethan and Daniel clambered aboard.

Mr. Stocking took Billy's arm and squeezed, forcing the

boy to turn and look at him. "Friends of mine is friends of yours, and you'll treat 'em civil, understand?"

Billy's cheeks reddened. He dropped his eyes with a murmured "Yessir."

"Good." Mr. Stocking flicked the reins and angled the wagon back and forth across the road until he'd turned it back the way he'd come. Once under way again, he cleared his throat. "Now, William James Michael Fogarty, this is Mr. Ethan Root and Mr. Daniel Linnehan, and it's them I have to thank for the pleasure of your company."

All three boys' eyes opened wide.

"Us?" Ethan asked.

"Them?" Billy said at the same time.

Mr. Stocking grinned at the boys' surprise. "Well, I confess I wasn't thinking on you fellas when I first seen Billy. He was sleeping under the bridge down by Factory Village, looking so decrepit I thought somebody'd killed him." One green eye disappeared behind a wink. "He taught me to play the Good Samaritan, didn't you, son?"

The tension around Billy's eyes softened as he straightened and thumbed his lapels. "You never been kicked so hard, I bet."

"Or so thoroughly." Mr. Stocking rubbed his shin as though it still hurt. "Tried to do the boy a kindness, and he assaulted me. Imagine. Kicked me and run off." The wagon seat groaned as Mr. Stocking turned sideways on it, so he could give the boys the full effect of his story. Phizzy plodded steadily along without the little man's guidance. "'Bad luck to you,' I says, and goes on to my business. Not two hours later, I'm down in the Patch, trying to sell a fine Gaelic lady one of my milk pans. I turn around and what do I see but this same rogue trying to carry away an entire tin kitchen!"

Billy's mouth spread into a grin. "Nearly got it, too, didn't I?"

Mr. Stocking made a humphing noise. "About as near as

Boston is to Timbuktu. Anyway, I sent him off with a kick on the backside to match the one on my shin, and figured our accounts was quits. But what do you think happened when I was down to the tavern having my dinner?"

"What?" Ethan asked.

Mr. Stocking bent closer to the boys, an elbow on his knee. "I come out, having satiated my appetite, and what do I see but this hellion had unhitched Phizzy and was trying to run away with him."

"What did you do then?" Ethan said.

Mr. Stocking spread a hand across his chest. "Well, boys, I was torn. Sorely torn. On the one hand, there's nothing worse than a horse thief. But you see, there were three other horses tied up outside that tavern alongside of Phizzy. This ruffian could'a chose any one of them horses to steal, but he picks mine. And that spoke to his character."

Billy's mouth pursed, softening the hard edges from his face. "Phizzy had a nice face, is all. I thought he liked me."

The peddler knocked Billy's hat askew to ruffle the boy's hair. "There, you see? The boy's a judge of horses, and the horse is a judge of boys. So I had him by the collar, wondering what to do with the rapscallion. And it was like trying to hold a wildcat, with him kicking and spitting and biting and cursing in that heathen tongue of his. By this time, a crowd's starting to collect. And that's when Providence steps in, if that's what you call that ugly layabout who walks up, grabs Billy out of my hands and commences to beating him for me."

"The constable?" Daniel wondered aloud.

The peddler shook a finger at the boys. "Now, you'd'a thought so, and so would I, but I'm familiar with the constabulary most places, and I hadn't seen this rogue before. So I steps up and says, 'Here now, sir. You're just going to have to wait your turn. I had him first.' The fellow turns to me and says

I couldn't have had him first, unless I'd had his mother, too. And if I did, he'd be sure and beat me, too, just as soon as he finished kicking the boy from here to Donegal and back."

"It was his da?" Daniel asked.

The little man nodded. "So he said. Well, if I'd been tore before, I was in a quandary now. I'm all for a father making his children mind, but if I'd'a stood there and done nothing, there'd'a been nothing left of Billy for *me* to thrash." He clapped his hand on the boy's shoulder. Billy grinned easily now, as if the story had thawed him. "So I waded in there between the two of 'em and said, 'Mr. O'Something or McThingamebob, how'm I to get my satisfaction if you beat that boy to death?'" Mr. Stocking turned the other way as he played Billy's father, lowering his voice to a fierce growl. "He says, 'To hell with your satisfaction.' That's when I tell the brute I'm more than willing to pay for my satisfaction. Cash money."

"Pay?" Ethan and Daniel repeated together.

The little man winked. "Got your attention, didn't it, boys? Got his attention too. I asked how much he wanted for me to take Billy off his hands."

"He sold—I mean—you—you *bought* him?" Ethan stared from the peddler to Billy and back.

"Hired, son, hired. Selling people ain't legal—leastaways, not white ones."

"So—so you hired him just so you could thrash him?" Ethan felt a wave of sympathy for the surly blond boy.

Mr. Stocking tipped his head to one side and frowned. "Thrash him? Now why would I want to do a thing like that?"

"Didn't you just say—"

"Well, now, maybe I did feel like slapping him around a bit on Phizzy's account, but there was this idea rattling around in my brain." He tapped his forehead.

"You see, when Billy started cursing in that Irish of his, it made me think of you boys." Mr. Stocking gestured toward Daniel. "I got to thinking how handy it would be to have Mr. Linnehan here along just so I'd know the exact nature of how I was being cursed. And that led me to thinking about how this particular curse"—he tugged Billy's ear—"could be turned into an asset. Ain't that right, son?" He winked at the boy.

The blond recited an incomprehensible string of words that sounded half like Daniel's magic language and half like a revival preacher that Mr. Merriwether had once invited to give the sermon.

"What did he say?" Ethan asked.

Daniel's lips moved silently before he explained, "He's praising Mr. Stocking's tin."

The peddler smiled. "So I believe. Though I only have his word for it—well, that and the coins in my pocket. Remember how I said I could use a boy like you selling tin to the Irish?"

Daniel nodded, his face growing dark and thoughtful.

"It don't hurt that Billy's got a sweet voice for singing the songs of the old country. Get one of them Irish ladies weeping about the green fields of home, and the next thing you know, you've sold a set of milk pans to a household that's got no cow nor pig nor even chicken in it."

Billy grinned. "We'll be rich. *And* I can ride Phizzy." The riding sounded more important than the riches.

Mr. Stocking took Billy by the scruff of the neck and gave him an affectionate shake. "Anyway, now I got some pleasant company and musical entertainment, and Billy's got himself some fancy duds and a trade to learn, and Phizzy has someone besides me to talk to." The gelding's ears pricked lazily up. Mr. Stocking bent half out of his seat to poke Ethan and Daniel on the shoulders. "And it's you fellas we have to thank for it. Billy's even teaching me a little bit of his Irish talk." A garbled sentence dribbled out of his mouth. Daniel's magical words sounded coarse and peculiar in Mr. Stocking's voice, like somebody trying to play a fiddle tune on the Jew's harp.

Billy giggled and said something that sounded vaguely like what Mr. Stocking had said, except that the boy's tones danced nimbly around each other instead of clattering together.

Mr. Stocking tried again, the words blending better this time, but still not right, even to Ethan's unknowing ears. "There. What d'you think?" He poked Daniel.

Daniel nodded reluctantly. He responded in Gaelic with something that sounded encouraging, though his words seemed sluggish and uncertain.

Billy giggled again, rattling off a long string of words that flew by like startled birds.

Pink scalded Daniel's cheeks. His words faltered as they came out, then stopped, as though he'd suddenly lost the way of them.

Billy howled with laughter.

Ethan waited for the boys to share the joke. But whatever it was, Daniel wouldn't tell, and Daniel wasn't laughing.

"Get up there! Go on, you old witch!" Daniel threw a clod of dirt that shattered against Nell's rump. Nell's horns clattered against Mary's, then Lily's. The cattle trotted raggedly toward the pasture, tails lashing, eyes wide at the unexpected pace Daniel had set them.

Ethan brought up the rear at a jog instead of the easy stroll they usually took down to the night pasture. He darted across the road, arms spread wide, to drive a wayward steer back into the herd.

"Come on," Daniel barked. "We ain't got all night." The

cattle stirred up a cloud of dust at the pasture's barway, blocking the road in a swirl of milling hooves, swishing tails, and clanking horns.

Usually, Ethan would come around from the back of the herd and help Daniel slide back the five horizontal rails that barred the pasture's entry. But usually the cattle stood in a quiet, sleepy-eyed straggle. Not tonight. The press of cattle made a solid wall across Ethan's path.

Up ahead, Daniel slapped and punched at rumps and shoulders, thumped his stick on horns, shouted and shoved his way through to the barway. If Daniel was cross now, Ethan thought, he'd be angrier still if Ethan wasn't there to hold the cattle at bay. Eager to get at the green grass, they often tried to charge into the pasture before the bars were down. He saw no way around the cattle in the road, so he climbed the fence to cut through the pasture. As Ethan hauled himself to the top of the fence, Daniel and Nell faced off against each other. The cow shook her head and edged forward toward the gate.

"Yah!" Daniel shouted, stamping his foot and waving his arms. The other cattle retreated. Nell stood her ground. Daniel shouted again. His lash stirred up the dust in front of the brindle cow. She backed slowly into the herd, her horns bobbing from side to side. Then she pivoted on her hind legs and turned her back on Daniel as if he were beneath her notice.

Ethan hopped down into the pasture, his stick tucked under his arm. "Wait for me!" he called out as Daniel turned to slide the top bar back. His mouth was grim and his shoulders taut as he grasped the pole and pulled.

"Fine. Do it yourself. See if I care," Ethan muttered, wondering what had made Daniel so cross.

Daniel shoved the bar back hard. The sudden release of weight as the bar left his hands pulled him off balance. He stumbled against the fence, grabbing for a rail to steady himself. Ethan saw Daniel's arms flail and his legs do a little dancing step as he tried to get his feet back underneath him.

Nell must have seen, too, because that was when she charged.

Chapter Twenty-One

"Daniel!" Ethan screamed as Daniel went down. He felt as though he were running underwater, unable to reach Daniel fast enough. He dropped to his knees at the gate, expecting to find a bloody heap on the other side.

Daniel lay motionless, his back pressed against the bottom rail, his body open to Nell's horns. For a moment, Ethan thought Daniel had fainted, but when he looked at Daniel's face, he saw the gray-green eyes opened wide, an eerily passive expression on his face.

"Come on, Daniel!" Ethan tugged at Daniel's braces. But Daniel made no move to help himself.

Nell lowered her head.

"No!" Ethan thrust his arm between the rails and jabbed his stick at the soft spot in the middle of Nell's nose. She retreated, eyes blinking with the sting of the blow.

Ethan grabbed Daniel again, trying to wrestle him through the fence before Nell recovered, or before the other milling cattle grew impatient and crashed through the gate. He threw his weight backward and dragged Daniel partway through the rails.

Nell lowered her head again.

"Daniel! You have to help!" Daniel didn't seem to hear. Ethan dug his nails into Daniel's arm, hoping the sting would rouse him from his stupor. Daniel looked at Ethan. His eyes narrowed slightly, his lips parted as if about to ask a question. Then his head turned back toward Nell.

She seemed to nod in response to a silent command. Her head bowed and she pawed the ground.

"Daniel!" Ethan punched him in the shoulder. "Come on!" At last Daniel rolled toward Ethan. Nell's waving horns slashed Daniel's sleeve from elbow to shoulder as he squeezed between the bars and slid through onto the soft green grass. He lay still, breathing deeply, steadily, strangely calm.

"You're crazy!" Ethan shouted, fists doubled. "You're crazy!"

"I never told you no different, did I, lad?" Daniel's voice was soft and emotionless.

"You didn't even try!" Ethan fought the urge to kick some sense into Daniel.

Daniel hauled himself to his feet. "S'pose we better let them cattle in, eh?"

Ethan gaped as Daniel stepped toward the gate, almost as though nothing had happened. Almost, except that his shirt hung in ragged bloody shreds at his right side and arm. Almost, except that the hands he laid on the bar trembled.

"What's wrong with you?" Ethan grabbed Daniel's elbow hard enough to make the older boy wince.

Daniel shook him off. "We got to do this first, lad."

Ethan eyed the cattle warily.

"We can't be leaving 'em in the road, now, can we?"

The boys worked together silently, Ethan keeping the cattle at bay while Daniel slid the bars back. Nell cast a baleful eye on the boys but kept her distance this time.

"What did I do to make you so angry?" Ethan asked, once the cattle were securely barred into the pasture and he and Daniel were on the other side of the fence.

Daniel leaned his forearms against the fence and rested his chin on the back of his hands. He squeezed his eyes closed. "It's naught to do with you, lad."

Ethan took out his handkerchief. He pulled the ragged tails of Daniel's shirt away to look at the gash Nell's horns had made along Daniel's ribs. Ethan mopped clumsily at the blood.

Daniel slapped Ethan's hands away. "Leave it." He bunched up a corner of his shirt and dabbed at the cut.

"She could'a killed you," Ethan said. "What's wrong with you? You been acting crazy since—since—" Ethan strained to pinpoint the moment. "Since we saw Mr. Stocking." For once, Ethan had no trouble keeping pace with Daniel as they walked. "That's it, isn't it? You're angry because you wish it was you instead of Billy working for Mr. Stocking."

Daniel spat out a humorless laugh. "I can't be working for no peddler."

"You could. You can talk Irish, just like Billy. You could be helping Mr. Stocking with his selling and all, and get away from here—"

Daniel pressed his lips together and closed his eyes. "No, I can't."

Ethan grabbed Daniel's sleeve. "Why?" Daniel tried to shake him off, but he clung fast. "Why?"

Daniel stared down at Ethan for a long time. "I ain't no Irish prince. I ain't even Irish no more. I'm just . . . just . . . nothing."

The revelation stunned Ethan into loosening his grip. Daniel tugged free and limped down the road. Fields and pastures yielded to a small rocky patch of woods watered by a narrow stream. Daniel trudged off the road and lowered himself at the edge of the water. He dragged out his handkerchief, soaked it, and dabbed at the scrape where Nell's horn had caught his arm.

"If you're not Irish, then what's that talk you do?" Ethan asked.

"It ain't proper Gaelic. That's why that boy of Mr. Stocking's was laughing. He said—he said I talk Irish no better'n a baby."

"What d'you mean?"

"I got the words muddled. I don't—I don't remember 'em proper no more. I didn't even remember—" Daniel rubbed the back of his hand across his face. He looked away from Ethan. He seemed to be searching for something far beyond the scrubby undergrowth and scrawny trees around them.

"What?" Ethan said, trying to recall Daniel before he drifted away into that place inside himself. "What didn't you remember?"

"That song the lad was singing. Me ma used to sing it—only I'd forgotten all about it. I didn't remember I even knew it until I heard him. And then I thought—" Daniel's eyes narrowed and he swallowed.

"It sounded like your ma singing?" Ethan asked.

Daniel shook his head. "She never sang as good as that. She only wished she could. But I thought—maybe—" He bent to soak his handkerchief again. "It's daft, lad. But I thought maybe the saints and all might'a given her the voice she wished she had while she was here." He shivered a little bit. "Daft," he repeated. "When I was little, I knew all the words. When I heard that lad singing it today, I couldn't remember what some of 'em meant. I couldn't even—" He pressed his eyes closed. "I couldn't hardly remember her face."

It was Ethan's turn to shiver. He couldn't imagine losing the picture in his head of Pa and Ma, the picture he summoned for comfort against the Lymans' scoldings and slaps and switchings. He sat with his knees drawn up under his chin, staring down at the brook, groping for something to say.

"If I went with that peddler, I couldn't talk to any of them people," Daniel said. "They'd all laugh, like that Billy. They'd think I was only pretending to be Irish."

"You can talk Irish to Ivy." It was the only comforting thing Ethan could think of to say.

"Oh, aye, she's a grand one for listening, but she ain't much for talking back now, is she? Not in Gaelic, anyway. I'll lose how a word goes exactly, and maybe I'll be getting it sideways or some such, and there's no one around to be telling me I got it wrong."

"I don't understand how you can forget how to talk—"

"Well, s'posing you was to be locked up in a room for six years and never could hear no one talking but yourself? Do you think you'd be remembering everything exactly right then?"

Ethan dabbled his toes in the stream, stirring it muddy. "I—I dunno."

Daniel rubbed the soggy handkerchief across his face. "I don't remember me ma's songs or me da's stories. And maybe someday I'll not be remembering *them*, neither."

Ethan hugged his legs to his chest and thought while Daniel scrubbed the dirt out of his cuts and the light faded behind the trees. It wasn't until Daniel rose stiffly to head home that Ethan spoke again. "Teach me. Teach me to talk Irish."

"We'll get thrashed. I've told you that before."

"We can be careful. No one will find out."

"And what good would that be doing me?"

"Maybe you'd start remembering better if you had someone asking you the words for everything."

"You won't know whether I'm telling you right no more'n Ivy does."

"But it would make you think about it, wouldn't it? Like you had to think about how to ride when you showed me. And maybe if you thought about it harder, maybe you could remember more. Anyway, at least you could practice, couldn't you?"

"I'll only be teaching you wrong."

Ethan shrugged. "That's all right. I won't know the difference."

Chapter Twenty-Two

"I'm the king!"

Ethan twirled on top of the haystack, arms spread wide as he surveyed his domain: the big white house, the flower garden and the kitchen garden, the cattle yard, the sheds, the smokehouse, the privy, and the corncrib; the barn and all the newly made haystacks hunched around it like old ladies huddled beneath mustard-colored cloaks.

"King of what?" Daniel asked from below.

Ethan gestured grandly around him. "King of everything!" He danced a little jig on his haystack. His feet slipped out from under him, and he slid down the haystack on his backside, landing in an unregal heap at Daniel's feet.

Daniel held up a wreath he'd woven from the hay. "If you're a king, I s'pose you'll be wanting a crown, then." He dropped the circlet on Ethan's head, where it settled over one eye.

Ethan shoved the prickly crown back from his forehead and stuck out his tongue.

"Lucky we got that lot of hay in today," Daniel said. He stretched, no doubt aching from a week's worth of mowing, raking, pitching, and stacking. "Them clouds're piling on something fierce."

The sky had been a perfect silken blue when they'd begun bringing in the hay that morning. Now flat-bottomed clouds piled up and rolled over each other like tufts of wool falling from the shearer's blades. Silas had been lucky to have most of the week fair and dry for his haying. The backbreaking work had seemed endless, but at last the hay was safely packed in the barn's haymows and in the surrounding haystacks, carefully sloped to shed water and keep the center of each stack dry.

Ethan scrambled to his feet, dusting off the seat of his trousers. "If it rains tomorrow, d'you s'pose Silas might give us a holiday?"

Daniel squinted. "For me, maybe. After I'm done sharpening scythes and mending rakes and such. But s'posing themselves come home from their grand trip tomorrow? I wager Lyman'll be wanting a turn at you in the store then."

Ethan's lower lip drooped. "It's not fair." He hoped it would rain long and hard and bottle Mr. and Mrs. Lyman up in Springfield for another week. Having only Silas and Mr. Bingham to answer to for eight whole days had felt almost like freedom.

"Well, I fancy he'd let you off if you explain to him about you being king and all." With a sharp tug, Daniel yanked the hay crown down over Ethan's face and leaped away.

"You—you—" Ethan spluttered. Pulling the crown off, he lunged after Daniel, trying to swat him with the twisted hay.

Daniel barked a laugh and dodged out of reach. He stretched one leg forward and bowed. "Careful, your dustiness, you're spoiling your crown."

"You—" Ethan grinned as the word came to him. *"Cráin!"*

"A sow, am I, now? Couldn't you at least be making me a boar?"

"Oh." Ethan frowned as he searched his memory for the proper word.

Daniel took advantage of Ethan's distraction to swoop him up and hold him upside down. Whenever he saw an opening between Ethan's flailing arms and legs, Daniel poked the ticklish spots along Ethan's ribs and under his arms.

"Put me down," Ethan tried to shout, but it was difficult to get the words out between his giggles.

"Not 'til you learn your words proper. Now, what am I again?"

"*Muc* . . . No . . . *Collach.*" ("Pig . . . No . . . Boar.")

Daniel stopped tickling but kept a firm grasp on Ethan's legs. "*Is fearr sin é. Agus Nell?*" ("That's better. And Nell?")

"*Bó.*" ("Cow.") Ethan's voice jogged as Daniel bounced him. "Can I get down now?"

"*Cad é Ivy é?*" ("What's Ivy?")

"*Capall.*" ("Horse.")

"*Agus cad atá tusa?*" ("And what are you?")

"*Rí!*" Ethan crowed. ("King!") He hung with his knees against Daniel's shoulder, Daniel's arms around his waist. He poked at Daniel's knee, wondering if there was a ticklish spot at the back of it. "*Is mise an rí!*" Ethan said. ("I'm the king!")

"*Ní tusa.*" ("You are not.") Daniel shook him. A handful of skipping stones fell out of Ethan's pocket and bounced around Daniel's feet. "*Tá tusa bunoscionn.*"

"*Cod 'ta mise?*" ("I'm what?") Ethan squirmed, trying to twist up to see Daniel's face.

"Upside down," Daniel translated.

Ethan couldn't find Daniel's ticklish spot, so he punched the back of Daniel's knee instead. "*Níl níos nío!*" ("Not any-more!") he said, as Daniel's leg buckled and the boys tumbled down into a laughing heap.

Daniel shoved Ethan off him. "*Tá tusa bunoscionn agus trom,*" he said.

"Say that again." Ethan rolled onto his belly.

"*Trom.* It means heavy. I taught you that one last week, didn't I?"

"No. The other one. The upside-down one. It's a funny one."

"Bunoscionn," Daniel repeated. He took a running start and launched himself at the haystack. "Now it's me own turn to be king, eh, lad?" A shower of hay spilled down as Daniel scrambled for the top.

Ethan recognized the word Daniel used when he reached the top. Daniel had always refused to translate it for him, so he knew it was a rude one.

"What?" Ethan called.

"Bloody hell, they're coming back already. Putting Ivy into a lather, too, to beat the storm." Daniel slid back to the ground. "Run and tell Lizzie they're coming. And wash up proper, not like you been doing all week. And have an umbrella ready for 'em, too."

The Lymans' carriage reached the house just as a streak of lightning brightened the yard. The ensuing thunder sounded ragged, like something tearing. Almost immediately, fat raindrops poured down, as if the sky were a great sack that had suddenly burst at the seams.

"Not a second too soon," Mr. Lyman said, tossing the reins to Daniel. Between the rapid pace Mr. Lyman had set and the storm, Ivy looked frazzled. She pawed and snorted anxiously, her eyes rolling until Daniel took her head and shushed her— in English, Ethan noticed.

Ethan had expected Mr. Lyman to be upset by the weather, but both he and his wife were grinning together. He rubbed his hands and laughed. "Well, I haven't raced like that in years. Quite the exciting ride, eh, Mercy?"

Ethan wondered if somebody had replaced Mr. Lyman with a twin. He never called Mrs. Lyman by her first name. Daniel had once speculated that they called each other Mr. and Mrs. even in their bedchamber. He'd never seen either of them look so jolly before.

"Ah, there's a good boy." Mr. Lyman smiled as Ethan held

the umbrella over him. "Thinking ahead, that's what I like to see, hmm?" He patted Ethan on the head as if he were a favorite dog. Putting his arms out, he helped his wife down and the two of them dashed into the house, hand in hand, Ethan trotting alongside with the umbrella.

"A good trip, sir?" Silas asked, greeting them at the front door.

"Excellent, excellent!" Mr. Lyman said. "Cheese and butter are up, cotton's down, and that investment in—"

"Papa! Mama! Did you bring us presents?" The three girls clamored around their parents.

"For pity's sake, let them in the house first," Silas said, shooing the girls down the hallway.

"Presents for everyone," Mr. Lyman said, swooping Ruth into his arms and giving her a kiss.

"Even Lizzie?" Ruth asked. "And Ethan and Paddy?"

"Everyone. And more to come," Mr. Lyman said. "Your mama's new cookstove wouldn't fit in the carriage, so I'm having it sent."

"A stove!" Lizzie exclaimed, her eyes wide.

"A cookstove *and* a heating stove for the parlor," Mr. Lyman said. "Silas, why don't you and the boys bring in the packages from the carriage?"

"What's it mean?" Ethan asked Daniel as soon as he could slip away to join the Irish boy in the barn. Daniel had been walking Ivy up and down the barn's central aisle to cool her off while Silas and Ethan had taken care of the boxes and carriage.

"Good days for a bit," Daniel said. The mare grumbled softly as lightning blazed and thunder shook the barn. *"Éist, a mhuirnín. Fil ach stoirm í,"* Daniel said. ("Hush, sweetheart. It's only a storm.") Even though Ethan knew what some of Daniel's words meant now, and could half say them himself, it didn't take away the magic as Daniel soothed the mare and cooled her down. The magic wasn't in the words after all, Ethan realized. Ethan could say them himself, and they'd have no power. But Daniel could say *fence post* or *doornail* or *ladder* instead of *There, lass, it's all right,* and the mare's nervous feet would grow still and her tail stop switching. "He could'a been easier on the lass, though," Daniel said, rubbing a rag across her sweaty neck.

"What's he so happy for? I thought he'd be cross about the rain."

"Some fellas need drink to brighten their moods. For Lyman, it's profits. He must'a sold high and bought low and made good on his speculations and such. That's all you need to know. If it'd gone the other way, though, you'd not be able to keep shy of his temper even if you was to be as perfect as the entire Holy Family altogether."

"How long does it last?"

Daniel shrugged. "No telling. Best enjoy it while you can, lad. If I was Silas, I'd ask for that new plow and the merino ram he's been wanting, though. Maybe two rams and a cow, then he'll be sure to at least get the plow and the ram."

"And what do we get?"

"A pocket of sweets, maybe. Perhaps a bit of a holiday from being thrashed."

At dinner the next day, Mr. Lyman approved the plow and one ram without debate. On the second ram and the cow, however, Mr. Lyman said, "I don't know. What would you say to a new horse?"

Ethan held his breath. *A new horse.* A horse that he could mind just as Daniel minded Ivy. He could already feel the velvety nose exploring his palm, hear the throaty whicker meant just for him.

"A new horse?" Silas repeated.

"Maybe two. A fellow in West Springfield has a pair of geldings for sale: fine, high-stepping animals. Coal black, and so alike you'd think they were twins. They'd be quite a sight drawing a carriage. Maybe a barouche, eh? So my girls can ride in style." Florella and Zeloda squealed with delight, and Mrs. Lyman beamed. "I've a mind to buy one of them, or maybe even the pair, if I can get his price down."

"And what about the mare?" Silas asked.

Mr. Lyman brushed some crumbs from the tablecloth. "We'd have to sell her, of course. No sense keeping three horses. She's fit enough to bring a good price, don't you think?"

Out of the corner of his eye, Ethan saw the tip of Daniel's knife quiver.

"If it's profit you want, you could keep the mare for breeding and the geldings for driving," Silas suggested.

Mr. Lyman's thumbnail rasped along his chin as he considered the proposition. His eyes flickered the way they did when he was summing up a customer's bill.

Daniel set his knife down next to his soup bowl, pressing the blade's butter-smeared end into the tablecloth. His other hand picked his roll into fragments.

Mr. Lyman finally shook his head. "No, no. I'm better off selling her. I'll make some inquiries. It shouldn't be hard to find someone who'll want her."

"I'll buy her," said Daniel.

Spoons crashed into bowls. Mrs. Lyman's glass of raspberry shrub teetered and nearly spilled.

"What did you say, boy?" Mr. Lyman's voice froze the diners in their seats.

"Sir," Daniel added hastily. "I'll buy her. Sir." His face glowed nearly as red as Mrs. Lyman's raspberry shrub.

Mr. Lyman snorted a laugh. "And with what do you propose to buy her?"

Daniel's swallow was nearly audible. Ethan watched a damp trickle creep down Daniel's temple, along his jaw, and under his collar. "When I leave," Daniel said deliberately, as though trying out words for the first time. "I'm to have me wages when I leave. I'll pay for her out of that. And if it ain't—" He cleared his throat. "If it isn't enough, I'll work for you until it is. Sir."

Mr. Lyman stared down the length of the table with raised eyebrows and creased forehead.

Daniel stared back, his neck and shoulders taut with his struggle not to duck his head and let the shaggy copper forelock shadow his expression. A muscle quivered under his eye.

The storekeeper broke his stare first, turning toward Silas, then toward Mrs. Lyman. He tugged at his ear. One side of his face slanted suddenly upward, an eyebrow lifting even farther, a corner of his mouth tilting up and parting. His hand thumped the table, rattling silverware and crockery.

Although Ethan had expected an explosion, the noise still surprised him. He hadn't thought Mr. Lyman could laugh so hard. Mr. Pease's braying laugh soon joined in, followed by Mr. Wheeler's soft wheezing chuckle. Zeloda snickered. Even Mrs. Lyman contributed a dry breath of a laugh. Silas and Lizzie exchanged a blank stare.

Finally, Mr. Lyman wiped his eyes with his napkin and spoke. "Now, boy, it's not that I don't credit your ambition and foresight, but your indenture runs another five years. It's not just the cost of the mare, but five years of the mare's board you'll have to pay, never mind farriers' bills and Lord knows what else. You'd be more prudent to wait and use your money to rent a place or buy a cow, or some sheep, or some tools. Something useful."

"I don't want a cow. Sir." Daniel's words were soft, but clear.

"Well, then, if you're that set on having a horse when you leave, you'd do well to wait. Then you can have the full value of your wages without losing anything for that mare's board. Get your horse then."

"I don't want a horse. Sir."

Frowning, Mr. Lyman leaned forward. "Now, wait a minute, boy. Isn't that what we've just been discussing?"

"I don't want a horse, sir," Daniel repeated. "I want Ivy."

Ethan hovered in the empty barn, waiting for Daniel to emerge from the house. It seemed he'd been shut up with Mr. Lyman in the study for hours. Finally, Daniel came out. He pulled his cap low over his forehead, so Ethan could see only the grim line of his mouth.

"What'd he say?" The question stuck in Ethan's throat, but he had to ask it.

Daniel padded through the barn. He stopped in front of Ivy's stall, empty now that the mare was out to pasture with the cattle. He stood with his back to Ethan, his hands gripping the top edge of the waist-high partition. "Only that I'm a fool."

"But he'll owe you the money when your time's up. Why can't he just give you Ivy instead?"

Daniel's knuckles whitened. "There'll be no money for me, lad. He showed me the numbers in that black book of his—not that I could make any sense of 'em. He says I'll be lucky if I'm not owing *him* when me time's through."

"But how—?"

"Breakage. Damages. Clothes and such."

"But he's s'posed to give you clothes."

Daniel stretched his arms apart as far as he could. "Lad, ain't you learned by now that 's'posed to' don't come that close to 'is' around here? He's s'posed to give me one set'a clothes a year. What I get is . . ." He plucked at his ragged shirt and looked down at his broadfalls, whose cuffs stopped well above his ankles. "And if I'm not tending 'em proper, that's me own loss, ain't it, now? Though it's the proper dandy I'd be if I had everything he's got writ down in that book of his."

"What're you going to do?"

"Same's always, I s'pose. Wait. Wait and see."

"Have you thought of what to do yet?" Ethan's pitchfork quivered with its sopping load of manure. He heaved the burden to the top of the manure pile. A wave of heat rose from the exposed center of the pile and flapped at his face, matching the heat from the sun that scorched his neck and shoulders.

"Maybe I would if you'd give me some peace to think, instead of asking me twenty times a day if I've thought of anything." With a fierce grunt, Daniel plunged his own fork into the pile as viciously as if he were stabbing a dragon to the heart.

"You're not thinking of stealing her, are you?"

Daniel leaned wearily on his pitchfork. "I been thinking of naught else all week, lad. But then I think of getting caught, and I lose me nerve. It'd be safer if I hunt for her when I leave."

"But that's not for five years!" The fork slipped in Ethan's sweating hands, dumping its load onto Daniel's toes.

"What's the point in me staying all of that now?" Daniel flapped his bare feet free of the dung. "No. I'll go after her soon's she's sold."

"Won't Mr. Lyman stop you? Your indenture—"

"Maybe he'll be glad to be rid of me. Maybe he'd not be thinking me worth the bother. Maybe it'd be different now."

"Different from what?"

"From when I run away before."

"Oh." Ethan stuck his fork into the pile and left it there. He rubbed his palms on the seat of his trousers. "What happened then?"

"What do you think? He thrashed me and Silas half to death, he did."

"He beat Silas, too?" Ethan said, astounded.

"Aye. It was two years or so after I come." Daniel planted his fork in front of him and gathered his fists at the tip of the handle, where he propped his chin. "Silas lied, said he'd sent me on an errand. He thought maybe it'd give me time to get clear. But Lyman found me and dragged me back. After he'd done with me, it was Silas's turn. His own son lying to him over a bit of Irish trash—that was too much for him, I fancy. Silas just took it without a word. And there was a bloody lot of it to take. He was so still afterward, I thought he was dead. Lyman did, too, I fancy. There was such a look on his face, I think he scared himself by what he done. He carried the lad inside and put him to bed. Silas couldn't work for nigh on a week. His da never touched him after that, not that I saw, anyway. But Silas never gave him cause to, neither."

"But you and me, we're just bound out. Silas is his son."

"I forgot. Your da don't believe in thrashings, does he, now?" He lifted his cap and swiped his hair back. Sweat had turned his hair into rusty damp spikes that stuck to his forehead and temples. It stood up in greasy ridges before his cap flattened and hid it. "You never knew any lads that got thrashed by their own das?"

"I—I guess." Ethan thought of some of the boys at school, who talked of switchings and strappings as casually as they spoke of chores and meals. But the ones who came to school with blackened eyes and swollen jaws, or who walked as if the mere touch of their clothes hurt them, those were the ones who said nothing at all.

"Lyman thrashed him same's he did me. Worse, sometimes. Maybe himself expected better from his own son, so it made him that much angrier when Silas done wrong. It's a wonder Silas didn't get all the sense knocked out of him. Not that he had much of it, when it come to being hit."

"What d'you mean?"

"I learned pretty quick to bite me lip so's I'd bleed a bit, then fall down and moan some, so it'd satisfy himself and he'd leave me be. All the things I taught you," Daniel said. "But Silas'd stand there like a post and take it until he couldn't stand no more. Never made a sound, never put up his hands nor made a move to spare himself. I never could figure out what he was at. Trying to show his da he wasn't afraid, maybe. Or maybe he was just hoping he'd get killed and that would be the end of it for good and all. I don't know."

Ethan shuddered. "It's—it's crazy." Not just Mr. Lyman's rages, but Daniel's and Silas's acceptance of them.

"It's discipline," Daniel said. His palm slid down the fork's handle, popping it loose from the earth with a little downward slap and catching it neatly as it bounced back up again, spattering a spray of dirt and manure around the boys' ankles. "So Lyman says, and ain't nobody who'll deny him."

"But Silas—"

Daniel looked over Ethan's shoulder. "Hush, lad. It's Silas himself coming up behind you now. No doubt wondering why we ain't gone to fetch up the cows yet." Daniel bent back to cut thick clods of manure from the base of the pile and toss them up to the hollow in the middle, where they'd pulled the mound open.

"Paddy?" Silas called.

"Give us a minute, Silas," Daniel said. "We're near done turning the dung heap. Then we'll go for the cows."

"No, that's fine. It's early yet. That's not what I wanted."

Silas kicked a clod of manure back into the pile. "Keep Ivy in tomorrow morning and clean her up well. Mr. Ward's coming for dinner, and he wants to have a look at her."

Ethan and Daniel exchanged wary glances. "Mr. Ward?" Daniel said.

"He's thinking of buying her for his boys to ride. Might do them some good. That older one especially could use some responsibility to take the mischief out of him."

"The older one," Daniel repeated numbly.

"She'll only be down the road," Silas said. He seemed more interested in examining the dung at his feet than in meeting Daniel's eyes. "Maybe Mr. Ward will let you visit her."

That evening, after the boys went upstairs to bed, Daniel thrashed about on the mattress, kicking at the sheets, punching the bolster, unable to settle down. It wasn't long before he pulled his trousers on and crept downstairs and out into the moonless night. Ethan peered through one of the tiny side windows that overlooked the barnyard. A shape a little less dark than the night stole from the house and slipped into the barn. Ethan shivered, wondering what would become of Daniel once the chain that bound him to the Lymans was broken.

Chapter Twenty-Three

Daniel thrust his arm under Ethan's nose. "What d'you think of that?" he asked, almost proudly.

Ethan started back in disgust, then forced himself to examine the swollen welt that arched across Daniel's forearm in a rainbow of painful color. Daniel rotated his arm, revealing a matching arc of bruise on the other side.

"Who bit you?" Ethan asked. But there was only one animal whose mouth was that shape and size. "Ivy! Ivy bit you?" His scalp tingled with horror.

Daniel was almost grinning. "Don't be daft. She's a lamb; you know that. But you really think it looks that way?"

"Oh, yes." Ethan breathed a little easier. He reached out a hesitant finger to touch the mark. It was puffy and slightly hot. Daniel sucked in his breath and flinched away. "It's real!" Ethan said.

"Of course it's real, you dolt! I couldn't hardly paint a false one on, now, could I? If himself found that out, he'd be giving me plenty of real ones for sure. Now d'you think it looks a proper bite or not?"

Ethan nodded. "But how will that help keep Ivy?" His eyes met Daniel's, gray-green and solemn and unblinking.

"You'll see soon enough. You still got that sling of yours?"

Ethan nodded. "Why?"

"I need you to be doing me a wee bit of a favor."

"What sort of favor?"

"Well, could you maybe arrange to be having a bit of a bellyache this afternoon? So no one'll be wondering why you're not about."

The sun beat down on Ethan as he lay on the chicken shed roof, watching the men come out of the house. Mr. Lyman and Mr. Ward talked merrily, laughing and puffing on their cigars. Silas and Joshua and Daniel stood a little apart from the men and from each other, their posture wary.

Daniel disappeared into the barn, returning with Ivy on her lead. The mare seemed to read Daniel's mood. Her ears twitched, and she moved with nervous, mincing steps. Daniel walked her around so that the men had to turn their backs to the chicken shed to examine her.

Ethan picked up a pebble and readied his sling.

Mr. Ward spoke first. "What's the matter with your arm, boy?"

"Nothing, I'm sure," Mr. Lyman said. "He's a clumsy boy, always getting into mischief. Walk her around there, Paddy."

Daniel tugged his cap brim and nodded. Ethan wound up his sling and whispered an apology. The pebble flew true. Ivy thrashed her tail. She pulled away from Daniel and tossed her head. A second stone had her kicking and snapping and looking around for her tormenter.

"Doesn't look very calm to me," Joshua said.

"Oh, no. She has quite a mellow temperament," Mr. Lyman reassured him. "Bring her here, Paddy."

Ivy snapped and stomped as the men checked her teeth and feet.

"What have you done to this horse, boy?" Mr. Lyman asked Daniel.

"She's only restless 'cause she ain't been out today. And maybe her season's coming on a bit soon. She'll be fine with a bit of a romp." He thrust the lead rope under Joshua's nose. "Hold her. I'll fetch her tack so you can take her for a run and see how nice she goes."

Ethan selected a sharp black stone. The pebble struck the mare just as Joshua stared down at the bruise on Daniel's arm. Ivy pawed the ground and clicked her teeth.

"She bites!" Joshua took a quick step backward. "Look at his arm!"

Ethan held his breath as Mr. Lyman ordered Daniel to hold out his arm. "Have you been provoking that horse?" he demanded. Daniel winced when Mr. Lyman pressed down on the bruise.

"No, sir. I must'a got hooked by one of them cows. Ivy never done it, I swear. Ain't you been driving her six years and never a bit of temper from her?"

"He's lying," Joshua said. "That horse is vicious. That's why they're getting rid of her."

Silas's voice rumbled so low that Ethan had to strain to hear him. "Careful what you say, Joshua. It's not only Paddy you're accusing."

Mr. Ward raised his hands in a conciliatory gesture. "Nobody's accusing anybody of anything."

"I should hope not." Mr. Lyman crossed his arms. "Haven't I always dealt fairly with you, Robert?"

Mr. Ward nodded. "I can't deny that. But this horse, George. This horse . . ." He reached for the lead rope. Ivy tossed her head and backed away. Mr. Ward made soothing noises in his throat until Ivy settled. When he tried to lead her around the yard, she balked, then followed with uneasy, choppy steps.

"She's never given you any trouble, George?" Mr. Ward said as he handed Ivy back to Daniel.

"She's always behaved for me."

"Hmmm, yes. For *you*." Mr. Ward took a long puff on his cigar, letting the smoke out in a leisurely *O* that floated over his head for a long time in the still summer air before it broke apart. "I'm not much of a horseman, but I suppose horses are like people in some ways. Some take well to change; some don't. Maybe you've got yourself one of those that don't."

"She's just showing a bit of spirit. Give her a little time—"

Mr. Ward rested a hand on Mr. Lyman's shoulder. "I'm sure Joshua could break her in fine. But I can't have the younger boys fooling with an unreliable horse. I'd have their mother to answer to if anything happened. And you know my Abby. No, George, I'm sorry. She's a fine horse, but she's a little too lively for the young ones. No hard feelings, now."

Mr. Ward shook hands with Mr. Lyman and Silas, then headed home with Joshua in tow. Ethan held his breath as the Wards disappeared around the corner of the house. His body trembled from the strain of keeping himself pressed flat against the roof.

Mr. Lyman flung his cigar in the dirt and trod on it. He spun on Daniel, gripping his bruised forearm hard. Ivy snorted and took a little hopping step away. "What are you playing at, boy?" Mr. Lyman said. "What have you done to this horse?"

"Nothing, sir. And she done nothing to me, I swear."

"That's a rather convenient bruise."

Daniel's shoulders bunched up as Mr. Lyman's fingers dug deeper into his arm. "It's just a bruise, is all, sir. Could'a been anything done it. Didn't I get thrashed just the other day for letting the sheep get into the flower garden?"

"And the mare? What's gotten into her?"

"Could be her season, like I said before. Or maybe she don't fancy Joshua. Can't say I blame her."

Mr. Lyman's free hand twitched as if he were about to strike Daniel.

"It's no secret there's bad feelings between Paddy and that Ward boy," Silas said. "The mare must have sensed it, and it made her nervous. I should have led her out myself."

Mr. Lyman's head tilted toward Silas. "Yes. Yes, you should have." He threw his hands up in disgust, shoving Daniel aside. "Aren't you a fine pair of dunderheads? I expected better of you, Silas, but I see that's too much to ask." Acid dripped from his voice. "I suppose I'm the only one who knows how to think around here."

"Yes, sir," Silas said. From the tilt of his hat, Ethan guessed that Silas was avoiding his father's glare.

"As for you—" Mr. Lyman turned abruptly to Daniel. The boy seemed to shrink without moving. The mare flattened her ears against her head and sidled behind him. "The next time someone looks at this horse, you make yourself scarce, understand?"

"Yessir."

"And keep your—your 'bad feelings'"—Mr. Lyman sneered around the words—"to yourself." He spun away and stalked back into the house.

Ethan waited until Mr. Lyman and Silas were gone before he stuffed his sling in his pocket and crept back into the house. Lizzie was alone in the kitchen, finishing the washing up. He waited until she headed downstairs to put some of the leftovers away. He slipped inside and pretended to be coming down the back stairs when she returned from the cellar.

She didn't seem surprised to see him. "Feeling better?" She brushed his hair back from his forehead, checking for fever.

He avoided her eyes. "I—um—yes." It wasn't entirely a lie.

"You were watching them, weren't you?" Lizzie said. "So was I." She tipped Ethan's chin up to look into his eyes. "He'll sell her eventually, you know."

"But not to Joshua Ward."

She gave him a little smile and released him. "No, not to Joshua Ward." She took a piece of bread and slathered butter and jam on it. "I suppose your stomachache's gone now."

Ethan shook his head. His stomach was still fluttering too much to put anything in it.

"Well, maybe Daniel's hungry," she said. Ethan's head jerked up at the forbidden name. Lizzie folded the bread around the jam and prepared another piece as serenely as if she'd said nothing unusual. She wrapped the jam sandwiches and four slices of cake in a cloth and held it out to him.

"You boys take a lot of chances," she said, her voice soft but firm. She slipped the bundle into his hand, then grabbed his wrist and pulled him close. Something brushed his hip. He looked down and saw his sling dangling from her free hand. "Maybe I should keep this for a bit," she said. The sling disappeared into her pocket. "No one will think of looking for it there, will they?" Her face glowed with smiles and secrets.

"You—you mean you won't tell?"

Lizzie's eyebrows arched innocently. "Tell what?"

Ethan ran to join Daniel and Ivy. Everything would be all right now. Joshua wouldn't have Ivy. And maybe it would be too late for Mr. Lyman to buy the black horses.

He wished he had brought some carrots to show Ivy he was sorry about the pebbles. Or maybe to show Daniel. He tossed and caught the little bundle of bread and cake that Lizzie had given him. Maybe Ivy would like some of that just as well as a carrot. Maybe she'd like it even better. Maybe Daniel would let him give it to the mare himself, and maybe it would make Ivy like him a little better.

He found Daniel and Ivy standing at the upper pasture gate, oblivious to the cows and sheep grazing around them.

Daniel's arms were wrapped around her neck, his face buried in her mane. The mare's ears tipped forward, quivering to catch his words. She looked easy now, her feet quiet in the long grass, her tail bobbing gently in the breeze, her eyes soft and calm. She rubbed her chin along Daniel's ribs and whispered back to him. It was only when Ethan got right up to the gate that he could hear Daniel murmuring, over and over, *"Tá brón orm. Tá an-bhrón orm."* ("I'm sorry. I'm so sorry.")

Chapter Twenty-Four

"Excellent! Excellent!" Mr. Lyman practically chortled. His fingers slid along his lapel as he grinned down at the pieces of paper in his other hand.

"Good news, sir?" Mr. Bingham asked from the other side of the store, where he and Ethan had been reading the newest letter from Mr. Bingham's brother in Ohio.

"Indeed. Two pieces of good news in one day's mail." He held up two letters. "Mr. Jordan in West Springfield has agreed to a price for his geldings, and Mr. Smead's cousin in Bland-ford expresses an interest in buying the mare."

"N-no one in town wants her?" Ethan said.

"Not since that blasted son of Ward's started telling tales about her temper." Mr. Lyman laid the letters on the counter and took out a pencil. "None of it true, of course." He nodded at Mr. Bingham.

"Of course, sir," Mr. Bingham said.

Mr. Lyman tapped the pencil on one of the letters. "Jordan says here he knows of a carriage for sale at a good price. Not new, but in good repair, and newly painted. For that, plus the horses . . . I'll sell the old wagon and chaise, too, but later . . . yes, it will do. It will do quite nicely." He muttered to himself and scribbled numbers on the back of one page as he figured his costs. "Now, if I send Silas to Blandford overnight, perhaps, or a day or two . . . Shouldn't take the first offer, I don't think. . . . Maybe he can get a better price than Smead's cousin will pay. . . . Twenty miles to West Springfield . . . hmmm . . ." He straightened and tapped his pencil on the counter. "Well, Lucius, I shouldn't wonder if we have horses and carriage within, say, two weeks at the most."

"Two weeks?" Mr. Bingham repeated. "Ah. Quite nice . . . quite nice indeed."

Ethan's heart plummeted. Two weeks, maybe less. He took a deep breath, gathering all his courage. He had to at least try to do something while Mr. Lyman was in a good mood. "S-sir?" he said tentatively, barely able to hear his own voice over the pulse pounding in his ears. "Couldn't you, um . . . maybe wait a little bit? Silas wants to get the rye cut soon, and there's ever so much work to be done before the end of summer."

"Wait?" Mr. Lyman frowned thoughtfully as he considered what Ethan had said, then his eyes grew warm and his lips curled upward. "Well, boy, Silas is making a decent farmer of you, isn't he? I could go myself, I suppose, but no, there's too much for me to do here, with the new goods due to arrive any day now. It'll have to be Silas. Mr. Pease can be in charge while he's gone." He laughed and snapped his fingers. "Perhaps I'll hire that boy of Ward's for a few days. I could discount his wages for the trouble he's put me to."

Ethan suppressed a shudder. How could things get any worse? Silas gone away to sell Ivy, leaving Ethan and Daniel with both Mr. Pease and Joshua Ward to contend with. Ethan swallowed the lump in his throat. If asking for a delay took all of his courage, asking for a reprieve surely would need a miracle. *Please,* he prayed. *Please help us.* . . . "D-d-d-do you really have to sell Ivy?" he asked. "She's such a good horse. C-couldn't you maybe think about changing your mind and keeping her?"

"There'll be two horses in her place. You and Paddy will

each have a horse to mind. What do you think of that?" Mr. Lyman hooked a thumb in his vest pocket, looking as kindly as Ethan had ever seen him.

"Da-Da-Da-Pa-Paddy—" Ethan stumbled over the hated name. "Paddy will miss Ivy something terrible."

"Tish—he hasn't seen these other horses." Mr. Lyman dismissed Daniel's feelings with a wave of his hand. "Once he sees them, he'll forget all about Ivy, and so will you. She's a nag compared to them."

Ethan couldn't help thinking about the bit from the Shakespeare book the peddler had given Daniel, the part Daniel read over and over to himself until he had it memorized: *She is pure air and fire. She is indeed a horse; and all other jades you may call beasts.*

"Anyway," Mr. Lyman continued, "it's not his place to say what I can and cannot sell, is it?"

"N-no, sir. But he—he loves her."

"She's a *horse*, boy," Mr. Lyman said with a laugh. "An animal. A tool. Would he love a shovel?" His mouth was still turned up in a half-smile, but his fingers drummed on the counter.

"Now . . . now, sir," said Mr. Bingham. "There's more to an animal than that . . . more than that, to those who're fond of 'em. My mother dotes . . . positively dotes . . . positively, on her cat."

Emboldened by Mr. Bingham's words, Ethan pressed on. "It'll break his heart if she goes. He loves her like—like you love your family. If one of them was gone—" Even before Mr. Bingham grabbed his shoulder and hissed him into silence, Ethan saw his mistake. Mr. Lyman's face went gray, and his hands clenched into fists around the letters, his knuckles as white as the paper, the light in his eyes smothered into bleakness.

"You know nothing, boy." Mr. Lyman's finger shook as he

pointed it at Ethan. Ethan stepped back against Mr. Bingham, certain that it was only the clerk's presence that kept his master's hand from turning into a fist. "You know nothing of heartbreak," Mr. Lyman said, his voice taut as a stretched wire. Then he stalked into the back room, slamming the door behind him.

"Two weeks." Daniel hacked viciously at the rye with his reaping hook. "Maybe less."

Ethan nodded. "Silas is going to Blandford tomorrow, or maybe the day after." The coarse stalks of grain prickled at his arms as he gathered them and bound them with a twist of straw.

"So that's why Silas was mad after making a start on the rye today," Daniel said. "He won't be liking having to trust the harvest to anyone else."

Ethan decided not to mention that Mr. Lyman wanted Silas to trust the harvest to Mr. Pease. Daniel felt bad enough already. Ethan looked around and saw that Mr. Pease and Mr. Wheeler were out of earshot on the opposite side of the field. "Daniel, I think . . . I think maybe there *is* a way for you to buy Ivy."

"Oh, aye? You been stealing bank notes down at the store, have you?"

"No, no. Remember how you told me Mr. Lyman showed you that black book of his—the one he carries back and forth to the store? Remember how you said he had all sorts of things written down there that weren't true? Clothes he said you got and things you broke and such?" The rye stubble pricked Ethan's bare feet as he tried to keep pace, binding the rye into sheaves after Daniel cut it.

"Aye. And he has the nerve to call *me* out for a liar." Daniel's work grew more ragged as he talked. He no longer paid attention to cutting the stalks evenly or keeping the grain from shattering as he worked. He waved the reaping hook carelessly, making Ethan fear that he'd cut off a finger along with the rye.

"I've been thinking," Ethan said. "If you could prove that Mr. Lyman's book is wrong, maybe—maybe you really would be able to buy her."

"And how would I be proving Lyman wrong?" Daniel straightened, his face red and dripping with sweat.

"Silas would remember, wouldn't he, if you got all the clothes Mr. Lyman says you did, and if you did all the damage he said you did?"

"Maybe . . . maybe some." Daniel pulled a handkerchief from his pocket and scrubbed it across his face.

"If we could get Mr. Lyman's book and show it to Silas . . ."

Daniel shook his head. "He wouldn't cross his da."

"He's not like Mr. Lyman. You said yourself Silas is fair and honest. I think he'll want to help. Remember—remember how you said he lied for you that time you ran away?"

"That was a long time ago, lad. I fancy he remembers the thrashing more than the helping." Daniel jammed the hand-kerchief back in his pocket and tested the edge of his reaping hook with his thumb.

"He's too big for Mr. Lyman to thrash now." The sweat running down Ethan's back felt like ice water at Daniel's talk of thrashing. But for Daniel to lose Ivy would be worse than any beating—maybe even worse than death.

"You don't go calling a man's da a thief and expect to get help from him."

"You don't have to call him a thief. Maybe just ask Silas if Mr. Lyman maybe . . . maybe made a mistake."

"A mistake."

"Then you can show him the book and let him figure it out for himself. Or if not Silas, what about Lizzie? She knows what clothes you really have. She's the one that makes 'em and washes 'em and mends 'em. I think there's something queer about that book, and not just what Mr. Lyman's written down about you. Nobody ever gets to look inside it but him—not even Mr. Bingham—and he writes in it most when—well, when certain people come in the store."

"Certain people?"

"People he cheats . . . I mean, I think he cheats. Measures their cloth short, puts his thumb on the scale. Not everybody. Mostly folks who aren't—well, who don't pay attention or who get confused real easy." Ethan fidgeted, thinking about his own father. If they looked in the black book, what would there be about Pa in it? "I think—I think maybe he cheats with his fig-uring, too. If we could show that book to somebody—maybe get Mr. Bingham to compare it to the ledgers in the store . . ." He'd been mulling the idea over all day, and it still terrified him. But what else was there to do?

"And how are we supposed to be getting our hands on this book?"

"He keeps it locked in his desk. We could go in there at night and—"

"Oh, aye, and break his desk open? Themselves'd sleep through that, sure enough. Anyway, what'll himself say in the morning when he sees his book missing?" Daniel stooped to begin cutting the rye again.

"Do you want to buy Ivy or not?" Ethan said, growing hot with the same anger he'd felt when Daniel had lost the race with Mr. Stocking. He kicked impatiently at a sheaf of grain. He'd tied it badly, and it fell open in a dry golden tumble.

"Aye, but she won't be doing me much good if I'm in prison, will she, now? We got to be sure we got time to show it to Silas or somebody we can be trusting before Lyman raises the alarm." Daniel rubbed his chin. "He'd notice the whole

245

book gone missing, but maybe . . . maybe we could just cut out some of the pages—near the beginning, where he wouldn't notice." He snapped his fingers. "Aye, that'd do it. You don't s'pose you could find a way to be getting at the key, do you?"

Ethan shook his head. "He never leaves his keys where anyone else can get 'em. But maybe we could use a little piece of metal to get it open. There's plenty of broken tools and things in the attic."

Daniel bent back to his work, his strokes steady and even again. "For an honest lad," he said, "you surely do a grand job of thinking like a thief."

Ethan heard the scratch of a lucifer and smelled sulfur, then watched the flame flare in Daniel's hand. He opened the lantern's little door so Daniel could light the candle inside it, though there didn't seem much need for the extra light. The full moon washed the room with an eerie pale blueness, so that Ethan felt as if they moved about inside a dream. "What if we get caught?" he whispered. Even though it had been his idea, his plan, he trembled like a cornered mouse.

"Fine time to be thinking of that." Daniel set the lantern on the floor next to the secretary. He pulled a bent fork from his pocket and maneuvered one of its twisted prongs around in the keyhole.

"Won't matter if we can't open—Here now, I think I've got it." The lock made a little snick, and Daniel pulled down the leaf that served as both door and desktop to Mr. Lyman's secretary. "Let's have that light here." He traded Ethan the fork for the lantern and set the light on the desktop. "We might have to put it out fast," he said, opening the lantern's door.

Ethan pocketed the fork and peered into the secretary at the six black ledgers lined up in a row against its back wall. He reached for one of them.

"Wait." Daniel opened the window next to the desk and propped it with a stick. "You stand there." He indicated the spot in front of the window. "Anyone comes, it's out the window with you, and me right behind. If I can, I'll shut things up, so he can't tell we been here."

"And then?"

"If they ain't seen us, we'll sneak back upstairs and pretend we know naught."

"And if they know it was us?"

"Then we pray, lad."

Ethan swallowed hard. He took his place by the open window. A languid breeze tried feebly to relieve the stickiness of the summer night. The chirps of crickets and frogs and the thrumming of cicadas that normally comforted him to sleep now sounded ominous.

"One for each year," Daniel said, glancing quickly at the first few pages of each book, then putting them in a stack in front of him. "Here, you take the oldest one and I'll take the newest." Daniel handed one of the ledgers to Ethan.

Ethan flipped through the book first, feeling daunted by the pages and pages of words and figures. He prayed that Mr. Bingham's lessons had taught him enough to help Daniel. A piece of paper slipped from between the pages to the floor. It had been folded by halves again and again until it was only a few inches square, like the notes that girls passed to each other in the schoolhouse. Carefully, he opened it. The paper was splitting along the folds and some of the ink had run, but the date was still clear: December 22, 1834. At the bottom was a signature in handwriting that was little more than a scrawl: *Matthew Linnehan.* His hands stopped shaking as he got caught up in the excitement of his find.

"Daniel, here's something about your—" He couldn't get all the words out before Daniel had clapped one hand over

Ethan's mouth and pinched out the candle with the other. Ethan's heart was pounding so hard that he had to strain to hear anything else.

They waited for an eternal second before Ethan heard it, too: the squeak of floorboards as somebody—Mr. Lyman, no doubt—lingered at the top of the stairs, perhaps trying to decide whether he'd really heard something or only imagined it, whether it was worth the bother of coming down. Then the decision was made, and footsteps began to descend.

"Out with you, lad!" Daniel whispered. He grabbed Ethan by the collar and the seat of his trousers and shoved him bodily out the window.

Ethan gritted his teeth so he wouldn't cry out when he landed. The stick propping the window open tumbled to the ground along with him and the sash slammed shut.

Chapter Twenty-Five

Ethan looked up to see Daniel's face in the window, contorted with an expression Ethan had never seen before. Resignation, cynicism, apathy—Ethan knew those expressions. But he'd never seen stark fear cross Daniel's face, not even with the worst of Mr. Lyman's thrashings. Daniel's mouth silently formed the word *Run!* as his hands scrabbled at the muntins, lifting the sash a few inches. Then he was jerked away from the window and disappeared into a darkness filled with growled curses and thumps.

Ethan rolled to his feet and ran. He trembled in the doorway of the back ell, unsure whether to run away or to hide in the attic as Daniel had told him. Stay, he decided. If he ran, they were both lost.

He slipped into the house and crept up the back stairway, crouching at the second-floor landing to see if there was anyone in the hall who might spot him. A group of ghostly figures clustered at the top of the stairs, white nightgowns almost glowing in the moonlight. Mrs. Lyman had her back to him, her arms wrapped around her daughters.

"George! Are you all right?" she called, her voice strained with worry.

"Mama! Papa!" the girls whimpered. "What's happening?" The baby wailed from his crib in the Lymans' bedroom, drowning out most of the noise from downstairs as well as Ethan's cautious journey up the stairs.

Once inside the attic, Ethan took a breath and unclenched his hands. He still held the mysterious paper that Daniel's father had signed. Pulling out his pocketknife, he ran to the bed, where he slit open a seam in the mattress and stuffed the paper deep into the straw and corn husks. He gulped at the humid night air, but his lungs refused to fill. It felt as though a giant fist squeezed his chest as he tried to figure out what to do next.

Pretend you know naught, Daniel had said. Ethan tried to imagine how he would do that. He closed his eyes and thought, but it was hard with the chatter of the girls below, the baby's shrieks, and the muffled thumping noises coming from the first floor. Was Mr. Lyman killing Daniel even now? It would be easy, wouldn't it? He could kill him and tell everyone Daniel had run away, and who would be the wiser? No. No, Ethan couldn't think about that just now. He had to think what to do.

He decided to pretend the noise had woken him up and that he'd come downstairs to find out what had happened. He scrubbed his hands frantically through his hair, shrugged one strap of his braces from his shoulder and pulled his shirttails out. Then he made his way back down to the second floor.

Mrs. Lyman was gone, leaving Florella and Zeloda teary-eyed in the hallway and Ruth huddled in a corner, sucking her thumb and clutching her rag baby. The noise from downstairs had subsided, though Aaron still wailed unattended.

Ethan stepped out timidly, rubbing his eyes and pretending to stifle a yawn. "What—what's happening? What's all the noise?"

"It's a burglar," Zeloda cried. "A burglar and he's killing Papa and Mama and he's coming upstairs to kill us all, too."

Florella rubbed Zeloda's back. "Hush. It'll be all right. Didn't Papa just say it was all right? Didn't he just call Mama downstairs?"

Ruth ran to Ethan's side and took his hand, her fingers moist and sticky with spittle. "Ethan and Paddy will help us, won't you?" She looked around the hallway. "Where's Paddy?"

"I—I don't know," Ethan lied. "Gone to the privy? He said—said he was going."

Zeloda snuffled. "He *would* disappear at a time like this. He just would."

"I wish Silas was here," Ruth said. She squeezed Ethan's hand hard.

Aaron's shrieks grew louder and more desperate. "Hadn't you ought to take care of the baby?" Ethan suggested.

"The baby!" Florella said. "Oh, dear!" She grabbed Zeloda's hand and dashed with her into their parents' bedroom.

"Is it burglars, Ethan?" Ruth asked, clutching her doll tighter.

"I don't know." Ethan went to the stairway and sat on the top step. Suppressing a shudder at the thought of how the banisters looked like prison bars, he peered between them, trying to see downstairs. There was no sign of light from the doorway of Mr. Lyman's study.

Ruth plunked herself down next to Ethan and nestled against him. "I'm scared," she said.

"Me too," Ethan replied, then realized he was supposed to be reassuring her. "But they—he—the burglar won't come up here." Of that, at least, he had no doubt.

Finally, the baby's crying subsided enough that Ethan could hear what was going on downstairs. A door slammed and a bolt rammed home. The noise sounded as though it came from the kitchen. He could hear somebody walking about there.

"It's all right, Mercy," Mr. Lyman was saying. "He's locked up good and tight now. A padlock and two good solid bolts between him and us, and a length of stout rope holding him fast."

"What's to be done with him?" Mrs. Lyman asked, her voice cracking anxiously.

"In the morning we'll take him to the constable, once Rufus and Phinney get here. Or have the constable come fetch him."

Ethan wasn't sure whether to be worried or relieved. Daniel was alive, at least, if Mr. Lyman had to talk about tying him up. If he was locked in the cellar, it shouldn't be too hard to creep downstairs and let him out, should it? He reached into his pocket for the broken fork Daniel had used to pick the lock on Mr. Lyman's desk. He wondered if it would work on a padlock as well.

An orange glow filled the hallway as the Lymans came out of the kitchen. Mr. Lyman took his wife's arm and escorted her up the stairs. "There," he said, his voice gentle though shaken. "We're all safe now. I'll go back in a bit and teach that wretch a lesson he'll not soon forget. Then—" His eyes narrowed as he saw Ethan sitting on the top step with Ruth. "Stay right there, boy!" he ordered, when Ethan stood up. "What do you know about all of this?"

"N-nothing, sir. I just came down to see what all the noise was."

"Oh, you're involved in this somehow."

"In what, sir? What's happened? The girls said there was a burglar. Did you catch him?" Ethan widened his eyes. At least he didn't need to pretend to be scared.

Mr. Lyman grabbed Ethan under the chin and forced him to look up at him. "Don't pretend you don't know who was down there." He squeezed so hard that Ethan could neither shake his head nor utter more than a squeak. "Where were you while all this was going on?" Mr. Lyman shifted his grip from Ethan's jaw to his hair. He shook him hard. "Well?"

"Up-up-upstairs in bed."

"None of your lies, boy! You were down there, too, weren't you? Just now sneaking up the back stairs, I'll wager." He shoved Ethan hard against the wall and pinned him there.

Ethan squeezed his eyes closed tight and covered his face with his hands. "No! I don't know what you're talking about! I swear!"

"He's not lying, Papa," Ruth said. Ethan opened one eye to see her tugging on the sleeve of Mr. Lyman's dressing gown. "I saw him come down when he heard all the noise. Please, Papa, don't be cross with Ethan. He didn't do anything. He was right here all the time."

"I d-d-don't even know wha-what's happened," Ethan said, his voice barely a whimper.

"Paddy tried to rob us." The lines around Mr. Lyman's mouth and across his forehead hardened. "You can't pretend you didn't notice he was missing, boy."

"Paddy?" Ethan hoped he sounded surprised. "I th-thought—He said he was g-going to the privy."

"That's right," Ruth chimed in. "It can't be Paddy either. He's gone to the privy. That's what Ethan said. Please, Papa, don't punish Ethan. It's not his fault."

Mr. Lyman pressed his lips together and collected himself. Loosening his grip on Ethan, he stooped and caressed Ruth's hair with his free hand. "All right, sweetheart. Go to bed now. It's late. Everything's fine now." His voice turned from steel to silk.

Ethan felt trapped inside a nightmare. It seemed as if Mr. Lyman were two completely different people at once: the one who had Ethan cornered and trembling, and the one who bent to accept Ruth's good-night kiss and give her one in return. Ethan almost expected to see the two Mr. Lymans split apart and the kindly father go with Mrs. Lyman to tuck Ruth in while the second Mr. Lyman stayed to torment Ethan.

"All right, boy," Mr. Lyman said, after his family had disappeared behind their bedchamber doors. With one hand, he captured Ethan's wrists and jerked them down so he couldn't hide his face. "The truth now." His voice was low, and even more menacing for that.

"I d-don't know. Paddy—he's not—he can't be a thief."

"I caught him in the act, boy. Rifling through my desk." His grip tightened, and he forced Ethan to his knees.

Tears welled in Ethan's eyes at the shock of his landing. Pain lanced from his knees all the way to the base of his skull, and it felt as though his wrists were being crushed to jelly in Mr. Lyman's palm. "C-c-c-aught him?" Ethan stammered, hoping his terror sounded like surprise, like innocence. "What—what—where is he now?"

"Locked up in the cellar. Don't tell me he didn't take you into his confidence." Mr. Lyman shook Ethan like a dog shaking a rat.

Ethan's head thumped hard against the wall. He choked on tears and phlegm, wanted to collapse to the floor and just sob with fear and pain. He thought then that he would just tell everything, if it would make Mr. Lyman leave him alone. But telling would only make things worse. How could Daniel always be so brave, he wondered. He swallowed back the glob of mucus in his throat, grasping for the right lies to tell. "I-I-I-didn't know. I didn't think he'd really turn out to be a thief. I hoped he wasn't so bad as everyone made out. I-I-I-I guess I was wrong." Ethan let himself go limp and drooped his head. "I guess you were right about him all along."

Mr. Lyman narrowed his eyes. "If you're lying to me, boy . . . Well, never mind for now. Upstairs with you, and I'll deal with you when I'm finished with the other one. Then we'll see how much you know and how much you're pretending not to know." He hauled Ethan to his feet and dragged him toward the attic stairs. He shoved him upstairs then slammed the door behind him and shot the bolt home.

Ethan lay on the stairway for a long time, letting loose the racking sobs he'd held back. Finally, head aching and throat raw, he dragged himself up the stairs. He thrust his shaking hands into the pitcher, dashed the lukewarm water on his face, rubbed it over wrists that felt rope-burned from Mr. Lyman's grip.

Fat and bronze, the moon's round face filled the eastern fan window, spilling silver-blue light across the attic. The moon's shadowy craters seemed to curve into a mocking sneer. Ethan turned his back on it and limped to the western window, where Daniel so often looked out over the spot that had once been his home. The stars were wan and feeble, overpowered by the moonlight. He clutched the sill, his nails digging into the wood. He wanted to ball his hands into fists and slam them through the window. Instead, his fingers brushed against Daniel's tiny horse. He rubbed the toy's wooden neck and sides, wishing it could be magic, that it could tell him the right thing to do, or that it could spring to life, grow to full size, sprout wings, and carry him and Daniel far, far away, beyond the mountains, or even to the moon.

Clutching the horse in one hand, Ethan flopped down on the bed and reached into the mattress, where he'd hidden the paper. The coarse straw and husks scratched his fingers as he groped for the smooth white rectangle. For all its raggedness, it had been important once—he could tell that even in the moonlight. Mr. Lyman had drafted it in his best hand, and the tattered paper had once been heavy and fine.

Ethan took a lucifer from Daniel's little table and lit their last candle stub. He tipped the paper so that the light shone more fully upon it. The document was full of important-sounding words like *whereas, hereby, wherefore,* and *witnessing thereof.* Four months ago, Ethan wouldn't have been able to make any sense of it. But from his lessons with Mr. Bingham, he knew that familiar words like *presents* and *satisfaction* had entirely different meanings from the ones he'd learned in school. He prayed that he'd remember enough of his lessons to sort it out, prayed, too, that it might hold some clue that would help Daniel.

He followed the letters with his finger. *Know all men by these presents . . .*

By the time the moon moved out of the eastern window and stood straight overhead, he'd studied the paper so long that he could see it with his eyes closed. It was just what he needed. The document was dated December 1834, the winter of the fire that destroyed Daniel's family and his home—the home that Daniel's father had mortgaged to Mr. Lyman. The home that Matthew Linnehan had redeemed only days before his death, the final payment and satisfaction of mortgage all documented by the paper Ethan held in his hands. But Mr. Lyman had taken everything anyway, taken Mr. Linnehan's money and his property. And his son. Taken them all and used them as if he had a right to.

He rose and returned to the western window, where the silhouettes of the mountains loomed like sleeping dragons. Surely the paper would be enough to prove who the real thief was. And surely Matthew Linnehan's land was worth the price of a horse. But what good would the paper do when it was locked up in the attic with Ethan, while Daniel was trapped in the cellar, maybe even now being thrashed to death by Mr. Lyman? And when Mr. Lyman came for Ethan, he'd find the paper and destroy it, destroy it and Daniel and Ethan all together.

Chapter Twenty-Six

With the moon hovering above the mountains, poised to sink behind them and yield to the sun, Ethan made his decision. He would have to tell more lies than he'd ever told in his entire life. He would have to tell Mr. Lyman he was sorry for not believing him. He would have to disown Daniel entirely and pretend that he was on Mr. Lyman's side, now that he knew Daniel was really a thief and a liar. It was the only way he'd get free. And then, once he was free, he could run home and tell Pa and Ma everything that had happened. Surely they would help Daniel. He frowned, remembering that people used to call Pa *Simple Gideon*, that Pa had relied on Mr. Lyman to sort out his accounts. Would he know if someone had been cheated? And would anyone believe *Simple Gideon*? But Ma—she'd know. She'd know and she'd figure out a way to help.

He slit the seam of his vest pocket and slipped the document in between the vest front and its lining, working the fabric between his fingers until the paper settled by the side seam, where someone searching his pockets wouldn't notice it. Then he braced himself for the thud of Mr. Lyman's footsteps on the attic stairs, practicing over and over what he would say.

Only Mr. Lyman didn't come. The eastern sky faded from black to gray, and the cattle and sheep grew restless for their breakfast. From the attic window, Ethan watched Mr. Pease and Mr. Wheeler and Joshua Ward and Lizzie come to do their chores. He watched Mr. Lyman talk to them in the yard, telling them all of Daniel's crimes, no doubt. He watched Mr. Lyman walk away after giving the men their instructions. He watched Lizzie go in and out of the barn with her milk buckets, and the Lyman girls go off to school.

As the sun crawled higher in the sky, the August heat filled the attic and stayed like an unwelcome guest. The cicadas hummed a constant vibrato that set his nerves trembling to the same frequency as the sound. The sound stretched and stretched and stretched, then snapped in a moment's silence, then started again.

An hour, maybe more, went by, and a wagon drawn by a piebald horse pulled into the yard. A middle-aged man with the sad eyes and droopy jowls of a hound dog drove. Constable Flagg. Mr. Lyman sat next to him, calling out for Mr. Pease as they drove into the yard. Ethan watched the three men disappear into the house, then return dragging Daniel, bound hand and foot.

If he hadn't known it was Daniel, he wouldn't have recognized him. His face was purple and swollen, striped with tendrils of dried blood. Dark stains splotched his tattered shirt, welts and bruises mottled his forearms. Mr. Lyman talked excitedly to Mr. Flagg and gestured as if recounting a fearsome duel between himself and Daniel. The constable glanced uneasily back and forth from Daniel's battered face to Mr. Lyman's unmarked one. Finally, Mr. Lyman and Mr. Pease tossed Daniel in the back of the constable's wagon like a carcass to be taken to the butcher's. Then all three men got into Mr. Flagg's wagon and drove away.

Ethan's throat clogged and his eyes blurred.

Noontime came and went, and still Mr. Lyman didn't return. Ethan could smell dinner cooking in the kitchen, but Mr. Lyman didn't come home for it, though Mrs. Lyman came out and stared down the road for a long time, as if that would summon him back. He saw the girls come home from school for their noon meal and leave again. He watched Lizzie throw the dinner scraps to the chickens. Then somewhere in all the watching, he fell asleep.

Ethan heard the bolt rattle at the bottom of the stairs. His head snapped up, and he dashed to the farthest corner of the attic, as if that would protect him. The tread on the attic stairs was lighter than Mr. Lyman's. No doubt it was Mrs. Lyman come to see if she could thrash the truth out of him. He set his jaw and tried to work up his courage to endure whatever she meted out. He began to rehearse his story in his head.

But it was Lizzie's voice that came to him from the stairway. "Ethan? It's only me," she said softly.

He sobbed with relief as he dashed over to her. "Lizzie! You have to let me out! Please!"

"Shhhhh," she said. "I brought you some dinner. I made you a plate while Mrs. Lyman had her back turned." She set a cloth-covered dish on the floor next to him and pulled knife, fork, and spoon from her apron pocket.

"I don't want it," Ethan said. "I mean, that's kind and all, Lizzie," he added when he saw her expression go from sympathetic to sharp, "but I have to get out. I have to help Daniel."

"It's too late for that, dear. Daniel's made more trouble than anyone can help him out of now."

"It wasn't his fault!"

"Mr. Lyman caught him right there, stealing from his desk. How could it not be his fault?"

"Please, Lizzie—"

Lizzie smoothed a tangle of sweaty hair away from Ethan's forehead. Her hands felt cool, even though they were strong and callused. "This is about Ivy, isn't it?"

Ethan nodded. "We just wanted to figure out how to keep her, that's all."

She tipped Ethan's chin up to look into his eyes. "Buying her with stolen money was a pretty foolish idea, wasn't it? Whatever made Daniel think he wouldn't get found out?" She shook her head. "I was starting to think he was different from what they all said. Now it turns out he's just a thief after all."

"He's not! He's not!" Ethan tore away from Lizzie's touch. "It wasn't money we were looking for. We were looking for Mr. Lyman's account books. We thought we could prove that Mr. Lyman owed Daniel enough to buy her."

"*We?*" Lizzie's eyebrows rose. "So he dragged you into it after all. Oh, Ethan!" Her hand rose to her mouth. "If Mr. Lyman finds out—"

"He's the one that's the thief. I can prove it if you let me out."

Lizzie shook her head. "It's not my place—"

"Please, Lizzie. You know what he'll do when he gets back. You saw what he did to Daniel, didn't you?"

Lizzie winced and looked away.

Ethan clutched her arm. "If I don't get out, nobody will ever know the truth. Daniel will go to jail. And he'll die. You know he can't stand to be shut up anywhere close. Please, please . . ."

Lizzie looked around as if she expected to find someone spying on them. Finally, she said, "Show me this proof, and then we'll see."

Ethan ripped the lining from his vest and took the paper out. He hesitated before turning it over to her. "You have to promise not to give it to Mr. or Mrs. Lyman. You have to promise to let me out first."

"All right. I promise."

Ethan fidgeted while she read the paper. How much time had they already wasted? Why couldn't Lizzie just trust him?

"This is terrible. Just terrible," Lizzie said finally. She got up quickly and put the paper into her pocket. Ethan grabbed for it, but she pushed his hand away. "If anyone tries to stop us, they won't be looking through *my* pockets, will they?" She pursed her lips. "But who do we tell?"

Ethan heard the sound of hoofbeats in the yard below. He tugged at Lizzie's sleeve. "Come on, Lizzie. We have to go now. Somebody's coming—maybe it's Mr. Lyman."

She stepped over to the window and looked out. "No. It's all right. It's Silas come back. We'll tell him. He'll know what to do."

"And where do you think *you're* going?" Mrs. Lyman demanded as Lizzie and Ethan came downstairs into the kitchen.

"We need to talk to Silas." Lizzie took Ethan's hand and headed for the door.

"You'll do no such thing." Mrs. Lyman stepped in their way, her arms folded across her chest, her tall, thin frame a solid barrier to their escape. "That boy is being punished, and you have no right to take him." She reached for Ethan's free hand.

Ethan jumped back as if she were a snake. Just as quickly, Lizzie stepped between him and Mrs. Lyman. "Don't you touch him." Although Lizzie held her head high and her eyes flashed angrily, her hand on Ethan's was shaking.

The slap sounded like a thunderclap to Ethan's anxious ears. He gasped and looked up to see Lizzie's cheek reddening with Mrs. Lyman's handprint.

"What do you think you're doing?" Silas's deep voice resonated through the kitchen.

Lizzie was wrong, Ethan thought, watching Silas's eyes darken with gathering ire. Silas would take Mrs. Lyman's side after all.

"What she's doing is defying me," Mrs. Lyman said. "This insolent baggage is—"

"Not her. *You*," Silas said, pointing to his stepmother. His mouth was set in a thin, angry line, and his hands opened and closed at his sides. "Do you think Lizzie's a bound girl for you to strike as you please? Apologize to her."

Ethan had never heard Silas defy his stepmother before, let alone order her to do anything. Neither, apparently, had Mrs. Lyman. For all the heat of the fire and the sweltering day, a cold trickle crept down Ethan's spine as he watched her face turn as red as the pickled cabbage that sat in a bowl on the table. She snatched up one of the wooden spoons from the table and struck Silas so hard across the jaw that the handle cracked.

Silas raised a hand to his cheek. A spot of blood appeared where a splinter from the spoon had scratched him. He stared at the blood on his fingers as though he didn't know what it was.

"You've gone too far, *boy*." Mrs. Lyman's hands flailed about as she talked, as if she yearned to strike the young man again. "You'd think the farmhands and the dairymaids were in charge of things around here."

"Farmhands? I trust I'm more than that, ma'am." Silas's voice remained cool, but it was a dangerous chill.

"Oh, yes. You're no more than a glorified farmhand. No more than that"—she snapped her fingers under Silas's nose—"to Mr. Lyman and me. You're only here on my sufferance—you and those—those *boys*." She said *boys* the way she would speak of vermin and wrinkled her nose at Ethan as if he were a piece of filth from the bottom of the slop-bucket. "And all because your father has a soft heart. He's endured you and those—creatures—out of pity. And look where it's gotten us. Robbed last night, and heaven knows but we might have been murdered as well. It wouldn't surprise me to learn you had a hand in it."

Silas blinked and shook his head. He looked suddenly confused by the course his stepmother's tirade had taken. "This is absurd."

"Is it? I know what you're capable of. I do indeed." Her eyes narrowed into glittering slits. "Your father may be blinded by sentiment, but I know his mind *and his memory.*"

The last three words seemed to lance through Silas, draining the color from his face.

"Silas?" Lizzie said softly.

With a visible effort, Silas straightened and collected himself. "Come along, Lizzie. I see we're not wanted here."

"You're not taking that boy," Mrs. Lyman said, moving toward Ethan.

Silas brushed her aside and took Ethan's free hand. "A thief takes what he pleases." He turned, and he and Lizzie marched out of the house with Ethan between them.

"Go, then!" Mrs. Lyman shouted after them. "But you'll answer to Mr. Lyman before long. I'll see that you do."

Ivy was tethered in the yard, still saddled and bridled. Silas took the reins, looking for a moment as if he wanted to leap on her back and race away. Then he shook his head and ran a hand across his face as if he were putting on a mask, his expression changing to an unreadable blank.

"What is it, Silas?" Lizzie asked. "What does she mean?"

He shook his head. "You heard nothing in there. Nothing. Understand?"

"No," Lizzie said.

Ethan tugged her sleeve impatiently. "We're wasting time, Lizzie," he whispered. "Daniel—"

"Daniel?" Silas repeated. "Yes, I've heard. The whole town seems to know." He spoke slowly, as if it took an effort to redirect his thoughts. "Turned thief. Well, I hardly have any right to judge him, have I?" He started to lead Ivy toward the barn.

"He's not a thief," Ethan said.

Lizzie took the reins out of Silas's hands and wrapped them back around the hitching post. "There's something you need to see," she said, taking the paper from her pocket. She glanced back at the house, where Mrs. Lyman watched from the kitchen window. Lizzie moved behind Ivy, so Mrs. Lyman couldn't see her.

If Silas had looked stricken before, he looked crushed after reading the paper. "My God, what sort of lie is this?" He clenched his fist around the document.

Ethan jumped forward to snatch it back, but Lizzie's hand was already on Silas's, gently uncurling his fingers and extracting the document. "I think it may be the truth. Ethan says it was in your father's desk. I think—I think it may be genuine."

Ethan blurted out the story of how he and Daniel had plotted to save Ivy, how Daniel had been caught, and how Ethan had escaped with only one piece of paper to show who the real thief was. "There's more in his desk. Those black books of his—I think the truth's in there."

Silas shook his head dizzily. "I don't know what to believe."

"Then look for yourself." Lizzie led Silas and Ethan around to the front of the house, so they wouldn't need to go back through the kitchen and face Mrs. Lyman again. As they entered Mr. Lyman's study, his wife bustled down the hallway, her wooden spoon raised like a truncheon.

"Out! Out of my house!" she shouted.

Lizzie stood in the study doorway, her chin lifted haughtily. "That's odd, ma'am. A moment ago, you didn't want us to leave."

"Why, you—you—you—" Opening and closing her mouth like a newly landed fish, Mrs. Lyman fumed her way down the hall. Just as she reached the study, Lizzie slammed the door in her face.

Numbly, Silas sat at his father's secretary while Lizzie bolted the study door against Mrs. Lyman. She pounded on the door and shouted for several minutes before giving up and going away, probably to fetch help.

"I don't know where the key is," Silas said, looking about the room. "No doubt He keeps it with Him."

"I—um." Ethan twisted his shirttail in his hands. "It's broken. It broke when we—" He fumbled helplessly, looking to Lizzie for assistance.

Silas raised a weary eyebrow. "And I'm to believe you're not thieves?" He pulled down the flap and looked at the row of books before him. As Ethan had the previous night, he reached for the first one and began to read.

Lizzie took a second book to examine for herself. "Look," she said, pointing out some entries to Silas. "Look at all the debits next to Daniel's name for new shirts and trousers. And a greatcoat? He doesn't have any of this."

Two sets of footsteps thumped down the hallway now, and two sets of fists pounded at the door.

"You see?" Mrs. Lyman's voice said. "Locked up in there, all three of them, searching your desk for banknotes, no doubt."

"Silas!" Mr. Lyman called from the hallway. "Open this door! What have you done to your mother?"

Silas slammed the ledger down on the desk, stomped across the room, and threw open the door. "My mother, sir, is dead. And it appears that Mr. Flagg has arrested the wrong man."

"Now, son, what lies has this—this boy been telling you?" Mr. Lyman waved a contemptuous hand at Ethan.

"It's you who's the liar," Ethan said, taking courage from Silas's and Lizzie's presence. "Daniel just wanted to prove it, that's all."

"I knew he'd lead you astray, boy. Well, he's going to prison now, where he'll do none of us any more harm."

"He'll die in prison!" Ethan said. "Wasn't it enough that you took his land? Do you have to kill him, too?"

Mr. Lyman took a second to control his face. "Took his land?" His laugh cracked around the edges. "What sort of foolishness is that? His father couldn't mind his books and couldn't pay his bills. I bought that land with a mortgage that Irish fool never repaid." Mr. Lyman's eyes darted around the room as though he thought Matthew Linnehan's ghost might jump out of a corner and challenge him.

Mr. Lyman was afraid, Ethan suddenly realized. A hopeful spark kindled in his heart. "He *did* pay you. I found the paper that says so. Only there was the fire, and he died. And then you never told anybody, so you got to keep his land. Daniel's land."

"Don't be ridiculous," Mr. Lyman said, stepping toward Ethan. "These things have to be witnessed. If there were any such paper, somebody else would know about it."

Ethan backed away. "Mr. Palmer witnessed it, but he doesn't live around here. Nobody would think of asking him."

At the mention of the teamster's name, Mr. Lyman's lips pressed into a tight, thin line. "That's absurd. There's no paper. I destroyed—" He caught himself too late.

"Destroyed what? This?" Silas said. He held up the discharge of mortgage. "Does this look familiar, sir?"

The storekeeper's face turned nearly the same yellowish parchment color as the paper.

"What—what is it, George?" Mrs. Lyman asked. "He's lying, isn't he?"

"Would you like me to show her, too?" Silas said. "Or does she know?"

"It's nothing, Mercy, nothing," Mr. Lyman said, his voice ragged. "It's all right."

His wife took his arm. "Of course. He's trying to blackmail you. You owe him nothing, dear. Nothing." She lifted her chin and looked down her nose at Silas.

"Nothing but the truth," Silas said. "That you're a liar and a thief."

Mr. Lyman's hand cracked across Silas's face. The young man stood as still and solid as granite. Ethan winced, but the only evidence that Silas had felt the blow was the growing patch of red on his cheek. Mr. Lyman's hand came up again. Silas caught his wrist, clenching it so tightly that Mr. Lyman's fingers spread wide and he let out a hoarse cry of surprise. Silas dragged him toward the secretary, sending him reeling into the chair.

"Stop! Help! He'll murder us all!" Mrs. Lyman shrieked. She ran toward the door.

"Oh, be quiet, you old cow!" Lizzie snapped, quickly stepping in her way.

Rising from his chair, Mr. Lyman clutched his son's elbow. "What are you doing?"

Silas shoved his father back down. He grabbed the arms of the chair, trapping Mr. Lyman in his seat. He jutted his chin toward the stack of black ledgers. "I'm going to take these to Constable Flagg. Maybe I should see what else is in here as well." He released his father and attacked the desk. Drawers crashed to the floor as he pulled out more papers and account books and stacked them in a pile. "Perhaps we'll find out who else you've been cheating."

The storekeeper recovered himself and stood up, fists doubled. "You're not too old for a thrashing, boy." He shook a fist under Silas's chin.

Silas stood his ground. "Nor are you." He parried his father's fist and shoved him away, returning to his assault on the secretary.

"You ungrateful lout!" Mr. Lyman said. "You mean to ruin me, don't you?"

"You're a fine one to talk about ruin, after cheating a ten-year-old out of his inheritance." Silas looked as though he was tearing the desk apart only to keep from doing the same to his father. His hands twitched as if they'd like nothing more than to turn into fists and pound at something.

"You're mad!" Mr. Lyman said, trying to grab Silas's arm and pull him away from the desk. "Who buried that boy's parents? Who kept him when nobody else would have him?"

Silas pushed his father off, like a mastiff shrugging off a nipping terrier. "Don't pretend you gave him any charity. He slaved for every stitch on his back and every mouthful of food off your table."

"I never treated him any worse than I did you."

"No, I'll say that to your credit. You never spared me the back of your hand, either." Silas loomed over his father as if he were about to repay him for every beating. "You should be ashamed of yourself." He shoved armfuls of books and papers at Ethan and Lizzie, gathered the rest for himself, and headed for the door. Ethan followed without thinking, dazed by Silas's fury.

"'How much sharper than a serpent's tooth . . . ,'" Mr. Lyman shouted after him. "It's fortunate your mother never lived to see you turn on me."

Silas's tan seeped away, leaving his face a sickly beige. The books and papers in his arms trembled. For a moment, he seemed to shrink. Then, in a blink, he was steady again. "You're right. My mother would weep to see what you've become."

But Mr. Lyman had the last word. As Silas neared the threshold, his father shouted after him, "It wasn't *my* sin that killed her!"

Chapter Twenty-Seven

Silas staggered, drawing his stomach in as if someone had just punched him. The books in his arms crashed to the floor.

"There, boy, there's the truth, isn't it?" Mr. Lyman said. "A fine one you are to be passing judgments."

"Don't listen to him, Silas," Lizzie said. "He's only saying that to be cruel. Everybody in town knows it was an accident. She fell—"

"Because *he* made her." Mrs. Lyman pointed an accusing finger at her stepson.

Silas turned away as if he couldn't bear Lizzie's gaze.

"You have no idea what it was like, do you?" Mr. Lyman said, his tone swaying between wheedling and cutting. "Seeing her in your face every day, reminding me she was gone, and who had killed her. I thought I could beat her out of you, but it was still her eyes looking at me out of your face, cursing me for what I'd done. I'd shut myself up and weep for her, and then despise myself for that softness. I vowed you'd never be that weak, suffer that way. I'd make you hard, as hard as Delia and I should have been. If we'd been hard, she'd still be alive, she and the baby. I vowed I'd make you hard. And I have, haven't I?" His voice was dagger sharp. "Damn you."

Ethan drew closer to Lizzie. She took his hand and squeezed it. But her palm was sweaty and her fingers trembled.

Silas's hands clenched until his knuckles whitened. "I've been damned, sir, for most of my life."

Mr. Lyman's bitter chuckle hung between them. "And bringing me down, that will redeem you?"

"No, sir," Silas said softly. "It's too late for that." He gestured toward the tumble of books on the floor. "But Paddy—Daniel," he corrected himself. "Daniel and the others. Maybe it's not too late for them." The two men's eyes locked for a moment.

Mr. Lyman's voice turned to steel. "You're still soft. Soft for these strangers. Can any of them do for you what I've done? Give you what I can give? Damn you, boy, I'm your father."

"I have no father." The hardness in Silas's voice matched Mr. Lyman's.

Mr. Lyman recoiled as if he'd been struck with his own switch. "How can you say that? Everything I've done—it's all for you. You only have to ask, son. Give up this madness and whatever you want is yours."

"I want the truth."

Mr. Lyman made a gurgling noise deep in his throat, as if someone were choking him.

Silas's eyes turned hard at his father's silence. "That's what I thought." He stooped to pick up everything he'd dropped. Mr. Lyman groaned as though Silas had torn a hole through him. He lunged toward the spill of papers and books.

Silas elbowed his father away. "Here," he said, pulling the books together. "The truth's in here, isn't it?"

"Ruin me, then. Ruin me, and ruin yourself as well. There'll be no farm for you to work, no house for you to live in."

"It's no more than I deserve." But from the ashen look on his face, Ethan suspected that Silas hadn't considered what exposing his father would really mean. Ethan himself hadn't thought of anything but helping Daniel get Ivy and perhaps finding out the truth about Pa's debts. He'd never imagined that hurting Mr. Lyman would hurt Silas, too.

Mr. Lyman pointed to his wife, her narrow face grown pale, her eyes no longer sharp. "Does your mother deserve—"

Silas cut him off with an abrupt sweep of his hand. "Your wife, you mean. I ruined my mother long ago, as you reminded me."

"And your sisters, your brother?" Mr. Lyman continued, gaining strength as he spoke. "You'd cast them out into the streets?"

Silas turned to Lizzie and Ethan, his face haggard. Ethan prayed Silas wouldn't give in. But how could he expect Silas to sacrifice his livelihood, his home, his family for Daniel? Mr. Lyman stood a little straighter, a little taller, certain that he had won.

Ethan swallowed the lump gathering in his throat. He hoped Silas would forgive him for what he was about to do. He hoped even more that Mr. Lyman was wrong about ruining Silas. He stepped forward. "It doesn't matter if you keep Silas from telling. I will," he said. His chest felt tight, and it was hard to breathe, but the words came out sure and steady.

Silently, Lizzie came to Ethan's side. She gave his arm a little squeeze, then knelt and began gathering papers and account books into a tidy pile. "I'm sure my father can make sense of these," she said. She took off her apron and spread it on the floor to make a bundle of the books and papers.

The tightness in Ethan's chest eased. He knelt to join her.

"You see, sir." Silas gestured toward Lizzie and Ethan. "It's not in my hands. They have no reason to protect you. Or me." He bent to help Lizzie and Ethan bundle up the papers and account books. Ethan noticed the tightly clenched muscles hardening the lines of Silas's jaw, making the tendons stand out like cords in his neck.

"Protect you?" Mrs. Lyman said. "From what, George?

You've never cheated anybody. There's nothing here. Nothing that can harm us." Her chin trembled. "Is there?" She went to her husband and put an unsteady hand on his arm.

For a moment, Ethan thought the storekeeper might lunge toward him and Lizzie and snatch the papers away. Then he turned to his wife and laid his hand over hers, his thumb tracing the blue veins that stood out on the back of her hand. "Leave us, Mercy, please," he said, trying to guide her toward the door. "You don't need to hear any of this."

"I think I do, George." Mrs. Lyman released her husband's arm. She groped for a chair and lowered herself weakly into it. "I need to hear the truth, whatever it may be."

He looked ready to crumple to the floor and weep. "The truth, then." He returned to his desk and slumped into his chair. "Since you'll have it whether I will or no."

Each time Ethan glanced at the storekeeper, he looked a little more faded, a little smaller. Ethan burst out with the question that had plagued him all day. "Why?"

"Why?" Mr. Lyman repeated. Ethan guessed that he'd never had to give a reason for anything before.

Silas rose and loomed over his father. "Yes, why? Why cheat an orphan out of ten acres of land that's barely good enough for potatoes? You didn't need it."

Mr. Lyman stared at his empty desk for a long time before answering. "It was Lucius who gave me the idea."

"Mr. Bingham?" Ethan couldn't believe it. Mr. Bingham was an odd man, but surely not a wicked one.

Silas growled in disgust. "So now it's someone else's fault. I should have known."

Mr. Lyman nodded. "Lucius gave me the idea and didn't even know it. A few days after the fire, he told me how sad it was that Linnehan had left the boy with nothing but debts. I never thought the man had made a secret of paying me. But he did. He told Lucius he wanted to see me about a Christmas surprise for his wife and children. Lucius thought he wanted credit to buy some frivolous thing or other. He said wasn't it just like a Papist to borrow money to buy presents when he should be paying off his debts. Then I remembered what Mr. Merriwether said about the fire. God's judgment, he called it. God's judgment on Papists for keeping Christmas like a pack of heathens. I saw God's hand in it, too."

Ethan shuddered, remembering the sermons Mr. Merriwether had preached about how Papists couldn't be saved, how God would punish them for their wrong beliefs. It made God sound as mean as Mr. Lyman.

Silas rolled his eyes. "God's hand," he repeated. "What did God have to do with it? Mr. Linnehan paid you."

"Yes, he paid me, and we drew up the papers. But your uncle Henry was away. He was Justice of the Peace back then, too. We needed his signature before I could file the papers at the courthouse. I told Linnehan to hold on to his money until then, but he had some superstition about starting the New Year clear of debt. He said he trusted me."

"He trusted you," Silas echoed sarcastically. He shook his head in disbelief, lifting his hands and then letting them fall to his sides.

"We had Seth Palmer witness the payment. He was handy, and Lucius was busy with a customer. I don't think Palmer even knew what he was signing. If Lucius had been the one signing, he'd have examined every letter, every comma. And he'd have remembered.

"I was going to take care of the discharge, get it registered. But the more I thought about it—" Mr. Lyman plucked at his son's sleeve. "There were ten acres of land in my pocket, free and clear, and the only one who knew I had no right to them was a dead man."

Silas yanked his arm away as if his father's touch would contaminate him. "There was the small matter of his son."

"The boy was dying. He had no family. There was no will. What was I to do, let the Commonwealth claim the land?"

"But he didn't die, George," Mrs. Lyman said, her voice fraying. The more her husband revealed, the more she bent inward on herself, as if she had eaten something that was tearing at her insides.

Mr. Lyman straightened in his chair. His voice grew indignant. "I did right by him. Didn't I keep him in my household and raise him like family? How many times did I send for the doctor? You know he'd have died otherwise. And Mrs. Nye in to nurse him day and night. Who do you think paid for all of that?"

Ethan bit his lip, sure that Mr. Lyman's accounts would show that Daniel had been debited for all of that and more.

Silas grunted. He folded his arms across his chest. "And while he was dying—rather, *not* dying—of fever, you stole his land. Daniel got his Christmas surprise all right, didn't he?"

"I waited," Mr. Lyman said, as if that should redeem him. "I put the paper away and waited. If anybody knew Linnehan had paid me, I could say I hadn't time to deal with it, what with the fire and the boy getting sick. But nobody said anything. When the estate went to probate, I waited until the last possible moment to make a claim. Nobody questioned me. God wanted me to have it. Why would He have let it be a secret if He didn't want me to have it? Why would He have brought Mr. Palmer to me at just the right moment?"

"And what else did you think God wanted you to have?" Silas said coldly.

Mr. Lyman looked away. He picked at a piece of blotting paper. "It was like a game in the beginning. A penny here, a penny there. At first I destroyed any proof of my doings. I thought I'd destroyed Linnehan's discharge. But then there were so many, I had to start keeping track. Each one needed to be handled differently. I couldn't risk getting them confused." A wisp of a smile tickled his mouth, a wisp of the master Ethan feared. "And for my own satisfaction, too. It was all very clever, Mercy." He leaned toward his wife, but she only stared at the floor, rocking herself. "Believe me, dear, you would have been impressed if you saw the method to it." Mr. Lyman looked to the others for confirmation. "I pursued it with intelligence and discipline. Yes. It was no more than they deserved, the fools." His voice grew strong, almost proud. He rose from his chair. "They had no discipline. If they couldn't mind their money, why shouldn't someone have it who could? They were better off without it, most of the time. Better off having the overseers of the poor look out for them. They couldn't look out for them-selves." Mr. Lyman nodded to himself, pleased with his speech. "Yes. Yes, I'm sure God wanted somebody else to take care of them."

"And you were only doing God's work, I suppose?" Silas said. "How many were there?"

"How many?" Mr. Lyman blinked as though Silas had recalled him from a faraway place. When he met his son's eyes, he began to shrink again.

"Will you tell Uncle Henry and Mr. Flagg how many people you 'took care of' the way you took care of Daniel?"

"I can't." Mr. Lyman took out his handkerchief and wiped his face. "You know I can't. Please, Silas. I can't go to prison."

"Why not? You'll be taken care of."

"Prison! George, what have you done? What will become of us?" Mrs. Lyman was weeping now. "My girls! My baby!"

"What do you want from me?" Mr. Lyman's voice cracked with despair.

"Go to Mr. Flagg," Silas said. "Tell him you won't pursue your complaint. Tell him to let Daniel go."

"I can't. What will people say?"

There was no joy in the smile that spread across Silas's face. "They'll say what a merciful and forgiving man George Lyman is."

"It's too late. They're gone. Flagg took him away hours ago."

"Away?" Ethan said. "Where?"

"To the sheriff's. In Springfield."

"Then we'll go to Springfield," Silas said.

Ethan and Lizzie followed Silas outside, with Ethan carrying the books and papers bundled together in Lizzie's apron. Silas looked as beaten as his father. His hands shook as he untethered Ivy and led her into the barn. He fumbled with the buckles on her bridle and didn't seem to know which one to undo first.

Lizzie's skirts rustled across the barn floor. "Silas?" Her voice wasn't much more than a whisper. "Silas, are you all right?"

Silas turned to face her. Ethan and Lizzie flinched at the despair that darkened his eyes. "Now you know the truth about both of us, Lizzie. A fine pair we make, a thief and a murderer. What right have I to judge him with all that's on my soul?" His voice was hoarse.

"Your father's a hard man. He only said those things to be cruel," Lizzie said gently. "It's not true." She approached Silas tentatively, the way she might approach a cornered animal. "Ethan, can you take off Ivy's saddle and put on her harness?" she asked softly.

Ethan nodded, though he'd only watched Daniel do it. He pulled Ivy's girth strap loose and slid the saddle from her back, surprised by its weight in his arms and by his own ability to manage it. It seemed odd that he was steady enough to work, while strong, competent Silas looked aimless and lost.

Silas shook his head like a wounded beast. "He may have lied about everything else, but not that. *I* killed her."

Lizzie took Silas's arm and led him to sit with her on the big toolbox in the corner of the barn. She put her hand on Silas's wrist, bent forward to look into his face. "I don't believe that," she said.

Fascinated and frightened at the same time, Ethan worked slowly and quietly so he could watch and listen to Lizzie and Silas. He put Ivy's saddle on its rack and took down the bridle and harness for the farm wagon.

Silas shuddered off Lizzie's hand. "You don't know, Lizzie. I was an evil child." He rested his elbows on his knees and stared grimly down at his hands. "I was spoiled. I was selfish and willful, and they indulged me. They never raised their voices to me, let alone their hands. If they'd curbed me early, at four, or three, or even two—"

"You're only saying what he's taught you. You were so young, how can you remember?"

"Oh, I remember that day, Lizzie. Something like that you can't forget." He stared out at some remembered horror that he couldn't help but watch. Once he started talking, the words flooded out as if he had to tell every detail as some kind of penance. "I remember it was raining that afternoon, so I couldn't go out and play. My mother was tired, so she sent me to my room. I was five. I didn't care about the baby coming. I only knew that my mother was big and clumsy and tired and cross."

Ethan tried to picture Silas as a child, but all he could imagine was a child-sized body wearing Silas's adult face.

"I tired of playing in my room, so I went downstairs. My mother was sleeping. I went to His secretary. I'd been forbidden to touch anything there, but I thought no one would know if I played at writing with His ink and quill. I passed the afternoon scribbling and drawing. I spoiled a mountain of paper and smeared ink all over my clothes and His ledgers and books. It was only when I heard her shriek that I saw the havoc I'd made.

"I leaped from the chair, and the inkwell leaped, too. There was a great pool of ink on the desktop, dripping down onto the carpet. She could barely speak for anger. So I—I fled. I ran up the stairs and into my room and huddled under the bed, waiting for her to come up and punish me. But she never did. She didn't even cry out. There was only a jumble of noise that ended at the bottom of the stairs."

Ethan held his breath, afraid to hear how the story would end. Still carrying Ivy's bridle and harness, he crept closer to Silas and Lizzie, careful to keep the buckles and rings from jingling as he moved.

"For a long while I was too frightened to look. When I did, I found her sleeping, I thought, in a funny heap at the bottom of the stairs. I was afraid, and ran next door to fetch my aunt Sarah. It wasn't long before the house was full of people whispering and hurrying around. They fetched Him from the store and sent for the doctor."

Ethan shuddered. When he closed his eyes to shut off the haunted look on Silas's face, he imagined his own mother lying in a crumpled heap at the bottom of the stairs, himself frantically trying to rouse her. His throat grew thick with imagined grief. He opened his eyes and looked at Lizzie, hoping to find comfort in her sympathetic face. She wiped a finger under her eye, her lashes sparkling with tears.

"I hid upstairs for a long time. I was so wicked I never gave a thought to what had happened to my poor mother. All I could think was that somebody would see the ink on my clothes, and I'd be punished." Silas rubbed his hands against his thighs, as if his fingers were still stained with ink. "Aunt Sarah cleaned me up and put me to bed without a word about what I'd done. The next morning, I finally came down, not out of concern, but because I was hungry." Silas laughed bitterly. "You see, Lizzie, the poor woman was dying under my bedchamber and all I cared about was my breakfast.

"The house was still full of people. Some were asleep on chairs in the parlor, and some were crying. No one had cleaned up the ink I'd spilled. My aunt was in the kitchen, but there was no breakfast. So I went to my parents' bedchamber. The door was shut, and I heard voices inside. While I tried to decide whether to knock, the door opened and He came out.

"His face was gray, but I was so lost in my selfishness that I couldn't guess why. So I asked Him if Mama was awake. At first, He didn't seem to know who I was. Then He raised His hand and hit me. He hit me until Aunt Sarah came and took me away. But you see, it was too late, wasn't it?"

Seeking confirmation, his eyes turned to Lizzie, then beyond her to Ethan. Lizzie made a soft, sad noise. Ethan looked away.

Silas continued. "They kept me away from Him for the next few days, until the funeral. Afterward, I stayed with my aunt and uncle. It was a week before He sent for me. He'd shut Himself up all that while. Aunt Sarah left me in the parlor waiting for Him. He came in and told me my mother and sister were dead and asked me if I knew what that meant. I didn't understand, then, about the baby, that I'd killed her, too. But I did understand about my mother—or thought I did.

"'They put Mama in the ground,' I said. 'She won't come back ever, will she?'

"'No,' He said. He asked if I knew why she was dead.

"'She fell,' I replied.

"'Why?' He asked.

"'Because I was bad,' I answered.

"He said I must be punished. I tried to suffer the strapping in silence, but after a while I couldn't help crying. I mustn't have understood what *dead* meant after all, because I called for my mother. He began to weep at that, and said that a boy who'd killed his mama had no right to call on her. The next thing I remember is waking up in my bed, hurting so much I thought I'd die. Perhaps it would have been best if I had. It must have been a torment to Him, to see me every day, knowing what I'd done."

The humid summer air clung around them like a suffocating blanket. Yet Ethan had to wrap his arms around himself to hide his shivering. Though the sun glared down outside and birds and insects sang all around, Ethan imagined he could hear the mournful drone of rain against glass and wood, and the sound of somebody crying.

"Oh, Silas," Lizzie said.

"I'm not telling you this to get your pity, but to show you I don't deserve it. He was right, only He was too late. If He'd curbed my disobedience a year, a month, a week earlier, she would have lived. All He's done to me was no more than I deserved. But all His discipline—all my work—none of it can undo—can bring back—" His voice broke, turned into a strangled groan. "I deserved every thrashing He ever gave me, but what about Paddy?"

"Daniel?" Ethan corrected.

Silas glanced over at Ethan and nodded. "Daniel. When something went wrong and He thought it was Daniel's fault, I was only too glad to see another boy take a beating instead of me. So I said nothing, did nothing to put it right. I could have stopped it, but I pretended I didn't see. A fine pair of liars and thieves, aren't we, Him and me?"

"It's not the same." Lizzie shook her head fiercely. "It's not the same at all."

"No, it's not. There's no fixing my sins." His voice strengthened with resolve. "But maybe I can undo His." He nodded at the bundle wrapped in Lizzie's apron.

"Sins?" Lizzie's voice burned with anger. "What sins? You were a child. A frightened child. You're not a monster or a murderer. Not then, and not now. You're a good man, Silas."

Silas's red-rimmed eyes narrowed with disbelief. "How can you say that after what I've just told you?"

"If you were all that wicked, it wouldn't torment you so." Lizzie timidly took Silas's hands in hers. "I remember a day, a long time ago. I was ten or eleven, and I was weeping fit to burst because some girls laughed at me and said I was fat and homely. You gave me your handkerchief and walked me home, and I thought you were the kindest boy I knew."

Silas opened his mouth to object.

Lizzie put her fingertips to his lips to silence him. "I've worked here for five years and watched you for longer. And I'm still fat and homely, and you're still the kindest boy I know." She seemed embarrassed by her confession. She looked away, her cheeks turning red, her eyes brimming with tears.

Lizzie's tears gave Ethan a prickly feeling in his eyes. He suddenly wanted nothing more than to make her stop crying. There was only one thing he knew that was sure to make a girl smile. "*I* think you're pretty, Lizzie," he said.

Lizzie's face turned redder still, and her mouth crumpled to smother a sob. She tried to pull her hands away from Silas, but he held them fast. He stared at her as if he saw her for the first time. "I think you're pretty, too," he said.

Chapter Twenty-Eight

"Look, Pa! It's Silas!" Ethan nearly dropped the milk bucket when he saw what had roused Scratch into a fit of hoarse barking.

Pa snatched the bucket away before the milk could slosh onto the ground.

Ethan raced toward the fence. He vaulted the rail and tumbled to the road in a heap. Gathering himself back up, he pointed at the carriage coming his way. "He's got Daniel with him!" Without a backward glance, he pelted down the road to meet the chaise.

Though Ethan had begged to go to Springfield with Silas, Lizzie had taken him home instead. The last few days had seemed an eternity of frustration as he'd waited for Silas to fetch Daniel back.

"Daniel! Daniel! You're back! You're back!" Ethan shouted, dancing at Ivy's side. The mare let out a high-pitched whinny, as if she shared Ethan's joy.

"Don't you think I know that?" Daniel said.

The words spilled out of Ethan in an ecstatic babble as he skipped around the horse and carriage, keeping pace with Ivy as she headed toward the house. "Isn't it wonderful? Did Silas tell you yet? I was right about those books. Besides cheating you, we found out that Pa didn't owe Mr. Lyman nearly so much as he said, and Silas made him forgive the rest or he said we'd tell Mr. Flagg, and when we looked through the books, we found out he'd been cheating a lot of other people, and Silas is going to make sure they get all their money back, and . . . and . . ." Ethan stopped jumping and stared at his friend's face. "What's the matter?"

Daniel's eyes were red and teary. He rubbed his face with his sleeve and shook his head. "It's the sun. It hurts me eyes. It was so awful dark in that cell," he said in an unsteady voice.

"Oh." Ethan sobered, perplexed that Daniel wasn't bursting with joy the way he was. Instead, he looked sad and weary and old, as though he'd been gone years instead of days. Though the bruises Mr. Lyman had given him were beginning to fade to green, he seemed to have one or two new ones, and his face looked a sickly gray where it wasn't bruised. When they reached the house, he needed Silas's help to get out of the carriage. "Are you all right?" Ethan asked.

"Just—just tired is all." Daniel looked over Ethan's head toward the house.

Ethan followed Daniel's glance. Maria and Chloe stood in the yard, staring at Daniel as if he were a monkey from a menagerie. Ma came to the doorway to see what the fuss was about. She clapped her hands to get her daughters' attention. "Girls! Your manners!"

"Good day, sir," Maria and Chloe said in chorus. They made their best curtsies, blushed, and ran away giggling.

Ma rolled her eyes and laughed. She stepped forward to greet Daniel and Silas. "I'm pleased to see you, Daniel," she said, holding out her hand. She gave him her warmest smile.

"Thank you, ma'am." Daniel took her hand lightly. He seemed to fear she might snatch it away and strike him instead.

"It's a while yet 'til tea, but you're welcome to—" Ma cast a glance toward Pa, who was just coming up with the milk.

Pa's face was solemn as he looked Daniel over from his tattered cap to his leathery bare feet. Daniel met Pa's eyes uncertainly.

Pa set down the milk pail and took off his hat. He thrust out his callused hand and cleared his throat. "Mr. Linnehan, I'd be honored if you'd take tea with my family."

Daniel stared from Pa's hand to his face. "Thank you, sir," he said finally. "I'd like that very much." He clasped Pa's hand firmly.

Ma squeezed Pa's elbow. "And Silas, too?"

Pa nodded. "Silas, too." He gave Silas one of his sternest looks, as if he'd been the cause of all the trouble instead of Mr. Lyman.

Ma took the milk bucket inside, then ushered the men and boys into the best room. She disappeared into the kitchen to find the girls and muster up a tea worthy of company. Every now and then one of the girls would run to the door and stare at Daniel with wide eyes until Ma pulled her away. The kitchen clattered with dishes and pots, and the smell of the fire newly started drifted out into the best room.

Daniel stared around the best room in a daze. He seemed unsure where he was or if he'd be allowed to stay. Ethan guided him to Ma's rocking chair. Daniel settled into the chair slowly, as if every movement hurt. He closed his eyes and ran his hands along the chair's arms. For a moment, Ethan thought he might go to sleep. Then Daniel sighed, opened his eyes, and curved his mouth into a slow, cautious smile. "It's true, then. It's really true."

Ethan smiled. The weary stranger was starting to turn back into the Daniel he knew. "Isn't it wonderful?" Ethan said. He plopped himself on the floor at Daniel's feet while Pa pulled out chairs for himself and Silas. "Of course, there's a lot nobody can prove, like when Mr. Lyman put his thumb on the scale and such, and Silas made Lizzie and me promise not to tell anyone but you and Ma and Pa—"

"It ain't kind to gloat, lad," Daniel cautioned, giving Silas a wary glance. "Not with the man's own son right here."

"But—but—" Ethan glanced at Silas. He, too, looked solemn and tired and old. But they'd won—Ethan and Daniel and Silas and Lizzie. They'd won, and Mr. Lyman had lost. Ethan wanted to sing with joy, while everyone else looked like they were at a funeral.

Silas looked down at his hat. He turned it around and around in his hands until he'd bent the brim out of shape.

Pa leaned toward Silas. "I've kept my peace until now, sir," he began, "only because Ethan and Lizzie begged me. But I need some explanations. Why should I help you hide what your father's done? He lied to me—to all of us. If half of what Ethan's told me is true—" He looked at Daniel's wounded face. "Mr. Lyman needs to pay for his crimes."

"He'll pay, sir," Silas said. "I'll make sure of that."

"How then, if you don't hand him over for the law to deal with him?"

"The law may see him locked up, perhaps impoverished as well, but it probably won't see anybody paid back," Silas said. "If he's prosecuted, he'll fight until he exhausts his appeals. Court costs and lawyers' fees will whittle away his fortune until there's hardly anything left to repay the people he's cheated." As Silas talked, Ethan noticed that his tone was different when he referred to his father. The *he*s and *him*s now seemed to begin with lowercase rather than capital letters. "If you let me handle things myself, I can use the income from the store and the farm, sell some land, perhaps, or even the house, to return what he's taken. It will take some time, but I swear to you I'll go over every page of those books and see that every penny's repaid, with interest and damages. The law can't promise you

285

that. Which would you prefer, Mr. Root, to see him jailed or to see restitution paid to his victims?" He spread his hands wide. "The law may not have room for both."

Pa lit his pipe and mulled over it for a long time. "And how will you pay all those people back without them finding out the truth and bringing the law down on his head anyway?"

Silas rubbed his jaw. "I've thought about that, sir. I think—I think they will hear Mr. Lyman has suffered a fit of nervous prostration, perhaps an apoplectic shock. If you saw him now, you'd not have a hard time believing it. It has unsettled his mind, caused him to become confused, agitated, accuse people of things they haven't done. Become violent, even." He gave Daniel a pointed look. "He will need to withdraw from his business affairs, of course, which I will take over. I expect I will find . . . mistakes in his bookkeeping. If he could manipulate the accounts to his favor, they can be manipulated the other way as well." His mouth curled in an ironic smile. "If he recovers, he'll not be able to return to his work. I expect he will devote the rest of his life to charity and philanthropy."

Ethan imagined how much it would torment Mr. Lyman to lose his power and to watch Silas give away his wealth to those he regarded as weak and undisciplined. But Silas would have to spend the next twenty years or more standing guard over a man he despised. The two would be virtually chained together for the rest of Mr. Lyman's life, their grand white house becoming as much a prison for its masters as it had been for Ethan and Daniel.

"New lies to cover the old ones," Pa said, his tone heavy with disgust. "How do I know you're not lying to me now?"

"If I don't satisfy you, go to Mr. Flagg. Tell him the truth."

"After you've destroyed those books, I suppose?" Pa raised a suspicious eyebrow.

"Silas isn't like that, Pa," Ethan said. "I swear."

"You don't know, Ethan," Pa said. "He could be fooling you just as his father fooled me."

"Wasn't I right about Daniel?" Ethan said.

Pa studied the smoke drifting toward the ceiling.

"There are the girls to think of as well, Mr. Root," Silas continued. "And the baby. They've done no harm to anyone. I'd like to keep a home for them, at least."

Pa tilted his head toward the kitchen, where Ma was teaching the girls a song while they worked. Ethan wondered if he was trying to put himself in Silas's place, considering what lengths he'd go to in order to keep a home for Benjamin and Maria and Chloe. *And me,* Ethan thought.

"I think maybe—" Ethan began, then stopped, not sure quite how to say why he'd agreed to keep Silas's secret.

"What, son?"

"Well, I wanted to hurt Mr. Lyman, too. Something awful, especially after what he did to Daniel. I even wished he was dead." He glanced at Silas. "Sorry," he said, then turned back to Pa. "But I was thinking of something Daniel told me once. Something his mother said: *If you wish someone ill, it only comes back at you in the end. So you're better to wish somebody good.* So maybe Silas is right."

"Aye," Daniel said. "From what I seen of that prison, I can't say as I'd be feeling any sorrow to have him locked away there. But what good would that do, if it don't undo the ruin he's caused to folk like meself?"

Pa made a little humphing sound and blew smoke out through his nose. "Very well, Silas. I'll hold my peace for now. But I'll be watching to see if you keep your promises."

"That's all I ask, sir," Silas said.

The four sat in uneasy silence until the comforting sounds of Ma and the girls singing and laughing in the kitchen wore the tension out of the air.

"What are you going to do now?" Ethan asked Daniel.

"I don't know." Daniel's shoulders sagged as if he couldn't get out from underneath the weight of all that had happened.

"You can stay with us. Can't he, Pa?" Ethan tugged at Pa's trouser leg.

Pa gave Ethan a reluctant frown. "I'd like to say yes, son, but I can't pay him. I can't ask a man to work for just his board. It wouldn't be fair."

"I'd not be minding, sir," Daniel said. "It's more than I got now."

"That's not true," Silas said. "You have ten acres of land."

Daniel laughed wearily. "And what'll I be doing with that now? I hardly think your da'll be wanting me for a neighbor."

Silas pulled a small cloth bag from his pocket. It clinked heavily as he pressed it into Daniel's hands. "Sell it to me. I've counted out a fair price for it. And I owe you rent for all the years we've been using it. I still haven't done the sums for that. Sell it and make a good start for yourself somewhere *he* isn't. There should be enough to buy you some tools or some live-stock or a little bit of land."

Ethan grinned and hugged his knees to himself. Now Daniel would be happy, he thought. Now Daniel could be sure everything was all right. Even Pa smiled at last.

Daniel sat for a long moment, weighing the purse in his hand as if he were afraid to look inside it. Finally, he opened it and took a cautious peek. He pulled out one of the coins and held it in his palm, watching the sun sparkle across its copper surface. "Is there enough here to buy a horse?"

Ethan turned the bone-handled knife over and over in his hands.

"Mr. Bingham told me which one you fancied," Daniel said.

"It's beautiful. I—thank you. Ta." He grinned up at Daniel.

"Take care of it. I'll not be around to buy you another."

Daniel's words smothered Ethan's joy in the gift and replaced it with a heaviness that sat in his stomach like a stone.

It was strange to see Daniel dressed in brand-new clothes made just for him. Ma had told him to have them made a little big, because he had so much growing yet to do. Even so, the bottle-green jacket looked especially fine. Lizzie'd been right about the color; it made his red hair seem a rich shade of copper rather than dull faded orange. The vest fabric she'd picked out was a soft fawn color shot through with copper threads that looked as though they'd been plucked from Ivy's mane. He slipped on a new green cap that matched his coat.

Perhaps he didn't look like an Irish prince, but he looked respectable compared to the ragged, bruised boy Silas had brought back from Springfield three weeks since. He even wore a pair of boots, although he shifted from foot to foot as though he'd rather have gone barefoot. He would probably shed boots, coat, and vest as soon as he was shy of town, but he'd said he wanted to say his good-byes looking like a proper gentleman. He'd already given parting gifts to Ethan's family. Now Ivy stood by him, ready for the journey, her saddlebags fat with supplies.

"I don't understand why you have to leave. You can stay with us forever if you want," Ethan said. He kicked at a stone and stubbed his bare toe. The dull ache matched his mood.

While Daniel had stayed with Ethan's family, his bruises had healed and his strength returned. He'd helped Ethan and his father harvest the rye and bring in a sparse second cutting of hay. Meanwhile, Silas and Lizzie had fitted him out with new clothes and goods for his journey. In between, the boys had somehow found time for swimming and fishing and, best of all, riding. Ethan had found it all great fun, until today. Until today, there'd been the hope that Daniel would change his mind and stay.

Daniel had spent one long morning with the Lymans—

Silas, George, and Henry. He'd returned with a dazed look on his face and a sheaf of legal papers in his hand: receipts for all his goods, so no one could accuse him of stealing; papers freeing him from his indenture to Mr. Lyman; letters of reference drafted by Silas, signed by George Lyman, and witnessed by Henry Lyman. Silas had wanted to make sure nobody would question Daniel's right to go or to own the things he carried.

Silas had proposed that Daniel go west to work for a business associate of Mr. Lyman's. There was, indeed, a letter from Mr. Lyman to a Jonas Farrow in Parma, Ohio, but Ethan doubted Daniel would ever use it. He'd want to avoid anybody remotely connected with George Lyman. Silas must have known that, too, for he'd provided Daniel with reference letters from other people as well. It was no surprise that Silas had included a letter from Ethan's father and an introduction from Mr. Bingham to his brother in Ohio. But he'd also managed to convince both Lizzie's father and Constable Flagg to write about what a hardworking, upstanding young man Mr. Daniel Linnehan was.

Daniel had read the letters over and over, shaking his head in amazement at the words. "I can't hardly recognize meself in here," he'd told Ethan. "You'd think I was Saint Daniel instead of me own self, wouldn't you, now?" Daniel traced his finger over Mr. Flagg's signature. "I'm surprised Silas didn't try to get one from the minister. But I fancy Mr. Merriwether wouldn't be recommending a bloody Papist for anything but a place in hell."

Daniel had carefully stored all his papers in a leather wallet and packed them away in Ivy's saddlebags. All but the most important one: the bill of sale for Ivy, which Daniel kept safe in the breast pocket of his new green coat.

Silas had brought the mare up from the Lymans', and Daniel had given Ethan a daily riding lesson. Now, just as Ethan felt confident enough to ride Ivy without Daniel's help, Daniel and Ivy were going away. It wasn't fair.

"Please stay," Ethan said. "Then you could be my brother for real."

Daniel avoided Ethan's eyes. "I'd be doing you no favors, lad."

"You can stay here, even if you work for somebody else," Ethan said. "Pa said so. There's plenty of folks around here who need a hand now and then."

Daniel shook his head. "And how would I be trading at Lyman's store, with all that's between us?"

"He won't cheat anybody again. Silas will make sure—"

Daniel raised an eyebrow. "How will I be living in this town, with no one wanting to hire me or trade with me, for fear I'll rob 'em or murder 'em should they turn their backs? Anytime someone's goods go missing or some such happens, and there's no one to hang the blame on, folk'll be looking to me 'cause I'm the lad as tried to rob Mr. Lyman."

"But you didn't do anything wrong. Everybody knows that now."

"And how will they be knowing, with you and Lizzie and Silas and your folks all keeping it secret?"

"They'll know 'cause you're free. They wouldn'a let you go if you were guilty."

"Oh, is that the way of it, now? Or will they be saying I'm free only because Lyman's a charitable and forgiving man, not because I done nothing wrong?"

"But—but—" Ethan hated the way arguing with Daniel felt like swimming upstream. Couldn't Daniel let him win just this once, when it really mattered?

"Come on, lad. Let's ride for a bit." Daniel swung himself onto Ivy's back. He kicked his left foot free of the stirrup and held a hand out to help Ethan get into the saddle in front of him. He pressed Ivy into an easy walk. "I know you mean well, but don't you see? How can I live easy here with all that's happened?"

Ethan looked toward the Berkshire foothills. Once Daniel crossed them, he might as well be on the other side of the ocean. He thought of Mr. Bingham's brother, who had always promised to return but never had. "Why do you have to go so far? Can't you just go to Westfield or Pittsfield, or—or—"

"Talk travels fast and far, lad. I want to go somewhere the talk won't reach."

"It's not fair." Ethan's lower lip jutted out.

"Ain't you learned that by now? Me da once told me that he come here so he could start new, with nothing hindering him from making his own way in the world. If he failed, well, he'd at least know it was all on his own account and not for someone keeping him back. I want to get far enough away so there won't be no Lymans or talk of Lymans to poison me life, somewhere I can rise or fall on the strength of me own hands, where I got no one to thank or blame but meself."

"Is there really such a place, even out west?" Ethan twisted to look up at Daniel's face.

Daniel's gray-green eyes were soft and distant. "I don't know. But I got to find out, don't I?"

Daniel circled Ivy to the west, then turned south along the river, past their old fishing and swimming spots. When they turned back east, he gave the reins to Ethan until they reached Daniel's thinking place. Daniel slid from the mare's back and paced the foundation, then sat on the mound where the chimney used to be. He pointed up at the Lymans' house. The sun sparkled off the big fan-shaped attic window.

"The first time I went home from Lyman's to see me ma and da," Daniel said, "I told me ma I could see our house from me window. She said she'd put a candle out where I could see it, so I'd know she was thinking about me. I'd watch nights until the candle went out, and I'd fancy she was saying her good-nights to me. It made me feel better, thinking I wasn't working up there for nothing, and there was someone as minded what become of me. But that was a long time ago." Daniel walked over to the lilac bush; the brambles Silas had weeded out had grown back already. He gently separated the shrub from the prickly shoots and uprooted the briars. "Sometimes—I—I fancy maybe I can feel 'em here, and they can hear me. Daft, eh, lad?"

"I don't know." Ethan squatted next to his friend and helped pull the brambles out. He grabbed the shoots carefully, trying to place his fingers between the thorns.

Daniel didn't seem to mind how the brambles bit his fingers. The lilac's seedpods rattled against the boys' shoulders as they worked. When they were done, Daniel started to wipe his hands on his trousers. He caught himself before he dirtied his new clothes. He gave Ethan a crooked smile and began to wipe his hands on the grass instead.

"Here." Ethan dug his handkerchief out of his pocket and gave it to Daniel.

"Ta, lad," Daniel said, brushing the dirt from his hands. "I just thought I'd come and tell 'em where I'm going. So they won't miss me, see. It's just a notion, mind." Daniel went back to the chimney mound. He closed his eyes and sat in silence for a long time, his face quiet as if he were listening to someone that Ethan couldn't hear.

Daniel let Ethan take the reins all the way home. But there was no joy in the honor, even though it was a perfect day to ride: sunny and warm, with a breeze stirring Ivy's mane. The light had made the shift from stark white to pale yellow that would eventually mellow into the gold of autumn. The whir of crickets and cicadas had risen to an anxious rattle, as if they knew they had less than a month left for singing. There would still be sweltering days ahead, but the season had crested and begun to slip toward fall. It seemed right to Ethan that the summer had chosen this day to begin dying.

Ethan could feel that Ivy wanted to run, but he didn't let her. The sooner they got back, the sooner they'd have to say good-bye. They'd nearly reached Ethan's house before he spoke. "Daniel—"

"Aye?"

All the way back, Ethan had been reflecting on what Daniel had said back at his thinking place: *It made me feel better, thinking there was someone as minded what become of me.* "I mind. I mind what becomes of you." The words stuck in his throat as though he'd swallowed some of the brambles they'd pulled.

"Do you, now?" Daniel took the reins and halted Ivy in front of the house. He slid off the horse and helped Ethan down. "That's grand, lad. That's what brothers are s'posed to do, ain't it?"

It was all Ethan could do not to fling his arms around his friend and beg him once more to stay. But he'd vowed he wouldn't shame Daniel or himself with tears. He held himself stiffly, ready to shake Daniel's hand like a man.

Daniel took something out of his pocket and slipped it into Ethan's hand. "Here. Take care of this for me."

Ethan unwrapped the knotted handkerchief. The little wooden horse nestled inside gleamed a mellow golden brown. He shook his head. "I can't take this. Your pa made it for you."

Daniel knocked Ethan's hat askew. "I didn't say you was to keep it, you fool." He swung himself into the saddle before Ethan could give the little horse back. "I'm just lending it to you. Until you can come and bring it back to me." Ivy danced and reared underneath him, eager to run and play. He whirled her away and down the road before Ethan could recover his breath enough to say "Ta."

Acknowledgments

As of this writing, *A Difficult Boy* is officially older than Ethan, its main character (although thankfully *not* older than Daniel!). Along the way I've accumulated a long list of people who've helped in various ways. If I've forgotten anybody, please forgive me.

First, I'd like to acknowledge the members of the Longmeadow Writers and Poets and the Oak and Stone Writing Groups, without whom this book would not have even been started. Nearly half of the story was written during workshop sessions, and members' encouragement and enthusiasm helped me see the book through to the finish. Their comments also helped immensely with the editing. Thanks to Julia Starzyk (for inspiring exercises and editing), Beth Clifford (for additional editorial advice), Lise Hicks (for yelling at me at a very critical stage), Anna Bowling and Melva Michaelian (my present Wednesday night support group, who've continued to see me through to the not-so-bitter end), Mary Jane Eustace, Maureen Kellman, Bill Lang, Amy Lyon, Melinda McQuade, Lauretta St. George-Sorel, Beryl Salinger-Schmitt, and Peggy Tudryn.

Thanks to Florence and Paul Muller-Reed for their constant and relentless encouragement and for making me write five pages a week, whether or not I felt like it. If my writing group comrades made me start the story, it was Flo and Paul who made me finish it.

Thanks to my agent, William Reiss of John Hawkins and Associates, for giving Ethan and Daniel a second chance. And thanks to my editor, Regina Griffin, for giving Ethan and Daniel a home, and to Assistant Editor Leanna Petronella for picking up where Regina left off.

A huge thank-you to Carol Munro, for friendship, cheerleading, continuity checking, helpful criticism, and diligent (and unpaid) editorial advice. Carol, I owe you big-time!

Thanks to Dennis Picard, historian extraordinaire, for saving me from anachronisms, illegal and improbable plot twists, and other historical faux pas. If I've made any errors, it's in spite of his help, not because of it.

Thanks to Thomas Moriarty and George Bresnahan for providing Irish translations.

Thanks to my early readers, who endured the telephone book–sized version: Dru Bronson-Geoffroy, Pat Cahill, Marlissa Carrion, Chris Creelman, Chris DeFilippis, John and Jo Ellis-Monaghan, Stan and Nancy Graziano, Fran Holland (thanks also to Fran for proofreading), Jessica Holland, Margaret Humberston, Judith Jaeger, Patti Millette, E. Catherine Tobler, and the Skarzynski clan—Terri, Jim, Cindy, and Stan. Thanks, of course, to my parents, Joseph and Rhea Plourde; my siblings, Rosemarie Plourde Buxton and Christopher Plourde; my Aunt Theresa and Uncle Joe Chevalier; and my husband, Joe, who had to read it because they're related to me.

Thanks to the PEN New England Children's Book Caucus for recognizing *A Difficult Boy* with the 2003 Discovery Award. Special thanks to Nancy Hope Wilson of PEN New England for advice and encouragement. And thanks to Jessica Holland for nagging me into entering the PEN competition in the first place. Thanks also to Jessica for encouragement, enthusiasm, timely nagging, and revisional inspiration, and to her writing group members Marlena Zapf and Kristin Kladstrup for helpful comments and long-distance support even though they've never met me.

Thanks to the University of Southern Maine's 2001 Stonecoast Summer Writers' Conference, where the manuscript first met strangers' eyes and, miraculously, did not crash and burn. Dennis Lehane and Karen Joy Fowler, both wonderful teachers, were inspirations. Remembering their words of encouragement kept me from giving up when things looked bleak. Thanks to fellow Stonecoasters for encouragement and lots of constructive criticism.

Thanks to Judith Jaeger for encouragement and advice on shameless self-promotion.

Thanks to the research libraries at Old Sturbridge Village, Mystic Seaport Museum, and the Connecticut Valley Historical Museum (where I've been archivist for the past eleven years). Thanks especially to CVHM, since it was coming across a document in the archives that inspired the story. Special thanks to Margaret Humberston, head of library and archives (and the best boss I've ever had), for flexible scheduling, encouragement, and extremely large blocks of chocolate.

Most important of all, thanks to Mom and Dad for giving me a passion for books.